# HONOR ROAD

## SEQUEL TO BLACK AUTUMN TRAVELERS

JASON ROSS

ADAM FULLMAN

ReadyMan
PUBLISHING

# THE BLACK AUTUMN SERIES

# PREFACE

A post-civilization world would astonish us all, gunfighter and gardener alike. In this novel, we tell the bare-knuckle truth—and this time, it might leave a scar. Forgive us for stripping away layers of literary comfort and dipping into stark tales of starvation and twisted honor.

Honor Road is the direct sequel to Black Autumn Travelers, the stories of Mat Best, Sage Ross and Cameron Stewart. We rejoin them in the nightmarish abyss of lost civilization, two months after the Black Autumn collapse.

Army Ranger Mat Best scrambles to defend the Tennessee town that struggled and failed to save his love, Caroline, from the ravages of gangrene. He stands between her orphaned brother, William, the town and tens of thousands of desperate, feral urbanites starving to strip the town bare.

Seventeen-year-old Sage Ross flees the charred and broken farm of the Holland family in western Washington state. He faces a perilous, winter mountain climb, then a chain of impossible choices that he must brook before continuing his homeward journey to Salt Lake City, Utah.

Cameron Stewart, the insecure family man, surviving on luck

and fury, flees a black-hearted polygamist enclave in northern Arizona with his family, then drops them into the gristmill of starvation. Hunger takes them down dark roads, and Cameron commits foul acts in the midst of his delirium. Will his wife and children pay the ultimate price for his dishonor?

"Sing to me of the man, Muse, the man of twists and turns, driven time and again off course, once he had plundered the hallowed heights of Troy.

Many cities of men he saw and learned their minds, many pains he suffered, heartsick on the open sea, fighting to save his life and bring his comrades home."

— HOMER, THE ODYSSEY

# 1

## CAMERON STEWART

*Six weeks before.*

**Highway 59**
**Outside Apple Valley, Utah**

Did you screw him?" Cameron seethed.

Julie answered low and angry, "We. Were. Married."

"Don't ever say that again. Don't you ever fucking say that again. You weren't married. That's just whacko cult shit. Did you screw him or not?" Cameron's hands flew up and down in front of his face like furious pistons.

She stole a glance at the pickup truck idling beside the highway. Four passengers stared straight ahead, avoiding their eyes. A man watched in the reflection of the driver's side mirror—the big, extended kind for pulling trailers.

"Yes, Cameron. I had sex with him. Is that what you want me to say? *I did.* They made me marry him and, yes, there was a wedding night. You were in a coma. The boys needed protection."

The sun set over Utah Mountain, and the chill of evening gnawed at the warmth coming off the blacktop. Cameron cradled his Mosin-Nagant rifle. Forty-five minutes before, he'd fled a polygamist colony in the confusion following the killing of their Prophet.

Cameron, Julie and the boys had been their prisoners, but he'd turned the priesthood inside-out with a killing spree. He'd made them pay to play. Oh yes, he had.

The rifle was all Cameron had in this world. Julie's hands were empty. They had no vehicle. No backpack. No buckets, bags or suitcases. She and the kids escaped with the clothes on their backs.

The boys milled around the shoulder of the highway, pretending not to listen to their mother and father argue.

Cameron stared hard at the pickup truck, idling, waiting for the couple to reach a decision. The asshole behind the wheel was the son of the dead prophet, the heir apparent to the cult. He'd probably called dibs on Cameron's hot wife as soon as they'd ambushed and captured his family six weeks before.

*What a difference a day makes,* Cameron thought as he shot daggers from his eyes at the round, blonde-haired face in the mirror.

They'd shot Cameron through the neck, stolen his wife, his boys and his supplies. But Cameron had his revenge. He'd broken the back of their cuckoo collective and left the remnants tearing at each others throats. No doubt, that's why this dipshit polygamist in his Shit-kicker-mobile had come along with his truckbed full of gear. He was making a run for it. After his father was exposed as a sex weirdo, then gunned down by the elders in a "blood atonement," the son grabbed what he could and got out of town. His other wife sat in the passenger seat, her hair piled up in a doo like it was the nineteen eighties. Three small heads bobbled around in the back seat.

Cameron pictured himself walking up to the driver-side window, pointing the Mosin at the man's head and blowing his brains into the polygamist chick's lap in a shower of blood and shatter-proof glass.

*Why do they call it shatter-proof glass if it blows into a million pieces?*

His mind did a little loop-de-loop. It'd been doing that a lot since he got shot and spent a week in a coma. *Maybe it'd started on the drive through Las Vegas,* he corrected. The last two months had been a horror show. He'd set a personal record for killing dudes. He'd gone from zero to...he didn't really know how many.

Not counting the Prophet Rulon—because he hadn't actually pulled the trigger on that crazy, old coot—he'd smoked six polygamists. *Seven, maybe?* Rulon's son, idling in the truck, would be Number Eight.

"You have to promise me not to hurt him, Cameron," Julie hissed, interrupting his loop-de-loop right at the top. He came crashing back to earth. "Cam. Can you hear me? We need to go. Right now. And you can't hurt Isaiah. You need to promise me that you won't touch him. He's got what we need to survive—stuff. Supplies. He has a place to go. He can't go back to town. They said they'll shoot him too if he returns. He's willing to take us with him, but you have to control yourself."

Cameron stared back toward town. Truck lights zoomed around like an anthill kicked over by a kid. Soon they'd send out trucks and horsemen, and they'd scour the red rock plains looking for the gentile who'd taken down their little heaven on earth. They weren't going to forget about Cameron. He'd shot too many of their stalwart sons and exposed too many of their dirty secrets. He felt the heft of the rifle, and the weight of the bullets in his pocket. He had just five more rounds.

"Boys," Cameron yelled. "Get in the back of that truck. Push stuff out of the way and make yourself a place to sit. You too," he said to Julie. "Tell your Celestial Husband that if he tries anything, I'll put a bullet in the back of his head."

"He's not like that. He stopped for us because he's decent, Cam. He's a decent man. Say whatever you want about the polygamists, but Isaiah isn't like his father. He stopped for us because he gave his word to protect me and the boys."

Cameron grunted. "I'll be sure and put him up for Father of the Year. Tell him what I said, Julie. And if you screw him again, I will kill him."

She glanced at the boys, probably to see if they'd overheard that last part. Cameron felt his face redden with shame.

*How could he say something like that in front of the boys about their mother?*

If his own dad had done that, he would've beat the shit out of him—no matter what his mother had done or who she'd screwed. He would've dropped his old man on-the-spot with a three-punch combination.

*Pop. Wham. Thud.*

"Nobody talks to my mom that way," he'd say.

Another loop-de-loop of the mind, and there he was, being a classic piece of shit, right in front of his boys.

Julie shook his shoulder. "Cameron. Please keep it together. We need you. It's life or death *right now* and we're scared. Real scared."

Cameron loosened his grip on the Mosin-Nagant. All the blood had been wrung out of his knuckles.

"Okay. Where are we going?" He stepped onto the truck bumper and over onto the pile of junk in the back.

Julie followed him up and into the truck bed. She wore the designer jeans he liked, the ones that showed off her long legs. A shockwave of jealousy ran up his spine.

Had she worn them for the polygamist? Had he peeled them off, with saliva in his mouth and lust in his eyes. *How many times had they done it?*

"Cameron. Did you hear what I said?"

"What?" The truck rumbled forward and gathered speed down the highway. The chilly breeze built a swirling tempest of wind around the shattered family.

"I said: he's taking us over the mountain to a place we can hide. It's an abandoned town his dad owned. He thinks we'll be safe there. He's not a bad person, Cam."

"Shit," Cameron scoffed. He pointed the rifle at the man's back, through the sheet metal of the truck cab. The kids were in the back seat. He pointed the rifle at the sky instead.

"He's decent," she repeated over the wind. "You'll see."

# 2

## SAGE ROSS

*Present Day.*

**Holland Farm**
**Wallula, Washington**

The burned farmhouse came as no surprise. Sage saw the orange glow on the horizon three days before. Even though every edible bit had been taken from the smoldering wreck, scavengers from the highway shuffled among the ruins, flipping over boards and picking through piles of blackened rubble.

Between the scorched remains of the two giant cottonwood trees, a charred body lay twisted in ankle-deep snow. He couldn't tell if the corpse belonged to the Holland family or if it'd been a scavenger who caught fire and burned to death. Whoever it was, the Hollands were either dead or on-the-run, which amounted to the same thing these days. Refugees were dead people who hadn't gotten the memo.

Sage had been a guest at the Holland's house when the refugees first came from the highway. The farmer's daughter died that first night. The rest either moved on or died later, defending the farm.

Sage hadn't been around to see it. He'd left them to their hapless cause. Nobody could survive this close to a highway, not with hundreds of acres of farm to protect. The desperate and dying citizens of Seattle, Yakima and Richland had come from hundreds of miles to pick clean the countryside, just as the frosts of winter crisped the ground and grayed the skies.

For now, Sage didn't have to worry about scavenge, though he would soon be a refugee himself. He carried a treasure trove on his back. His Grandpa Bob had set him up with enough food and equipment to last at least three more months. For six weeks now, he'd kept his head down, living in a cave carved into a crust of stone, hiding behind a camouflage wall of tumbleweed and sagebrush.

The same equipment that kept Sage alive also kept him rooted, unable to travel toward his family home in Utah. No matter how Sage packed and re-packed his gear, he couldn't carry more than six days of food on his back, and to get home, he needed to cover 600 miles between Washington State and Salt Lake City. Even at twenty miles per day, a pace unlikely given the weight of his pack, his food would hold out for 120 miles—480 miles short of home.

But even more than calories, the peaks gave him a lump of cold lead in his gut. The Blue Mountains soared five thousand feet on the eastern horizon, looming between this place and the farmlands that stretched between Wallula and Utah.

He'd backpacked with his father and sisters many times, but it'd never occurred to him that live-or-die backpacking involved a damned-if-you-do, damned-if-you-don't calculus of weight and calories. The more calories, the more weight; the more days he could hike, but he'd make less distance because of the weight. The less calories, the less weight, the fewer days he could hike, but then he would make more distance.

There was the variable of footwear to consider as well. No matter how good the pair of boots, he knew his feet would blister and foul if he carried too much weight too far too fast. The immutable bedrock of math, physiology and calories anchored his journey to the inexorable conclusion: six days of food and thirty pounds of pack weight were all he could carry, and that wouldn't get him even a quarter of the way home.

He couldn't stay in eastern Washington much longer. He'd been dipping into his Grandpa's food less and less because of the rabbits, onions, and roots he'd added to the stew pot. But very soon the snow would bury edible plants and force animals into hibernation. He'd already noticed that lazy rattlesnakes and sunning lizards had vanished. It was more difficult for him to dig up onions left by the harvester in the stiffening ground. Most of all, he burned more calories working in the cold. His hunger after foraging gnawed at his ribs in a way he hadn't felt during the friendly days of fall.

Snow had given him an advantage when it came to snaring rabbits. He could tell where the rabbits lived and travelled. After each snowfall, Sage tracked rabbit prints between field and burrow. With the tracks, the mystery surrounding the hunt thinned; he now knew where the rabbits lived and where they scampered. Armed with a sure knowledge, the pace of trial and error quickened. He deduced the best snare wire—barbed wire proved too thick, but light fishing line worked perfectly. He learned he'd been losing rabbits because his loops were too large—a loop the size of his fist caught more bunnies. Snare height mattered too—three fingers above the snow yielded best results.

To learn those lessons required hundreds of repetitions, but Sage had nothing better to do in his autumn hermitage than supplement his food with wild game and edible vegetables. As a result, he only burned through about half the freeze dried he'd brought with him from the Olympic Peninsula in his now-rotting car.

But against a 600 mile trek, he feared that starvation would seize him like a cougar on a mouse—skillful trapper of rabbits or not. He'd watched from afar as hundreds had died of starvation on the interstate. At seventeen years old, he'd come face-to-face with death more times than he could count. He knew how quickly the Reaper would take a man, and he'd lived hard enough over the last months to see the truth: he was *not* his mama's special snowflake. He was grist for the mill—another fleshy body Mother Earth would grind apart in her churn through the relentless seasons.

Given the skills he'd learned this fall, Sage felt cautiously optimistic he could extend his food by a factor of two. That'd get him 240 miles before he became another beggared refugee.

As he watched the half-dead stragglers pick at the burned-out farmhouse, a heavy sigh escaped him. Even with good forage, he'd die if he stayed here much longer. The winter would commit, the winds would embolden, luck would weaken and his life force would dribble away into the cold earth. His cave would become his tomb if he stayed.

The farther he ranged to set rabbit snares, the more likely he'd kick over a nest of refugees with enough spunk to hit him over the head with a rock or stab him with a knife. Eventually, he'd be discovered and he'd have to defend himself.

If the refugees caught him, they'd kill him for his backpack and his rifle. They might even eat him. He'd seen that recently too. Cannibalism. Human bones picked clean. Most of the refugees from the interstate had already surrendered to hunger, violence and disease. They were a peril slowly resolving itself—a self-licking ice cream cone, as his dad used to say.

Sage hung the binoculars on their harness around his neck and looked about, making sure he hadn't been spotted by vagabonds.

He let out another deep sigh and lingered for a moment, grieving the fate of the Hollands.

He cinched the sternum strap on his backpack and trudged east across the fields paralleling Highway 12. Even walking the dirt roads near the interstate could lead to a confrontation. With only a slight crescent moon, he couldn't travel at night yet, which would've been his preference.

Fortunately, the crop land of eastern Washington was crisis-crossed with irrigation canals. Walking in the deep irrigation ditches seemed the best compromise between speed and security, even though the route wasn't always direct. He could pick his way along the frosty, ice-pocked bottoms of the empty canals and generally follow the highway toward the unwavering base of the Blue Mountains. The farmlands of Eastern Oregon beckoned beyond, but the climb might take his life. He gave himself fifty percent odds.

The agricultural communities on the other side of the mountains called to him. Not just for resupply, but as a chance to prove his worth. As Sage moved along the gridwork of frozen canals, he pictured himself as an ancient, wandering young man; cast between huddled caverns and riverside hovels. At the dawn of time, teenage males probably wandered these same wildlands in hopes of finding a cluster of humanity that might welcome their hearty hands and willing souls. If, perchance, a young lady caught the eye—one who hadn't yet been claimed by a seasoned, mature man—so much the better. Young men had probably always burned with a desire to *arrive,* to contribute and to mate, and it had propelled them into the frozen unknown for aeons.

He could contribute to a community. If he could feed himself, as he had these last two months, he could help feed others. He ran his hands through his lengthening, brown hair as he journeyed away, forever, from the Holland farm. His ultimate destination would be Utah, but he would mount a mighty struggle against the space in between.

Sage recalled the promise he'd made to his dad, the last time they'd spoken over the phone. It seemed like years; another lifetime ago, but it'd only been six weeks. He'd promised his father that he would do whatever it took to survive. Somehow, his old man had known the journey would crumble into a gauntlet of terrors. The world had only just begun to burn at that point, but his dad must've sensed it falling into a pit of chaos that would devour cities and render men down to blood and grease.

In that nearly-forgotten world of telephone calls, before the collapse and while still a rebellious teenager, Sage's word hadn't meant a hill of beans, so he hadn't considered his promise overmuch at the time. He'd broken his word to his parents more often than he could count. Now, after all he'd survived, he made good account of his promise, every word. He would claw a living from the nap of the earth in order to survive, but in the ice fields of winter, he wasn't fool enough to believe he could do it alone.

Those lonely young men who dwelt in caves and hunted wooly mammoth had undoubtedly learned the same lesson as Sage in the stoney swales of eastern Washington: foraging alone through the winter was a death sentence. Cooperation was the first, elemental tool of survival. Without the ties that bind men to clan, Sage would forfeit his promise to his dad, and surrender his ghost somewhere on the snow-bound plains of Oregon or Idaho. He'd learned enough to be useful, but survival would require much more than skill. He must wrap himself in the threads of civilization—find a tribe, a town, or a family with a fighting chance of survival, and then ally himself to them.

The entire region—the eastern onion fields of Washington— had been too close to the pandemonium issuing from Seattle and Portland. The frank physics of the internal combustion engine and the size of a tank of gas doomed the Hollands and their farm, along with every hearty family between the Cascades and the Blue Mountains. The death throes of the old, broken society plowed them under. Sage had no choice but to cross over the towering dam of earth that'd held off the blood tide from Seattle. The tsunami of feckless men and their huddled women couldn't venture beyond the limits of a tank of gas, but with his new knowledge and his backpack, Sage likely would.

Beyond the Blue Mountains lay a mystery. Sage regarded the snow caps in the distance, peeking over the ledge of his irrigation canal. It'd take him a week to reach the foothills, and he knew he could survive that far. He had less confidence in the five thousand-foot climb over the snow-socked crags, but what lay beyond offered him a chance to reconnect with real people—and to resupply his backpack.

Sage glanced over his shoulder, hurrying away from the red and orange painted sky. With the icy hands of sunset already pawing at the back of his neck, he searched for a nighttime refuge. He wouldn't have time to set many snares before sleep, but he would try a few. His own tracks in the light snow, overlaying the tiny tracks of the rabbits, might betray his passing, and attract the human carrion-eaters. He would craft a way for his tracks to lead *away* from his sleeping den.

He sighed again, the only complaint he allowed himself these days. Everything in this new, ancient way of life required meticulous consideration. He wondered how many calories he burned just thinking about it all: minimize threats, conserve energy, and reap life-force energy from the land. Survival was a colossal pain in the ass.

He smiled against his internal bitching. He'd been alone for a long time, and his mind, he supposed, had subdivided into several personalities in order to argue with itself.

*Good God*, he swore. *He'd give his left nut for someone to talk to.*

He swept a too-long lock of dark hair out of his eyes and kicked a tumbleweed, then chided himself for the wasted energy.

He spotted the rotted, hanging door of an old root cellar, and in the distance, an abandoned-looking farmhouse. The root cellar had been dug into a hillside, probably fifty years before, ten yards off the irrigation canal. No cars, other than a rusted-out old truck, sat around the farmhouse. Sage thought he might take shelter in the root cellar. Refugees would hit the farmhouse before they'd search the surrounding grounds. He'd hear them and make his escape if it came to that.

Sage adjusted the straps over his shoulders again and back-tracked along the canal bottom until he cut a rabbit trail. He traced it to a den, set two snares, then looped around in the dark, in a spiral pattern, to the half-collapsed cellar. He'd leave enough prints circling his final sleeping place that anyone following would alert him passing by. He'd learned not to walk straight to his bed.

Surviving alone was a lot of work. He wouldn't miss that part if he ever found a new home, or God-permitting, made it back to his family.

## 3

### MAT BEST

**Highway 79**
**Northeast of McKenzie, Tennessee**

The *rats* had human faces. Mat Best caught glimpses as they vanished, screaming, under the bumper of his behemoth, deuce-and-a-half truck. His knuckles popped white on the steering wheel. The face of the third rat of the morning flicked from anger to defiance to horror as it grunted and disappeared beneath the army green hood. His rat companions dove off to the shoulder at the last second. They must've convinced themselves that the truck would stop or swerve, and that they'd score a tasty meal—maybe a roadside BLT or a *ham sammich.*

*Not today pals. No stopping this train between here and the slaughterhouse.* Mat pretended he hadn't heard the bump-and-crunch from under the rear tires.

Highway 79 reminded him of an Afghan goat trail. The Tennessee Transportation Authorities' incomplete repairs had stripped the road bed to nothing. Heavy rains in October demolished the remaining track.

*The same rains that killed Caroline,* Mat churned. *The same rains that dumped her bike and gave her a lethal dose of flesh-eating bacteria.*

The jacked-up road and thirty-mile-per-hour speed of the convoy allowed plenty of opportunity for rats to attempt an ambush.

*But not today, rats. Today, you get a giant helping of O.D. green radiator grill right over your filthy mugs.*

Mat was lead security for the convoy—out in front of a livestock hauler full of pigs. *The Porky Pig Fun Run,* his security team called it. This was the first of two trips slated for the day that'd bring a hundred live hogs into Mckenzie to be butchered, dried and preserved; 27,000 pounds of pork on the hoof. The Tosh Farms complex held thousands more pigs, and they had to be protected-in-place. The pigs were the key to survival for the town of McKenzie —an immense bank of living, breathing, eating, shitting post-collapse wealth. They were also an up-at-dawn security nightmare. Thousands of starving refugees surrounded the farm and the town, knives out.

Mat's four-vehicle, seven-man convoy should've been sufficient for the pig transfer between Tosh Farms and McKenzie. The convoy team was made up of his best men. Mat was the only guy with actual combat experience in town, and he'd been asked to lead security, which was a lot like being thrown into the middle of a swamp with a pocket knife and asked to eradicate the alligators.

Seemingly, word had gotten out about The Porky Pig Fun Run. Thousands of rats lined the roadside to watch the truck-loads of meat cross the vulnerable five-mile gauntlet between the "mutual security zones" of McKenzie and the neighboring berg of Henry, population 475. The town of Henry handled the pigs. The town of McKenzie handled the security. That was the deal.

The rats were castaways from the urban hellscapes surrounding the small towns: Memphis, Nashville, St. Louis and Louisville. When the economy took the Big Dump, thousands of city people flooded into the Tennessee countryside, where food actually grew.

The watchers along the road weren't Mat's problem. They could have their drooling fantasies about pork chops and applesauce. Today, though, the rats had grown a pair. Mat had never seen them coordinate like this before. It was a ragged attempt, but the new motivation was obvious. Somebody was leading them.

Up ahead, two rats pushed a big baby stroller onto the road.

*What the fuck?* Mat's foot bobbled on the accelerator, then kept steady pressure.

"Please don't be a baby. Please just be an IED," he prayed.

*Did a tiny hand rise from the buggy?* Mat prayed in monosyllables to an unfamiliar god.

"No-no-no-no-NO!"

A skeleton-thin man lit the baby buggy on fire, then pushed it, into Mat's path. It exploded in flame, like it'd been doused in gasoline or lighter fluid. He hit the stroller at thirty miles per hour and the flame blasted in all directions. Mat couldn't see anything but fire cascading up and over his windshield, but there was no meaty thunk under his tires, no tiny hand slapping against the glass. It'd just been an ingenious, trash-tech IED: an empty baby carriage, and the ploy had almost worked. Mat had to think hard before reaching the conclusion that he hadn't, actually, shit his pants.

*Would he have slammed on the brakes if he'd seen a baby?* Mat honestly didn't know.

The buggy engulfed the hood and bullet-resistant glass in flame. Mat worried about the vulnerable wires and hoses under the hood if gas seeped inside. He hoped the wind sucked it all away.

Would it be weird if a few coke bottles of gasoline killed a military vehicle? Mat had seen weirder things than that over in the sandbox. For now, the truck seemed okay. The engine growled and the road flew past.

As the smoke cleared, the second phase of the ambush appeared.

"Fuck me!" Mat gasped as he leaned toward the windshield.

The highway between the two towns was arrow-straight, except for two curves that snaked between a pair of bogs. Before the first curve, the rats had launched the buggy trick. Past the bend, a line of dead cars suddenly appeared across Highway 79.

Mat roared obscenities as he stood up on the brakes.

---

*THREE WEEKS **earlier***

**McKenzie City Hall**
**McKenzie, Tennessee**

*Joint Security Committee and Food Committee Meeting*

THE TOWN OF McKENZIE, Tennessee, population 3,547, had responded as well as any town could to the collapse of America. They moved straightaway to preserve food, water and energy resources. They even struck a mutual security agreement with the neighboring hamlet of Henry—five miles Northeast on Highway 79.

Henry, Tennessee had 475 people and 3,500 pigs in various stages of fattening. Securing Tosh Farms commercial hog complex meant the survival of McKenzie. Losing it meant starvation—the numbers weren't complex.

"Sheriff Morgan?" The mayor wouldn't start a meeting without Morgan. Maybe the mayor had always deferred to the sheriff. Mat didn't know. He'd been living on the East Coast before the Big Nosedive. He'd wandered into McKenzie, weeks before, looking for medical help for his girlfriend.

Gunmen like Mat were held in awe in McKenzie. Mat had a gun, and a sterling resume as a U.S. Army Ranger, so their unquestioning respect suited him fine. He'd lost the girl to gangrene and ended up with her little brother as his ward. *So what if she had turned out to be the love of his fucking life?*

"Sheriff, we're ready to start." The mayor smiled and sat down.

Mat wasn't clear on how town committees worked. This committee was apparently a mishmash of security people and food people meeting to discuss defense of the hog farms.

"Protecting an area of operation the size of the pig farms, five miles from town, is probably more than we can handle," Mat said, launching into his area of expertise. It was what Sheriff Morgan had asked him to cover. "Can we move the pigs into town?"

"*Sounder*," Charles Jones, Senior corrected.

"What?" Mat asked.

"A group of pigs is called a *sounder*." Chuck Senior was dressed in well-worn green coveralls with a toothpick in his mouth. He looked every inch the swine farmer.

"How large of a *sounder* can we move in a semi truck?" Mat asked.

"We can move fifty butcher-ready hogs in a livestock trailer," said Charles Jones Junior.

Chuck Junior wore a collared shirt and jeans. He carried himself like a businessman.

"But even if we could move them, McKenzie couldn't keep them alive in city limits. And we can't slaughter them all-at-once. There's nowhere to refrigerate that much pork. If we're going to keep 3,500 pigs—and hopefully at some point breed them—we have to house them where we can care for them: *at the complex in Henry.* That many pigs can't live in peoples' yards. The pigs would get sick and so would the people."

Mat raised his hands in surrender. "Alright. Sounds like we'll be running convoys and patrols between the two towns." He studied the map spread out on the meeting table. "That's a five-mile umbilical cord between two secure zones. Chuck Senior and Junior, how many of these farms are there and how far apart?"

Chuck Senior pointed at the map they'd spread out: "Hogs are spread over six locations within three miles of Tosh, here in the center. That's the sow farm. That's for breeding, mind you."

Chuck Junior held up a hand and made eye contact with each of the pig farmers in attendance, including a frightened-looking executive in a wrinkled suit from Tosh Farms. "We think we can pull back to headquarters, plus two wean-to-finish farms just outside of town. We'd shut down the others to make a smaller perimeter."

"Wean-to-finish?" asked Mat.

"After a pig is weaned from its mother, it goes to a wean-to-finish farm to put on another two hundred and fifty pounds. Bottom line: we can pull the operation back to a mile-wide circle around the town of Henry. We've already started."

Mat sucked in a breath and exhaled. Chuck Senior was no country bumpkin. He'd already seen the vulnerability of their situation and taken action, but building a perimeter around a mile circle, plus the four-mile-radius around town, was a security nightmare. The twin towns would be like a Forward Operating Base with a combined eighteen miles of perimeter and a five mile cordon in between, with a steady stream of indigenous threats, numbering in the tens of thousands.

"What heavy vehicles do we have for convoy duty between here and there?" Mat looked up from the map.

Deputy Wiggin answered. "Um. There are a few box trucks in town, but I think we can do better. The Feds gave us a deuce and a half. A military truck." He grinned like a kid. "I'm not sure why."

The heavy truck made no sense for a small-town sheriff's department, but nobody had understood the Federal Government, then or now. It was a homeland security thing, and Mat was now very involved in homeland security. The deuce-and-a-half would be perfect.

Mat spoke up, "Sheriff? We don't have veterans with combat experience, right?"

"Combat experience?" repeated Sheriff Morgan. "Smith and Rickers served. They drove trucks or counted band aids or something. We have Gulf War vets in town, but they're old as the hills."

Mat nodded. "I spoke with Smith and Rickers. They worked convoy duty in Afghanistan, so that's good. But they've never been in a gunfight," he added. He could see in their eyes they didn't understand. Driving truck and gunfighting were about as closely related as pet grooming and bull riding.

The town's Gulf war vets were over fifty years old by now and probably a few thousand beers past their *Best If Used By* date. War was a young man's game. He needed young, experienced combat vets. High school and college-age kids might have to do. Then again, he didn't have any bullets for training. He barely had bullets for fighting.

---

*"ROADBLOCK! ALL STATIONS: RUN THE BASTARD!"* Mat keyed his radio and stomped on the accelerator. He aimed the deuce-and-a-half for the seam between two of the dead cars.

Four sedans had been parked end to end across the road. If the rats had used twice the number of vehicles in an overlapping pattern, Mat would've been in deep shit. As it was, he had a pretty good chance of spinning two of the cars out of the way by hitting the gap. The convoy might sail through.

The deuce-and-a-half hurled into the roadblock and only the

three-point belt kept Mat from face-smashing the windshield. Upon impact, his torso yanked back so hard against the harness that his brain smacked around inside his skull. For two seconds, his mind struggled to re-load it's operating system.

When he came around, he saw he was through. The deuce-and-a-half had only lost ten miles per hour. Mat had lost five IQ points.

He lurched around in his seat to check the rearview mirror. The livestock hauler behind him clipped the nose of a sedan. Then the driver, Chuck Jones Junior, massively over-corrected. The rig performed three, ever-increasing swerves until the trailer flipped over. Then it took the cab with it. The engine screamed as the drive wheels clawed at air and the rig slid across the road base on its side. The engine died as the rig skidded to a halt in a storm of gravel and shredded blacktop.

Mat slammed on the brakes and the deuce growled to a stop. He ground the gears into reverse and stomped on the gas. He roared back to the livestock hauler just as the sheriff's cruisers skidded up behind it. The rig was like a beached and bloodied whale.

Deputy Smith leapt out of the cruiser and bounded up the side of the big rig. He reached inside the shattered window and dragged Chuck Junior up and out of the cab. Mat and Deputy Rickers took up defensive positions behind the ruined quarter panel of the truck, scanning the road with the barrels of their AR-15s.

The screaming of the pigs was deafening. Mat's neck pulsed with the blow he'd taken when he'd hit the roadblock. Around the corners of his vision, he saw flashes of light and dark, squiggly shapes. He could barely see, much less think tactically.

"Sarge!" Deputy Smith screamed for Mat. "He's hurt bad, Sarge! He's... I think he's dead! They killed Chuck Junior. They killed him!"

Smith cradled Chuck Junior's green coverall-clad body against his chest. Chuck's head hung in a position that made no anatomical sense.

"Goddamn rats," raged Deputy Rickers.

The rats were in chaos after the violence of the collisions. They sprinted across the fields, ducked around the smashed up cars and generally flitted around like a flock of pigeons when an old man shows up with a bread bag. It gave Mat's team time to recover the body of Chuck Junior and get it in the passenger seat of the police cruiser.

The six surviving men ran back to the capsized truck. Halfway there, some rats opened fire on them. A dozen rats had taken cover behind the roadblock. The majority carried improvised weapons like clubs, even a few spears, but few had firearms. What was left of the convoy—the deuce and two cruisers—was trapped on the McKenzie side—the flipped semi sealed the roadblock.

"Just leave! Take your people and go!" called a rat voice from the roadblock.

A chorus of hoarse, panicked voices joined. "Just leave. Don't fight us! Please. We need the food! Just leave the pigs and go!" The rats pleaded rather than threatened.

"Shut up! Shut up!" boomed the first voice—a man behind one of the smashed vehicles. "It's over, cops. Take your people. We won't shoot you if you leave your guns."

That last demand must've been a visit from the Good Idea Fairy. Mat doubted the original plan had anything to do with stealing firearms from cops. The rats had a leader, and he had a pair of brass balls, but the promise of food trumped all. The gun thing was icing on the cake.

Even through the thundering percussion in his neck, Mat felt pretty sure he had the measure of the enemy. They were near panic, and a counter-attack would flatten them like a pup tent. They sure-as-hell weren't getting any guns from Mat and his guys. The rats would be lucky to leave with their lives. The two deputies carried AR-15s and the sheriff had loaned Mat a SCAR Heavy rifle. The brothers, Juan and Jesus Cabrera, had been issued pump shotguns from the sheriff's gun locker. All six men wore soft body armor.

They could Alamo-up and try to hold this ground for the forty-five minutes it'd take to scrounge up another hauler from Henry and salvage the pigs. They only had the one hauler on the McKenzie side and now it was tits-up, blocking the road. Or, they could ditch the pigs and light out for McKenzie. But this wasn't Indian country—this was their precious link to the pig farms. After his latest success, Mister Loudmouth Leader would ambush them again and again. Better to destroy the threat now. Mat knew right where to find the guy. He might never get this chance again.

Deputy Rickers shouted at Mat, "Sarge, they're coming. Holy shit. They're *ALL* coming."

Thousands of refugees sprang from the muddy fields and rushed from the treeline. What Mat had mistaken for a vanilla tactical problem, flashed suddenly into an apocalyptic shitstorm.

He'd read stories about British soldiers fighting African tribal nations in the 1800s—when a handful of Brits would be attacked by thousands of spear-wielding natives. Even just reading about them, his throat had tightened; a couple dozen men, circled by the carcasses of their wagons, facing the fury of five thousand enraged warriors. But in real life, the cavalry never came. In most of those desperate battles, every white man died dangling from the end of the enemies' spear.

Until that moment on the road, behind the dead big rig, witnessing waves of humanity pouring across the mud-soaked fields, Mat had thought of this as a standard contracting gig.

*Teach a town to defend itself. Help them build a perimeter wall. Tighten up security, then get back on the road.* One-and-done. Over-and-out. Mat Best rides off into the sunset, once again.

What his eyes beheld buggered that idea all to hell. He had not been trained for this. They didn't teach Army Rangers how to defeat thousands of Zulu warriors with fifty rounds of ammo, twenty men and six, broke-axle wheel carts. The army had you read those Zulu stories so you wouldn't be stupid enough to get in those situations in the first place.

Just the rats from the immediate vicinity of the ambush numbered in the thousands. The mud fields crawled with them—scrambling, high-stepping, clawing toward Mat's position. The rats *right in this bog* outnumbered the residents in town. There had to be ten or more times that many refugees in the woods, surrounding McKenzie.

A filth-ridden man and woman launched out of a tall stand of grass toward Mat. They clambered onto the road and swung home-made clubs in one hand, steak knives in the other. She wore a filthy, gold and purple dress—like she'd fled the big city wearing the nicest thing she owned.

Mat's hands operated automatically—they flicked off his safety and put two rounds, center mass, into each of them. The couple crumpled off the road and rolled back into the muck.

Two more nasty-looking creatures crouched in the bushes behind Mat's position. He didn't see weapons, but he couldn't allow the flank. He fired two rounds into each through the grass, and they pinwheeled backward—a woman's scarf trailed magenta and saffron. Mat shook his head at the weirdness of it, which sent his thundering neck ache up to his brain pan. The cacophony in his coconut went from bongo drums to acid rock.

The man he'd just blind-shot behind the bush cut loose with a soul-wrenching keen of anguish. The dude jumped up, alone now, and rushed. Both Mat and Rickers put rounds into him and he went down hard, flipping over backward, just like in the movies.

A refugee in orange coveralls broke into a sprint along the shoulder, right down their throats. Juan Cabrera blasted him with buckshot and the guy vanished off the road and into a pile of trash.

*Was that a prison jumpsuit or an orange dress?* A flicker of color in the tall grass caught Mat's eye. *Yellow silk? A child's coat?* There were children in those fields. Mat despaired, *Please God, don't make me shoot kids today.*

He breach-checked his rifle in order to yank himself back to reality. His mind had flickered for a moment, right in the middle of a firefight. He poked his head over the fender of the semi for a tactical assessment.

The fight had lulled. The rats numbered in the thousands, but they were no fierce Zulu warriors. They wanted a meal, not victory. He and his men had killed a dozen or more of them—their bodies littered the road. The slayings gave the field of refugees pause. Without religious fervor or a warrior's creed, they were legion, but confused.

Mister Loudmouth Leader shuffled around behind the wreckage. He wasn't going to leave well-enough alone. The bastard screamed, inciting the masses, "They're trying to take our food! Stop them! Stop them! They're taking the pigs away! Get them! GET 'EM NOW! GET 'EM NOW!"

Thousands jumped from the winter-dead, knee-high grass and stormed toward Mat's team. The ARs and shotguns barked a steady, murderous rhythm, and the rats stumbled over each others' bodies. The rush faltered and the rats slunk backward behind clumps of shrub and tall grass. The dead and wounded littered the ground. Their moans were like piles of sorrowful demons, torn from the breast of hell.

*Snick-snick-snick*, Mat's guys consolidated ammunition from half-empty mags.

The air tasted of burned powder and the sweat of his mens' terror. The pigs' screams had almost vanished like the background noise of a busy dungeon.

The armed rats behind the blockade fired willy-nilly at his team.

Mat shot two young women rushing onto the road, one wearing what looked like a green ball gown and the other in a cocktail dress. The woman in the ball gown hurled a spear before a round punched her chest. The makeshift spear clattered to the ground at Mat's feet.

*Was that a Zulu, a woman or a mirage?* The sparkles around the edge of his vision had graduated into lightning bolts. He rubbed his eyes so hard it made them ache.

A wave of rats attacked from the roadblock. Guns, knives and clubs flashed. Mat's knot of men answered with a wave of thunder. Deputy Smith ran out of rifle ammo, drew his revolver and fired into a man's belly at the same moment he jammed a stick into Smith's eye. Smith shrieked, and fell back into Juan Cabrera, who killed two guys with one blast of his shotgun. The wounded remnant of the rat attack scurried back to the smashed-up cars.

Mat needed to end this. Things weren't going well. He didn't know if the problem was the whiplash from the crash or the absurdity of the jacked-up zombie bullshit. He knew he couldn't keep this up for another forty-five minutes.

He sprinted for the semi trailer without telling his guys what he was doing. The time was ripe for some special forces, Hail Mary shit. The dumped-over pig hauler rocked with the violent thrashing and ear-piercing wails of the swine.

He bounded up on the trailer, which was now on its side, and yanked the last remaining cross-pin free from the half door. The trailer gate crashed to the ground. Pigs shot out, like fat, pink cannonballs, scattering in every direction. The first wave of hogs bowled over a knot of refugees rushing Mat. One guy hit his head so hard on the asphalt Mat could hear the *plack* sound from atop the hauler.

The rats' attention flashed to the bolting food. "The pigs! There they go!"

A mighty torrent of three hundred-pound animals streamed from the trailer and into the fields. The refugees dashed after them, but the pigs blew through them like living, stampeding, wrecking balls. Rats in the field went down in swaths. Yet others swarmed into the melee, trying desperately to get their hands on some bacon.

"Rickers and Jesus, cover fire on the roadblock," he screamed. Now, Mat knew what to do. It was high time to roll up the HVT—the High Value Target. Mr. Loudmouth Leader was fresh out of cannon fodder, and by demanding the guns, he'd put himself in Mat's gunsight. Mat couldn't shoot thousands of refugees—at least not today—but he sure as hell could take down the party planner.

Mat ran to where Deputy Smith lay sprawled on his back with both hands over his eye. Mat hauled him to his feet and half led, half dragged him to the passenger side of the deuce-and-a-half. Then he circled his hand in the air, the signal for Wiggin, Rickers, and the Cabrera brothers to rally on him.

Two of the rats at the roadblock fell to their gunfire. That left five rats focused on the gunfight, and only four with guns. Mat alone was worth twenty armed rats.

"Juan cover Smith and provide overwatch. You three push the center of the road. Don't take any risks. Move up, cover to cover. Keep a steady pace of fire. I'm flanking to the right. Don't fucking shoot me. No shooting toward the right shoulder of the road. Got it?" It would be a test of Mat's brilliant new idea: the quick-and-dirty L-ambush training-under-live-fire. *What could go wrong?*

Mat signaled forward, and his three shooters pressed up the center of the road, leap-frogging to the police cruiser and then pushing toward the blockade. The AR15s sent steady waves of lead into the roadblock. The rats managed only wild, unaimed shots in return.

Mat slid down the road embankment and darted forward. The hundreds of rats on that side were otherwise occupied with the hog rodeo. He didn't wait to see if anyone would notice him. He sprinted forward and slid around the side of the barricade with his rifle at the ready.

All but two of the rats took rounds. Mr. Loudmouth Leader surrendered, throwing down an SKS rifle, and raising his hands above his head. Mat's men moved in and overtook the blockade.

Jesus Cabrera waited until the leader's arms were zip-tied behind his back, then he smashed the douchebag's nose with an elbow.

Mat shouted, "Cabrera! You're with me and Mr. Loudmouth in the deuce-and-a-half! Jesus and Rickers." He turned to the deputy. "Take the cruiser. We'll leave the other cruiser here for now."

To Rickers he rasped, "You're on point. Don't stop until we hit the checkpoint. GO."

The pigs had run off the field and into the tree line. One rat dangled around a hog's neck, stabbing it like a prison fight. The running, squealing pig shucked him off and disappeared into the trees. Another man shot a pig with his nine millimeter to no apparent effect. Somehow, someone had gotten a single pig on the ground and a brawl broke out over the carcass.

*Rats one. Pigs forty-nine.*

Even hungry and desperate, people were no match for the pigs. Eventually, the refugees would probably get most of them in the stew pot, but it'd take time and ingenuity. In any case, Mat's team had bought back their lives with those fifty pigs. There was little doubt how the Zulu siege was going to end.

Mat did a tactical reload and hoisted himself into the driver seat of the deuce-and-a-half. The big truck had been idling this whole time, wasting fuel. Mat rocked it into gear, punched the accelerator and lurched for town.

"Juan, make sure those new guys withdraw to McKenzie with us. Radio the northeast checkpoint, and have them call in at least twenty more guards in case the mob gets any more big ideas."

As Cabrera completed one radio call, Mat gave him another,

"Radio McKenzie HQ and have the next shift start now for all checkpoints. Double coverage. Have HQ warn the hospital we're coming in with Smith. Someone's going to have to tell the family that Chuck Junior's dead." Mat would give anything not to be that guy.

There was a moment when he feared the heavy vehicle might stick in the wet gravel. Mat pushed the deuce through a loose spot in the half-deconstructed highway. The wheels caught and in a few seconds he was grumbling toward the safety of town. He mashed the gas pedal to the floor, but the deuce barely noticed.

*After what he'd just seen—countless thousands of rats, pouring toward the promise of food—how safe was town, really? How long until the rats made their big push?*

It wasn't just the ringing in his ears or the war drums in his raging brain stem; Mat had landed in the middle of an unwinnable fight. McKenzie would inevitably fall, like the Battle of Isandlwana when the Zulu crushed the mighty British with 20,000 spearmen. Everyone here would die—either at the hands of the refugees or in the famine that would follow. The winter had only just begun. The hunger could only get worse, all the way through April.

Mat needed to put a shine on his personal exit strategy or this contract would be his last. He'd hoped, at least, to stabilize this place and leave them with a fair, fighting chance. He owed Caroline at least that: to leave her brother William in a good home, preferably with a wall around the town. At that moment, Mat couldn't see it happening—couldn't make the numbers work in his head.

*A quarter-finished HESCO barrier around town. Thousands, maybe tens of thousands of famished refugees. Very few guns and little ammunition.*

Mat thought of himself as being pretty damn clever, but big numbers have a power all their own.

Juan Cabrera must've read his mind. "We need a better plan, Sarge."

*Indeed,* thought Mat. *A better plan for the town and a better plan for Mat Best.*

———

FIFTY-FIVE MINUTES AFTER THE AMBUSH, Mat knocked on the open door of Sheriff Morgan's office. He walked in without waiting—still a little rattled and adrenaline-drunk. Sheriff Morgan looked up from the conversation he was having with a man Mat didn't know.

"Here to debrief?" Sheriff Morgan smiled grimly at Mat. "How's Smith? Can they save the eye?"

Mat shook his head. "The doc didn't think so. Smith asked me to tell you he'd be back on duty tomorrow. I don't doubt he means it."

"The man's got grit," the sheriff agreed.

Mat continued his interruption. "I sent a team to reconnoiter the ambush site. The cruiser's gone; probably stolen for its gas. We're going to need some kind of wrecker to get the pig hauler back on its tires. It's blocking the whole road."

"What the hell happened out there?" The sheriff knew the outcome, but he hadn't been briefed.

Mat flicked a glance at the man sitting across from the sheriff.

"This is Jim Jensen," the sheriff explained. "He's our kids' science teacher. I've asked him to join the security committee. He has some ideas about chemical weapons." *You can speak freely,* the sheriff seemed to imply.

Mat hadn't "spoken freely" with anyone since Caroline's death, and he already didn't like where this was going. He'd gone to war to stop Sadaam Hussein and chemical weapons, and it put a bad taste in his mouth to even hear them mentioned on American soil. He accepted the man's outstretched hand for a handshake. The science guy didn't stand up to greet him, which was *strike two* in Mat's book.

"We've met," Jensen said. "His younger brother William comes to my class." Meeting Mat's eyes the science guy said, "Good to see you again." Mat had no memory of ever meeting him.

Mat moved on to the sheriff's question about the ambush. "We had bad operational security. The rats knew where and when to hit us. I underestimated them by putting the convoy trips on a fixed schedule. They're organizing."

"Okay," said Sheriff Morgan. "What was your oversight?"

"More of an assumption than an oversight," Mat said. "I assumed a leadership vacuum among the rats..."

Sheriff Morgan cleared his throat. "I don't like that name. *Rats*. These are people. I don't like dehumanizing the refugees."

Mat didn't like being pulled up by the short hairs for political correctness, but he respected Sheriff Morgan—even liked him. Mat let it slide. Jensen sat up a little straighter, almost like he was taking note of the micro-fracture between the two men. Mat continued, "I had assumed the refugees weren't coordinated. We didn't vary our route and timing. It was my mistake."

Morgan leaned forward onto his desk. "Who was leading them?"

"We captured the guy. We're going to want to keep him in a cage, or put a bullet in his head." Mat described Mr. Loudmouth Leader's coordination of the ambush and his use of a couple thousand rats as cover for his operation. Mat had spoken with the guy for a couple minutes after they reached McKenzie. His name was Jared, and he was definitely a problem.

"The guy doesn't have any formal training. Just big ideas," Mat reported. "He's smart enough, and he got people to follow him. We should interrogate him and see what he knows about leadership in the other camps. We're totally blind when it comes to how they organize. I assumed they were nothing more than mobs. I don't want to make the same mistake twice. I've got a job to finish and an organized enemy's going to make it harder."

"Leave the interrogation to me," Sheriff Morgan suggested.

"Each man to his profession. I have a sixth sense for criminals—in my own, small town way." That was okay with Mat. He'd never interrogated anyone.

Jim Jensen spoke up. "The refugees want our food. They'd kill every last pig in an hour, given the chance. The meat would spoil and they'd be hungry again in a day. The guns they demanded at the ambush—they would've been for this guy, Jared, and his inner circle. That's how tyrants work, historically."

There was a pause as the conversation reset. Jensen had stated the obvious and thrown in a bit about history; a willowy academic trying hard to be relevant in the presence of two men-of-action. Mat noted the irony; social posturing survived even when the rest of civilization had gone down the shitter.

Sheriff Morgan nudged the stalled conversation forward. "Right. Good point."

Encouraged, Jensen went on. "The rats..." He turned to Morgan. "I'm sorry sheriff but it's not an unfair moniker given the situation." He turned back to Mat. "These rats—these threats to our safety and our food supply—will be increasingly dangerous as more arrive and as they become more hungry and desperate."

*Yeah, no shit,* Mat thought. The guy kept talking.

"Winter is here, which means desperation will peak in a couple months. It'll be mid-January before the die-off of refugees crescendos. Common colds will lead to pneumonia. Bad water will cause dysentery and probably cholera. I've asked to be added to the security committee, because I can accelerate the natural draw-down of the refugees. Speed the process."

Mat couldn't quite follow the doublespeak, but it sounded like some Doctor Mengele shit.

The sheriff interrupted, "Now, Jim, I'll repeat what I said before, so we're crystal clear: allowing you to present these ideas to Sergeant Best is not an endorsement. I have misgivings. I want to hear his thoughts from a military perspective. If Mat doesn't support your plan it's unlikely I'll support it either."

Jensen seemed unfazed by Morgan's reticence. In fact, it seemed to excite him. "Fair enough." He turned his chair to face Mat, which was also weird—Mat was standing up and the science guy was sitting down. "I was there when you came into the town meeting to warn us of the threat from Louisville gangs. You put the scare into me—let me tell you. It got me thinking: how can we defend ourselves from a numerically-superior enemy? Now two months later, we've now got a refugee problem instead of a gangbanger problem. This rat problem is probably worse than gangs, because there are so darned many rats. But that's the beauty of it. My idea works even better with thousands of them." Jensen paused expectantly. He obviously wanted Mat to inquire about his "big idea."

Mat hated this shit; hated the long, puffed-up preamble guys like this had to deliver before they shared intel, or gave up their salsa recipe, or whatever they were using to hold an audience captive. Mat had plenty of experience dealing with guys like this in the army officer corps; he usually let them bloviate for a while, until eventually they gave up some bit of meaningful intel. Then he could get to his transport and get shit done.

Right now, Mat's head felt like it was full of wet rags, slowly going to mold, and he didn't want to play the pretend-to-kiss-the-officer's-ass game. Science Guy could sit there with his eyebrows raised, with a slight, stupid grin, for as long as he liked. Mat had just killed six people. He wasn't in a mood to stroke egos.

Jensen detoured. "Okay, so my background is chemistry, but I also teach biology. I was thinking, *what can I do?* I'm no warrior. I mean, I can do my part with a gun if it comes to that, but that's not my expertise." He paused again.

The sheriff broke before Mat did. "Jim, let's get to the point. You're talking about anthrax, right?"

"Right!" exclaimed Jensen, pleased by the audience participation. "But not exactly. Anthrax was the first thing I thought of, yes, but then weaponizing anthrax is not a simple process. I can do it, and my tests are underway. I looked into botulism, too. That's the weapon I propose we use first against the rats."

"Refugees," corrected Sheriff Morgan.

Even the word "botulism" sent a chill down Mat's spine. Botulism had been the pathogen that had likely killed Caroline. She'd been gone eight weeks and the wound felt as fresh as yesterday.

Mat crammed the watery-gut sensation down and interrupted Science Guy, "Whether we call them refugees or rats, we need to admit that the camps pose an existential threat to McKenzie. Deputy Smith lost an eye on a milk run, and that run will only become *more* dangerous. The shit heads in those camps will be eating pork tonight, and that's a serious problem for us. Today's ambush will sound like Washington crossing the Delaware to people eating pork for the first time in two months. And, we failed to complete the supply mission. With all due respect, Sheriff, calling them 'rats' is a love letter compared to the words my security team uses to describe them. The rats are the enemy." Mat pointed out a window of the sheriff's office in the direction of the strand of road between McKenzie and Henry. "I don't know if bio-chem weapons are the right idea, though. Can we even control a biological weapon this close to the town?" Mat recalled the holy fear of bio-chem put into him by the Army. Poison gas and viruses killed indiscriminately; like how botulism killed Caroline. She'd scraped the deadly bacteria off the asphalt in a motorcycle crash. Letting something that vicious off the leash should terrify them. But after what he'd seen in the killing fields that day, he wasn't crossing anything off the list.

"...which is precisely why we're discussing food-borne botulin toxin instead of anthrax," Jensen explained. He leaned forward, apparently getting ready to restart his monologue.

Mat held up a hand to stop him. "I'll keep an open mind until Science Guy here does his presentation to the committee."

"Jim," Jensen corrected.

"Right." Mat wasn't in a big hurry to accept that kind of responsibility. The committee might even be worth something, if they could off-load the guilt of poisoning a bunch of women and children.

Mat hated the idea of botulism, but one of his men was just killed and another blinded. A damned stadium-load of people had just come at him like an Egyptian plague. If not for the pigs to distract them, those fuckers would probably be cooking Mat's corpse over a campfire right about now.

Sheriff Morgan sat back and observed the two men, probably assessing them in his "own, small town way." He lurched forward and stood. "Very well, Jim. We'll hear you out at Thursday's meeting. Sergeant Best, would you mind staying for a minute?"

Jim Jensen left the office with awkward handshakes. The sheriff returned to his seat and sipped from a coffee mug with a government seal on the side. Mat wasn't sure what made a good sheriff at the end of the world, but he thought the big man was probably dead-center in the middle of the target.

"How are you and William settling in?" the sheriff asked.

"Good. The house you loaned us is perfect. I appreciate it."

"Good. And how are you two getting along with the town?"

Mat shifted in his chair. "No problems."

"Is this home yet?"

"Our house or McKenzie?" Mat stalled.

Morgan held Mat's gaze for a few seconds. "Mat, you said *I've got a job to finish.* Before."

Mat raised his eyebrows.

"That's what you said a few minutes ago. 'I've got a job to finish.' What's the job and how will you know when it's finished?"

Mat scooted forward in his chair. "You asked me to protect this town, to reinforce it, to defend against invasion and that's what I'm doing. The eighteen full-time and reserve officers are insufficient to protect the town. Now, we have 150 men and women on the security force. I haven't had time for much training, but we've got checkpoints on every ingress and egress point. We have patrols and we have perimeter guards. We're stretched thin between here and Henry, but we'll add another hundred security personnel over the next few weeks. I'm considering candidates for a quick reaction force. We could've used a QRF today."

The sheriff held up a hand to pause Mat's report. "If I was a fancy therapist, I'd wait for you to see this on your own, but I'm just a cop, and we don't have time to do this the slow way. So, hear me out."

"Okay, Sheriff," Mat said.

"Son, I don't know what you believe about God, but I believe you're here for a reason. We're grateful an expert on warfare came right when we needed him. You saved us, I believe. At the same time, this town can save you. But you have to let it."

Mat's jaws clenched so tight it took effort to move his mouth. "You mean like the town saved Caroline?"

Mat hated these kinds of conversations—the "let's talk about all the feelings you're not seeing," kinds of conversations. People were on high alert for PTSD in a combat veteran—like a Where's Waldo of amateur psychology: *where's the PTSD? Let's probe around until we find it.*

Sheriff Morgan didn't match Mat's sudden tension. Instead, his voice went soft. "I am sorry for your grief." There was heartbreak in his voice, not as fresh and violent as Mat's, but true empathy.

Morgan continued, "I'm talking about how this town saved a miserable, divorced, alcoholic patrolman from Louisville. Like how it took him in, gave him a home, a family, and a path back to his creator. This town saved me, but I had to let it in first. I had to open myself up."

"Sheriff, I don't..."

Morgan raised a hand. "You've been here two months. How many of your neighbors can you name? Aside from today's team on convoy duty, how many of your security guys can you name? I mean proper names, not Fat Dude, Toothpick or Science Guy. How many of their wives' names do you know? People want to trust you, Mat, but you have to trust them, too. They can smell it when you don't. They can smell it when you're not all in."

Mat stood up. His face felt hard. "I've got to make my rounds to the checkpoints. Anything else, Sheriff?"

"Just this, and I'll let it be: a man has to have a home. A place he claims folks as his own, and where he lets them claim him."

Mat pulled the office door open to leave. "I'll see you later, Sheriff. If there is a later. What I saw today was two thousand refugees pop straight out of the woods for a whisper of a prayer of a meal. We might want to hold off planning the village *hugfest* until we're no longer surrounded by 10,000 near-cannibals."

Sheriff Morgan smiled. "I respect a man who meets an attack with a counter-attack. And while I was born on Tuesday, I wasn't born *last* Tuesday. Any fool can see you need us as much as we need you, Sergeant Best. You have the look of a man being chased by ghosts."

Mat went to close the door, but the sheriff stood from behind his desk, so Mat paused. Respect for elders was a thing in Mat's family, and it definitely was a thing in the army. He'd never close the door in the face of a man like Sheriff Morgan.

The sheriff met Mat where he stood. "I'm on your team," he said. "We're staring into the shittiest bucket of choices I've seen in my sixty-two years on this planet. I want you to know that I'm with you, and when push comes to shove, I'll have your back. This is me giving you my word of honor."

Mat covered the emotion that rose in his throat by looking away down the hall. What Morgan just said sounded like something his dad would say. Mat suddenly missed his family. He missed being surrounded by people who had his back. If he was being honest with himself, he did need a place to settle the whacky shit that'd sprung up in his battered head.

"I appreciate you saying that," he admitted, in a voice that sounded too low and husky.

The sheriff clapped a hand on the crook where Mat's shoulder met his neck. "Stand or fall—we're brothers now."

Mat nodded, stepped back and slipped into the hallway.

# 4

## CAMERON STEWART

"So then, royal son of Laertes, Odysseus, man of exploits, still eager to leave at once and hurry back to your own home, your beloved native land?

Good luck to you, even so. Farewell!

But if you only knew, down deep, what pains are fated to fill your cup before you reach that shore, you'd stay right here, preside in our house with me and be immortal. "

— THE GOD CALYPSO, THE ODYSSEY

**Grafton Ghost Town**
**Southern Utah**

Cameron, Julie, Isaiah, his first wife Ruth, and the kids survived in a one room, old-timey farmhouse in Grafton, Utah. The little cluster of wood plank buildings was a ghost town, and they were its resident ghosts.

Cameron's wife, Julie, kept her distance from her Celestial Husband, so he hadn't felt the need to kill the man yet.

During their six weeks in Grafton, two important truths clarified in Cameron's mind. Isaiah, the polygamist, was a nerd; and not only because of his weirdo religion. He would've been a nerd in any religion. The second thing was that they didn't have enough food to make it even half-way through the winter.

They'd been slowly starving for two weeks now. The four adults rationed themselves about a thousand calories a day, and the kids were getting about half of that. When they arrived, the other wife thought they could stretch the food until spring. Her assumption had been that springtime would bring crops, a renewed wave of wild game and a reprieve from the biting cold at night.

In any case, Ruth was wrong. Even at a thousand calories a day, the food wouldn't last to the end of February. Everyone could see that now. They were down to half of what they had when they arrived even though they'd been eating like sparrows.

Isaiah sat across the rough-hewn table from Cameron, his eyes sparkling with excitement. A candle burned in a sawed-in-half aluminum Pepsi can in the middle of the table. Everyone else had gone to sleep. Hunger did that—made a person want to sleep all the time. Cameron didn't understand how Isaiah could muster the energy to be enthusiastic about anything, much less boring local history.

The polygamist nerd whispered his way through a detail-plagued story about the ghost town and its former residents. The nerd got off on Old West history, particularly stories that involved his forefathers. Their three-building ghost town was founded by the ancestors of the polygamist cult they'd just fled.

In the flickering candlelight, Isaiah's eyes pleaded for Cameron to like him, and in the snarls and grunts of the human wolf pack, that meant power. Power to Cameron. So he played along with story time.

"George C. McGammon was the superintendent of the coal mine. He was my great-great-great grandfather on my mother's side. He built the barn in the south pasture."

"Coal mine?" Cameron asked. He waited impatiently for Isaiah to get to the point—say anything that would lead to more food. Cameron thought if the coal mine had bats, they might be able to eat the bats. They'd already caught, killed and eaten all the rabbits on the property. "Where are the caves?"

"No, silly," Isaiah chortled. "They're pit mines. There are no caves. It's a big hole in the ground, over yonder across the river."

*Nerd*, Cameron thought. "What's George C. Backgammon, great-great-great-nutter to your mother's third cousin have to do with food?"

Isaiah waved his hand through the candlelight. "He built the impoundment up the river. Well, not this impoundment, but the previous impoundment that got washed out. The dam washed out thirteen times between 1875 and 1915 when they finally built the concrete impoundment."

Cameron made the "get on with it" motion with his hands without lifting them off the table.

"The impoundment dammed the river, and if we restore it, we can divert water to grow crops," Isaiah explained.

Cameron sat up in his chair and ran his hand through his dark hair. "There's a dam?" His thoughts went immediately to fishing. Maybe a pond behind a dam would hold fish. They fished the Virgin River but caught only finger-length chubs. They'd eaten them, of course—muddy-tasting and slimy, but they were food.

"Well, yes. There's a dam down by the town of Hurricane, but that's not going to help us." The polygamist pronounced Hurricane as *hurry-kin*. "I'm talking about the old, washed out impoundment above here."

Isaiah gave Cameron the lay of the land and the scuttlebutt on what'd been going on in this valley since the collapse. Rockville was the next town up the Virgin River. Rockville and the town down-river, Virgin, were embroiled in some kind of war over water. The families were close enough to hear the shooting but far enough away to have nothing to do with it. The only bridge for miles had been blown up by Rockville to block raiding parties from Virgin.

The warring towns were ten miles apart, and the ghost town of Grafton sat squarely in the middle—but on the wrong side of the river for anyone to give-a-shit, which was lucky since between Isaiah and Cameron, they had seventeen, twenty-gauge shotgun shells and five bullets for Cameron's Mosin-Nagant. If they had to fight, it'd be a short battle.

The other side of the river might as well have been the dark side of the moon—it was alien territory, where men from the towns had the energy and bullets to scrabble for advantage. On this side of the river, the two families slowly starved for lack of anything to put in their bellies.

"So what are you proposing we do about the dam? We barely have enough energy to walk across the yard," Cameron argued.

Isaiah nodded. "I know. Hear me out. We don't need to rebuild the impoundment to stop the river. We just need to scoop a little water out of the river and run it down the old bits of pipeline, then channel water into the stock tank at the top of the pasture."

"Then what do we do with the water once it's here?" Cameron felt ornery at the thought of work, so he made Isaiah explain.

"We dig a greenhouse into the ground and run water to it from the stock tank. We use the seed bank to start a garden," Isaiah said.

In the back of Isaiah's hastily-loaded pickup truck had been a can of "survival seeds;" an assortment of pre-packaged, vacuum-sealed vegetable seeds for a typical American garden. Neither Cameron nor Isaiah knew anything about gardening, but Ruth had kept a little garden in Wacko Wonderland. Growing a garden in the middle of winter seemed far-fetched, but an ear of corn sounded like Jesus in a gold chariot right now.

When they arrived at Grafton, Ruth had planted a dozen corn kernels, some tomato seeds and several squash beside the pioneer house on the sunny side. Each morning, her two boys carried water from the river in five gallon buckets.

A few of the seedlings had sprouted, and the tiny, green shoots looked like the first fruits of salvation punching through the dark, red soil. But the weather shifted. A few nights after the shoots emerged, a chill descended upon red rock country, and the morning mist froze to the ground like fairy dust around the tender seedlings. When the sun came out, it turned the crystals to vapor and the tender shoots twisted and crumpled, surrendering their energy back to the soil.

The daytime temperatures often soared into the sixties, but the night returned with the chill of the distant, snow-capped mountains. The awkward clan of straight-necked polygamists and jaded Southern California urbanites clung to the edge of Nevada desert on one side, and Utah alpine on the other. They broke a sweat working in the day, but chilled to the core at night. It was early December, and the life-robbing cold of night would likely worsen in the months to come. A garden seemed all but impossible.

Isaiah continued with his history lesson. "Mary Allen Mayfield grew turnips in the winter in Rockville. That was 1892, I believe, before the big flood of '95…" Cameron sighed forcefully and Isaiah hurried to his point. "Anyway, Mary Allen Mayfield dug trenches in the dirt and covered them with panes of glass. She had glass left over from the cabins that the flood destroyed. She glued the pieces together with clay." Cameron sighed again. The nerd was unstoppable once he started. "Anyway, she built glass boxes over them and the sun warmed the ground enough for the shoots to survive the night frost. She grew turnips for Christmas dinner for everyone in town, which was only four families at the time."

Turnips sounded very, very nice, but his reaction to anything out of the wife-grabber's mouth was always the same. Disagreement and argument. "Even with miniature greenhouses, we would need water, and not water from the river. We'd burn more calories carrying water than we could grow in vegetables."

Isaiah shifted in his seat and Cameron could guess what he was thinking. Carrying water was a sore subject. The polygamist kids always did the work while Cameron and Julie's two boys watched.

What else would they expect? Isaiah and Ruth's ten year-old daughter and twin eight year-old sons had grown up in a farming commune. Cameron's boys were raised in a sea of tract homes. They didn't know how to do chores. To get them to work, Cameron had to watch over them every second. Now that his boys were starving as well as incompetent, their usefulness had diminished to the level of house-cats. But they were still Cameron's sons, and if his boys got to save precious calories while the polygamist brats did most of the work, that was no skin off his ass.

The polygamist kids were slowing down, too. Work and hunger went hand-in-hand in a downward spiral. The more the polygamist kids did chores, particularly carrying water, the hungrier they became.

Health issues arose. That afternoon, Ruth fell and hit the table in a dizzy spell. Several of the children were suffering from dry, flaky skin, and everyone was dragging ass. Rebuilding the dam sounded about as likely as getting the Umpa-loompas to make a candy forest.

"We could partially dam the river and channel some water with metal pipe. We could run it down the old canal bed."

There was a lot of galvanized corrugated pipe laying around the river, rusting into oblivion. Cameron chalked it up to past attempts at damming.

The highway on the other side of the river led to the Zion National Park, ten miles up the road past Rockville. Steep escarpments and pink sandstone monoliths framed the green, winding riverbed. Titanic stacks of boulders dotted the landscape. They stood out ruddy and bulbous above the desert grasses, thick stands of saltcedar and the towering willow trees. It would've been beautiful if it wasn't killing them.

When the power stopped, so did the water to the towns up the Virgin River. An ancient truth emerged: a man can have water at his feet, but unless he has *water pressure* in pipes, he's got *squat-nothing*. As the unlikely family of refugees discovered firsthand, carrying water was slow suicide.

"If we can channel the water from a hundred yards upriver," Isaiah continued, "we can fill the cattle cistern at the top end of the pasture. We can run PVC tubing down to the garden and water vegetables. I have a roll of clear plastic sheeting in the back of the truck, and we can use it to make half-buried greenhouses, like Mary Allen Mayfield."

It took Cameron a second to remember who that was. The greenhouse lady. Turnips.

The candle guttered. It was one of their last. Soon, their days would end with the setting sun.

Like the candle, Cameron could see their energy failing. They would have one more chance to get ahead of starvation, if that. The pantry was down to a bucket and a half of raw wheat, eleven cans of beans, two cans of spam and a bottle and a half of home-canned peaches. It reminded him of his bank account when he'd been out of work six weeks. Down, down, down—less every time he checked it, which he'd done ten times a day.

They would stretch the food pantry, but calories were calories were calories. Energy out required energy in. Every twitch of their muscles drew down the pantry, and very little was being done to add back.

They had no electricity, no refrigeration, no cooking gas and barely enough sleeping bags if they spread them out and slept in family stacks. There was sage brush and cottonwood firewood nearby to last them months, maybe even the winter, if only to cook and to take the edge off the coldest of nights.

They were refugees, plain and simple. Cameron knew from personal observation: refugees were the walking dead. The supplies Isaiah and Ruth had tossed into the back of their truck as they fled Colorado City were the only things standing between Cameron's family and the same, slow death that'd devoured the rest of America.

They had this ghost town. The forty acre spread didn't hold any wildlife to speak of, but it was protected by the bridgeless river. They could ignore the *pop-pop-pop* of small arms fire, but they couldn't go anywhere. It was a prison, and homicidal, small town prison guards wandered the outside world ready to shoot on sight.

Cameron tossed out his pride days ago. He'd admitted the truth to himself: the weirdo polygamists were his only hope of surviving until spring, but he would have to make them work. If he let them sit around like rag dolls, they'd all die.

He'd begun to think of them as slaves. This bright-eyed fool across the table from him was a calorie bank for his family, and it was up to Cameron to work him down. The weirdo had put his blond-haired dink in Julie, and that had sealed the deal. Cameron would use the man as a workhorse, get as much out of his horse-flesh as possible, then let him perish. The polygamist had been living on borrowed time, anyway.

Cameron sighed and closed his eyes. He didn't enjoy being the madman, the slave master. He couldn't help it. It was a mad world, gone back to the ancient ways of survival. If Cameron had gleaned anything from a dozen documentaries on the Roman Empire, it was that slavery got it done.

His dreams of slavery thinned when he considered the polygamist wife and kids. They were being worked down too. His wife Julie wasn't a tenth as useful as Ruth, and Julie had a bad habit of disappearing when work needed to be done. Cameron had no idea where she went.

If he was going to use this man up, it might as well be to get water to a garden. Cameron didn't have any better ideas.

"We can go look at the wreckage of the dam tomorrow. We'll see if anything can be made of it." Cameron slapped his knees and got up from the table.

Five minutes later, the candle flickered out on its own.

---

IT TOOK them a half-hour to walk the river to the old dam. It was the first time Cameron ventured so far off the property. They moved slowly, deliberately, like the starving men they were.

They'd eaten a quarter cup of boiled wheat kernels each, with a small pour of peach syrup. Cameron guessed it amounted to three hundred calories. His stomach snarled as it pounced on the little knot of nutrition. He could swear he was hungrier after eating it than he was before.

As they picked along the riverside trail, the winter sun strengthened. It might've reached seventy degrees—enough for the crickets to animate, move around, and dine on the dried algae on the edge of the water. The men scrambled for the crickets, then shoved them into their mouths straightaway.

"We shood cash sum for da women and kiz," Isaiah spoke around a mouthful of insect.

"We'll get them on the way back," Cameron replied. He flipped over a rock and found five crickets. Four made it into his mouth.

"Eeeech!" Isaiah screamed. Cameron stood. The polygamist pointed at the base of a red boulder and danced from one foot to the other. "Rattler!"

Cameron stepped back. "Kill it so we can eat it."

"No way. I'm not getting near it," Isaiah gasped as he backpedaled, as though the snake might launch itself at him.

"Don't be a wussy. We can eat that. Kill it," Cameron commanded.

"Hunh-uh, urgh." Isaiah stumbled over the river rocks and danced back toward the trail.

Cameron didn't want to get near it either. He'd never seen a rattlesnake outside the zoo, so he didn't know what to expect. Did they chase after people?

He picked up a rock and approached. The polygamist's screaming had sent the rattlesnake into a coil. The beaded tip of the tail had the unmistakeable hallmark of a rattlesnake, but it hadn't yet rattled. It raised its triangular head, seemed to change its mind, uncoiled and slithered toward a stand of reeds.

As soon as the head stretched out, Cameron threw. The rock struck the neck and the snake coiled again. This time it rattled furiously. Its head hung crooked. He picked up a sun-bleached stick and approached the angry, damaged creature. The broken head followed him warily, but didn't uncoil. Cameron reached in with the stick and smashed the head to the rocks, pinning it against a river stone. The body writhed and the fangs gnawed at the air. With his free hand, he grabbed another rock and hammered at the head until it fell away from the body. Still, the headless serpent twisted and fought.

Cameron pinned it with the stick. Without the head, he wondered if there was still poison, somewhere. Isaiah was on the trail watching the thick, writhing rope with eyes the size of teacups.

No, Cameron concluded, there couldn't be any venom outside the head. He was safe to treat it like any other dead animal. Cameron grabbed the still-rattling tail and lifted. It stretched from the top of his hip to the ground and weighed several pounds. He could scarcely remember what meat tasted like, and his mouth watered. The severed end splattered blood on the rocks and his shoes. He didn't know if reptile blood was edible. He let it drain.

"Stay away from me with that," Isaiah said, shuffling along the trail. "I don't like snakes."

"Yeah. No shit." Cameron waved the dangling body up-river. "Let's see this impoundment of yours and get back to the house for some real food." He held up the writhing cord of flesh.

Isaiah nodded without conviction, and skittered away up the trail.

---

CAMERON WAITED to gut the rattlesnake until they returned to the homestead. He wanted it seen by the clan before he diminished it by removing the guts. He'd made their first kill in weeks and Isaiah couldn't claim to have anything to do with it. The polygamists weren't the only valuable members of the group after all.

Everyone except Isaiah gathered and watched as he gutted. Ruth handed him a paper plate for the entrails, one of the last plates that hadn't fallen apart after being washed in the river a dozen times. Cameron had no idea what they were supposed to do with guts, but he dumped them onto the plate as directed.

From the inside out, the snake was ribs, muscle and skin. If he removed the ribs and the skin, there wouldn't be a whole lot left.

"We lay the skin down on coals," Ruth spoke, in answer to Cameron's hesitation. "We'll pick the meat off the bones with our teeth."

The skin would act as a frying pan of sorts. Cameron cut the snake in eight-inch sections with Isaiah's knife, so they wouldn't have to coil it to fit in the skillet. Ruth piled up some dry sagebrush in the fire pit off the wood porch. She cooked outside unless it was raining or snowing. It was easier to work over a fire pit than to work inside the cramped fireplace in the one-room house.

The sagebrush burned down quickly, and Ruth laid the sections of meat, skin down, on the glowing coals. Everyone sat on the porch and watched while the rattlesnake meat cooked in its strange smell. Cameron considered taking an extra portion for himself, or demanding an extra portion for his boys. But, an innate understanding of the pack intruded, wordlessly, on his thoughts. He would give them all a portion equal to their size. He didn't know why, but he felt certain. As the sections of rattler sizzled, he divided them up in his mind in a manner he knew would be seen as fair.

As Ruth pulled them off the coals, Cameron received them on the paper plate, then cut them into precise portions, and handed them out, each according to the person's size.

As Julie, and then Ruth, took their piece, a brute electricity crackled between he and the women. Cameron's eyes focused and he understood a little better. The women and children were a pack of sorts. He and Isaiah stood apart from them, and not necessarily as compatriots. In the darkening shades of sundown, the cold returned, as did a primitive gloom. Each person retreated to a corner, to gnaw down their portion of snake flesh until it was just charred skin and gleaming bone. It was a profoundly personal ritual. The raw loneliness of starvation cast a feral contention in their midst.

The group skipped eating from their stores that night, as though two hundred calories of snake meat apiece was enough. As Cameron stumbled to the edge of the river to take his nightly piss, Ruth approached out of the shadows.

She said nothing, but walked right into Cameron, breast to chest. She looked up into his face, and he saw the flash of something ancient and bestial in her eyes; the meat had awakened another feral hunger. She shoved her fingers into his hair and pulled his face down onto her tits. She wore her high-necked dress, as always, but the message was clear. He breathed hot breath onto her nipples through the fabric, and she moaned. The sound fired blood into his cock and he went hard in an instant. She turned, laid her head back on his chest and pushed her rump against his penis. They pressed against one another like animals in a pen, possessed by the carnality of male and female. She grasped at her skirts and bared her ass. Cameron shoved his pants to the ground and seized her hips. She'd already discarded her underclothes before seeking him in the dark. He penetrated her from behind, and reached around to cup her clitoris. He probed into the damp crevasse with his fingers and pressed hard. She groaned again and instantly tripped a cascading, helpless collapse. He filled her with molten life, arched against his grip on her hips and loosed an animal shudder from the base of his spine to the back of his throat.

He couldn't care less who might hear.

# 5

## SAGE ROSS

**South of Lowden, Washington**
**Southeastern Washington State**

As so often happens in the wilderness, a seemingly small problem became a life-threatening problem within an hour. Sage's boots had filled with ice-cold water. His socks slurped and sloshed in his boots and on the skin of his feet. Water-logged and soft, the skin of his feet was wearing into fleshy pulp at an alarming rate. He could feel wet blisters bulging with every step.

The tongue of his boot had been scooping up the slightest scrim of snow with each boot rise. Then the snow wicked its way down to his foot via the sock. Even the tiniest kernel of snow, scraped with each step, thousand of footfalls a day, eventually became a boot-full of water.

He'd dumped his boots and wrung out his socks a dozen times so far that morning, and even so, he hiked in a constant state of wetness. There was no way his feet would tolerate even a hundred miles of backpacking like this, much less *six* hundred.

After two and a half days of hiking through the snowfields of eastern Washington, Sage's feet had reached the end-of-the-line. He'd learned that his brain, not the contents of his pack, was the ultimate survival tool. He needed to stop and think.

A rough circle of vehicles sat ahead under a cluster of giant elms, and the snow around it remained smooth and untouched. It looked good for the night, but he stopped and waited anyway. An ironclad rule; Sage always spent ten minutes glassing an area before approaching.

He counted down from 600 while watching the cluster of cars through his binoculars. Nothing moved. If he could shelter in one of the vehicles for the night, it'd partially block out the light of a fire. He didn't need the warmth to sleep—he had many layers of clothes for that—but fire was the only way to dry out his socks and boots.

He finally approached with his 30-30 rifle leveled, safety off. He found no surprises, the new-fallen snow was untrampled and the cars were frosted with several inches. Nobody had been there in days.

Sage yanked open a car door with his left hand, covering the inside of the car with a one-handed grip on his 30-30. In the bottom of the footwell lay a small, dead dog. The cold must've preserved the corpse, since the smell of decay barely registered.

The loneliness hit him so hard he almost had to sit down. The sight of the little, mangy mutt, so well preserved, sparked a ferocious hunger for companionship. He wished the dog would look up and blink back death.

*Who the hell would leave a dog locked in a car to starve?*

These days, if someone came upon a dog, even dead, they'd probably eat his rotting corpse. Sage leaned on the door frame and set the 30-30 against the side. It struck him for the first time, the sheer amount of *resource* contained in a modern automobile. As he looked around the passenger compartment for food, he made note of the treasure trove—plastics, vinyl, stuffing, containers, oil products, flammables, hardware and elastics. The quantity of manufactured goods made him think: *how could he solve his boot issue with car parts?*

He assumed, since they'd been abandoned, that none of the cars contained enough gasoline to travel, so he wouldn't bother trying to find keys or check the tanks. Driving down a road, in any case, would be like begging for bullets. He hadn't seen a moving vehicle in weeks.

It was still early in the afternoon, maybe three o'clock, and Sage had his work cut out for him. He got a fire going in the center of the circle of cars and set his boots on elmwood spikes, unlaced with the tongues open, to encourage them to dry. He dug around in the snow for stones, and put them under the burning sticks, where the coals would heat them. While the fire dried his boots and heated the stones, he went to work on the cars, cutting away raw materials with his heavy Glock knife.

After trimming and testing the pliability of the seat leather, floor mats, and headliner, Sage settled on the headliner of an Aerostar minivan as the best material for boot gaiters. It provided the best combination of flexibility and impermeability.

While he'd sloshed along earlier that day in his boots, it'd dawned on him that he'd seen, but never used, boot covers for hiking in the snow. In a mental "gap," he'd even remembered the name for them: "gaiters." They were like stretchy tubes that sealed the space between boots and pants. If he could make a pair of gaiters, it'd stop the snow from scraping into his boots.

After almost two hours of trial-and-error around the firelight, Sage produced a pair of gaiters made of headliner and seatbelt cinches. After testing them for a couple days and making modifications, he'd finish the hems with his tiny sewing kit.

By the time he completed his gaiters, night had fully descended. At first light, he'd leave this camp behind, so if he wanted anything more from the dead cars, he'd need to get it now. Dead cars were everywhere along the highway, but Sage forbid himself from going anywhere within 300 yards of the blacktop. It was far too dangerous —far too likely to lead to an encounter. He could out-run most full-grown men, but he harbored no illusions; they were almost all heavier and stronger. It would be years before his long, lean body could match theirs in a life-or-death struggle. Running and hiding was his survival advantage, for now.

Sage ripped up the rear seats of the Aerostar, popped out the zig-zag seat springs, and began construction of a pair of snowshoes. The snow in the flatlands were just the first frosting of winter—six or eight inches in most places and a little deeper in the shade. The mountains that loomed ahead had been basted by snow for over a month. He expected it to be several feet deep. He'd need to float on top instead of crunching through, like he'd been doing in the irriga-tion ditches.

Fear crept up his spine as he pictured the flickering light of his fire traveling across miles of snow-glassed ground. Even surrounded by cars, it might be visible from the highway. The snow-shoes would have to wait. No matter how much he enjoyed the warmth, the fire wasn't worth the risk now that full night was upon him.

He stamped the fire out, spread the coals and bundled himself against one of the elms. He scraped out the stones from the fire, dusted off the cinders, and plopped two hot stones in each drying boot.

Then, he watched and waited for an hour to make sure nobody approached. When he was sure he was still alone, he set up his bedroll in the Aerostar and drifted off to sleep.

Sometime during the witching hour, he awoke to snow flakes drifting down from the heavens. To his sleep-addled mind it felt like entombment. Even in his shallow wakefulness, he heard the gentle pattering of Mother Nature piling obstacles ahead of him.

The coming storms would conceal his path home in the maddening drudgery of snow and solitude.

He thought about the little dog. His face flushed and his nose ran. A lone tear burgeoned in the corner of his eye, then lost its battle with gravity and chased a path down his cheeck, off his chin, and onto the floorboards. He lay awake for a while, in the steel chill of the Aerostar, worrying the decision whether to forge on without the snowshoes or to dedicate the morning to their construction. There was no right answer, and nobody to help him decide.

Life and death hinged on decisions such as these. For once, it made sense to worry, but his worry tendered nothing but lost sleep.

---

**Blue Mountains, 4300 feet elevation**
**Southeastern Oregon**

As MUCH AS the road beckoned him, Sage saw it for what it was: a deathtrap. With the warm blacktop melting away the snow, the surface of the highway presented much easier walking than the forest—maybe half as difficult.

Sage floated on top of the snow in his homemade snowshoes, but it was no easy thing to traverse uncut snow.

Back at the circle of dead cars, he'd used the aluminum seat tubing as frames and the zig-zag seat springs of the Ford Aerostar as platforms for his homemade snowshoes. He sunk into the snow only four inches, but even that sapped his strength a lot more than walking on asphalt. He would've traveled twice as far on the mountain road, but then he could almost guarantee a bullet to the back of the head or a sudden ambush of bat-wielding men. Sage walked the path less travelled, always. To do anything else was a death wish for a five-foot ten-inch seventeen-year-old boy.

The snowshoes were already proving critical. Six times, he

silently circumnavigated knots of desperate people stumbling along the snow-patched highway up the Blue Mountains. Sage ghosted around the groups, unnoticed. He'd yet to see another footprint out in the snowfields that paralleled the road. He traveled alone, so he traveled carefully.

But he ached to join one of the groups. He sometimes paused behind a snow bank or a screen of pines to listen to their chatter. They blathered, argued, jockeyed for control, complained about food or dreamed loudly about the "old days." They were all desperate, untethered people. Sage knew if he threw in with any of them, his food would be callously devoured and he would be cast aside.

He seriously considered it anyway. He wondered if a person could literally die of loneliness. He had no choice but to stay in the same canyon as the winding, climbing highway. Scaling up and over, into an empty canyon, would burn too many calories and run the risk of an avalanche or a fall. The road passed through the easiest crossing of the mountain range—alongside a small creek that eventually opened onto a high snowfield up above.

Sage reached the top of the Blue Mountains in three days, never lighting a fire or even heating water. He ate freeze-dried meals cold, with only filtered water from the creek. Because he shared the canyon with other travelers, he minimized flickers of light, flashes of color and wisps of scent. He slept in his camo-pattern tent, partially collapsed to reduce its profile, and covered it with sticks and branches.

He got better and better at shaving risk off his movement, economizing his food and perfecting the silent catechisms of putting up and taking down camp. He traveled more and more at night. He was covering ground, but the truth became increasingly clear: he couldn't keep this overland movement up forever.

Moisture plagued him, a relentless nemesis. Every sleep time, no matter how he configured his tent, condensation accumulated along the tent wall and dripped onto his sleeping bag. Sage woke up every hour to dab runnels off the ceiling with his dirty clothes, but the tent was like sleeping in a light sprinkle. His bag grew more and more damp, and he got colder each night as the insulation compacted. He already slept fully-dressed. The next, and perhaps final, defense against the cold would be sleeping in his coat and boots as well. He gained altitude every day, and the nighttime temperatures hardened past freezing.

It was with palpable relief that he finally reached the high saddle of the Blue Mountains. He crossed the open meadow in the moonlit dark. The half-moon hadn't set until three a.m. that night, and he'd come to see that moonlight was almost as good as daylight for overland travel, and it was undeniably safer.

Other than five nights on each side of the new moon, he enjoyed a few hours of workable moonlight. Each month, fully half of all nighttime hours were bright and navigable, particularly across snow. There wasn't enough natural light for fine tasks, like tying snare wire, but if he shadowed the rising moon, he no longer required a flashlight. He could travel, set up camp, sort his pack and prepare meals without artificial light. Stuck within the walls of the canyon, amidst shiftless strangers, his nocturnal habits armed him with the double-edged sword of secrecy and solitude. But his emotions despised his isolation. His mind buckled and bent. He awoke once, weeping, inconsolable. Another night, he became convinced he saw his mother in a group of stragglers mumbling around a fire. Like a castaway alone on the seas, his mind became parched from lack of connection.

On the east-facing side of the mountain range, Sage paralleled the path of the highway along a stream bed. He caught glimpses, now, of the rising sun as it freshened the day from its home below the horizon. He could see several hundred miles to the east, out across eastern Oregon and Idaho.

Mankind had gone insane, but the Earth remained the same. Somewhere out there, past the rising sun, his family waited for him.

Having crested the mountain range, Sage picked his way through pine forest, searching the moonlight for rabbit tracks and listening closely for human sound.

He decided to push ahead without hunting or fishing until he reached the next farming valley, but searching for rabbit sign had become a ceaseless habit. His eyes did it of their own volition, only alerting him when there was a promising convergence of track, or a likely rabbit warren.

It was a dim night, with the half-moon dipping in and out of the thin clouds, and he had two hours left until the moon set. He forced himself onward, not stopping to place snares or wet a line in the snow-banked creek. He could easily get trapped by a snowstorm at high elevation, caught in an endless white-out of blinding snow, buried beneath more powder than his snow shoes could navigate. Better to mimic the deer and elk, he reasoned, and descend without delay. So far, he'd lucked out on this climb—nothing but ice-cold sunshine. Other than a few, errant flakes, it hadn't snowed.

Sage heard a human voice and froze. Voices carried a long way in the canyons, and his course along the river was never more than a couple hundred yards from the highway. He padded quietly around a snow-basted hillock and crouched.

He heard a laugh. *Male. Young adult.* More talking. *At least three men.*

Sage waited as the voices grew in volume then faded, bit-by-bit, up-canyon. They traveled uphill, walking in the dark, heading God-knew-where. The west side of the Blue Mountains couldn't possibly be better than the east side. Seattle and Portland seethed toxic humanity to the west. Why would anyone cross the mountains from east to west? It wasn't the only group he'd encountered heading west, and it worried him. What could be so bad in the south-eastern corner of Oregon that people would flee toward the big cities?

While he waited, the perspiration under his jacket chilled. The moon shadow of the lodgepole pines grew long. Soon, he'd lose light and it'd be time to dig in. It wasn't safe to walk along the stream in pure darkness. The snow concealed small crevasses.

Up ahead, he spied a dark, pine hollow that ran perpendicular to the main canyon—a small tributary to the main stream. He had to cross the tributary to get there, but the heavy pine overhang in the hollow would hold heat and maybe hide a tiny campfire. He'd pitch his tent under a drooping fir and protect it from the winds. More than anything, the side canyon would buy him distance from the highway—maybe three or four hundred yards.

Sage waded through snow alongside the creek until he came abreast of the feeder canyon. The moonlight had all but disappeared behind a cloud. Waiting while the group passed had made him late to make camp.

He worked his way up the tributary to the stream and searched for a crossing in the undulations of snow. The waterway looked about as wide as Sage was tall, with a curling cornice overhanging both sides. Even though the stream was too wide to jump in snowshoes, the cornices closed the gap. Sage backed up and launched into a flopping, snowshoe sprint.

The moment he planted his first snowshoe to jump, the cornice collapsed, dropping a three foot section of snow into the creek. His momentum carried him forward, unable to recover with his boots bound up in the snowshoes. He went down to his knees and fell forward, slamming his forearms onto the mossy rocks on the bottom of the creek, barely holding his face from plunging into the stream.

He struggled upright. The snowshoes were seized by the flow of the water. They threatened to drag his legs downstream. As the icy chill filled his jacket and pants, Sage heaved air. His diaphragm spasmed from the intense cold. He grabbed a pine root sticking from the bank and hauled himself over the four foot wall of snow on the opposite side, hand-over-hand. He gained the far bank and flipped over on his backpack.

The chill of the water and sub-zero mountain air went immediately to work killing him. As much as he wanted to lay there and catch his breath, there was no warmth whatsoever to be had in the snow, yet he so wanted to stay still, curled in a ball. Every movement exposed his flesh to the frigid cold of his soaked clothing. Staying perfectly still minimized the discomfort, but the specter of death nudged him with the back of its scythe, urging him to move; to push through the galactic pain of the ice that frosted his skin. *Move or die,* Father Death seemed to say.

Sage worked his snowshoes underneath him and plunged his wet gloves into the snow. He hunted for anything solid to help him stand, but the snow gave way with every thrust. Nothing held his weight enough to push against. After compressing the snow with a dozen vain attempts, he created his own snowpack and finally floundered to his knees, then to his feet.

Without a fire, death from hypothermia would come in a few hours at most. Other than his head and his left arm, ice water covered him, gobbling up his body heat. The moon was only an hour from setting. Soon, it would be completely dark.

The feeder canyon towered over him, too far to reach deep cover before hypothermia sapped his will to live. He could feel ennui coming over him, like a slothful demon occupying his mind, slipping in behind the freeze.

Sage's teeth clacked together in the worst shiver he'd ever experienced. He stumbled and shivered for a hundred yards, heading toward a pine with a skirt of dead branches at its base—fuel for a fire. He reached it, then set to work bending and popping the dead branches from the tree, clearing a small area under the pine canopy. Starting a forest fire was the least of his worries. In his frozen state, lighting the whole damn mountain range on fire didn't sound like an entirely bad idea.

He was making a lot of noise, snapping branches off the pine. Several of them cracked like rifle shots, but he had no choice. Death by cold was imminent. All other contenders would have to wait their turn.

In five minutes, he had enough pine boughs. He'd read the Jack London story about the man who'd died in the same scenario; alone, wet, and huddled beneath a pine. He remembered the guy running out of matches while he willed his frozen hands to function.

Sage spoke out loud just to bolster his grit, "Fuck matches. I'm using the JetBoil."

He piled a teepee of pitchy pine twigs then dug into his frozen, stiff backpack. He removed the camp stove and dumped the pieces onto the packed snow around his knees. His hands struggled with the threads on the burner head to get them to line up with the propane tank. He finally got a smooth twist, ran the head home, cranked the valve, and clicked madly at the piezoelectric igniter until a flame burst to life. The warmth hit his hands like acid, but he sighed with relief. Sweet warmth—but it would be short-lived. The propane bottle felt light.

He pointed the stove at the teepee of twigs, and the fire from the JetBoil hissed long and strong, a flame thrower dousing the twigs in curling, greedy tongues of flame. He kept it on the twigs until they caught solidly. He tossed the loose parts of the stove back in his pack without repacking the case, then alternated warming his hands and adding pine boughs until steam spun night-ward from his frozen sleeves and pant legs.

With death no longer imminent, another brand of chill ran down his spine. It'd been a half-hour since he'd fallen into the stream and since he'd considered any risk other than hypothermia. He sat next to a blazing fire, the smell of smoke traveling up the mountain on the prevailing breeze, announcing his presence to any threats nearby.

He hadn't so much as looked up from the fire in thirty minutes —a soft target if ever there was one. He snatched up his 30-30 rifle from the pack and worked the lever to make sure it hadn't frozen shut. He ran it six times, ejected the rounds onto the snow, wiped each round with a dry spot on his fleece and reloaded the rifle. His hands were growing cold again. He'd shucked his gloves off to dry them by the fire.

Still soaked through, he couldn't leave the flames. He'd freeze again within minutes. Yet, the men he'd heard on the road could come at him any second. Reluctantly, he got up and walked away from the flickering light, collecting more firewood while he listened for movement.

If they were stalking him, they wouldn't speak. He might hear the crunch of compacting snow, but that would be all the warning he'd get.

Sage set a bundle of wood beside the fire, added a few sticks and spent a moment in thought. Full-dark would descend any moment. The moon perched now on the rim of the mountain range and would soon vanish. The odds of being ambushed because of the light signature and smell of the fire, this close to the road, were high. He'd die faster from an ambush than hypothermia. If he sat by the fire, warming himself, he might not even hear the bullet that would take his life.

In frozen agony, he pulled off his pants and underwear and hung them in the pine tree over the fire. He had no extra coat or dry, insulated jacket, and both pairs of pants were soaked through. Naked from the waist down, he unclipped his sleeping bag from the base of the pack, put on his one pair of dry socks and slipped back into his wet boots.

The blood in his hands had returned to ice water. He struggled to dig his tent sack out of the pack, then to extricate the rain cover— a dome-shaped tarp. Luckily, he'd stuffed it on top the last time he'd broken camp. He repacked the backpack and turned again to hanging his clothes. Every micro-movement of packing and unpacking, undressing and dressing, required four times as much effort as normal. He moved like a zombie, and he had to force himself to stop groaning. He yearned to quit, wanted nothing more in the world than to slip away from the frozen hell into oblivion.

Instead, he shucked off his wet wind shell, his fleece, his acrylic sweater, then his soaked thermal underwear top. He stood bare-chested and balls-out to the frigid breeze, but he had no time to warm himself. Marauders could be stalking him. He dangled the thermal top from a branch alongside the sweater. He climbed back into the wet fleece sweatshirt. Amazingly, it was warmer, even wet, than the thermal top had been. But warmer was a far cry from warm. Taking care not to damage the delicate Gore-tex with flame or sputtering cinders, he hung the wind shell on the underside of the pine, where it too would dry.

With the sleeping bag, sleeping pad, and rifle in-hand, he left the fireside. His boots plunged into the deep, mountain snow as he followed his snowshoe tracks. With every step, he plunged almost to his naked balls. To escape each hole, he launched himself up and out, and threw himself forward. He back-tracked his own trail almost fifty yards without making any prints outside of his own snowshoe tracks. He found a spot beside his trail where a snow-berry shrub convoluted the snowfield, and he jumped clear of his trail and came down in the disturbance beneath the shrub. Then, using the brush to conceal his new prints, he picked toward a small pine thirty yards off the trail. If someone stalked up on the fire, following his tracks, they'd walk past him, hiding under the little pine.

He tucked his foam pad up and under the tree and teased the sleeping bag from its stuff sack. Miraculously, only a corner of it had gotten wet. He'd jumped out of the creek so fast that water hadn't fully saturated his belongings.

A wet corner on his already-damp sleeping bag was dangerous enough. He had no idea if the sleeping bag would be enough to warm him. He was chilled, wet and wasn't wearing most of his clothing. The wet fleece would compromise the bag even further. The temperature had to be at least five degrees below zero, plus the damnable wind chill factor.

He was so fucking cold he could barely think. His shin bones felt like they'd hardened to stone and the marrow was struggling to break out. It was like having an ice cream headache in his legs. His teeth clacked so hard he worried he might break a tooth. He leaned the rifle against the small pine and scrubbed the snow off his naked legs. So much of it had frozen to his leg hair, that he had to scrape at it with his fingernails. It had to be done. He couldn't afford to bring any more water into the sleeping bag. Small failures now, could be life-and-death factors later. Finally succumbing to the desperation of hypothermia, he climbed into the bag, only realizing then, that he hadn't done anything with the rain fly from the tent. It was still laying in the snow.

He closed his eyes and sighed. It was no time to succumb to weakness. He'd made a promise to his father. He would do everything he could to survive.

Sage climbed out of the sleeping bag, stood naked in the snow, lifted up the foam sleeping pad and set them aside. He laid the tent's rain fly half-inside the snow print of the pad. It would serve as a vapor barrier, blocking heat vapor from rising up and away from the bag, but first it would have to be anchored. He laid the pad down on the fly, then the sleeping bag on top of that.

He removed his wet socks, stepped onto the pad, wrung out the water and spread the socks over his shoulders. He would warm, and maybe dry them with body heat in the sleeping bag. The bottom of the sleeping bag was already the wettest. If he was going to get any part of the sleeping bag damp, he reasoned it'd be better at the top.

Finally, he climbed once again into the sleeping bag, then wrapped the rain fly around it. He tucked it over and around, then under the pad again like a rip-stop burrito.

The warmth didn't come for a long time. He knew better than to expect it. He was hypothermic, and it would take his body the better part of a half hour to accumulate warmth in the bag and the vapor barrier. Despite the foam sleeping pad under him, he could feel his heat pouring straight through and into the snow. Naturally, the pad compressed wherever his body weight was greatest. There was no stopping it.

Chattering violently, he stilled himself and focused on making micro-movements in the sleeping bag, tensing muscles up and down his frigid legs. Little by precious little, they loosened. Numbness abated, and pins and needles stung like wasps around his calves. He welcomed the pain. There was no sensation in his feet, other than the throbbing ache of the bones.

The 30-30 was tucked alongside him, outside the burrito, but he didn't dare extricate his arms from the bag to breach check it. He felt certain he'd breach checked it, reflexively, before climbing into the bag.

He worked muscles, up and down his body. He listened and waited. He didn't so much sleep as fade in and out of consciousness for the rest of the interminable night. He heard the distant fire crackle and pop as it burned down to a restless pile of ash. He worried about his half-dry clothing, hanging under the big pine, fifty yards away in the inky dark.

He could've unpacked himself from the bag, and restarted the fire. He weighed the cost against the benefit. Even at its warmest, the sleeping bag burrito didn't stop the relentless cold from gnawing at his feet and ears. If he unwrapped it to restart the fire, he'd have to rebuild body heat all over again.

He hadn't heard anything on the silent snowfields around him. The threat of marauders, paramount minutes before, now drew back into the dead of night.

The night was crystal clear, which explained why the cold seemed so bitterly disposed to killing him—there were no clouds to hold in yesterday's warmth. When morning finally arrived, so would the sun, and it'd come blazing out of the east on this downs-lope of the mountain range. His clothes would need to be pulled from under the pine boughs. If the morning came strong, they could be arrayed in the saplings and snowberry to sun themselves in the sparkling, hopeful light of day. He decided to take the entire next day to dry his things—if he survived the excruciating night without frostbite.

He couldn't tell if he would lose his toes or not. He attempted, a couple times throughout the night, to burrow into his bag with his head lamp and look at his feet. They didn't look any different than usual, which belied the torment of the freezing bones. If they hurt that bad, he reasoned, they might not be dead yet.

As dawn's first light colored the horizon, Sage drifted in and out of a stupor.

He flashed awake.

*Had he heard something crack?*

He stared, wide-eyed, into the underside of the pine hanging over his ice burrito. He dared not move a muscle.

He listened, then heard the airy crumple of snow. Then a *woof* —the snow compacting under a footstep. Then nothing.

A whisper.

He pictured them. Men, following his snowshoe prints; stopping when they saw flashes of color through the pine trees—his clothes drying.

Another *woof*. Then another. They were picking up speed. Moving in for the kill.

Sage sat up slowly. He could hear the footfalls, clearly now. He couldn't see them. The ambushers were on the other side of a screen of trees and they were closing in on his cold campfire. He wriggled out of his sleeping bag and quietly breach-checked his 30-30. Brass glistened.

Bare-footed and half-naked, he rolled out of the sleep burrito and stepped into the holes in the snow left by his boots the night before. His dick and balls dangled free, and the cold was almost unbearable, but his blood was up and he couldn't afford to worry about exposure.

The men had passed his bivouac under the little pine, and followed his trail right to where he'd left his clothes drying—along with every bit of food and gear he had left. He cursed himself for not keeping the pack with him.

Why leave it fifty yards away? If he lost the pack, he might as well shoot himself.

Hopefully, they would double back on their own trail. He didn't know how many men—two to four, he guessed—but if they cut new track and continued on from his camp with all his gear, he was done-for.

People didn't usually do that, though. People usually went the easiest route, which would be back the way they'd come.

He reached the trail and crawled on his knees behind a snow-basted clump of wild rose.

He could hear them mumbling over a rise in the snow. He pictured them gathering up his stuff. Their whispered voices jumped up an octave. They were probably excited about the freeze-dried food. The voices grew louder as they approached. As predicted, they'd doubled back on their own trail; his own snow-shoe trail from the night before. He'd get the jump on them. He might have no choice but to kill them.

*No.* He told himself. There would be no time to think it through. If he waited to decide until the moment presented itself, then it'd be too late. The other guy might decide first.

*If they have a weapon, they die,* he decided.

The voices echoed louder now. Bolder. They were returning, confidently, on their back-trail. Men were brazen on ground they knew.

Behind the wild rose, Sage hid. It was trail they'd covered just minutes before. It wasn't a threat anyone would expect.

A head appeared over the rise in the trail. Then another, walking single-file to take advantage of the packed snow. A third head wobbled into view over the drift. Three men, whispering loudly.

"Maybe he fell in the crick," one of them said. "And froze to death."

*Not far from the truth,* Sage thought.

His hands shook like palsy, a combination of galloping nerves and killing cold. The sun still hadn't shown its face. The morning hung, cold and muted, like a bear still groggy in April.

"Naw. Those clothes were set out to dry," the first guy—the smarter guy—corrected.

All three were in the clear, now, thirty yards from Sage's ambush.

*Any weapons, I shoot,* he reminded himself.

He stood up from behind the wild rose.

"Show me your hands or you die." Sage's dad had taught him defensive shooting. His dad taught him: *watch the hands. Nothing else matters.*

Piles of gear thumped to the snow. The first guy dumped his arm-load and raised his empty hands. The second guy did the same, but his right hand came out from under the falling gear with a black pistol. Sage couldn't see the third guy's hands, because he was behind the other two.

*BOOM!* The 30-30 thundered.

"Oh shit," Sage swore. He hadn't meant to pull the trigger.

*Or had he?*

The first man dropped to the ground and rolled into a ball. The second fell sideways and the third fell over backwards.

"Don't shoot! Don't shoot! Don't shoot!" the first man screamed. "We're sorry. Don't shoot me."

Sage had racked the lever on the 30-30 reflexively. He almost racked it again but stopped himself.

"Let me see your hands! All of you," Sage bellowed. His voice cracked.

The first man had his hands up and his head down, still half-rolled into a ball. The second guy was on his side, not moving. Sage couldn't see any blood on the front of his green jacket, but the guy's eyes were open, staring hard at the blue-on-blue sky. The black handgun had vanished into the snow.

The third man writhed in a fan-pattern of blood and snow. Thousands of red droplets surrounded him, vivid against the sparkling whitescape. Most of the blood must've come from the man in front of him in line, who still hadn't moved.

The third guy mewled, "I'm shot, I'm shot..."

Sage kept the 30-30 trained on the group, mostly on the first man who didn't seem to be injured. He'd only shot one round, but two men were down. He'd never seen a bullet do that, but he'd only shot men twice before in his life, and all since Black Autumn.

The mewling guy rocked back and forth on the snow, holding in his guts. The rocking slowed, then slowed some more. He stopped mewling. His hand fell away from the ragged hole in his jacket. Tufts of white down lifted in the breeze. The guy's face went slack and his head rested against the snow. Sage focused on the first man. The only one left alive.

His eyes darted around wildly, like a leg-snared rabbit. "Don't shoot me, dude. I didn't mean any harm by it. Look, my gun's right here on my hip and I haven't touched it. I haven't even tried. See? I'm a good guy. I'm no threat."

Sage didn't know what to do. When the second guy went for his gun, Sage's hand automatically made the decision to kill. Somewhere between his lower brain stem and his finger, his body acted on its own. But this man didn't have a weapon—not that he'd touched.

"Just tell me what you want me to do and I'll do it," the guy yammered. "I promise. What do you want me to do?"

"Just wait. And shut up," Sage said, the iron sights danced across the guy's chest.

His bare feet were blocks of ice and he needed to get them warm very soon.

"Check your friends' pulse. Keep your hands where I can see them."

The guy struggled up out of the snow. He didn't stop talking the whole time. He remonstrated Sage in a loop about how much of a good guy he was, how he didn't mean to steal his gear, so-on and so-forth.

The talker looked to be in his late thirties. He wore expensive-looking winter-wear, like stuff from REI. It was noteworthy that none of the guys were wearing rugged clothes: Carhartt or Wrangler, like rural folks would. These were all white collar guys.

The third man, who'd probably bled out now from the gut wound, was much younger. Maybe twenty.

The talker put a finger on both of their throats, one after the other, and declared, "Dude. They're dead. You killed them both. Please don't shoot me. What do you want me to do with my gun? Please don't shoot me."

Sage realized that he'd let him keep his pistol on his hip this whole time. The crushing pain in Sage's feet—locked in four feet of snow—was beginning to cloud his judgment.

"Pull your pistol out with TWO FINGERS, and drop it on your buddy's chest." Sage motioned to the guy laying on his back.

He complied.

"Now, put everything back in my backpack. Take off that guy's clothes and bring them to me." He waved the gun barrel at his gear, spread around the snow. "Are there more of you?"

"No. I mean, yes," the guy sputtered as he loaded dirty clothing, freeze-dried food, and the JetBoil back into Sage's pack. "There are women and kids. No other men. We're just travelers, man. We weren't going to hurt you."

Sage doubted that very much. Desperate men with women and children would almost always hurt a solo person if it meant their family got to eat.

"Pick up all that stuff and walk back to my campfire," Sage ordered. Before anything else, he needed to un-freeze his feet and put on some dry clothes. He had no doubt: his toes were now frost-bitten. As he walked by the bodies, one dressed and the other one naked, Sage picked up the handguns. He had no pockets, so he hooked the stiff fingers of his left hand through the trigger guards. At least that way he could still keep two hands on the rifle.

As he moved past, he stole a glance at the two dead men—just regular guys. There was no sign of evil in their slack faces.

Sage worked the tactical dilemma in his mind as he forced the talker at gunpoint to rebuild the campfire and light it with the JetBoil. He ordered him to sit opposite him, across the fire, while Sage sat on his pack and put his bare feet toward the flame. The pins and needles were excruciating.

He considered his situation: a gun had gone off in the canyon, and now there was woodsmoke. If anyone was within a mile, they would come to the ruckus like coyotes to a wounded rabbit. These days, people gravitated toward distress, and humans were the worst kind of opportunists.

Others could follow the well-trodden path in the snow and come across the two dead men. They'd either turn back, at that point, or stalk up on him while he had his shoes off. For the thousandth time since the world died, Sage wished he had a dog.

The women, and maybe the kids from the camp might come, and that'd be a holy mess.

"How many women and children?" Sage asked the talker.

"Um. Joey's wife, Becky. Their five year-old boy, Robin and a toddler, Gershwin. Ryan didn't have any kids. Just his wife, Tanya."

Sage hated this. He'd killed a father and a husband, but what the hell else was he supposed to do? They had guns. The one guy had drawn on him.

"Switch sides with me." Sage needed to watch the trail and put his back up against a tree. A stalker would probably shoot the talker first.

They switched sides around the fire, which was a several-minute process of putting his boots back on, moving the backpack and then setting everything up again under the pine.

"What are you doing out here anyway? Why were you and your friends heading west?" Sage asked with accusation in his voice. There had been no need to kill those men; the father and the husband. He wanted someone or something to blame.

"They're not really my friends. We got kicked out together, is all."

"Kicked out from what?"

"Union County. Sheriff Chambers sent us packing. Told us to leave," the talker suddenly ran out of things to say.

"Why?" Sage asked.

"They have a rule against entering empty homes. I knew the family—I taught their kid basketball at middle school. I was checking the house to make sure they didn't have any pets that were starving or anything, you know?"

Sage nodded. It sounded like bullshit, but he didn't really care. He preferred this version of the story; the one where the men he killed were exiled looters.

"A lot of people were out of town when the thing happened. My wife. Lots of families. The harvest was mostly in, and people had gone out of town. They left their places empty without making arrangements. Ya know? Because they thought they'd be right back."

"Where are the women and children?" Sage lifted his chin toward the road.

The talker pointed. "We left them about a mile or two up."

So, they'd passed Sage, then doubled back when they smelled the smoke from his campfire.

"Do they have food?" Sage hated asking the question. It would lead down paths he would rather avoid: guilt, responsibility, risk, entanglement.

The talker shook his head. "Man, we don't have nothing."

Sage studied his own feet. They didn't look like they were frost-bitten. They were the normal color now that they were warmed up. His toes had been sloshing around so much in the snow they were whistle-clean for once. He had to ask. "Will the sheriff take them back without their husbands?"

The talker shrugged. "Maybe. Probably. Joey's wife is pretty hot and what's-her-name, Tanya I mean, is young. Their families lived in town for a lot of years. The girls were locals. The sheriff will probably go for it. I mean, it's not like the town doesn't have enough food."

"Food?" Sage asked.

"Like I said, they just got the harvest in. There's a shit-ton of wheat and hay still in Grande Rhonde Valley. They'd just begun shipping it out when America went tits-up. There's a lot of food, if you don't mind eating animal feed," he said with a laugh.

Grande Rhonda Valley sounded like civilization. Sage felt the crushing belt around his chest easing. If he could find a safe place to resupply and, *please God*, warm up—he could continue into the next leg of his journey without feeling so damned desperate; maybe he could find some traveling companions. Maybe even a dog. If they had plenty to eat in that valley, maybe they hadn't eaten the dogs yet.

"Tell me more about this sheriff and the valley. What do they need? What can a newcomer offer them that they'll want?"

The talker slapped his knee. "I can tell you this much—if you can kill two men with one shot, they will definitely want you in their militia."

"Militia?"

"Yeah. That's how they keep the valley bottled up. From North Powder in the south to Meachum in the north, they got the valley sealed up tighter than a frog's hoochie-hole."

"Why didn't you join the militia then, instead of raiding farmhouses?" Sage pressed. It made him uncomfortable to talk to an adult like that. He was calling a grown man a liar, which he almost certainly was. It was the first time Sage had talked to another human being in a long time, and he felt like he might be doing it wrong.

"I did join," the talker explained. "They didn't want me. They said I was too fat and slow. I don't know why that mattered. All I ever did was stand guard at the roadblock. Why does a man need to be skinny for that?"

Sage noticed the loose skin around the guy's neck. He'd probably been fat, back before the collapse.

"And you think they'll take me in the militia?" Sage confirmed.

"Yeah. You're definitely skinny enough."

# 6

## MAT BEST

**Highway 79 Road Block,
McKenzie, Tennessee**

Anything you say can and will be used against you..."

Mat looked down from atop the HESCO barrier at the two sheriff's deputies. They twisted a long-haired, twenty-year-old man into handcuffs, and read the guy his rights.

"Sweet Jesus in a shopping cart," Mat swore.

He scanned the crowd of 250 refugees pressed against the barricade. The town had built the hasty HESCO barrier across most of Highway 79 and out a hundred meters to each side. It was the start of what Mat hoped would be the final word in town defense: a fortification surrounding the majority of the small town's homes and businesses.

This was exactly how the army did it in Afghanistan, in all the army's rarefied wisdom. They set up forward operating bases surrounded by HESCO barriers, perimeter guards and heavily-guarded points of ingress.

They'd only completed a couple hundred meters of the barrier since Mat took the job. The mob of rats could go around the wall if they waded across the mucky fields, but it was a good start. They'd also cobbled together barriers across both sides of Highway 22 and Highway 79. All together, Mat figured the town had completed about 500 meters of HESCO barrier. There was a long, long way to go before the town was fully encircled. He sucked at geometry, so his mind left it at "a long, long way to go." But the majority of town was surrounded by ankle-deep mud—the post-apocalyptic remnant of the hay fields that'd been plowed under for the winter; and it'd been a rainy fall for Tennessee, they told him. The mud and muck could be considered a half-assed moat of sorts. The rats stacked up at the highway gates and they avoided stepping off the roadway into the mud.

This barricade at the northwest corner of town got the most pressure. The refugees pressed against Mat and his erstwhile soldiers in hopes of a handout from the people of McKenzie. A handout wasn't going to happen. The town couldn't feed even a fraction of these refugees, even for a week, without killing itself. He sighed as he watched the cops arresting the long-haired guy.

"To a hammer, everything's a nail," his commanding officer in Iraq liked to say. Mat had been an Army Ranger—a death-dealer for the United States of America, and one hell of a hammer himself. But the country he defended no longer existed. His area of operation, these days, was the fields and bogs around McKenzie, Tennessee, chock-a-block full of the filthiest, most-desperate human beings he'd ever seen—and he had seen some real trashlickers.

Fortunately, most of the refugees had wasted away during whatever hellish travail brought them to the outskirts of McKenzie. They'd exhausted themselves pursuing the ever-dwindling world of modern possibilities and landed in the mud, outside the small town. Exhausted was good, but even dull-eyed zombies were capable of superhuman acts of desperation, in Mat's ample experience. They were the enemy, and while they weren't Zulus, they could easily kill them all if they got the wrong idea.

"Hey, he didn't do anything wrong!" some, filthy, city schmuck shouted from the crowd.

Mat didn't like the look of the crowd gravitating toward the arresting deputies. He couldn't allow this to become a pre-apocalypse "protest" with people bitching about police brutality. He had to nip that shit in the bud, right away. People hadn't entirely forgotten "their rights"—it'd only been a couple months since the nation vanished out from underneath them. The last really big race protest had been in Los Angeles, then Baltimore and Detroit, and that was right before the bomb turned everything ass-toward-the-sky. That'd been October and this was December. People still remembered how to demand shit from "the man," even though the original copy of the Constitution had probably been used to wipe some looter's butt by now.

Mat climbed down off the tetanus-infested jumble they called a HESCO barrier and hurried to where the deputies were about to fold the unruly guy into a patrol car. The town's eighteen cops, including six auxiliary officers, plus two dozen volunteers, were all Mat had to work with on the barricade. Half of those men and women were spread like wandering ants across the top of the HESCO. If this crowd got big ideas, and came at them like Mat had seen the Sudanese do, his guards wouldn't even be a speed bump. They'd go right up and over the barricade and pour into town.

The wall was a HESCO in name only. In this section, they'd stacked hundreds of otherwise useless vehicles, three tall. The tires were removed on the bottom so there wasn't space to crawl under. The top car was flipped over and mashed as flat as possible with the bucket of a backhoe; it gave the guards a flat surface for high-ground defense. Three cars, stacked and crushed, added up to nine feet of wall. They had welded sewer pipe to the outside of the cars and extended the height of the wall another six feet with chainlink fence. Near the highways, they added razor wire on top of that. It was the ugliest HESCO imaginable—uneven and full of holes, like a kids' tree fort made out of pallets and trash cans.

Mat climbed down the HESCO and trotted toward the deputies. "Stop!" His voice was loud, firm, and calm. "We're not arresting people today." The portion of the crowd within earshot quieted. He could sense hope rise. They probably thought the police would back off, lay down and give the "protest" room to burn out like the old country used to do. But hope in this circumstance was bad for the town. Very bad.

The deputies hesitated. Town cops still answered to the sheriff, not necessarily to Mat.

"He refused to comply with a lawful order," one of the officers argued. "Sheriff Morgan said we maintain the peace."

Mat leaned into the man and lowered his voice. "Yes. But this is an indigenous population, not your normal arrest. Peace requires strength on this side of the wall."

The cop looked confused at the word "indigenous," but he stopped trying to cram the guy into the patrol car. Mat looked hard at the refugee. He was thin, filthy, and frightened, but in his eyes, resentment mingled with fear. Mat had seen the same steam coming off young, pissed-off Afghans. Resentment was the last thing Mat wanted to see in these people. Resentment meant they thought they were owed something. It was one thing for people to beg, it was another thing for people to act like they were being ripped off by someone. Old, bad habits still smoldered in tumble-down America. The collapse of everything was still not enough to stamp out victim culture.

Mat didn't ask the guy's name. He gave him a new name in his mind: "Mr. Example."

He turned Mr. Example around and frog-marched him to the front of the crowd. Mat was exposed, but it wasn't the first desperate throng he'd faced. The rats shouted and griped a blue streak, but they weren't a mob yet. They hadn't gone over the top of the emotional spillway. With luck, Mat's gambit would settle the waters.

From behind Mr. Example, Mat raised his voice. Those in front could hear him. The back of the crowd muddled around with low energy typical of extreme hunger.

"We will not be arresting you today," he called to the refugees within earshot. Mat felt hope rise like a sheet in the wind, as anticipated. He removed the deputy's handcuffs from Mr. Example, stepped back and delivered a vicious side kick to man's kidney.

Mister Example must've believed he'd won this round of "who's entitled to what" because when Mat's kick connected, he was as loose as a noodle. His back arched in an impossible S-curve and he snapped face-forward into the road.

Mat's Glock sprang into his hands and he searched for targets in the first row of the crowd. Mister Example gasped like a fish out of water and twisted at Mat's feet. Mat didn't think he'd broken the dude's back, but he would walk like an old man for a couple days.

"NOW! BACK THE FUCK UP!" Mat didn't dare fire a warning shot. If he fired his gun at this point, it'd flip a switch—and maybe trigger a cascade. There were undoubtedly firearms in the crowd. His men were outnumbered, and they were not prepared for battle. In his peripheral vision he saw the security detail had drawn their weapons. "Hold!" he ordered his team.

The crowd couldn't back away. They were hemmed in by other refugees on all sides. Mat backed up, finally with some breathing room. Without turning his back on the crowd, he led his team in an orderly retreat through the gate and behind the barricade. The big rig they used to block the entrance across Highway 79 rumbled forward, scraping the sides of its trailer along the HESCO. The local welder had added steel plates to the underside of the trailer so nothing bigger than a cat could slip beneath.

Mat's security guys stepped through the gap before it closed, then ran up the ramps to the top of the HESCO.

The crowd roiled forward into the space Mat had made with his antics. Rats piled against the big rig and the HESCO, mashing their front row into the wall. Mat gave orders to employ the greased poles if anyone climbed.

The greased pole idea had come to Mat a few days before. He and Sheriff Morgan had been discussing the town's major source of meat, the pig farms in Henry, five miles to the Northeast. The mental association of pigs led to greased pigs, like at the county fair, then to the greased pole the Army had Mat and his fellows attempt to climb in training. If a man couldn't climb a greased pole, he sure as hell couldn't rip one out of another man's hands.

Mat issued the McKenzie defenders six-foot fence posts from the lumber yard and tipped them with half-spherical caps. An enterprising deputy filled the middle of the tube with concrete for weight. The top three feet of the blunt, heavy lance was smeared with axle grease to prevent attackers from yanking it out of a defender's grasp. The post focused the punching power of a snap-thrust into a two-inch ball of regret.

Someone in the crowd shouted, "They got plenty to eat in there, while we're starving out here," and that was all the crowd required to go high-order. The throng surged up to the semi trailer, but they could get no purchase on the slick, metal-sided wall. They overflowed onto the fields on both sides of the road, and then scrambled up the stacked cars that served as walls.

There were plenty of footholds, but climbing the curved surfaces of car fenders and hoods proved tricky—as many rats fell away as made it to the chainlink topper. As they climbed, the fence wobbled and waved. The weird motion shucked off rats like sand off a shaken beach towel. They plummeted into the mass of people surging against the HESCO.

A female police offer punched her ramrod through the fence

and took a jowly-looking man in the sternum. He toppled backward and bounced down the stack of cars. A woman rushed to him and went down to her knees. The crowd loosened around them.

Another guy flew away from the fence, probably gut-punched by Juan Cabrera's ramrod. He fell all the way to the ground and lay there heaving, like trying to suck breath through a straw. Several others fell part way off the fence, bounced down the cars, and rolled into the mob.

On the opposite side of the gap across Highway 79, the crowd thickened and surged up the car-wall. Their chainlink waved rhythmically as six men climbed at once. A college-aged kid from town fought furiously with his ramrod, punching repeatedly through the fence without dislodging any of the climbers. The welds holding the corner fence pole cracked like a shotgun and a fifteen-foot section of fence gave way. The six men fell. One swung into a crushed Oldsmobile. The naked hood armature impaled him through the side of the gut. He slid off the metal stake, bounced once on the car below and fell to the ground. The mob swallowed him and his body disappeared as they flowed back away from the wall.

The attack on the wall waned. Hunger left the rats with short fuses and even shorter endurance. Mat nodded satisfaction. The ramrods were working for now. The refugees backed up and took to yelling insults.

"What the heck was that you did down there?" a civilian volunteer asked Mat. He was pretty sure her last name was Carter. Gladys Carter. She'd been the high school basketball coach before the shit hit the fan. Before that, she'd played in the WNBA, which is why Mat remembered her name—that and the fact that she towered over his six-foot frame. Now, she looked pissed, her fists on her hips. Mat felt like a schoolboy being called to task by his mother.

"Are we beating people up now?" she pressed. The whites of her eyes swam beneath her knotted brows. "I don't think they would've attacked the wall had you not kicked that guy's ass." She was referring to Mr. Example. That was minutes ago, practically forever in battle time. "Now some dude has an Oldsmobile ornament up his ass. That was unnecessary," she said.

"We're saving lives, ours and theirs," Mat argued. "You mind if I keep at it?" Her fierce eyes relented and she tilted her head to the side as if to say *"Go ahead, mister, but this conversation isn't over."*

Mat smiled as he climbed up a ladder at the back of the semi trailer. He enjoyed having someone around with the guts to call him on stuff. He'd always liked having a second set of eyes— someone to tell him the scuttlebutt on any team he led. He decided that he'd ask the WNBA player to train with the quick reaction force. She could end up being a decent 2IC—second in command— if she could learn to keep her mouth shut until *after* an operation was in the bag.

From on top of the semi trailer, Mat could survey the bulk of the crowd. He was exposed to gunfire, but this next part couldn't be done from behind the barrier. He wanted the rats to see him. He knew how he looked to them: dark haired, muscular, tattooed, bearded and well-armed. To the starving hundreds of barbarians at the gate, he must come off like Zeus, fresh down from Olympus.

The frothing sea of humanity had become a stagnant pond of just a few, focused acts of violence. He patted himself on the back for his judgment. It'd played out more-or-less as he'd hoped.

"This town is closed!" Mat bellowed. "There's nothing for you here! There is only death. Move on. We do not want to hurt you, but we will. Old Paris Road will take you south. This town is closed."

Mat repeated the message three times and then thumbed his radio. "Highway seventy-nine detail this is Best, repeat my last, tell the refugees they must move south on Old Paris Road."

Mat waved the basketball pro up to take over shouting the message. She shook her head, but did it anyway. She shouted a lot louder than Mat. It only bothered him a little.

Fifty people detached from the back of the crowd and drifted toward Old Paris Road. Mat mentally urged more to leave. The remaining six hundred or so ignored the commands.

In the distance, down Highway 79, a thin, staggering mass of refugees trickled in to replace the few that had left. They'd be at 700 in the next half hour, and then maybe 900 by nightfall. They'd start the day tomorrow at well over a thousand. Mat's showmanship had bought them just thirty minutes of reprieve.

Mat turned and found Deputy Rickers crossing behind the semi trailer. He called down to the Deputy.

"Yo, Rickers. Go get the dry food wagon. Let's offer the food-for-guns trade while they're tuckered out." Rickers saluted and hustled off down the highway toward his cruiser.

*Every little bit counts,* Mat tried to make himself feel better. If he was being honest, this was like fighting forest fire with coffee piss. He didn't need a new plan, he needed a whole, new playbook.

He contemplated the enemy arrayed before him on the roadway. Nearly all of them had run out of gas driving through snarled traffic between the big cities and McKenzie. There were 700 here, but at least ten times that number squatted in make-shift camps in the woods, surrounding the town, like an invading army preparing for siege. Mat had no idea what led some people to gather in one camp as opposed to another, but smoke columns rose from at least thirty clusters of trees, mostly toward the north and the east in the direction of Louisville, St. Louis and Nashville. The refugees had overrun the farmlands around McKenzie and chased almost all the farm families into town.

The rats were "just people," a never-ending sea of accountants, receptionists, day care workers, cab drivers, parking lot attendants and paralegals. They weren't gangbangers, mostly, and they weren't militia combatants. They were very hungry, regular folks.

Mat remembered the old movie with Kevin Costner—*The Postman*. The bad guys had been a militant gang of preppers with a megalomaniac tyrant for a leader. What Mat wouldn't give for such an enemy. At this moment, staring down at the mulling, sulking crowd of discontents at the foot of the wall, clear battle lines and black-and-white evil would come as welcome relief. At least he could fit that situation into his wheelhouse of past experience.

"The food-for-guns wagon's here," Gladys Carter had climbed up the semi trailer to tell him. She could've yelled from the ground, but she hadn't. "Sorry for getting in your face earlier. It probably could've waited."

"Yep," Mat agreed. "But I appreciate your candor."

"The food wagon's here," she repeated. "Do you want me to crack the gate and let the refugees know we're open for business?"

"Yeah. Thanks. That'd be great. Every little bit counts," Mat said. On some level, they probably both knew it was B.S.. Sometimes, "every little bit" didn't add up to *diddlysquat*.

# 7

## CAMERON STEWART

"No winning words about death to me, shining Odysseus!

By god, I'd rather slave on earth for another man—some dirt-poor tenant farmer who scrapes to keep alive—than rule down here over all the breathless dead."

— ACHILLES, THE ODYSSEY

**Grafton Ghost Town,
Southern Utah**

I t took two men to carry an eight-foot section of twelve inch, corrugated pipe, or Cameron would've made Isaiah move two pipes to his one. Cameron reminded himself throughout the day: if he wanted to survive, he must do less and eat more. It was the only way to make it to spring. If he burned fewer calories than the polygamist, he would come out on top.

But if Cameron did no work whatsoever, Isaiah would balk and the water project would grind to a halt. Isaiah would never quite tell Cameron "no," but he had his own way of slowing down and playing dumb when he felt jerked around.

Cameron could point his rifle at the man and order him to work as a proper slave, but then the polygamist would dig in his heels and his ideas for food would cease. So far, the weirdo had a lot of ideas, and some of those ideas held promise. Even starving, the polygamist chatted incessantly while they carried pipe—reciting endless factoids of local history, picking them apart for some survival advantage. If Isaiah had spent half as much time reading about Native Americans in the area, they wouldn't be so focused on cultivation. They might find a natural food source that they could eat now, without having to work so hard. Even by Isaiah's accounting, the first Mormon settlers in the area struggled to feed themselves by planting the soil. The Indians had done it for eons by wandering around. Cameron would give anything to know what they knew.

But the clan's best idea so far was to grow crops. They'd have to divert water from the Virgin River, a hundred yards above the homestead, and channel it to the rusty stock watering tank at the high end of their pasture. While they worked on the big pipes, the women and children dug out the foundations of the farmhouse for the cold frame greenhouses. Isaiah swore the ground heat would keep the plants warm enough to survive overnight.

Like everything else in their red rock prison, the crop project was subject to survival math: calories in and calories out. They'd run their food pantry down to a single bucket-and-a-half of raw wheat, six cans of beans, and a half bottle of peaches. A mouse had chewed through the sidewall of the wheat bucket, eaten its fill and pooped in the bucket. Cameron's boys sorted through the wheat kernels one-at-a-time and picked out the mouse poop. Cameron found where the mouse hid in the floor, ripped up the planking, and caught an adult and three baby mice. They ate them all for breakfast.

Two hundred calories were burned lifting the floor. Fifty calories were gained eating the mice. That was mostly how it worked. They burned twice what they reaped. Every calorie in the natural world, it seemed, had evolved an infuriating system for protecting itself from consumption.

Cameron killed two more snakes while they moved pipe—another rattler and a gopher snake. A mouthful of snake possessed a slight greasiness that landed in the stomach more solidly than starches. Cameron couldn't fathom why meat would be better than wheat. In any case, they steadily starved notwithstanding; no matter what they picked off the ground, dug out of a rotted log or smashed with a rock.

Cameron and Isaiah were forced to search for irrigation pipe farther downriver, where the willows and cottonwoods shaded the black soil and riverside grasses. For once, they found calories free-for-the-taking: bugs. Lots of bugs. They sent for Isaiah's ten year-old daughter, Leah. She came with a sleeping bag stuff sack to collect the bounty.

Under every fourth or fifth pipe they lifted from the wet ground, they found seething, green masses of stink bugs—sometimes two or three pounds under a single pipe. Like everything else on the ground, they were both somewhat nutritious and somewhat disgusting. Stink bugs tasted like green apples sprayed by a skunk. They choked them down anyway.

Under the canopy of the cottonwoods, they overturned white grubs, cockroaches, earthworms and assorted insect larvae, all of which went into the fry pan. No matter how much nastiness he swallowed, Cameron felt no difference in his predatory hunger. Even when they had bugs and worms, the level of wheat in the bucket continued to drop, because without the grain every day, he and Isaiah would not be able to work. There simply wouldn't be enough calories in their bodies.

Under the trees, with young Leah present, Cameron found himself doing his share of the work, despite his strategy to work less and eat more. If he stopped to let Isaiah wrestle pipe on his own, the girl stopped and stared at him watching her father. Her brown eyes framed no malice, but they tracked him with an unblinking judgment that gave Cameron the heebie-jeebies.

"What do you and my first-mom do down by the river? Are you looking for bugs?" Leah asked as Cameron caught his breath in the shade of a cottonwood.

It was an unusual question, made more unusual by the fact that nobody in the group, except Isaiah, spoke unless it was a necessity. Thinking burned calories. Talking burned more. Cameron reminded himself that taking a long time to answer didn't make him look guilty. Everyone took a long time to answer now.

"We're looking for frogs," he lied.

Her eyes betrayed neither suspicion nor doubt. "Did you get some?"

For a moment, he wasn't sure what she meant. He was definitely getting some, but that couldn't have been what she meant. She was a naive polygamist kid.

"No. We can hear them, but we haven't found where they're hiding."

She seemed to accept the explanation. "Are you the prophet here?" she asked.

"I'm not a prophet," he replied without really considering what the word "prophet" meant to her. He chuckled. "I don't think God throws in with guys like me."

She cocked her head and watched as her father dragged a section of pipe, then dropped it in exhaustion. "We're proud to labor for the prophet," she said with a question hanging in her voice.

Cameron walked to the pipe, bent over and lifted his end. Isaiah followed suit and they duck-walked it toward the old canal bed.

They'd decided to place all the pipe first, then dam the river later. There was no sense building a dam if the salvaged pipe wouldn't reach the stock tank, but it looked like there would be enough. They were half-way, and dozens of lengths of pipe still littered the property.

Neither of them had ever built an irrigation system before, and a solemn terror stalked Cameron—some unknown gremlin would skulk in the rudimentary mechanics of their plan. It always did, for Cameron. He hadn't ever done a project that spanned a football field like this one, but drawing upon his one, disastrous attempt to repair his own broken sprinkler system back home, he knew how insidiously uncooperative water could be.

Six years after discovering that his lawn in Anaheim was dying, he still watered it by hand. He tried at least half-a-dozen times to find the problem with the sprinklers only to give up after hours of digging. He refused to call a landscaper, mostly because he couldn't stand the idea of his wife seeing an immigrant yard worker succeed where Cameron had failed.

Worries about this jumbo-sized irrigation system sprouted like weeds in his mind. For one thing, there were no fasteners to lock the pipes together. Someone had come along before the apocalypse, unbolted the couplers, took them away and left the pipe corroding in the sand. Cameron found a few rusty nuts and half-moon brackets hidden in the weeds, so he knew that's how the pipes were supposed to be connected. Without couplers, they just nested each ten-foot section of pipe, precariously, inside the other. He hoped water would rush down the bottom of the pipes and only splash out a little at every seam. He figured it'd be less water loss than just letting it go down the dirt canal, but he had no way of judging how much of the water they'd lose before it reached the pasture. He supposed they could build a bigger dam if the water petered out too soon.

There was a stack of old, three-quarter inch PVC tubing on the edge of the pasture, and every plastic section came with a one-to-one straight connector. He didn't think they'd have a problem getting the water from the stock tank to the trenches with that tubing, but he had no idea how they were going to attach the PVC to the drain spigot at the rusty tank.

They had a single envelope of turnip seeds from the "survival seed bank"—maybe two hundred of them—but he didn't know what percentage of those seeds could be expected to sprout. The seed bank looked to be at least five years old. Would seeds last that long in a can?

Then there were questions about winter. It seemed like greenhouses should work in Southern Utah—it mostly only froze at night. The days were moderately warm, even as Christmas approached. But what about the daylight hours and the angle of the sun? Cameron could swear that the days were shorter and the light was a little more autumn-like than summer. Did vegetables mind less sun? Did the angle of the sun matter?

The irrigation plan could be a catastrophe—tens of thousands of calories sweated away for nothing, or it could be their salvation. His worry soured his stomach.

"If you're not the prophet, then why does my father do most of the work?" the little girl's voice yanked him out of his whirlpool of worries.

He'd dropped his end of the pipe, but Isaiah continued yanking on it like a stubborn dog with a rope. He tugged the pipe three inches, rested, tugged the pipe three more inches, rested again. The man wasn't much of a physical specimen, but he was no quitter. Cameron's old man would've admired the kooky dipshit. He had spent half his childhood getting reamed out by his dad for running lackluster Little League laps, hating his math homework or slacking off on make-work chores his dad gave him at home. "Stewarts never quit!" his old man would scream from the bleachers while little Cam pumped out sluggish, floppy burpees. Little Cameron seethed against his dad when he did that. He wanted to smash his fucking face.

*Someday*, Cameron had promised himself. *Someday he would be big enough to shut that mouth with his fist. One-two punch combination. Blood jetting from the lips of his old man. The nose too. He pictured his pops toppling to the side, surprise in his eyes.*

"Brother Cameron," she repeated. "Are you quitting? Should I tell my dad it's time to quit?"

*Had she read his mind?* She turned and watched her father yank at the pipe, worry in her brows. She walked toward him, as if to pick up the end of the pipe.

"I'm not quitting." Cameron lurched away from the cottonwood that'd been holding him up. "I needed to catch my breath, is all." He stepped past her and resumed carrying his end of the pipe.

"Cameron," a woman's voice floated from the distance. It was Julie. "Cameron. Come quick." She burst through a stand of reeds. "Denny's sick. He's in a lot of pain."

Cameron and Isaiah dropped the pipe at the same time, and it clattered to the ground. They rushed to the farmhouse.

*This is where it begins,* Cameron fretted as he broke into a run. *This is where the dying starts. Not Denny. Anyone but Denny.*

Cameron burst into the dim cabin and the dust motes swirled in the shafts of light from the door. Denny was on the floor, twisted in a sleeping bag.

"Ow, ow, ow," he moaned. "It hurts."

"What hurts, little man?" Cameron dropped to the floor beside him. "Tell me what hurts."

"It's my stomach. It hurts so bad."

"Is anyone else sick?" Cameron asked the gathering.

Julie and Ruth shook their heads.

"Everyone else seems fine," Ruth answered. "But come look." She waved them outside.

The farmhouse had been a restored structure—an artifact from when the Grafton ghost town had been part of the Mormon cotton mission. The outhouse had been restored too, but not to any useable standard. When they arrived, Isaiah had made a half-hearted attempt to carve the pit toilet a bit deeper, and that'd been the extent of their effort toward proper sanitation. The outhouse smelled like raw, human sewage, freezing and reheating with each night and day. At least the cold at night killed off all the flies.

Ruth had apparently climbed down into the shallow pit and displayed a scoop of the sewage on the chunk of wood she'd used as a shovel.

"Look close." She pointed at the watery slop, her finger trembling.

White worms threaded through the turd like maggots in the compost.

"Roundworm," Isaiah said, and Ruth nodded. They'd obviously seen it before.

"Is that bad?" Cameron's throat tightened like a noose.

"We don't know if this is his poop," Ruth said. "This could be from one of the others. We might all have it. It's not a big deal, usually. The infirmary back home would give the kids Vermox for it. They'd sometimes get the white worm from playing in the fertilizer or swimming in the canal. But we don't have Vermox here. We don't have any medicine."

"We can go to Rockville and ask," Julie blurted. "If Hildale had it, then Rockville will have it." Her eyes stood out like the ragged eyes of leg-broke cat.

"Slow down," Isaiah urged. "We need to think. Balance risks against benefit. Rockville does have a dispensary, but they're probably not going to share with us. We could get shot for even asking."

Cameron knew he should take control of the situation. He was the father, but his hunger coupled with his terror left him mute.

"I'll go," he blurted out. Cameron grabbed the Mosin-Nagant from against the wall.

"No, wait a second." Isaiah urged with his hands. "They always had roundworm here. I think the Mormon settlers had a remedy from the Indians." His eyes went vacant and he rubbed his chin for a moment, deep in thought. Then he was back. "I think I remember. Give me an hour before you do anything, okay? I need to check on something. Promise me you'll wait an hour before you go into Rockville, Cameron."

Cameron nodded, then stormed back to the homestead, to suffer with his son.

---

ISAIAH RETURNED WITH LEAH, both bent over under bulging cloth wraps.

"We need help," Isaiah blurted as he dumped his pack on the table. He pulled open the knots in the cloth and shook out over a hundred dried gourds, like mottled-yellow racquetballs onto the tabletop. Leah did the same. Dozens overflowed onto the floor and rolled around the cabin.

"Crack these open and separate the seeds from the duff," Isaiah urged.

Everyone except the sick boy jumped to cracking the dry gourds on the floor or the table and separating out the loose, dry seeds.

"Why weren't we eating these?" Julie stuck some in her mouth.

Isaiah shook his head, "They were all dried up. It's not the season. I didn't think about the seeds. But don't eat them yet. We need them for medicine, for Denny. Leah—stop what you're doing and go find a rock and a board. We need to grind these up into powder. I remember the Natives used pumpkin seeds to get rid of parasites. These should work the same."

The boy moaned on the floor, rocking back and forth inside the sleeping bag. Cameron clawed at his hair in desperation. He'd never felt so helpless.

The turd Ruth had dug from the privy had been riven with worms, almost a rope of them coiled around what little nutrition the boy had left in his poop. Cameron pictured the worms in his son's intestines, writhing, sucking, hunting for nutrition.

"Focus, Cameron!" Isaiah almost shouted. "Open these and pick out the seeds. Stop fretting and work."

Cameron blinked back the desolation that threatened to swamp him and focused on the gourds that Isaiah swept off the table and dumped into his lap.

*Crack, split, dump.* He forced his hands to the simple labor, though his senses drowned in liquid terror. A knot formed in his stomach, and Cameron pictured it as his own parasite chewing him from the inside out. He welcomed the pain. He imagined it drawing agony away from the boy, taking it into his own stomach.

*Crack, split, dump.* The crashing waves of love and terror could not be contained, but he could execute the gross functions of smashing the tiny, smelly pumpkins. The girl, Leah, knelt beside him and picked the clustered seeds out of the dry pile of fiber in front of his aching knees. It was good that she did because his fingers buzzed with adrenaline—insensate and thuggish. He couldn't force them to pick out the seeds if he tried.

There was no escaping the truth: his family was completely exposed to the horrors of Mother Earth unbound. She was revealed, vengeful and cruel, and Cameron knew she wouldn't hesitate to devour his son from the guts out. His son suffered, and Cameron could marshall no salvation but to follow the orders of the awkward polygamist.

Fifty-foot waves of crushing love swelled and then dropped into hundred-foot troughs of despair. Cameron hated himself for hating Isaiah. If he repented for his abuse of the polygamist family, maybe God would save Denny.

They were all so hungry, so close to the edge of oblivion. Denny had become a bony, stick-figure version of the Little League short-stop he'd been four months before. He would not survive an onslaught of parasites. Like the rest of them, he was dying by degrees already.

*Crack, split, dump.* In the hazy hunger and arrhythmic thumping of gourds on the floor of the dim room, Cameron despaired. His sin had brought them here. He had succumbed to slavery and abuse, at least in his heart. So, the devil feasted on his family, given leave by God because Cameron had abandoned decency. He was like Job in the Bible, if Job had been a soulless sonofabitch.

"I'm sorry," Cameron heaved the words out. The saliva in his mouth turned to slurry. He'd been weeping without realizing it. Everyone paused their thumping and cracking. "I'm sorry, Isaiah," he repeated. "I've been a dick."

The pause lingered. Isaiah looked up and nodded acknowledgement, but he was probably too tired from collecting the gourds to speak. One-by-one, they went back to thumping and cracking.

# 8

---

SAGE ROSS

**Elgin, Oregon**
**C-Zers Drive-thru**

S age hadn't ever been to a job interview before. It probably
wasn't good that his first-ever job interview would be
live-or-die.

They'd moved him to the dining area of a drive-through burger
shack, and given him a burger, which felt about as strange as being
interviewed naked. Over the last two months of eating rattlesnake,
wild rabbit and shriveled, discarded onions, he'd assumed
hamburgers had gone extinct.

The police captain pulled into the parking lot of the burger joint
in his cruiser. He got out and shook hands with the militia officer
supervising Sage. The two bullshitted for a bit. Sage couldn't hear
what they were saying through the glass, but he watched as they
guffawed and knee-slapped like old fishing buddies, which they
might have been.

Sage had sent the one dude he hadn't killed—the talker—back

to the women and children two nights before. Then he hightailed it down and out of the canyon in the dark. The moon had been waxing, so he had an extra hour of light. At all costs, he wanted to avoid facing the women and the kids of the men he'd killed.

The barricade guards arrested Sage at the mouth of the canyon. They handed him over to the officer—a forty-something-year-old guy with a paunch, wearing old-school, green and brown military camouflage. They locked him up in an office at a plywood factory that appeared to be the centerpiece of town. The "jail cell" was just a room with a deadbolt; not much of a jail, really. It was cold in the room, but they gave him a couple blankets and warm food. His toes came back from being numb for a week. Nothing seemed frostbitten. Some skin sloughed off, but the flesh underneath looked pink and healthy.

When Sage told the officer he wanted a job with the militia, and that he had firearms training, the man cocked his head and nodded. It seemed to be the right thing to say. They fed him real food and told him to wait until the police captain could come around and "get an eyeball full of him."

The captain leaned up against his cruiser in the parking lot of the burger joint, never casting a glance toward Sage, laughing it up with his friend. Sage took the opportunity to wolf down the rest of the burger and start in on the fries.

Through the glass panes, the sound of the conversation clarified and Sage picked up bits and pieces: the militia had mixed it up with a Mad Max gang from "south-a-Boise." The militia had known the gang was coming and had shot them to pieces as they passed through Powder River Gulch, wherever that was. Apparently, it'd been a one-sided engagement. The militia slaughtered the biker gang and left their corpses on the asphalt of the interstate as a warning to the next biker gang.

That probably explained how a string of farming communities

like Union County, Oregon, hadn't been overrun by starving city folk—they killed anyone who tried kicking in the door.

The captain wrapped up with his buddy, in perfect time to catch Sage licking the grease off the wax paper in the bottom of the burger basket. Sage dropped the paper when the captain came through the glass door.

"So, young man, they tell me you know how to shoot? They say you killed Joey McCullum and his brother with one shot. That true?" The captain looked too carefree to be the man in-charge. He had a little gray showing on the fringes of his full head of hair and his jaw was a sharp, square line. He looked like a casual athlete who hadn't given up his every-day run, even during the apocalypse. The man exuded vitality.

"I guess so. I didn't mean to hit them both, but the first guy definitely pulled his gun on me."

The captain waved away the explanation. "Neither of those boys were going to make it out there. These days, you're either part of the team or you're dead. The McCullums were never part of the team. They were the losers selling weed under the bleachers at half-time. They actually did that in high school. Those boys weren't going to survive in this new, improved world." The captain smiled his winning smile, which must've been a habit, since he didn't need to sell Sage anything.

Sage didn't know what to say. He felt like he might be a murderer, so he just nodded.

"We're looking to hire out-of-towners," the captain said, changing the subject. "Ya know, for the department." He indicated the police cruiser. He wasn't wearing a uniform—just a captain's department coat and a T-shirt underneath that said *Ironman Coeur d'Alene Finisher*. "We got all the locals we need on the force, and we're bulking up the squad with new blood. You want in?"

Sage hadn't been prepared for it to be this easy, but he liked the captain. In any case, there was nothing to think about. He nodded eagerly.

"We'll get you all your stuff back. Your rifle too. Ferguson already topped off your 30-30 ammo and we'll get you set up with fatigues—that's the department uniform now that we're the police, army, navy and air force, all rolled up in one." The captain got up from the table and held out a hand. "Welcome aboard, Sage Ross. You'll be on my personal cadre." Sage shook on it.

He hadn't been this lucky in a long time. He'd almost forgotten what it felt like to have things click. He'd been carving out his existence with sheer force of will for months. This turn of events felt like normal life. It felt like all those years when his mother made sure he had no complaints. *Easy street.*

"Thank you, sir. I won't let you down." It sounded cheesy.

The captain smiled and punched him lightly on the shoulder. "Just because it's the apocalypse, doesn't mean it's gotta suck." He smiled again and Sage smiled right along with him.

---

**Grande Rhonde River Settlement Ponds**
**La Grande, Oregon**

THE OTHER GUYS in the police called him "Stack," and Sage hated it. Word spread around the militia that he'd killed two men with one bullet, and that became his calling card, whether he liked it or not: Stack.

Today, he ran security on work parties putting up the greenhouses. He wished he could help with construction, but his orders were to stand around the workmen and "look like you're paying attention." Apparently, theft had been an issue in the past.

To Sage's eye, La Grande city teetered on the edge of being too big to control. He didn't know the population numbers—maybe ten thousand or so—and there seemed to be fissures in the spirit of cooperation, to put it mildly. An us-and-them gulf persisted between the law enforcement and the workmen on the project.

Snow had begun to fall in dribs and drabs in La Grande. It was early December and, while it hadn't "stuck" yet at that elevation, they got a few light frostings every week. The sky clamped down around the valley, a sullen gray lid to a powdered sugar pot. The primary focus of the town was winter food production.

The agronomy professor from the tiny Eastern Oregon University oversaw the construction of fifty hoop greenhouses, clad in heavy, clear plastic, along the settlement ponds of the Grande Rhonde River. Ten of the greenhouses were to be dedicated to winter greens, but the majority were being tasked to grow russet potatoes in trash cans that were, even now, being collected from every home in town. The town subsisted on the last of the fall harvest, the local herd of beef cattle and twelve grain elevators alongside the railroad tracks. They would need more than that to make it through to the next harvest, and nobody in La Grande, so far as Sage could tell, had any illusions about the federal government coming to save them. This far from urbanity and this close to the furrow, people accepted a harder existence. They probably always had.

But not everyone was a farmer in La Grande. In the other towns of Union County, the ones off the "beaten path" of I-84, almost all the residents tilled the ground or ran cattle. A good number of those grew stupid stuff like golf course-ready Kentucky bluegrass, or peppermint for essential oils—stuff not even the cattle would eat. No matter what they grew, though, the majority of Union County grew something.

In La Grande, what they called "the city," there was another class of human, and Sage could pick them out of the work crew like picking green jelly beans out of the bowl. Only this bowl was mostly green jelly beans.

They were the people who had once provided services for the people who tilled the ground: waiters at the local eateries, drug dealers, furniture salesmen, pizza delivery guys, even the tellers from the local bank. They were people who didn't make anything anyone could eat, and they fell into a new class that the farmer class called "Klingons," as in "freeloaders."

What struck Sage as particularly strange; he and the other militia guys called them Klingons too, even though most of the militiamen didn't plow either. The police department, which had combined with the county sheriff's department and ballooned from thirty men to almost four hundred camo-clad warriors, hovered over them in a class by itself. Not even the farming class dared challenge their dominion over the county.

Chamber's militia made sure the farmers were left alone to grow whatever food they could with winter looming. That meant keeping the Klingons out of their pastures and from stealing their livestock. It also meant keeping the rest of the world out of the Grande Rhonde Valley.

Captain Chamber's uncanny foresight, prior to the collapse, made it all possible. He'd been locked, cocked and ready-to-rock when the curtain fell on the modern world; a bona fide prepper with guns, ammo and even a solar system powering his ranch at the edge of town. His forethought and personal magnetism had unified all law enforcement under his control: city police, sheriff's department, even the two forest rangers who lived in La Grande.

The day the stock market closed, the other deputies whispered to Sage, the captain ordered every shop, store, gas station and storeroom buttoned up tight. He pulled his department back into La Grande and put a gunman in front of every store and ordered them closed indefinitely. La Grande, Oregon entered the apocalypse without even a run on toilet paper.

When it became apparent that the crisis was permanent, it was the most-natural thing in the world for the police to assume control of all manufactured goods and gasoline in Union County. As a result, nobody went hungry and they had reserves of fuel. Chambers organized soup kitchens and bread lines in eleven locations around La Grande, and shipped out regular deliveries of red winter wheat to the outlying towns. A lot of modern amenities, like fresh veggies and disposable batteries disappeared, but everyone ate, assuming they got with the program.

Unless they produced food on a farm, every Klingon checked in, every morning except Sunday, with their assigned work crew. Mostly, they built greenhouses, rounded up trash cans and assembled watering system for the potato project. Sometimes, they were trucked out to help farms with mission-critical manual labor. Of course, the Klingons bitched. They had no way of knowing how bad it was outside their valley. All they knew was that they were now the lowest social class, and they were being forced to work with their hands and backs.

Sage grew accustomed to getting the sideways stink-eye from the Klingons working the greenhouse project. It was part of working for the department.

He overheard their complaints about the captain "robbing the town blind," but as far as he could tell, Chambers took nothing extra for himself. He didn't need anything—his ranch was sitting pretty.

Sage caught remarks, tossed over shoulders, about "getting run out on a rail." When break time was over, the Klingons would say passive-aggressive shit like, "Better get back to it, boys, or the captain's henchmen, here, will run us outa town. Won'tcha?"

It came as no surprise to Sage; the first men he'd met coming out of Union County had been exiles. If a man couldn't bring himself to cooperate in the game of bare-knuckle survival, he was sent away to try his luck against the elements. Goodbye and good luck. The captain's force was on-track to deport all malcontents, for one reason or another. Being unskilled wasn't a crime in Union County. Being a bitch about it was.

Hovering over the work crews alongside the frigid river, Sage had a lot of time to listen, observe and think, and it began to make sense why the captain sought out-of-towners for this band of merry enforcers. As more and more people were shown the road, in a small community like La Grande, every local officer would eventually come up against a hard pill to swallow; somebody the officer knew and loved—a family relation, a high school pal, or the childhood babysitter now married to a coke addict. Eventually, a local cop would be forced to exile someone he cared about from the county.

Marching men, women and children to the county line was no picnic. Sage had taken his turn at it like everyone else. Those people knew they were being walked to their death. South of the county line was a one-way ticket to Rapeville for the women and Murdertown for the men. The biker gangs controlled everything south, around Boise.

North, over the Blue Mountains, the masses of starving Seattle-ites and Portlanders hid in ambush, hungry for fresh meat, but only if the exiles could first survive the snow-piled summit. They called it "exile" but it was a barely-cloaked execution.

The deputies debated duct-taping their exiles mouths, including kids. Listening to the begging, the arguing, the sob-soaked entreaties to give them just-one-more-chance; it was almost more than a man could bear. Sage couldn't imagine what it was like for an officer who had grown up as part of the community. Any officer who could—those with their own farms—had already left the force.

Sage shrugged his La Grande Police coat up around his shoulders. At least if he could help with the work, he wouldn't be so damn cold. He hated watching men work. Through a relentless campaign of shaming, his dad had instilled in him a phobia about standing around while there was work to be done.

"Hey, Goldbricker," his dad would shout in front of Sage's friends. "A man looks for work. Only a lazy piece of shit stands around with his hands in his pockets."

Sage shifted back and forth on his feet while the Klingons worked on the greenhouses. One of them walked by carrying a twelve-foot bundle of PVC over his shoulder, but the balance was off. Half the PVC slid out the back and clattered to the ground. Sage pulled his rifle sling over his head, settled the 30-30 on his back and trotted over to help. The Klingon gave him a quizzical look. They rebundled the PVC and carried it together, over their shoulders, into the greenhouse. Sage dropped the load and walked back to his post by the water bowser.

"Hey. Stack!" The senior officer put his hand on Sage's shoulder. "Don't do that again. There's plenty of Klingon-power to get this done. We have more hands than we have work. You're skilled labor." He tapped Sage's rifle barrel. "Don't get in the habit of carrying pipe. It's a waste, and it fucks with your mission readiness. You copy?"

Sage nodded. "Sorry. My dad didn't raise me to stand around, ya know?"

The officer chuckled. "Me too. But this ain't the world our dads raised us for. Not no more."

# 9

## MAT BEST

**Mat & William's House**
**McKenzie, Tennessee**

It'd been two weeks since the ambush on the road to Henry. Since then, the convoy had been hit six times. Subsequent ambushes hadn't been as coordinated, with the loudmouth ringleader cooling his dangly parts in the McKenzie jail. They hadn't lost any hogs, but two volunteers had been shot—both grazing wounds or frag. Luckily, neither of them died.

Mat was deep in thought about the stretch of busted up highway as he approached his house on the sidewalk, stepped onto his front porch and reached for the screen door. A girl's voice snapped him back to the present. Mat entered to find William on the edge of the couch with a pretty brunette.

The girl's words trailed off as the screen door squeaked. "Horizon Zero Dawn is not so much a first-person shooter. It's more..."

William had been so engrossed in the conversation he hadn't noticed Mat's approach.

"Hi, Mat!" William chirruped. "This is Candice."

"Hello, Candice." Mat waved. "Bro, you didn't notice me walking across the yard. What did I teach you about situational awareness?"

Mat was fully aware that it was a weird thing to bitch about, but these weren't normal times. No matter how *Leave It To Beaver* things seemed in town, there were thousands of despairing scarecrows massed outside the town limits, poised to ransack every cupboard.

William's face flushed with embarrassment. Nevertheless, Mat doubled down.

"You're not eating a burger and fries at Hardees here. We're surrounded by thousands who would kill you for a stick of gum."

William's face painted itself a deeper red. He stood up as he snapped at Mat, "I know that. I don't know why you're making such a big deal."

"Hello," the girl interrupted. She offered a handshake. Her other hand touched the small of William's back.

If Mat knew anything, he knew women. Females of the species had been de-escalating conflict between males for 10,000 years. Her touch calmed William like a magic spell. He leaned slightly toward the girl, and his posture relaxed. The girl had sent an unconscious message that the dominant male's correction hadn't diminished her interest in him. With the lightest touch, she smoothed over the wrinkle in their social grouping.

Candice filled the physical space between Mat and William with words. "My step dad is Jim Jensen. He organized the new classes at the high school. He's a big fan of yours, sir. He says with you we stand a good chance of holding back the refugees."

Instead of reading too much into the compliment, Mat mined for intelligence on Jim Jensen.

"What's he teaching these days? Are they spending half of class talking about Ancient Mesopotamian gender roles and inclusive diversity among urban Aztecs?"

She laughed at the awkward joke like an adult woman might. William just looked confused. Mat guessed she was a very mature thirteen year old.

"Jim knows that times have changed," Candice answered. "He's smart. He knows that no one cares about Shakespeare and political correctness right now. Classes are just a few hours a week—practical stuff like science, math and biology—how to care for livestock and how to make useful chemicals. We'll probably all be farmers for the next hundred years." She laughed again. Mature or not, only a child could laugh at the loss of so much.

Mat heard Jensen speaking through the girl and it unsettled him—like she worshipped the science teacher or maybe feared him, which was weird given the guy's balding head, oily complexion, and funky little pot belly. *Who would fear that guy?* Most kids her age were pushing back against their parents, not praising their wisdom.

"Jim's trying to preserve as many of the modern technologies as possible, and hand them down to us. That's the role of education now: to hang on to what mankind knew."

She must've listened to her stepfather give that post-apocalypse education speech many times, and she recited it faithfully. Jensen was more politician than Mat liked, but the words made sense. Science Guy might be a good ally after all, egghead or not.

Mat could get the townsfolk up to speed on security. He could teach them what he knew about defending a forward operating base, but he needed an exit plan—someone to take over when he headed west. Jensen might be good at herding the committees.

Mat was no civic leader. He was a tool. When you were done with a tool, you put it away, or in Mat's case you gave him a truck full of dried pork and waved as he drove away into the sunset.

The girl had stopped talking. Mat put his daydream about

leaving on pause and replied, "I've met your dad. He's right about the future. It's going to take a long time to come back from what we've lost."

Candice looked away and blushed. "Jim's my stepdad. We're not related by blood or anything." The pink in her cheeks tipped into red.

"What's your mom's name?" Mat changed the subject.

"Dina. She doesn't live with us anymore. She's in Louisville."

William shot Mat a knowing look.

*Louisville*: they'd passed through that hell hole. There was a good chance Candice's mother was dead or enslaved by gangs. The girls eyes, though, begged for hope. Mat wasn't going to shit in the middle of her hope parade.

"It's a big city." William said, comforting her. He picked up one of Candice's hands.

*It's to hand-holding,* Mat noted. *Things must move faster with kids at the end of the world.* Or maybe Mat had been too busy to keep an eye on the boy's love life.

Candice drenched William in a grateful smile and gave him both her hands. "You're sweet," she said. William swelled.

The boy had turned twelve a few days after Caroline died—more than two months ago. At that time, neither of them had been in a mood to celebrate. Sheriff Morgan's wife, Beatrice, insisted on making him birthday pancakes. It took less fuel to heat a griddle than a whole oven.

From grief-sprinkled birthday pancakes to consoling a young lady suitor in just two months. Life and death came fast, and so, apparently, did love. William was smitten, and that might just be a bomb-proof emotional shelter from the catastrophe all around them. It made Mat glad. It gave him hope.

"Hey, Will." Mat shifted to the slightly-more-adult version of the boy's name. "Why don't you walk Candice home? It'll be dark soon.

I've got some people to see before night patrol, then I'll be outside the wire with the new QRF. Please be back by dark. I'll see you in the morning. Maybe we can get something to eat together? Maybe talk about things?" Mat glanced at the girl, trying to send William a sideways message. *"I want to hear all about your new girl,"* the subtext read.

William nodded, barely paying attention.

<hr />

YOUNG WILLIAM WALKED the tree-lined lane back toward home, reliving the last three, amazing minutes. It had been perfect. When they reached her door, she'd turned and taken both his hands in hers.

"Thanks for walking me home, Will," Caroline had said. "I'm really glad you and Mat came to town."

Then she'd *leaned in,* just like in the movies. William hesitated at first, but it was a clear signal: the *lean in.* He took the chance. He'd kissed her.

Candice had kissed him back. Her soft lips had held his upper lip for the sweetest, most exciting of moments. His first kiss, and it was perfect. He'd nailed it.

"Good night, Will," Candice had said. She'd turned to the door, then looked back. "Umm... Don't tell Jim about that, okay?" He'd nodded. Then she'd disappeared inside, and the night had dimmed in her absence.

Twenty minutes later, William mounted the steps to his home. The house was dark. The whole town was dark.

He remembered they had candles. A few days earlier, Mr. Jensen held a candle-making class and Will brought home six of them. He rummaged through the kitchen drawer for matches, lit one of the candles and built a small fire in the hearth. Firewood was scarce—dangerous to haul in from the woods—but he wanted light and heat. Just tonight. He fell asleep tending the fire, contented, with her smell lingering on his sweater.

———

CANDICE WALKED into the house and eased the door closed behind her. She didn't want Jim to know she was home. She needed a few minutes to collect herself. Jim couldn't find out.

She soft-shoed down the hall and through the kitchen. At the door leading to the basement she paused and took a deep breath. She retrieved her cell phone from her pocket. There was no service, of course, but she still carried the phone, a reminder of a past life. Her phone case had a mirror on the back. She checked her face and made sure she wasn't flushed. She didn't want her face to give it away; her scarlet cheeks that fairly cried *I kissed a boy.*

When she was ready, Candice headed down the stairs. Jensen was there in the basement, tinkling with glass beakers. For most people, having a laboratory in the basement, full of biology experiments and hazardous chemicals, would seem odd. But Jensen was head of the high school science department. The lab was only a *little* strange. She was the only person in the world who knew he'd gone on an ego-fueled binge after watching the show *Breaking Bad.* He'd taught himself how to cook crystal meth, just like Walter White. But he'd never achieved the perfect, mythically-blue product. He'd gotten spooked and sold all his meth stuff to a drug dealer in Oklahoma City.

That was far from their only secret—she and him.

Jensen was popular with the kids and the townies thought of him as a harmless "science geek." If the town knew half of what he was doing in that basement, they would freak out.

Candice paused at the bottom of the stairs. Jim tinkered at a counter, facing away from her. She knew he'd heard her, but he wouldn't stop and acknowledge her until he finished his current task. That was his way.

The basement lab was big; the same footprint as the house, packed to the gills with boxes, barrels of liquids and chemicals in glass or plastic containers stacked on industrial shelving. Jim kept his secrets from the town, but he bragged to her. She was his "special girl" and she'd been allowed into his private world of potions and science, genius and deviousness.

Her mom—a cocktail waitress at a bar in the town of Paris—had begun to disappear, a little at a time, over a year before. At first, Candice imagined she might be jealous of the teacher-student vibe between Jim and her daughter. Now, looking back, Candice saw her mother suspected the truth, but wasn't strong enough to confront it. She had drifted toward friends in Louisville and left her daughter behind.

At first, Candice had felt the tiniest bit triumphant as Jim lavished attention on her in her mother's absence. Over the months her mother waned even further, spending more and more time at "scented candle conventions," and then an astral projection convention. She came home days later with bags under her eyes and a gray pallor to her skin. Her mother wasted away in front of her eyes. She and Jim pretended it wasn't happening.

When the crash stopped everything in its tracks, her mother was in Louisville, and Candice was left in the hands of her stepfather. Bit by bit, in the weeks that followed, Candice suspected she'd discovered a new, insidious hell.

The lab contained explosives, of course. Not just useful chemicals that happened to explode when mixed wrong, but actual explosives, cooked up by Jim on purpose. Even before the collapse, he'd bragged about experiments with biological and chemical weapons. It was common to find dead rabbits in the trash bin. He kept a hutch of them in a dark corner of the lab.

Without turning, Jim said "Hey, sweetie. You're back a little later than I expected."

"I was with William."

"That's a good girl. You made friends with him? Is he beginning to trust you?"

"Yes."

"Excellent." Then he paused for a moment, as if thinking. He set an instrument down on the counter and turned to her.

"You sound like you're hiding something."

"I'm not."

Jensen crossed the room in three strides. He reached out and touched her cheek. It took everything she had not to flinch. He hated it when she flinched.

"Then perhaps you'd like to explain why you're wearing such a guilty face?

Candice couldn't look him in the eye. She looked at his chin instead. "No reason. Will introduced me to his guardian, and I talked with him about you. Just like you asked me to do."

"*Will* is it? Such a grown-up name."

"William. He... we were at his house waiting when Mr. Best came home."

Jim was obsessed with Mat Best. He wanted Candice to engineer a friendship between them: the genius scientist and the brawny soldier. Maybe Jim had seen a movie like that or something, but it was all he could talk about these days.

She offered him some hope. "I think you'd like what I said. I talked about how smart you are and how much you could help the town. Mr. Best said that your farming and chemistry classes were an amazing idea," she embellished a little.

Jenson smoothed a lock of unruly hair with his fingers. "What did he say?"

"Mr. Best seemed really interested. He said he liked where you were going with things."

"Good girl." His smile almost reached his eyes. His expression hardened.

"You said Mat came home. So you were alone with William in their house? Where in their house?"

"I made friends. Like you said. We were on the couch. In the front room right by the door."

Jensen took Candice's cheeks in his hand. He stroked her hair with his fingers. "You won't forget that you're my special girl? You'll remember that only a man like me can protect you now? A dominant, smart man. An alpha male. I'm the only one who can help you find your mother. When we finish our work here, and we have what we need to pacify the barbarians around the town, we'll get her and bring her back. We need to put the rats down, then we can go find her."

"Yes. I know that," she said, and she wasn't lying. Her mom was adrift on a sea of chaos. She could almost feel the pulsing, hateful terror gathered around them all. Candice floated on a tiny island amidst a sea of abject horror, with only this minor fiend to terrorize her. This was survival, she told herself: enduring his repulsive hands in order to save her mother from the unspeakable evil of the world.

"Don't worry. I'll protect you." He pulled her into his chest in an embrace. The front of his pants was soft, and that was good.

"Thank you," she said. Part of her meant it.

"Excellent. Now give me a hand with this tank of ethylene. Then we can head upstairs."

# 10

## CAMERON STEWART

"Of all that breathes and crawls across the earth, our mother earth breeds nothing feebler than a man.

So long as the gods grant him power, spring in his knees, he thinks he will never suffer affliction down the years.

But then, when the happy gods bring on the long hard times, bear them he must, against his will, and steel his heart."

— ODYSSEUS, THE ODYSSEY

**Grafton Ghost Town,
Southern Utah**

The Buffalo gourd seeds saved Cameron's son. After ten days of choking down powdered seeds in his willow tea, Denny finally stood up.

Every time the boy shit, it was a clan affair. They picked it apart with twigs, counted the worms, and dumped the black mess in the pit latrine. After a glut of white, wriggling worms during the first week, they began to vanish from his poop.

Everyone in the family ate the seed powder, and they harvested many more backpacks of the wild-growing desert plant. The seeds were both medicine and slight nutrition. They probably burned more calories collecting gourds than they consumed, but the medicinal value made up for it.

The spectacle of worms in Denny's poop triggered a renewed focus on sanitation. They hardly had the energy to spare, but they did it anyway, sensing that the boy's sickness was but a canary in a coal mine for the rest of them. If they didn't make changes, they would all sicken and die. They couldn't afford even run-of-the-mill dysentery. They were starving in earnest now, and diarrhea meant death.

Nobody in the group knew anything about sanitation. It'd been the sole purview of civil engineers and health departments back in the old world. The four adults washed their dishes in hot water, which turned out to be a sobering investment of calories: collecting wood, building a fire, boiling water to kill water-borne parasites, then using the cooling water to wash the dishes. They'd run out of paper plates long before. Now they used blown-off wood shingles as plates. Rough wood was exceedingly hard to sanitize.

Like a tyrant overlord, boiling water for dishes and drink taxed them half-to-death. They had no modern filter, and they couldn't rely on their layered, homemade "survival filter" of sand and charcoal to remove parasite eggs from the river water. Plus, none of them knew how to make charcoal. Every time they tried, they ended up with mostly ash. So they boiled all their water—for drinking and washing. After Denny's sickness, nobody suggested they play Russian roulette with the questionable, silty water from the Virgin River.

The boy was on his feet now, but he was greatly diminished.

Denny barely lifted his feet as he shuffled around the yard. He no longer played with the other children, choosing instead to watch with half-lidded eyes. The worms had depleted all his reserves.

Julie peppered the boy with questions until the truth slowly emerged. At first, Cameron argued viciously with his wife about what she'd found, and he personally verified every aspect of the story. The revelation terrified Cameron, and he resisted the truth of it until he had no choice but to see.

Denny had been hoarding food. He'd found a dead muskrat by the river and sneaked a kitchen knife to pare away pieces of the rotting flesh. He started his own fire with stolen twigs from the family fire, then cooked the carrion where nobody could see or smell. He'd eaten the dead animal down to bones. A week later, he sickened.

Cameron could scarcely comprehend how an eight-year-old boy could grow hungry enough to render a dead animal into food. But the true horror was the abject selfishness of the boy's act. He'd hidden food from his own family—if a dead muskrat could be considered food.

Cameron's personal guilt tripled as he poked around the dried bones of the muskrat down by the river, seeking some clue as to how his bright, beautiful boy had come to cheat his own blood. *The apple doesn't fall far from the tree,* Cameron's unruly mind repeated, over and over.

Cameron had screwed Isaiah's wife dozens of times. The only reason they hadn't been caught by Julie or Isaiah was because nobody had the energy for suspicion. Rude survival commanded all their attention, and they had little enough energy to spare for that.

Cameron didn't know and frankly didn't care why Ruth came to him—pulling him away into the darkest shadows, always offering herself from behind. There was nothing about a starving person's breath that made one want to kiss, but he doubted either of them would kiss anyway. They hadn't exchanged a single word of love or even explanation. They humped. He hadn't a clue why she initiated it. Most nights, he could barely achieve an erection, and his climax grew tepid and watery. Still, he took the carnality offered.

Ruth had probably never been an attractive woman, even before the deprivations at Grafton, but the gathering of her skirts and the animal draw of their rut gave Cameron momentary reprieve from his self-loathing. For a few seconds, in those interludes, he was a man—dominant, hearty and fierce. After sex, he flopped in on himself again, but not in shame over violating his marriage—Julie had grown so surly with hunger that Cameron could hardly stand the sight of her. Strangely, he felt shittiest about Isaiah.

The man had been an unfailing friend, aside from having stolen Cameron's wife before all this. That time seemed so distant now, a glimmer on the lip of the past. After who-knows-how-many weeks in this square of grass and redstone, Cameron could barely recall his hatred of the polygamist. They'd suffered much together, and Isaiah had rallied to save Cameron's son. The man had become like a faithful, albeit witless, Labrador retriever, and Cameron had grown fond of him, even thankful for him.

That inkling of brotherhood over the weeks of starvation hadn't discouraged Cameron as he piled up Ruth's dress and seized his thin seconds of reprieve from on-marching death. The picked-clean bones of the muskrat evoked the same echo of treachery. Cameron's ignobility reverberated in Denny. His son, at *eight years old*, had hidden food for himself.

Cameron rubbed his bearded face. Beneath the growth, he could feel his skin, thin and papery. Something important was missing in their diet and it made their skin crackly. They could only guess at what it was, but it wouldn't matter even if they knew. They were already eating everything they could find of any nutritious value whatsoever. They'd taken to eating strange weed roots, without any knowledge of their toxicity or nutritional value.

While Denny fought his parasites, Cameron and Isaiah

completed the water project. The stock watering tank overflowed with cloudy river water. But this morning, the flow down the eight-inch pipe slowed. The river must've risen to the challenge of their stone impoundment and attacked the pile of rocks they'd stacked against it. That was to be expected. They would need to repair and rebuild the dam almost daily against the stubborn will of the river.

However, the delicate sleeving of forty sections of pipes worked better than Cameron had hoped. Even though they lost splashes at each joint, the bulk of the eager water clung to the walls of pipe, and rushed the hundred yards into their catch basin with a happy willingness that surprised him. The stock watering basin had overflowed before they could stagger back to the homestead to check on it.

The drain spigot at the lower end of the big tank had been repurposed to fit the PVC pipe that stretched down the pasture to the cold frame greenhouses, set in the ground around the one room farmhouse. Cameron twisted the ball valve and the PVC jumped as though electrified. Ruth, at the far end, leapt up and down, waved her arms and shouted.

"Stop, stop, stop."

Cameron closed the valve and went to see what'd happened.

The PVC tubing stopped just below the cold frames. They wanted to see if it'd actually work before completing the final distribution of the water. Now, a miniature delta of washout surrounded the cold frames. The pipe had delivered too much water, too quickly—what Cameron would call "a champagne problem."

"It's good," Ruth explained. "Just too much. It's going to wash away all our trenches. We need to divide up the stream somehow."

A hundred feet across the pasture, the stock tank was already overflowing again. They had no PVC cement nor PVC junctions. The PVC tubing they'd scavenged had flared ends and one piece fit into another, but splitting the tube into multiple runs would require plastic tees and ninety-degree turns. Cameron wracked his brain to devise a way to split the stream coming from the stock tank without the proper joints.

"Maybe we could run the tube into a five gallon plastic bucket and send the water out the bottom into three tubes." Isaiah scratched his ruddy-blond beard as he examined the washout. "We'd use one of the old five gallon wheat buckets as our three-way splitter fitting."

"How would we attach the PVC to the bucket without glue?" Cameron asked.

Isaiah retrieved a five gallon bucket. "Maybe we can carve three holes in the bottom with the pocketknife, exactly the size of the PVC tubing. We have plenty of extra PVC. With short pieces, we can run it through the hole with the fitting on the inside of the bucket. The fatter end of the tube will mostly seal the hole like a funnel in a bottle top."

Cameron could see it now. Isaiah's solution was really quite clever. It'd split the flow into three streams and any extra water pressure would overflow the bucket harmlessly onto the ground. He considered complimenting Isaiah, but Ruth was there, and his dick wouldn't allow it.

"That'll work, I think," Cameron said instead. Even with the thin praise, Isaiah gleamed. "You can plant your seeds and set the frames now," Cameron said to Ruth.

Over the past two weeks, the women had gathered together wood for the six frames that would hold the milky sheet plastic around their grow beds. Built with a mishmash of lumber they'd pried off the barn, the cold frames looked like clubhouses constructed by children, but they'd function all right.

The grow beds stretched two-to-a-row, and three across, making six ten-foot-long planters. Each cold frame lifted away, to be set aside in the warmth of the sun. Every morning, if the weather was nice, they'd set aside the six cold frames and then replace them at night. Hopefully, the warmth trapped in the earth would keep the tender shoots from freezing.

Isaiah had already gone to work carving the three one-inch holes in the base of the plastic bucket. He removed the tiniest, pinky-fingernail shavings with his Boy Scout pocket knife, and checked progress every few minutes against a chunk of tubing. He kept a flat sandstone nearby and sharpened his knife frequently, swirling the blade in a tiny puddle of spit. The man really was quite meticulous. In a world where no scrap could be wasted, patience had become a survival skill.

*But it still wasn't what got a man laid.*

Cameron hated himself for the thought, but he couldn't deny it: something primeval had taken over, and he stood at the apex of the clan. Isaiah either didn't know or didn't care.

The polygamist looked up from his work and noticed Cameron watching him. Isaiah smiled, then returned to his craft. Cam sighed.

He walked away, toward the impoundment dam to check on it. He'd fix it himself this time.

It looked like the water system was going to work, and they'd get water to their garden seeds. What happened then was anyone's guess, but it was a victory, as was Denny's recovery.

As he walked, he faced facts: both victories could be placed squarely at the feet of Isaiah. His kooky, Asperger personality had uncovered the solutions, and his dogged work ethic had driven the construction of the water system and the winnowing of the boy's medicine. Cameron owed him everything, and he couldn't remember having a more long-suffering friend.

Cam jumped over a dry, weed-choked ditch and came down hard on the other side. His head swam for a moment and he almost sat down. The hunger made him dizzy. It made him maudlin too. Maybe he was giving the polygamist too much credit.

The spinning in his head passed and he continued toward the

river. He reached the wide spot in the waterway where they'd stacked rocks to channel a side stream into the corrugated pipe. The water level had risen and rolled away the upper stones atop the little dam. The side stream poured over where it hadn't before. One stone at-a-time, Cameron carried rocks from the bank and filled the gaps. The flow nudged them around until they settled, or rolled over the top and tumbled downriver. He added dozens of rocks until the impoundment again rose into the side stream. The flow into the pipe strengthened. Isaiah had warned him; if they allowed water to overflow the top of the dam long enough, it'd tear it down. They needed to maintain the impoundment above the waterline so that the flow would go around and into the pipe instead of over the top.

Cameron had taken Isaiah's word as gospel truth. In many ways, the polygamist was the brains of the operation. Cameron tried to muster the passion to hate him for his practical, unselfconscious competency, but he failed. Cam was so hungry, he could barely feel anything at all. He kicked over a log with his foot—a log he'd kicked over several times before. A new, white grub appeared in the damp. He bent over, slowly, and plucked it up.

*Had it even been worth the energy to bend over?*

He didn't know and didn't care. He almost popped it in his mouth, but remembered the white, writhing worms in Denny's poop. He stuck the grub in the pocket of his dungarees instead. He'd cook it over the fire, and maybe share it with Denny. Maybe he'd give the boy the whole thing.

He wondered how Denny would feel about that—his father giving him food even when the boy had been holding out on them all. He probably wouldn't spare a thought for it. Kids took what they wanted, especially when suffering. Their parents weren't real people to them, truth be told. Parents were caregivers, without their own agonies. He could remember feeling the same about his dad, and to some degree, about his mom.

Cameron staggered toward the homestead, exhausted. He

scratched his head feverishly to unseat the dry skin that plagued his scalp. A chunk of hair came free and drifted away on the breeze.

*So starvation does that too,* he noted.

But there was hope, today. The water system worked. Denny was back on his feet. Soon, maybe, there would be fresh, green, edible shoots in their grow beds. They might be eating sprouts in a few days. It wouldn't be much, but it'd be something.

The wheat in the bucket was almost gone, but they ate a few tablespoons every day. Before the bottom of the bucket showed through, maybe the turnips would fatten and the corn stalks would thicken. Spring would come, albeit not for months, and the nightly frost would give up its siege against all things living.

Isaiah and Ruth's ten-year old daughter, Leah, met Cameron at the edge of the pasture.

"My mom asked me to find you. We're ready to turn on the water. To test it in the beds."

"Okay. I'm coming," Cameron drawled, then shuffled forward. But the little girl didn't move.

"Have you found any frogs?" she asked.

"Huh?" He had no idea what she was talking about,

"Frogs. You and my mom look for frogs. Did you find them?"

"Um. No."

"Then you should stop looking," she said with stony eyebrows. She was a strange child, like she'd grown up too quickly in a world where toys didn't exist. Maybe that was because of their weirdo polygamist cult. Maybe it was because of Cameron. He couldn't get it straight in his mind. Hunger blurred the timelines.

"Maybe we should stop looking," he agreed. The man and the girl turned and meandered side-by-side across the straw-colored pasture toward the homestead.

# 11

---

SAGE ROSS

**Wallowa Town**
**Wallowa County, Oregon**

Sage didn't know whether to shit or go blind. Hound dogs yowled behind him, followed by gunmen. A police Blazer waited for him at the bridge with its lights flickering orange and blue. If he waded the creek, and somehow avoided being seen, he'd be forced to build a fire and dry out his stuff. In other words, it was only a matter of time before he was caught.

Sage had royally screwed up the first real mission Captain Chambers had given him. Some Wallowa shit-kicker had seen him, which wasn't a tremendous surprise. Wallowa Valley was considerably higher than La Grande, and the mountains surrounding the string of tiny hamlets was winter-bound in snow even though it was early December. Someone must've been staring out their kitchen window when Sage slunk by on the hillside.

He'd been skirting the towns and pastures of Wallowa for three days, trying to get a count of the neighboring county's cattle for

Captain Chambers. Sage hadn't asked why the captain wanted to know. Counting another county's cattle could be seen as a prelude to theft, but Sage hadn't drilled down. It wasn't his place to ask.

This was his first "solo mission" with the captain's militia, and after only three days in the field, it looked like he was going to get scooped up by the Wallowa locals. Based on what he'd seen so far, they weren't going to stop searching for him, and unlike his cold, wet ass, they could go home and dry out. Sage had no change of boots in his backpack.

A snowstorm brewed over the big mountains to the north. It was going to dump overnight and he didn't love the idea of being buried in a tent while they searched for him. The moment he started snowshoeing again, working deeper into the valley, someone would cut his tracks, as sure as there's shit in a goat.

The good news about a snowstorm: it erased tracks. The bad news about a snowstorm: new tracks could be picked out from five miles away.

He'd gone around the roadblock Wallowa County had placed across the county road by cutting straight across the foothills of Sacajawea Mountain on snowshoes. He'd climbed up and scooted down at least six steep canyons before the Wallowa Valley opened before him like Elysian Fields, where heroes go to die. Sage literally rubbed his eyes when he first saw it.

The Wallowa Valley spread out from a mountain pass, meandered for five miles, then disappeared at the foot of majestic, ice-capped mountains. As far as he could tell, there were three villages plus a couple clusters of homes. There couldn't be more than three thousand people in the whole county, and Sage could see them all in one glance from the side of the mountain. It looked like a postcard of Switzerland.

There was only one paved road into Wallowa, and the people of Wallowa County had sealed it up tight, not allowing visitors or trade with Union County to the west. Not a soul had passed their roadblock, in either direction, since the collapse. Nobody in La Grande could explain why, and Captain Chambers wanted answers.

"What are they doing in there, and how many cattle do they have in that valley?" he'd asked Sage.

That's what the captain wanted Sage to find out, and after three days of cross-country snowshoeing, Sage still didn't know the answer.

He'd seen a ton of cattle—so many they weren't even countable. Tens of thousands, at least. Hay dotted the snow-patched fields, in giant rolls that looked like massive Cinnabons made of dry grass. Sage watched the ranchers move the big bales around with heavy equipment and cover them with white plastic. He worried the captain wouldn't be satisfied with his reconnaissance of the valley. He pictured the conversation.

"What did you find out?" the captain would ask.

"They have thousands of cattle," Sage would answer.

"How many?"

"Best guess: forty thousand head of cattle." Sage figured that using the term "head of cattle" would make him sound a lot more certain than he felt.

"Okay, and what were they doing in there?"

"Minding their own business," Sage would say. He didn't know if that answer would fly, but it was all he had.

Maybe getting arrested by the local-yokels would give him something more to report. Or maybe they'd shoot him as a spy, which was precisely what he was.

Sage doubted it. Even in Grand Rhonde, they didn't execute people by firing squad. They just kicked them out.

He sighed and gathered up his rifle. He'd probably lose the 30-30 this time. A guy can only get arrested so many times and expect to keep his rifle. The hounds grew louder on his trail. It was probably better to surrender to the authorities than make them track him down. In the snow, with dogs, it wasn't going to be hard—no matter if Sage swam the creek or not.

He stood and walked toward the flashing police cruiser. Next to it on the bridge, a man in a cowboy hat leaned up against an old pickup truck, chewing the fat with the uniformed police officer. As he got closer, Sage read the door of the police blazer: *Wallowa County Sheriff.*

Sage slung his rifle across his back and raised his hands. The men watched him descend the hillside, but didn't halt their conversation. The cop stood with his hands on his hips and the other guy leaned against his fender, observing Sage's long, embarrassing snowshoe flippity-flop across the slope.

"Well there's the fox you been chasing, Sheriff." The man took the stalk of hay out of his mouth and said, "Doesn't look like much up-close, does he?"

"No, can't say he looks like I thought he'd look. I imagined he'd be a special forces type or something."

"You've been chasing this fox for three days?"

"Yup. Ever since we seen him cross at Minam. Hey, son," the sheriff yelled. "Why don'tcha slide that rifle off and set it against that little pine for me?"

Sage complied, then continued toward the bridge. When he got there, the men looked him up and down.

"You got any more guns?" the sheriff asked.

"No."

"Did Chambers send you?" the man in the cowboy hat asked.

The question knocked him off balance. He hesitated, then answered honestly. "Yes."

"He wanted to know about the cattle?"

Sage gave up any idea of being clever. "Yes."

Cowboy Hat man nodded and tossed away the stalk of hay. "Just a matter of time, right Tate?"

The sheriff nodded.

"How about this, then?" Cowboy Hat stood up from against his truck. "I'll buy you a burger and answer all your questions. Maybe you can answer a few for me, too."

"Yessir," Sage replied.

"Put your ruck in the back of my truck," Cowboy Hat said and walked around to the driver's side. The sheriff leaned into his cruiser and called off the dogs over the radio.

Arresting people and feeding them a burger must be a thing in Northeastern Oregon, Sage concluded. The shame of capture had already begun to fade.

Visions of a hot burger, after three days of eating freeze dried, went a long way to salving his wounded pride.

---

"I'M COMMISSIONER PETE, by the way," the man reached a hand across the plastic table outside the "Blue Banana" diner in Lostine, Oregon.

They'd driven to the village in the center of the valley, between the towns of Wallowa and Enterprise. Townspeople had set up dozens of Costco-style plastic tables and chairs in the parking lot around Sage and the Commissioner. Sage gathered that the people of the town came to the parking lot of the tiny restaurant for group supper. Given the gray clouds massing over the ice-bound peaks, they'd need to move this daily routine under cover, soon. The snow on the hillsides hadn't quite blanketed the south-facing fields yet, but after another storm or two, it would.

"So, let's hear it. What does Captain Chambers want to know about us?"

"He asked me to figure out what was going on here. You haven't let anyone through your road block."

"I don't see why he should have any questions. That's his county.

This is ours...never mind. It's just old men and their politics. It doesn't matter."

"He wants to know about trade between the counties," Sage offered.

"Ha!" the Commissioner barked. "As if we needed anything from the city." Commissioner Pete sat back and thought a moment. "That's the problem, see? We have plenty of cattle, feed and grain. We only have three thousand mouths to feed and there's no need to complicate our lives with Chamber's brand of nonsense. By hook or crook, everyone ends up working for him. Ain't that true?"

Sage blanched. He didn't know if it was true or not, but Captain Chambers certainly seemed like a man-with-a-plan. If there was someone else in charge, Sage hadn't heard his name uttered.

"Um. I just got there—in Union County. I'm from Salt Lake City and I'm passing through on my way home. I only just met the captain a couple weeks ago."

"Okay, then tell me: what kind of government do they have over there in Union County?"

Sage hadn't seen or heard of any government other than the police department. He assumed there were elected guys, but Sage didn't know their names. His confusion must've shown on his face, because Pete waved the question away.

"Don't sweat it. Let me show you something—pick someone. Anyone." He waved around at the people setting up supper tables. Sage pointed toward a middle-aged lady walking past.

"Joan," Pete called out, stopping her. "What kind of government do we have here?"

She smiled, looked at Sage, recognized him as an outsider, and answered. "It's a Constitutional thing. We elect you sweet-talking politicians and you tell us what to do."

Pete laughed. "Then how come I feel like you're always telling ME what to do?"

"Because that's the natural order of things, Pete. You men run the show and we women run you."

Pete belly laughed as Joan went back to work setting the silverware. "Ain't that the truth?" he asked Sage. He seemed to realize he was talking to a young man—too young to know how the world really worked—and he looped back to his point. "We didn't get creative here in Wallowa County when the outside world came crashing down. We pulled up the U.S. Constitution and clicked *copy* then *paste*." Pete smiled. "Can't say the same for our neighbors in Union County. They've got their own style of guv'ment, and Ron Chambers is up to his armpits in it." He held up his hands in surrender. "But they can do whatever they want. Don't get me wrong; Union County is Union County and if they want to run it like the Russian mafia, that's none of our business."

"It's not like that," Sage argued. "They're doing what they have to do to survive the winter. They have a lot less food than you do and a lot more hungry people. I saw what it was like over the mountain into Washington—after the stores closed and the water turned off. Mister Commissioner, they were eating people. I swear they were."

The Commissioner's eyes widened. "I'd heard stories on the shortwave, but I didn't know it'd gotten so bad, so fast. I'm sorry you had to see that. You're lucky to be alive."

"Yes I am. Thousands are dead. Probably millions. Just over the Blue Mountains." Sage didn't know what point he was trying to make, but he kept talking because the Commissioner seemed to be listening. "I killed a couple guys. Mostly by accident. Guys from over in Elgin. They tried to rob me." Sage's throat tightened with emotion.

Commissioner Pete reached across the table and put a heavy, calloused hand on Sage's shoulder. "It's okay, son. It's war over there and you did what you had to do. It's okay. Just breathe. Oh, hey, here's your burger." He took the paper plate with a burger and fries on it from Joan as she passed by. She looked at both of their faces—Sage's an emotional mess—and retreated to the kitchen.

"Did I mention I've got a daughter your age? And, a son a few years older. He was in Boise at the university when the crash happened. What are you, nineteen? Twenty?"

Sage wiped his nose with his sleeve. He hadn't reached for his burger yet. "Seventeen."

"Wow," Pete remarked. "Have you been outside this whole time? More than two months?"

Sage nodded and stuck a fry in his mouth. The oily saltiness of it shocked his taste buds.

"It aged you. Turned you into a man too soon." Pete glanced around at the crowd as though looking for his own son and daughter. "We've been blessed here. Very blessed...and we're in no hurry to spit in God's eye. We don't want to screw this up, and mucking around with Ron Chambers is playing with fire. I don't know if you noticed, but we're trapped here. There's no back door out of this valley. We either go out through Union County, or we go out over those mountains. This place is our first and last stand. Please ask Captain Chambers, politely, to sock all his ambition into saving Union County and leave us the hell alone. They've got nothing we want or need."

Sage sighed and tucked into his burger. He felt bad about taking the man's food, but he'd be a fool to pass up fresh beef.

He had a sinking feeling Union County wasn't going to leave Wallowa County alone. After all his time in Union, Sage had only eaten beef three times, but the smell coming from the kitchen didn't lie—the townsfolk would be enjoying something with meat in it, and that was likely a daily deal.

*Beef, it's what's for dinner - if you live in Wallowa.*

If his guess was correct, there were at least ten cattle for every man, woman and child in this Valley. Chambers wouldn't leave that alone. He had a lot of men, and a lot of mouths to feed.

Commissioner Pete appeared to enjoy watching Sage eat. He was proud of his little county, that much seemed clear to Sage.

After Sage wiped out the burger, the commissioner spoke. "Sheriff Tate will be coming by in a minute with your rifle. He'll take you to the county line." He got up from the table. "I wish you well, Sage Ross from Salt Lake City. Keep your eyes open, son. There's more than one way to cannibalize people. I think we'll see them all. Even here."

# 12

MAT BEST

McKenzie, Tennessee
Southwest HESCO Barrier

He should've fought harder to cut the Reedy Grove neighborhood outside the wall. Mat swore at himself for his moment of weakness, six weeks before. It'd cost them over a mile of HESCO barrier and they were way behind schedule on the south side of town. They were way behind schedule everywhere.

"Nobody will come looking for a handout from Memphis," the longstanding residents promised. "Memphis people are better than that." Mat didn't know Memphis people from Martian people, but he knew even a noble race like the Afghans—mountain warriors all —would tear the throats out of a troop of Girl Scouts if their families were starving and it meant feeding them. People from Memphis, it turned out, were not better humans than Afghans.

The first wave of the mob came straight up Highway 79 from the direction of Memphis. Who knew if they actually came from the city or if they'd circled around from one of the "less reputable" cities like Louisville or St. Louis? They were a mob, and hunger was their birthplace.

The first wave of a thousand rushed up the highway and into the HESCO barrier. They were repulsed by a few shotguns and the ram rods. That's when the perimeter guards called Mat and the quick reaction force for help.

The QRF were a group of twenty pipe-hitters—high school and college boys with more grit than good sense. Mat trained them a few hours a day. His well-fed twenty could hold off a mob of a hundred; from behind a HESCO, maybe three times that many.

Up to that point, the rats were too uncoordinated to attack the town all-at-once from multiple points of the compass. Mat could hold his best guys in reserve, in the center of town, on a two minute alert. When a push came—and they came every couple of days now —the QRF rushed to the hotspot and hit them with the town's best guns, best shooters and the strongest hand-to-hand fighters. The QRF all ran AR-15s from the sheriff's gun locker, wore soft body armor and trained daily on radio communications. Radio waves were free. Bullets were irreplaceable.

The town of McKenzie had more food than firearms, given the partnership with the town of Henry. They had more hogs than people, with more piglets born every day. They traded dried pork at the highway barricades for guns and ammo, but that added to their stock of bullets *and* forced them to use them. Handing out pork led to arguments, theft and riots. Riots *always* turned against the town. That was exactly what'd happened at the 79 South gate; they'd been trading dried pork for bullets and a fight broke out in the refugee camp up against the HESCO wall.

Mat and the QRF arrived just in time to see the mob overflow into the flooded hay fields, and churn toward the Reedy Grove neighborhood. Construction on the wall hadn't made it that far. It was still only a quarter-mile long on that side of town— inching across the Bartlett's hayfield from the Hilltop trailer park toward the cluster of suburban homes called "Reedy Grove."

Mat argued as hard as he dared at the security committee back when they'd decided the boundaries of the wall. He wanted the wall tucked up against Hopper Lane—which would've saved them over a mile of HESCO. It would've also required the mayor's brother to move his family to a shitty, abandoned home in town instead of his pretty Reedy Creek rambler.

The mayor didn't get much for his trouble, serving as mayor. He was considered an empty smile and a free handshake, particularly when compared to the larger-than-life personality of Sheriff Morgan. This time, the mayor had thrown down: the Reedy Grove subdivision would be wrapped snugly *inside* the HESCO barrier "or his name wasn't Bradford P. Caldwell." Mat relented and the line on the map became yet another political boondoggle.

Now a thousand pissed off vagabonds trudged around the unfinished wall and straight toward the mayor's brother's home.

"Your brother's shitting in his Levis now, Mister Mayor," Mat said under his breath. He clicked the push-to-talk button on his radio. "QRF. This is Mat. Move out to Reedy Grove Road. Let's flex our muscle."

The QRF made a series of turns in their off-road vehicles and got them pointing back toward town. The fight wasn't going to be at the HESCO this time. They'd be fighting between swing sets and trampolines—exactly what Mat had hoped to avoid.

By the time they looped back south into Reedy Grove, the opportunity to rake the mob with gunfire while they slogged through the muddy field had elapsed. The front wave of incursion had already reached the trees and the backyards of Reedy Grove.

Mat and his fire teams poured around the five homes that bordered the hayfield. Rifle fire crackled. It sounded like 5.56 from his boys, but Mat listened hard for handguns or shotguns. The rats would have firearms. Hopefully, not more than a few.

He rounded an air conditioning unit to catch a cluster of bat-wielding rats bursting from the trees and onto the dead grass of a family's backyard. Mat lit them up, one-at-a-time. The last figure was a woman in a bright, green wrap. The tasseled edges were painted in mud.

*They're forcing me to slaughter them,* Mat screamed inside. *They were literally on the porch of that house. The family was probably inside, scared half-to-death. No choice but to shoot the intruders. No choice!*

Three more rats sprinted from the trees for the house. Mat shot a man's knee out the side of his leg. He pitched into a stone fire pit, full of rainwater. Mat didn't wait to see if he'd drown. He placed controlled bursts into the other two. One turned back, maybe wounded.

The rest was a blur. Mat noticed each mag change, but his gaze danced across the enemy.

*Trigger, trigger, trigger—scan for threats—trigger, trigger, trigger. Lull in the fight. Tactical reload. Scan again. Shift to new cover.*

For some reason, the mag changes always stuck out in his mind. After four mag changes, the rats stopped appearing from the tree line. The flow must've turned back toward the highway. The rattle of rifle fire had done its job and convinced the marauding thousands of the futility to run toward death.

The mayor's brother stumbled up and thanked Mat personally. He even said, "I'm the mayor's brother," as though it was a thing people said when surrounded by stinking, shitting, dying people.

The mayor's brother carried a big, Dirty Harry revolver. Now that the gunfire had stopped, more town folk poured out of the homes. Every adult had a gun of some kind, but they hung back from the killing fields. They'd stayed in their homes while Mat and the QRF did the work of death.

Mat understood the logic: stay inside as a last line of defense if the rats break in. Stand between their family and the threat.

But, still, he hated them for making him and his boys take life. If only the families had moved *inside* town, this could've been avoided. The HESCO barrier wasn't a magical force field, by any means, but it gave the rats a serious reality check. Without it, the rats drifted in and out of no-man's-land, catching bullets for their trouble. A ramrod to the solar plexus meant a few days of bruising. A bullet hole, pretty much anywhere, was a death sentence in the refugee camps.

Mat needed to get the fuck out of this town. He'd been forced to shoot people who, just three months before, might've served him his bacon and eggs at the Pancake House.

It'd be one thing if the town of McKenzie would follow his advice to-the-letter. Mat might be able to live with the killing if it was always absolutely necessary. But this shit here in Reedy Grove —this was lethal stupidity. Those lives were wasted in the name of hayseed politics.

Who had Mat been kidding? No town—no group of Americans —was going to set aside their compulsive opinion-making and bow to Mat's expertise. It was not something Americans did. Not then. Not now. For every six Americans who followed good advice, three more would pitch a hissy fit when told what to do.

If he stayed in McKenzie, Mat would be forced to kill, with ever-greater prejudice, in the name of local-yokel, municipal theater. The good folk of McKenzie would have their big opinions, and Mat would be forced to do the killing.

Mat cleared his rifle and caught the spinning brass as it catapulted out of the breach. He turned his back on the killing fields as he watched the neighbors collect in conversational knots in the street. The townies did their best to act like carrying a gun came easy.

Mat slipped the loose round back into the mag and stared down the stack of brass. He couldn't remember if he'd depleted this mag or not. He looked into the dark space around the bullets in the AR-

15 magazine, and it felt like gazing into the pit of his own soul. Time skipped a beat.

Mat keyed his radio. "QRF. This is Mat. Let's get the hell back to town."

———

MAT MADE his rounds to the check points—perhaps more quickly than usual, but with no skipped steps. Then he checked in with Carter at her home, as usual. This time, he asked her if she'd take William when Mat left town.

"Are you absolutely sure that's what you want?" she asked.

"It's not so much about what I want as what William needs. He's lost everyone he loves: his father, mother and sister. He needs a home and a family. That's not something he's going to get with me. Caroline would want it this way."

She shook her head like he was the dumbest genius she ever met. It was a common refrain between them. Gladys barked a laugh, apparently amused at his dumb jock logic. "Wouldn't she want *both* of you to find a home and a family?"

Mat launched into a list of reasons why leaving William with her, when he got the mission under control, was the right thing to do.

In the end, she reluctantly agreed.

Mat left Gladys' house feeling a weight lifted off his shoulders. He'd settled the question of William. She'd agreed to take him in.

If it weren't for the fact that she towered over him by six inches, he'd probably make a move on her. He'd never knocked boots with a professional basketball player. In fact, he hadn't been in the sack with anyone since Caroline. It was probably a personal record since puberty—going without the no-pants-dance for three months. It was like being on deployment.

It wasn't that Gladys wasn't hot. He could definitely "get there" with her, but he needed her even temperament and steady wisdom for the job. She'd become Mat's back-door channel to the gossip tree. She told him stuff nobody else wanted to tell an Army Ranger. If he was the father of the QRF team, she was the mother. So what if mom and dad weren't pounding the punnani pavement? Mat couldn't risk screwing up the friendship for sex.

In any case, he thought Carter might be a lesbian, but he really had no reason to think that. He was probably just being a prick. He automatically thought of a woman as gay if she didn't come on to him within the first seventy-two hours. Mat chuckled at himself.

She was a solid human and he was glad to leave William in her capable hands.

---

MAT WALKED from Carter's house to his appointment with the sheriff. When he came into the cell block below the town hall, Sheriff Morgan had Jared, the rat leader from the ambush, in a chair with his hands zip-tied behind his back. He'd been "simmering" in a jail cell for weeks, and looked a lot better-fed than when Mat first grabbed him.

After the Reedy Grove incident and the B.S. about Memphis refugees being somehow better than St. Louis refugees, it occurred to Mat that they might have a glossy, vague idea of the rats—as though they were one, homogeneous enemy. Like the bands of Afghan goat farmers, there might be more to the rats than he beheld. Maybe they could be turned like a wagon, instead of swatted like flies. Then he'd remembered the prisoner... Jared Loudmouth. Mat had radioed the sheriff and suggested they take another crack at intelligence gathering from the guy. It was the least the fucker could do, given what he'd cost the town.

The town cell block hadn't been modernized, and it reminded Mat of every jail he'd seen in movies; low-slung, concrete, with slit windows peeking above the ground outside. It was past midnight, and the sheriff had two kerosene lamps lighting the cold, gray room.

"He refuses to give me his last name," the sheriff's grin looked ghoulish in the light of the lamp.

Jared, the deposed rat leader spoke with more confidence than the situation warranted. Feeding him three meals a day hadn't made him any more cooperative.

"Names should be stories that tell you who a person is. I'm writing my story, and making my name. You can't intimidate me. I studied political philosophy at Penn State. I fought in the streets with Antifa."

Mat laughed. "Have you been down here communing with the ghost of Nelson Mandela? Have you been writing your prison memoirs on the back of toilet paper?"

The big sheriff leaned his chair back against the wall and smiled. He said, "Sergeant Best, I think maybe the right ear."

Mat's gloved fist smashed into the side of Jared's head. Cartilage crumpled flat against his skull. Jared's chair flew sideways to the ground. Mat hauled him upright, and stood behind him again where he couldn't see the next blow coming. The guy sputtered, cried and coughed.

"Young man," said Morgan, "I don't think it'll be necessary to torture you." Morgan stood up and settled his bulk in a crouch in front of the prisoner. "I don't know what you think you've wandered into, son, but this ain't a story about a young Che Guevara, hero of the apocalypse. Your ears will never be the same after Sergeant Best is done with you. They'll look like cauliflowers, and it's the first thing the ladies will notice from now on."

"Screw you and screw this town," Jared seethed.

"Left ear please."

"Wait no! Damnit!" he cried as Mat pivoted and delivered a soul-crushing blow to the other ear.

Jared gasped for a full minute, sideways again on the floor, then said, "I thought you weren't going to torture me."

The sheriff chuckled. "Son, this isn't torture. Sergeant, here, learned how to break men in Afghanistan. He knows how to destroy the body and the mind of true believers. Water boarding. Electric shock. Even those fanatical hard cases eventually became babbling babies. So far, I'm in charge of this interview. If I find your attention wandering again, I'll leave you with Sergeant Best for the real deal. You cost a friend of mine an eye, and Sergeant Best asked me for both of your eyes in trade. You don't need eyes to talk."

It was all bullshit, of course. Mat had never interrogated anyone. His army job had been to snatch the bad guys out of their compounds and hand them to legitimate interrogators.

"What do you want me to talk about?" Jared mewled.

Morgan nodded his big head in the lamplight. "If you're helpful, then we'll see about getting you a better meal and maybe even a shower."

"That's your best offer?" Jared spat.

"It's the only offer you're going to get, son. Now you're going to tell us what's happening in the refugee camps. We already know plenty, so don't even think about lying. If we know more about how the camps form and organize, we can save lives—theirs and ours. We just killed two dozen of them this afternoon. It was probably unnecessary. Now, please educate us. Pretty please. With a cherry on top."

———

THE EASTERN HORIZON grayed with the coming dawn as Mat trudged down Center Street on his way home. The nighttime rain had tapered off to a sprinkle. He was exhausted, but the breaking dawn made the streets seem peaceful. The smoldering camps hadn't yet colored the sky with their columns of daily smoke, ringing the town with peril.

The night patrols confirmed Jared's intel—at least the locations of some of the larger camps. A lot of days had passed since Jared had been locked up. Mat needed to act on the intel now, before it became even more stale.

Mat would move on the higher value targets that coming night. He needed to split forces and send one team, probably made up of deputies led by Rickers, to roll up leadership of three camps. Mat could lead the QRF to hit the big one.

The HESCO wouldn't be done for at least a couple months, even with the whole town working on it every day. Mat was no mathematical genius, but he'd learned: when you drew a circle around a town, that perimeter ended up being fuck-all long. Two times pi "r" equals *fuck-all long*. That's what his high school geometry teacher should've taught him. That would've been good to know.

Even if they cut away the "suburb" neighborhoods, Science Guy estimated it was twelve miles of perimeter, plus another five miles around the Tosh pig farms. To put it in grunt terms: if Mat jogged the perimeter during his morning workout, he'd be dragging ass by the end.

The townspeople were a wonder with heavy equipment, and they seemed to have a ton of raw materials to cobble into a wall, but even with almost every able-bodied man and woman working on it, they could only complete a tenth of a mile a day—about five hundred feet. The wall would be great, but the longer it stretched, the more obvious it became that it wasn't very useful without men on top and men on patrol both inside and out. Mat would give his left nut for a few dozen crew-served machine guns.

He turned down the last block toward his home, and the sky peaked yellow over his street. He planned to drink a liter of water, grab five hours of sleep, eat lunch, then kit up for the evening raids.

They'd go in the witching hour—about nineteen hours from now. The cops and the QRF would have their warning orders waiting for them when they woke up.

Mat stepped inside the door and was greeted by the scent of pancakes and burning plastic.

"Hey Mat. Surprise!" William called out from the fireplace. A frying pan perched on the coals with the plastic handle slowly melting.

"Just a minute more, and I'll have breakfast ready," William said over his shoulder. "This pan gets really hot."

Mat flopped onto the couch. Tired as he was, he watched William's culinary struggles with a smile.

William placed two plates on the coffee table, with matching sets of palm-sized pancakes: one pancake, burned to near inedibility, two dark brown pancakes with centers of uncooked batter, and one nearly perfect golden brown masterpiece. William cheated by giving Mat the best of them. His own were even worse.

*How to make a pancake.* Mat sighed. There were so damn many things to learn in this life. He wondered if William would survive long enough to learn half of them.

"There was still light in the sky last night when I ran over to Mrs. Morgan's house for pancake batter," he said, sheepishly. "I didn't *technically* go out after dark. Mrs. Morgan gave me the ingredients and told me what to do. I had to serve the burnt ones because there wasn't enough batter to make more."

Mat's eyes felt dehydrated, like his lids would stick closed the next blink. "This is great, little bro, but give the Morgans back the flour from our own rations, or as close as you can."

"Oh yeah," William said with a smile. "I was planning on it. I knew that's what you'd say, so I kept track how much. I just didn't know if pancake batter and flour were the same thing."

*So much to learn,* Mat mused to himself.

The two sat quietly, chewing crispy pancake.

"So, what do you think of Candice?" William queried. The scene clicked into place in Mat's head: the boy waking up early, making breakfast, waiting at the door to talk to his guardian; the closest thing he had to a father and best friend. It all made sense now. William was in love with the girl.

"She's a cutie, little bro."

William blushed. "Umm... I kissed her."

Mat slapped him on the back. "Was that your first real kiss?"

"Yeah." William smiled so big Mat could see burned pancake in his teeth.

"You picked a good one."

"She's *the one*, I think."

Mat chortled. "Yeah! the one for today. I hear you. There's lots of fish in the sea, though, Tiger."

William's face fell. It was the wrong note to strike.

*Damn,* Mat scolded himself. *You're not throwing back drinks with the bros.* It was a nice kid's first kiss. William had notions of riding into the sunset with the young, sweet-smelling brunette.

Mat fumbled, attempting to recover. "She's perfect. She seems smart." He almost said, *she looks like she'll have a great rack someday,* but he caught himself. That would've been Level Ten Creepy. Mat was too tired to have this conversation, but he had no choice. The boy wasn't going to put it down.

William talked around the pancake cinder in his mouth. "With Candice, it's like I want to keep her safe. I think I love her."

Mat sighed. He'd felt the same way about Caroline, William's sister. The world ate her up anyway, no matter that he was a big, bad Army Ranger.

Mat changed the subject. "I saw Gladys Carver last night. What do you think of her?"

"She's awesome; part schoolteacher, part fighter, like those girl warriors in Black Panther."

"Do you think you could make this place home? McKenzie, I mean?" Mat asked.

"Sure we can. I like it here," William said.

"I've been working on getting you set up here," Mat emphasized the word "you." "You deserve a family and a home. Traveling with me—there's not a bright future for you in that."

William's brow furrowed and tears sprang to the corners of his eyes. "You're leaving me?"

"Well, not for a while. I've got a lot to do on this job. Don't worry. Gladys Carver agreed to take you in. I've fixed it. You won't have to leave town or leave your new girl."

William seemed not to hear. "But I'm coming with you, right?"

Mat stuck to his guns—what he always did when things got dodgy. "No. You don't have to leave. You have a home here. I'll make it safe, or as safe as I can, before I go. You can stay with Gladys, and here in town with Candice."

The boy's eyes stood out like twin silver dollars. The tears glistened on his cheeks. It was no longer the face of an adolescent basking in the glow of his first kiss. This was the look of terror.

"No, please. We're going to be Army Rangers. You promised."

"William, I know what I said, but that was before. I can't stay here. I don't know how to be a family to you."

"Why? Just because your girlfriend died?"

Mat's face flushed. "What would you know about that, kid? One kiss and you're an expert?"

It was a bush league retort, Mat felt the sinking in his gut already. *Regret.* But he had to power through this conversation, this mission. He opened his mouth to speak but he stopped short.

He'd seen William's exact expression in Kabul when a boy's dad got blown up by an IED—the eyes swimming in loss. The chin quivering. The cheeks so slack that they drooped.

"My big sister was the only mother I had left. I can't lose you, too."

Mat's stomach churned with ice. He couldn't face this right now. This talk had gotten out of hand. He was too tired, and the mission was spinning out of control. The big mission—protecting the town —had become like trying to rub off beach sand with hands covered in sunscreen. Every move made a bigger mess.

Mat flanked the threat. "I want you to start sleeping at Gladys' house when I am out on night maneuvers."

"That's most nights," William barked.

"It'll be good for you. And safer." *Get used to it.*

William wore the same eyes that day in the clinic when his sister died. But this time, the kid's eyes went hard.

He'd seen this a lot on deployment in the Middle East. Arabs were a romantic people, and they ran around in the flush of romance over every-damned-thing. Love, food, friendship, religion. But, if you hit them hard enough, the romance compressed to flint; dense, dumb and razor-sharp.

Mat stood, carried his dish to the bucket on the kitchen counter, and went to get his four and a half hours of sleep. He forgot his water again.

The unresolved conflict with William felt like a threat, and no matter which direction Mat pointed his rifle, this one came from his six.

———

**Town Jail**
**McKenzie, Tennessee**

SHERIFF MORGAN CONDUCTED the interrogations of two of the three rat leaders.

The snatch and grabs had gone easy enough—no casualties and

nothing more than minor scuffles. Unlike Afghans, who bunkered inside walled compounds to prevent incursions, the rats lived like bags blown by a storm. Mat's assault teams marched into the camps, guns out, shuffled through the tents, and took HVTs into custody. No fuss. No muss.

One of the men fingered by Jared turned out to be little more than a bully with violent tendencies. So far, that'd landed him temporarily atop the hierarchy of his camp.

"I'm not too worried about that one," Sheriff Morgan told Mat. "I think we can take a page from the old cop playbook with a strip and dump."

"What's that?"

The sheriff smiled. "Guys like this tend to make enemies out of followers. They survive through brute force. When I started in law enforcement in the 80s in Louisville, his type led local gangs. If we couldn't get enough for a conviction, we'd hold them for two days, strip them naked, and dump them in their territory. One of their lieutenants always went for a shot at the title; sure as the Tin Man has a sheet metal dong."

"And the second guy? The men in his tent could almost be considered a security detail; four armed dudes watching over their primary."

"Cordell is his name."

Mat nodded.

"He's too dangerous to release," the sheriff agreed. "He's got the making of a post-apocalyptic warlord. We'll keep him here, and may he rot in peace."

"You got room for about 6,000 more in those cells?"

"I don't think any of the refugees would complain about three hots and a cot. For now, shooting at 'em or poking them with your greased javelins is the best idea we got. Do you want to join me for the conversation with this last guy?"

Mat nodded. This last guy defied post-apocalyptic stereotypes.

Dr. Abraham Hauser had given them his name straightaway, despite being restrained in flex-cuffs. He even spoke to them with the old kind of respect toward law enforcement.

Mat recalled Jared's description of Hauser: "You don't have to worry about that sheep Hauser and his crew," Jared had said. "They've got a snowball's chance in hell of mounting an attack on your town. He's got them building utopia in the forest. He wouldn't let any of his people participate in the run on your convoy. He told them they wouldn't be welcome back if they went with me."

Tonight, Mat sat across from Hauser, at a picnic table in the atrium of McKenzie city hall. In front of each man was a half a peanut butter sandwich and a cup of room temperature tea. Sheriff Morgan had asked Mat to take lead on this interrogation. Morgan sat in a folding chair off to the side, watching.

Mat ate his sandwich, sipped his tea, and looked for an opening.

Finally Hauser spoke. "I don't believe I've committed any crimes, officers. I have family back at the camp."

Mat replied. "I'm not a police officer." He had declined Morgan's offer to deputize him. It felt too much like agreeing to a permanent thing. "You're not under arrest. My name is Mat Best. I'm in charge of town security. We're trying to figure out how much of a threat you and your camp pose."

"We aren't a threat to anyone."

Mat offered a grim smile. "Being within walking distance of McKenzie makes you a threat."

"We haven't attacked you," Hauser said. "And we could just as easily be an asset as a threat."

"Do you deny that some of the food your people are eating is stolen?" Mat pushed back to get the measure of the man.

"Scavenged, certainly," said Hauser. "Our campfire council made it clear to all our people that stealing from occupied structures will get them shunned." It was a technical answer, but it made sense. This guy couldn't deny his followers the chance to catch and eat loose pigs in the forest, even if the pigs had come from an illegal attack.

Mat changed direction. "Tell me more about your camp and its council. Have a bite of your sandwich first."

Hauser looked to be in his late sixties; white, wispy hair, bespectacled and trim. While Hauser ate the sandwich, savoring each bite, he talked about Creek Camp.

After his wife died four years earlier, Hauser sold his medical practice in Jackson Hole, Wyoming and moved to Bowling Green, Kentucky to be close to his daughter, son-in-law, and granddaughter. When the American economy collapsed, Hauser convinced his daughter and son-in-law to pack their emergency supplies and run away from the city. Without a bug-out destination, they drove as deep into the countryside as they could. They ran out of gas on the outskirts of McKenzie with a month's rations, nowhere to go and no way to get there.

"The camp was a cooperative accident. The Baylors and Smiths were traveling together and happened to run out of gas at the same place as us. Tom Baylor and his two teenage sons are eagle scouts, and I mean the real kind, like we had in Jackson. James and Linda Smith are avid hunters."

Mat offered a platitude to keep him talking. "Good people to know these days."

"Yes, they are. But mostly they're just good, honest people. That's proven to be the most important survival skill—being a good person. The selfish ones, they're your enemies, Mr. Best."

"Sergeant Best. I'm army, retired."

"We could use combat veterans who've been 'in the shit.'"

Mat laughed. "What makes you think I've been in the shit?"

Hauser looked pleased with himself. "I know I don't carry myself as a veteran today, if I ever did, and I don't blame you for not recognizing me as one. The Army sent me to medical school. I served in VA hospitals stateside for twelve years and retired with the rank of major. I never deployed in combat, but in Germany, I treated men back from the Global War on Terror. They looked just like you."

"And your campfire council?" Mat asked. "How did three families become Creek Camp?"

Hauser had finished his sandwich. "How about I show you?"

Matt nodded. "You're free to go. Sorry about the rough treatment."

Hauser tidied up his napkin and plate. Mat reached across the table and took them from him. "I'll come by your camp to see you soon."

———————

FOUR DAYS LATER, Mat met Dr. Hauser at Creek Camp. When he arrived, Beatrice Morgan, the sheriff's wife, and another woman from town were there in the camp, standing in the mud, talking to Hauser. A boy from town unloaded empty fifty-five gallon metal drums from the back of the Morgan's pickup truck. The drums had been torch-cut in half.

"Mrs. Morgan. A word please?" Mat called as he moved into camp with his security team. The sheriff's wife should not be outside the HESCO. It was a security risk and totally unacceptable.

She paused her conversation with a touch on Hauser's arm and followed Mat to one side of a large, dirty tent.

"Mrs. Morgan, are you trying to get yourself killed? What are you doing in the camps?"

"We're delivering cook pots that the sheriff made in our garage. I can call him over if you like. He's around here somewhere giving first aid. Living outdoors, even minor injuries can fester."

Mat glanced around, but didn't see the sheriff. He didn't want to talk about post-apocalyptic first aid. He wanted them back inside the wire.

"I've got no problem with your charitable work, per se. Has the food committee signed off on this?" The look on her face told him she hadn't checked with any committee, and she had no intention of doing so. Mat didn't care about permission either, but if townspeople got kidnapped by refugees, it'd be Mat's team called in to mount a hostage rescue. "You can't be out here without security. My team and I could have delivered the pots for you."

The pots were brilliant, really—primitive tech he'd seen in the hinterlands of Iraq among the Kurds. Hauser had organized the Creek Camp into tent clans around campfires with ten to twenty people, and the big pots would become social pivot points for each clan.

The camp smelled of pork. The domesticated pigs they'd lost at the ambush a month back would avoid capture for a time, but all fifty of the escaped pigs would eventually end up in the stew pot—if the camps had stew pots.

Stewing meat in a big pot was far more efficient than roasting it over a fire, where most of the precious fat dripped away. The stew pots the Sheriff and his wife had crafted were a game-changer for the refugees. They could add bits of meat and handfuls of greens to the pot for weeks, or even months, so long as they kept the fire going. It was hard to find fault with Mrs. Morgan's initiative.

The camp looked safe enough. Tetanus or cholera were probably bigger risks to the Morgans than being kidnapped. But even on that score, Mat noticed, each grouping of tents had a tidy pit latrine with a privacy curtain. Someone had taught Creek Camp proper sanitation. Probably their physician leader.

Mat sighed and Mrs. Morgan waited patiently.

"May I ask," Mat hazarded the question, "whose idea was this? The stew pots?"

She didn't answer directly. "Did you know that my husband is a deacon at First Presbyterian?"

"Indeed, I didn't," Mat admitted.

"He does what he must, for his job, you know," she explained. "But before all, my husband's a Christian." She patted Mat on the forearm, just like she'd done to Hauser, then she turned back to her work with the refugees.

*You think you know a guy,* Mat thought to himself and shook his head.

———

THE MEMBERS of the Security and Food Committees sat on folding chairs in the foyer of McKenzie City Hall, taking advantage of the natural light streaming though the plate glass windows. It was cold outside, and raining again, but they kept the front and back doors propped open for a breeze to carry away the body odor.

The town was on one-day-in-three rationed water because it required electricity to pump water to the top of the cisterns. Electricity required a gas generator, or solar power, and solar was harder to move around where it was needed.

Every three days, a pickup truck with a propane generator drove around to each of the water towers and pumped them full of well water. When Black Autumn struck, there was a lot of propane in town. The outlying farmers used the gas for heating and cooking. A huge propane storage facility sat on the edge of town, and it'd just been topped off. Now that all the outlying farmers were crammed into town for protection, the propane could last for years if they were judicious.

Formerly, the town had placed a lot of hope in their stack of solar panels. In the weeks that followed the collapse, the town had been given a crash course in how hard it was to turn solar, DC power into "normal" AC power. It would've been fantastic to pump water into the town cisterns with solar power, but for love or money they couldn't find the right DC water pumps, or big enough inverters to run AC.

Even with lots of propane, the generator struggled to run the huge water pumps—and there were only two large, propane gennies in town: one primary and one spare. The townspeople practiced volunteer water rationing so as not to burn them up. The old luxury of daily showers became the new social virtue of body odor. If you smelled bad, you were being a good citizen.

Mat arrived at the committee meeting with a plan for blunting the threat of the refugees, but it wasn't a simple plan. It was the kind of thing the CIA tried on-the-regular in Afghanistan—the kind of thing that sometimes ended with really pissed-off Afghans.

After the formalities, the sheriff turned the floor over to Mat.

"We can get the refugees to go look for food elsewhere, if we can convince them the grass is greener on the other side. We sow rumors of FEMA supply warehouses far enough away that they can't make it back here."

The committee stared back with confusion.

Confusion was never good.

"When their scouts follow our directions to the first food cache, about thirty miles north of here, they'll find plenty of evidence to support the FEMA story. We'll stock a warehouse with food and make it look legit."

Benny Miles from the local hardware store interrupted. "I don't see how a pile of our supplies is going to look like a FEMA supply depot."

Mat repeated himself, "We use an empty warehouse outside of a town. We fill its shelves with dry food—the stuff we've been setting aside because it's expired. We make a FEMA sign and hang it inside; really sell the idea that it's a long lost supply depot. We leave clues pointing to another supply depot even farther away."

The hardware guy shook his head. "If we give them our food, won't the rats just come back to us for more?"

"They won't know it's our food. The food cache will be thirty miles from here—a two or three day walk. It'll look like a lot of food, but it'll only be a couple days worth. Then we leave a map for them to find another location."

The more Mat said it out loud, the more the plan sounded cockamamie even to him, but he was fully committed. *And wasn't this the kind of shit the CIA brewed up to destabilize indigenous populations?*

"If there are FEMA supply warehouses, shouldn't we go get the food and bring it back to town?" a woman asked. Her salt and pepper hair was piled on her head in a bun.

Mat stopped himself from groaning. "There aren't any *real* FEMA supply warehouses. We're just telling the rats that so they go someplace else. Once they walk far away, it's unlikely they'll walk back. The farther they walk, the better. They become another town's problem."

"So we lie to them?" she asked. Her face screwed up in a twist.

"In intelligence, we call it *disinformation.*" Mat had never been in intelligence. He'd been an assaulter. But he'd been around CIA shenanigans long enough to have a feel for the business. Still, he was doing a piss-poor job of pitching it to these hayseeds. Mat decided to punt.

"Here's the vote: can I use 3,000 of our oldest, crappiest dried meals? The expired stuff?"

The last meeting, the hardware guy had given a report of their food stores. They had enough food to last the winter and the spring if they butchered half the pigs. By then, they could replace the butchered pigs with new, weaned piglets. In short, they were okay on food if they didn't lose the pigs and if the town wasn't overrun by rats.

Hardware Guy finally picked up on Mat's plan and nodded. The other six food committee members glanced at him and a couple more appeared amenable, whether they understood the plan or not.

"If we don't want to spend bullets on these people later, we need to spend a little expired food *now*." Mat put the final shine on his argument. "Can I have the food?"

The food committee people voted in favor. Some of the security committee people voted for the idea too, even though it wasn't their decision.

*Slam!*

Jim Jensen, the newest member of the security committee, slammed a glass jar on the table. Everyone startled at the dramatic gesture.

"This is mustard gas."

"Good Lord in heaven," bun lady exclaimed. Her hands flew to her mouth.

Mat hadn't sat down yet, but he couldn't think of anything else to say. He'd been caught off-guard and upstaged by Science Guy.

"Don't worry folks, so long as I don't crack this lid, we're all one hundred percent safe."

Mat doubted the yellow dust filling the jar was really a nerve agent, but given that Jensen was a scientist, it was possible.

"You brought that shit in here?" Mat asked.

Jensen smiled as though proud of himself. "I produced it with the sheriff's permission to develop poison weapons for future use. We're now in the future."

Mat wondered if Jensen had a conversation with Sheriff Morgan other than the one he'd heard because the sheriff hadn't given permission to do anything, and they had been talking about botulism at the time. Something about Science Guy's white-knuckle grip on the jar made Mat withdraw any objection for the time being. *Best to let things roll,* he decided. *No need to get in an argument with the dude using nerve gas as a gavel.*

"Okay," interrupted Sheriff Morgan."That concludes this part of the meeting. Thank you very much, members of the food commit-tee. We will take a short break. Security Committee Members please stay close by. Mr. Jensen, please stay as well."

The sheriff handled the appearance of nerve gas as a procedural speed bump, not as an evacuation event. The guy really was great under pressure, Mat noted. Mat had almost drawn his Glock when the guy slammed down the jar, which in retrospect would've been the wrong response to mustard gas.

The members of the committees mulled around for a moment, everyone keeping an eye on the jar full of dirty, yellow dust. Back in the old days, threat of a chemical agent would've cleared the building in two minutes flat. These days, it barely raised eyebrows.

Mat thought through what might happen next. Sheriff Morgan had the security committee locked down pretty tight, with four of the seven members on his same page. Morgan had stopped Jensen's drama train in order to get the question of poison gas under control and away from the emotionally-wobbly food committee. The smaller the group to vote on a charged topic, like WMDs, the better. Mat and Sheriff Morgan were two of the seven votes, and the trucking guy was a Viet Nam vet who probably wouldn't vote for anything stupid.

Mat had mixed feelings about the nasty-looking jar. This wasn't Iraq and they weren't engaged in symmetrical warfare. The math of the apocalypse was rather rudimentary, when seen through the lens of a jar filled with poison gas: there were several times more people than there was food to feed them. The back-of-napkin solution was to reduce the number of people to match the supply.

Mat didn't pretend to be that rational. He wasn't a numbers guy, nor could he claim to understand chemical weapons systems. He'd never thought of them as anything other than bad. But that jar on the plastic table could very well be the key to him getting out of this town and away from this job. Maybe, if he combined his skills and that jar, this hashed-up mess could take a turn toward victory.

After ten minutes of back slapping and goodbyes, the food committee members were gone and the security committee settled into their plastic seats.

Sheriff Morgan stood and said, "As you know, Jim Jensen would like to share something he's been working on. But first let's have a conversation about discretion, and what it means to be part of the security committee. For starters, we keep our damned mouths shut." He drilled Jensen with a reproachful stare. The six men and one woman of the committee looked around, scenting the butt-whooping on the wind. "We don't talk about plans, strategies or weapons outside of this committee. Jim, you crossed a line putting a weapon in front of the food committee. If you do that again, you're off this committee."

Jensen nodded, but Mat got the sense that he didn't really care, and that the mustard gas dog-and-pony show had been entirely intentional.

The sheriff went on to impress upon all present the importance of not discussing meetings with friends and family, and he requested a raise of hands from all members indicating their promise to keep the committee's confidences.

As soon as the sheriff paused in his exhortations, Jim Jensen stood up and went straight into his schtick. "We all appreciate what Mat has done to secure McKenzie, but we have to acknowledge a difficult truth: what we've asked of him isn't really possible, not so long as we're surrounded by thousands of starving refugees. It's only a matter of time before we're overrun, our food taken and our loved ones murdered." Jensen flicked a look at Chris Jackson. Jackson was definitely NOT one of the committee members the sheriff had on-lock.

Jackson's house, on the outskirts of town, had been raided by refugees. They'd taken everything edible and raped his daughter. Young Nancy Jackson hung herself the next day. After that, Chris Jackson asked to move from the food committee to the security committee and, despite the sheriff's reluctance, the committee had voted to do it. Jackson hadn't said much since joining.

After a perfectly-timed pause, Jensen continued. "Even an Army

Ranger can't prevent attacks like the Jackson house and Reedy Grove, so long as desperate people surround us. The numbers are simply too great—by an order of magnitude or more."

Mat didn't know what that meant, but it sounded like a lot.

"While Mat's plan to draw refugees away might temporarily remove ten or fifteen percent of the threat, that still leaves ten thousand or more refugees poised to invade our town. Fighting them hand-to-hand and one-bullet-at-a-time isn't possible given the sheer numbers. Even with the HESCO barrier finished—which is at least three months out—we'll still be threatened from every point of the compass." He swept his hand around the inside of city hall, casting the specter of rats surrounding them, even here and now.

"We must employ science to protect our town. That or die."

Jensen banged two more glass jars on the table. *Bang. Bang.*

The one jar, with dark, yellow dust, Jensen had already identified as mustard gas. Another jar was full of mud—brown and viscous. The third looked like it contained a cloud; white and fluffy. Jensen had everyone's undivided attention.

"I propose we encourage the organic processes of Mother Nature to reduce the refugee numbers. Even without our involvement, bacteria will fester in the camps. Whenever thousands of people gather without meticulous sanitation, nature counterattacks with a one-two punch of bacteria and disease. Cholera. Dysentery. Botulism..." He tapped the lid of the jar that looked like mud. "Even anthrax from the hides of the animals they're hunting in the fields." He flicked the jar filled with white. "Nature is our greatest ally. Nature resists man when we gather in the thousands, without civil sanitation systems. Nature marshals its microscopic armies against humankind. We can help that process along—give those bacteria a nudge in the right direction. But we must do it *before the refugees invade our town.*"

In the face of Jensen's livid speech, Mat's plan to send rats out chasing FEMA camps sounded tepid and weak, even to him. The three jars, in all their terrible glory, promised the resurrection of a dead god: the god of science. They looked like an old lady's canning jars on the outside, but the slurries they contained heralded miracles of modern technology—mass solutions for mass problems.

Mat shook his head to break the spell. They were weapons of mass destruction, and they only *looked* good on paper. Mat had never seen WMDs used, but he knew there was a damned good reason mankind had universally deemed them evil. But Mat didn't have a presentation with visual aids and polished talking points. If he disagreed right now, he'd sound like a gun fighter arguing that guns were the answer. His FEMA plan had already been approved. He had no other grand strategy to offer in counter-point to Jensen's poison potions.

Sheriff Morgan cleared his throat. "What are you proposing, Jim?"

Jensen waved his hands around like a showman. "We all know there's no future for anyone living in the refugee camps. We can't care for them, and food isn't going to suddenly appear in government trucks. The danger to us *isn't* that they'll die. The danger to us is that they'll die *too slowly*—by disease, theft, murder, and God forbid... even cannibalism. The refugees will bring all of these to our doorstep as the winter deepens. After that, they'll still die, only we'll be dead too."

Jensen was winning. Mat now saw how words were weapons, sharper than steel and ferocious as a Viking army. Jensen commanded a platoon of dazzling options, a brigade of ideas and an army of verbs stretching to the smoke-riven horizon.

Jensen picked up the jar of mud and looked upon it fondly. "The botulinum toxin is not difficult to grow. It spreads via food, and it'll take the fight out of the rats within a week, maybe days."

Greg Schultz raised his hand, "Mr. Jensen, are you proposing we give the refugees poisoned food?"

"I am," Jensen said confidently, without even a hint of embarrassment. "Some of you already know a bit about clostridium botulinum. Perhaps you've learned how to protect against it when canning fruit. I'm sure Mrs. Morgan's famous blackberry jam is safe as can be. But the spores of botulism are all around us, in the air and in the soil. I've concentrated a small amount in my lab and I could grow more. Much more."

Greg Schultz spoke again "I don't know if I'm comfortable poisoning people. There are children out there."

Chris Jackson stood and Jensen eased himself into a chair, almost as if this were a planned hand-off. The grieving father addressed the wall on the far side of the room. His eyes hovered like spotlights over the committee.

"Two of the rats had handguns. At first we thought they'd just take our food. We'd have to rely on the town to eat, which would still be okay. Marta begged me not to fight them. I didn't want to hurt anyone, so I told the rats where to find the canned food." His eyes glistened and his mouth worked soundlessly, like he'd forgotten how to speak.

"Then they grabbed our Nan, we... we could hear her crying, calling for her daddy."

Jackson dropped back into his seat, but missed. The folding chairs were set close together, so he fell half-way into the lap of Marjorie Simms. She propped him up as he sobbed, and steered him into his own chair.

"I should've made them shoot me. I should've fought to the death. Anything would be better than this," Chris Jackson wailed. Marjorie Simms and Greg Schultz helped Jackson into the next room. The crying tapered, then muted as the door closed behind them.

Mat now fully understood the sheriff's misgivings about Jackson on the committee. When big feelings were involved, anything could happen. After Jackson's horrific outburst, the committee would gladly put botulism in baby food.

After the group composed itself, Scientist Guy—now "Mad Scientist Guy" in Mat's mind, continued. "The rats *will* starve. The only question is: how many of us will they murder first?

Mat didn't need to drench himself in a father's grief to understand the value of devastating weaponry. He'd spent his career under the canopy of hellfire missiles and AC-130 gunships. Winning was always better than losing, whatever it took. Nevertheless, Mat could see that many, if not most of the people in the room needed some justification to use chem-bio weapons; they couldn't move forward without an easing of their consciences. Mat had little respect for politicians, but he appreciated the Mad Scientist's skill. He'd struck the perfect note to sway the civilians on the committee.

But lethal force wasn't like Chick-fil-A: *the more the better*. Escalation was a two-way street. When one side introduced nasty shit, the other side would see their evil and raise them an atrocity. The rats hadn't tried half the nefarious shit Mat would've tried if he'd been one of them instead of an employee of the town.

So far, the rats hadn't gone to war—certainly not the kind of war they'd bring if they were attacked with anthrax. These days, Mat's men could still patrol the countryside with no more than an awkward wave to the refugees. The town wasn't under siege. Not yet.

"I like bad ass weapons as much as the next guy," Mat spoke up. "May I point out, that having weapons of mass destruction and using weapons of mass destruction are two different questions? We can approve this guy," Mat pointed at Jensen, "to produce chem-bio weapons, but we need to think long and fucking hard before we use them." Marjorie Simms gasped a little at the swear. "My apologies, ma'am. If we jump to weapons of mass destruction, I would expect the survivors to fire bomb the town or some proportionately-forceful response. Trust me: even using anthrax or mustard gas, there will be survivors. Lots and lots of survivors. They will be outraged and brimming with revenge. If we kill their families, the gloves will come off."

Mad Scientist Guy went to interrupt and Mat held up a hand. "Let us remember: the refugee camps drift around out there in the forest and fields. It's tough for my patrols to even keep track of them all. They're spread over fifty square miles. I couldn't attack them all-at-once if I wanted. We, on the other hand, are very easy to locate. We're stuck to this spot. All they gotta do is decide on a day and a time and ten thousand pissed off rats with nothing to lose will come screaming over our junkyard wall. I am very reluctant to give them a reason to do that. Revenge, by the way, has started more wars than money. Keep it in mind."

Mat delivered his whole speech leaning back in his chair while Mad Scientist Guy stood at the front of the room twiddling his thumbs. When Mat finished, Mad Scientist Guy seized control.

"The supply depot trick is too risky to be our only plan. If it works at all, it'll move a small percentage of the rats away from town. The majority—thousands of them—will still think of us as their meal ticket."

"All right," interjected Sheriff Morgan. "Let's vote."

"Wait a minute, Sheriff. We haven't heard from you," Greg Schultz said. He always voted with the sheriff.

"No, you haven't, and I plan on keeping it that way. I'll be the seventh vote. Who votes to approve the manufacture of biological and chemical weapons, with approval specifically denied for the *use* of those weapons until we have another vote?" The way Sheriff Morgan framed the vote, it contained nods to both experts; Mat and the Mad Scientist.

Chris Jackson drifted back into the room, now composed. Five of the committee voted "yes." Mat raised his hand as the sixth. The sheriff didn't vote.

Mat looked over at Mad Scientist Guy. Jensen would've probably preferred that his weapons get carte blanche from the committee, but this was almost as good. He had permission to make the nasty shit in his basement—every science nerd's dream. For his part, Mat was glad that the sheriff had put Jensen on a leash. Something about the guy felt askew, like when a confidential informant in Afghanistan compulsively picked his ear while giving up intel.

It was obvious by their body posture; the committee members regarded Jensen differently than before—like a demigod with terrible powers of destruction. The man's street cred in the community had risen dramatically, and the shifty tosser seemed well-aware of it. He barely suppressed a grin as he scooped his jars off the table and placed them in a plastic bottle carrier, each jangling like a milkman walking up the step. Mat didn't know the first thing about the manufacture of those substances, but he figured it must be difficult, and must require a long list of chemical agents. The slick prick hadn't made mustard gas from Liquid Drano, baking soda and Axe body spray. Mad Scientist Guy had produced not one, but three weapons all by his lonesome in his damned basement. Mat wondered what other secrets he might be keeping.

# 13

## CAMERON STEWART

"Nevertheless I long—I pine, all my days—to travel home and see the dawn of my return.

And if a god will wreck me yet again on the wine-dark sea, I can bear that too, with a spirit tempered to endure.

Much have I suffered, labored long and hard by now in the waves and wars.

Add this to the total—bring the trial on!"

— ODYSSEUS, THE ODYSSEY

**Grafton Ghost Town,
Southern Utah**

Cameron jerked awake to screaming, but the first thing he noticed was the hunger, thrumming in his ear and thundering in his overtaxed heart. His blood felt like mucus and his mucus felt like sand.

"What, wha, what's happening?" he asked the darkness, but the single room of the pioneer home jolted from sleep into chaos, a melee of shouts and cries.

"Stop talking," Isaiah shouted. "Where's Leah?"

Nobody replied.

"Leah?" he called, terror vibrating in his voice.

Nothing. Cameron could hear the cries of his own two boys, as familiar to him as the sound of the wind.

"You in there," a man shouted outside, from a distance.

Cameron struggled to orient himself toward the door. He stepped on a child in a sleeping bag as he scrambled in the pitch black for the Mosin-Nagant against the door frame.

The magazine carried five rounds and nothing more. His pockets were otherwise empty. He knew it for a fact since he slept in his pants now. As thin as he'd become, he wore every article of clothing to bed to keep warm.

Cameron slammed into Isaiah on their way to the door. He pushed the polygamist out the door first.

The moon flooded into the room. Cameron finally found his rifle, next to Isaiah's twenty gauge shotgun, he grabbed both and stepped onto the porch behind the polygamist.

"You in there," the voice repeated. "We have your girl. If you want her back, give us a box of food. A heavy box." A muffled girl's scream carried between the tree line on the river and the homestead. Cameron guessed they'd grabbed her when she went out to use the privy.

"We'll give you everything we have, but it's not much," Isaiah shouted into the darkness. "Just give her back.".

"No we won't," Cameron hissed.

"They could rape her," Isaiah argued.

"We don't have enough anyway. They won't give her back, no matter what we do."

"You don't know that."

"Yes I do. Men who take a girl would kill a girl."

"You don't know that," Isaiah repeated himself, panicked.

"Give us the food now or we take her as our toy," the man in the trees threatened.

Cameron rushed back into the house, and a chorus of barks and shouts followed as he bumbled through the dark, searching for the last of their food. All they had left was a few handfuls of wheat and one can of beans.

Cameron let Isaiah get all the way inside before shouting to the raiders. "We don't have any food, so you're just going to have to let her go."

"Bullshit. The other guy said you have food," the man fired back. "Give us whatcha got."

"We have some. We have some," Isaiah screamed from inside. "Just wait a minute."

"Nah, we got jack shit," Cameron cupped his hands around his mouth. "Do what you're gonna do, fuckers. Get on with it."

"Fine. Say goodbye to her, then, assholes. She's ours now." Three men in the cottonwoods laughed.

Cameron had put the bucket of wheat on a high shelf right before bed in hopes of keeping mice out. Isaiah probably hadn't noticed, so his bumbling search continued in vain. Minutes later he found the bucket and bolted onto the porch.

"I have it. Hold on. I have it here!" his voice warbled.

Ruth burst out the door with Isaiah's shotgun. Cameron grabbed her arm and restrained her before she flew off the porch, into the night and to her own death.

"They're gone," Cameron said. "You're not going to stop them. Not with this." He grabbed the little shotgun from her hands.

"No! I have your food. Take it!" Isaiah yelled from inside the house.

"Shut up," Cameron hissed. "Just shut up, Isaiah. They're gone. Put the food back inside. I'll follow them. I'll go after her. You stay here."

Isaiah wept, "My girl. Oh, my girl."

"Pull it together." Cameron grabbed him by the shoulders and shook. "I need you in the game. Focus."

Isaiah's whimpering lessened. Cameron comforted him. "I'll follow them, okay? You stay here in case they come back. Get inside and guard the door until I return."

Isaiah searched for the shotgun around the inside of the doorframe. He couldn't see it in Cameron's hands because of the dark.

"Stop. Say it, Isaiah," Cameron ordered. "Say that you'll stay here and guard the rest of the family. I'm not going after Leah until you say it, and we both know who the better fighter is between the two of us."

"I'll stay," Isaiah mumbled through the phlegm. "I'll guard the rest."

"Good. Hide the food. If we lose the food, we die." Cameron stepped off the porch and cut a beeline across the pasture for the edge of the cottonwoods.

---

THERE WERE THREE MEN. Their three to Cameron's one. But it was worse than that. It was God-knew-how-many bullets in their guns to his five. It didn't matter, he had no intention of fighting the marauders.

The marauders kept moving all the way to the river, then upstream toward Rockville. He'd followed them mostly to keep Isaiah from giving away their remaining food. Without that food, they would all surely die. Cameron still believed they could all survive, and if not all of them, certainly his own family. With the girl gone, as tragic as it would be, there would be one less hungry mouth. Their odds of survival would increase.

*Heck, the girl's odds of survival were probably better with the marauders, raped or not.*

The men couldn't walk and cover the girl's mouth at the same time, and they probably tired of carrying her and gagging her because Cameron could now hear her sobbing through the trees. It made them easy to follow. When they went to cross the Virgin River, he caught up. He poked his head out of the brambles and watched in the moonlight as two men waded across the river, one carrying the girl over his shoulder. A minute or two later, the third man crossed behind them.

Once on the far side of the river, the marauders gave up any semblance of stealth. They joked and talked, sticking to the dark fringe of cottonwood trees. Maybe this was Sherwood Forest for this fucked up Robin Hood and his Band of Merry Rapists. In any case, if they left the riverbed, they'd be in open country—with no more cover than occasional sagebrush and limestone monoliths. It made sense to stay under cover where nobody could see their silhouettes to make a shot.

When the raiders set up camp a half-mile south of the town of Rockville, Cameron stopped and listened.

He could've let the men go when they crossed the river, but he hadn't. He'd crossed behind them and stayed on their trail. He could've doubled back and claimed to have lost them. Isaiah and Ruth would've made a fuss, but they would've come to terms.

The pitch dark of the riparian forest and the loud banter from the men had made it easy to follow them, and by their conversation, it sounded as though they carried spoils of earlier raids. Cameron told himself he followed them on the outside chance of stealing their food. It had nothing to do with the girl.

He crouched against a tree in the dark, listening to them brag about their escapades. His stomach grumbled so loudly, he was afraid they might hear.

They talked about coming from Las Vegas, and bumping from town-to-town, picking at the dying outskirts of the communities of Mesquite, Santa Clara, Saint George, Hurricane and soon, Rockville. They slept during the day and raided at night; farm houses and survivalist "bug out locations"—too far from town for their victims to call for help. By switching to nocturnal activity, they found they could pick their targets with impunity.

Cameron hadn't seen a glimmer of man-made light the whole time he followed them. He had no idea how they managed. His own night vision was so damaged by starvation, he was a stumbling wreck.

He found himself wondering what he'd do if they turned their attention to the little girl. Would he sit by and let them rape her? The asshole at the ghost town had said, "...or we take her as our toy." Cameron remembered Leah's words to him; cautious optimism not yet overcome by cynicism. "Are you the prophet here?" He pushed the thoughts from his mind. That kind of sentimental bullshit would get him killed.

Eventually, the bragging slowed, overtaken in three measures by snoring. Cameron considered hitting them right then. One man against three, him with only five bullets. He had no idea how they were armed, but based on their stories, he knew they had guns and plenty of experience using them.

He had a good idea where they were: three bends above the impoundment dam he and Isaiah built, nestled deep in a bend in the river. The marauders hadn't lit a fire, but Cameron could smell them anyway. As he'd starved these last weeks, his sense of smell had transformed into a superhuman ability. At a primal level, the smell of any other mammal was the smell of meat. Their cloying body odor might as well have been a neon sign, pointing the way to their camp.

His brain worked slowly, and thoughts came like oatmeal being poured out of a tea kettle. He reached the conclusion that to attack these men alone would be suicide. In the dark, amidst the brush, he couldn't see to shoot his rifle. Even if he had a thousand rounds of ammunition, hitting one of them would require more dumb luck than he'd experienced in months.

Cameron worked his way to a standing position using a tree as a handrail, and shuffled through the brush, away from the camp. He had no choice but to move very slowly—if he did anything more than stop-start-stop-start he got winded. Being three-quarters starved forced a man to be sneaky. He made no surplus movement, and no surplus noise. When Cameron waded back across the shallow, sandy river, dawn colored the eastern horizon.

---

HE HEARD Isaiah's wailing as soon as he emerged from the cottonwoods. The man sat on the homestead porch, his legs dangling over the side, kicking at the air. He reminded Cameron of a boy whose dog just got ran over. He was a weeping, snotting basket case. He didn't judge the man, though. One of the first things they'd lost to starvation was control of their emotions. Cameron had undergone his share of crying jags.

"Wipe your face and pull yourself together," Cameron wheezed as he caught his breath against the porch. "We're going after her."

"You...you know where she is?" Isaiah's tearful eyes glinted with hope.

"Yes, but we need to go now. Just you and me. They're over a mile away."

In starvation terms, it was a long, long way.

Isaiah gathered his shotgun and poked his head inside to let the women know where they were going. Cameron didn't bother to climb the stairs. He'd need every ounce of energy just to get back.

"Do they have food inside?" he asked.

"Yeah. Wheat kernels."

Cameron nodded. "We need to eat before we go. We should eat the women's portions too. This is a winner-take-all kind of deal."

Isaiah ducked inside again and came out with four bowls of cold, wet mash. They didn't bother with utensils. They poured the joyless slurry down their throats and abandoned the bowls on the porch.

"Let's go," Cameron said and waved Isaiah off the porch.

---

CAMERON FOLLOWED his nose the last two hundred yards into the snoring camp. The girl must've fallen asleep too because there was no simpering.

On the way, he'd worked up a plan, but not the kind of plan he would be sharing with Isaiah. It was the man's daughter at issue, and it was only right that Isaiah should take the goat's share of the risk. It wasn't as though either of them had the energy to debate it anyway.

"You go around that way," Cameron whispered. "Hit them from that side and I'll come at them from this side." He motioned Isaiah along the back trail. The night before, the raiders hadn't so much set a sentry as made one guy sleep on their back trail—a human tripwire of sorts. Cameron sent Isaiah on a collision course with the sentry while Cam prepared to shoot the other two in the back.

Isaiah's shotgun was barely big enough to kill a rabbit. The twenty gauge shotgun was a lot smaller than the twelve gauge shotguns police carried. The big, stumbling, half-crazed polygamist wasn't going to do much in a fight, but he could draw attention while Cameron went to work winning this thing. To Cameron, that felt as square as a preacher's soul. Isaiah should be grateful Cam was willing to risk his life at all. The marauders were hardened, practiced killers. So was Cameron, but it was three-against-one—or three-against-two if he counted Isaiah, which he really didn't.

He'd told Isaiah to "hit them from that side," but those instructions would mean next-to-nothing to the man. It sounded more promising than "go over there, stumble around like an ox, trip over their trail guard and wake them up."

In the strengthening morning light, Cameron could already see one of the sleeping men through the underbrush. He'd shoot that guy first, the instant Isaiah made himself known. He held his rifle against a tree and peered at the sleeping man through the ancient riflescope atop the Mosin-Nagant. The other two bastards and the girl weren't visible. The three were spread out in the dimples of sand beneath the canopy of the cottonwoods. There were no tents, or tarpaulins. They'd settled to ground, bundled up and fell asleep like animals. It made them exceedingly hard to find.

The sleeping man shucked off his sleeping bag in the mounting warmth of the morning sun. The movement startled Cameron and he pressed the trigger by reflex. Luckily, the safety was set and nothing happened. He exhaled and quietly clicked the safety lug to fire. The sleeping man settled in and shifted his rifle to the other side of his sleeping hole. Cameron caught full view of the black AR-15 rifle, as well as the handgun strapped to the man's belt. They slept armed, and it made sense they'd have the most-lethal firearms available. They'd been raiding and upgrading for months.

"We have you surrounded," Isaiah bellowed. "Come out with your hands up." The copse of trees erupted.

The man Cameron had in his scope sprung from his bed and flashed through the understory of brush like a cat pursued by a vacuum cleaner. He didn't get time to shoot. Cameron side-stepped through the brush, trying to find a window to shoot the running man in the back.

"Who the hell was that?" an unfamiliar voice rasped.

"Shut up," another whispered.

His gun leveled, Cameron hunted for a flash of cloth or wisp of hair. He sought a target—any target, now that the element of surprise had been blown.

The once-sleeping man wore camouflage like a soldier, and it forced Cameron to pick apart every shape in the undergrowth. New windows flashed open with every shift of his weight. Sticks, logs, sprigs of grass—the men would probably be lying down or crouching. They'd be buried in the thickest cover.

"Squeech!" a shrill voice squealed under Cameron's feet. He stumbled back. The little girl, Leah, scrambled away from him, gagged and awash in terror. He'd stepped on her. His head jerked up in alarm. The raiders had certainly heard the squeal and they'd be looking his way.

"If you don't surrender now, we're coming in shooting," Isaiah yelled again. "We're from the Rockville militia and we're going to shoot you without a trial unless you drop your guns and come into the clearing."

It was a clever gambit, Cameron admitted, but it'd have the raiders looking in all directions. He wasn't nearly as safe as he'd planned, and he hadn't seen so much as a clump of hair dance in the breeze since his target flushed. The three marauders lay low in the duff, and low meant invisible.

The little girl scurried away on hands and knees. Cameron couldn't afford to watch her go. Taking his eyes off the raiders' whispered voices could prove fatal. Then the three went silent. Cameron strained for the slightest shush of grass or crackling of a twig. If they remained still, and if he moved through the brush, he wouldn't see them until he was right on top of them. He was ten yards from the trampled-down bed, which meant they were likely very close. His best play was to wait for Isaiah to do whatever Isaiah would do, no matter how long that took. Cameron stopped, waited and feared.

The adrenaline had already hit him in the back of the head like a cricket bat when Isaiah yelled and the sleeper bolted. Now, the juice turned sour in his bloodstream. His legs wobbled and his breath came in strangled swallows. At best, the riflescope was milky and blurred around the edges. With a horse's dose of stress galloping around in his head, all he saw in the scope was green blobs and watery patches. The optic became an utter liability—a pencil hole punched in wet newsprint. Without iron sights, he'd have to see the threat with the naked eye, find it in the shitty optic, then shoot. It'd take a long, long time.

The raiders whispered again. He placed them a little better. Twenty-five yards out, under the trunk of the thickest cottonwood.

"Gwaaah!" Isaiah bellowed and crashed through the branches. Motion flickered in the weeds. A man's head—red, turbulent hair stuck out from under a black beanie cap. The horrible scope forced Cameron to lean against a tree trunk to steady himself. The red hair came into focus in the wet hole of the optic.

*Boom!* Cameron's rifle barked.

*Boom-boom-boom, boom, boom, boom-boom. Zzzzt. Boom.*

Cameron's legs folded like a rusted-out camp chair. He forced them, *willed them*, to do their job. He pushed up and rose against the gnarled bark of a cottonwood. His eyes flicked from knot to knot of shaded glen, mistaking sticks and logs for the gun barrel that would end his life.

A crouching man rose and aimed in the direction where Isaiah had rushed them. Cameron found him in the scope and pressed the trigger, but the trigger refused to budge. *Had it rusted solid?*

Cameron glanced down. The safety knob looked weird. He crouched to repair his rifle.

He ran the bolt and an empty, brass cartridge popped out, cartwheeled through the air and disappeared in the thick grass. He hadn't reloaded after his shot at the redhead. He'd dropped to the ground instead. He had no idea if he'd hit him. He hadn't even run his bolt. Something felt knocked askew in his brain, and he felt like a visitor in his own body.

His hands eased the bolt forward. He could feel the liquid resistance of another cartridge sliding into the breach then snicking home. He came up out of his crouch. The man with the black assault rifle crept toward Isaiah, more upright now. More confident.

Cameron centered the crosshairs on his chest and squeezed.

The rifle barked and the man vanished.

*Boom-boom-boom-boom-boom-boom-boom-boom-boom-boom.*

The bitterbrush around Cameron scythed apart with incoming rounds. He flopped face-down in the sawgrass. Bits of bark and chaff thickened the dust motes like a fairy war. Bullets came in waves, scores of them chopping through the thicket like invisible machetes. His face pressed into the understory. He smelled dark soil and sage. Gunpowder and sweat.

Some gauzy part of his mind knew that the pauses in the maelstrom were his enemy changing thirty-round magazines, but his legs refused to do anything useful with the information. The bullets zipped and hacked through wood and stem, little-by-little reducing the thicket to mulch.

*Da-boom!* Another shot echoed from the forest to the desert and back. The rifle fire from the marauders ceased. A man screamed, long and ceaseless, like an old fashioned train whistle. Another man moaned. Cameron pressed his face deeper down into the black soil.

"Cameron...are you alive?" Isaiah called from beyond the world of dank leaf litter and raw terror.

Cameron's muscles were locked down like a ship in the storm, every joint seized in a curl of self-protection. At first, Cameron couldn't even make his jaw function. When he finally forced it to unlock, his voice refused to obey. If he made a sound, the maelstrom might resume.

But he wasn't shot. He knew that much for certain. There was no dull pulsing of hashed flesh. He'd been shot before, and he remembered the pain. He was still whole at the moment. His body was hollowed out by starvation, but no blood leaked out of him.

The thought of food gripped him even tighter than his fear of having his head blown open. In the middle of a gunfight, sex, looming death, it didn't matter. Food was his god. His holy creed.

His salvation. The raiders would have some food, probably. They might be dead or wounded, and if so, he could eat their food.

Cameron crawled to his knees and looked around. More light poured through the canopy than before. It was mid-morning.

"Cameron?" Isaiah called for him, but his voice wheezed and tapered.

Nobody was shooting and there was a chance they'd won, but how was he supposed to know for sure? Isaiah was probably shot and the girl might be shot too. The marauders had fired hundreds of rounds in every direction. Cameron sure as hell wasn't going to rush over and attend to Isaiah. The hero had been knocked out of him by the apocalypse months ago.

He'd needed to locate the three marauder assholes before he did anything else. Their food wouldn't be far from them.

Cameron army-crawled on his hands and knees through the shattered green and toward where he'd heard them whispering. There were no whispers now, but that could mean a lot of things. He wasn't going to jump to conclusions. He'd only barely survived. His consciousness wobbled and memory intruded on the tiny battlefield.

"Don't stand around giving each other hand jobs until the game's good-and-proper won," his dad used to say, way-too-loud, when ten-year-old Cameron's Pop Warner football team was winning a game at half-time. The other parents always treated his dad to sidelong glances, even though Cameron was typically one of the best players. His old man was one of "those parents" at games, and if he were totally honest, Cameron might be a similar parent now, with his own boys.

"Don't stand around giving yourself a hand job," Cameron whispered to himself as he stalked the blown-apart grove. "The game's not good-and-proper won yet."

Ahead, through the grass, he saw a boot against the base of a tree. It was attached to a leg, both motionless. The camouflage pant cuff had slid up to expose a white tube sock and a hairy leg. Cameron pushed his rifle out in front like a spear, finger on the trigger. He felt fairly certain he'd racked the bolt this time. He believed he had three bullets left.

A man stared back at him from the ground. His expression was difficult to read, but it seemed to ask some mundane question like, "Did you remember to pack the salt shaker when we left camp?"

Cameron noted the red hair. The black beanie was gone. The back of the man's head had been raggedly removed. Another dose of adrenaline climbed up his spine. Cameron shivered. It was the emotional shockwave of victory. He'd slain this man. Definitively.

He struggled to re-engage his brain. He needed to think about what to do next. Isaiah called out for him every minute or two, but Cameron filed it away under "not my fucking problem."

*A better weapon.* Of course. He needed a better weapon.

Cameron slid up behind the red-haired corpse and used it like a protective sandbag. There was an AR-15 next to the body in the dirt. He didn't think the guy had shot it before Cameron clipped him in the dome, but he slid the magazine out of the receiver and checked. A stack of brass stared back at him from the depths of the curved magazine. He couldn't tell how many rounds, but it was more than a few. Enough, probably. And the rifle's scope was modern, open and clear. A little, red light gleamed in the middle of the optic. Cameron dumped his Mosin-Nagant in the dirt.

He took his time searching the man's body. It was a damned treasure trove of equipment. These bastards had probably improved their gear with every home invasion. Redhead had tricked himself out like a special forces operator.

He forced himself to stuff the foil-wrapped energy bar that'd come from the man's pocket, still warm, into his own pocket. For now, Cameron must attend to the threat of death. He needed to find the vipers in the lawn before he turned his eyes to the chicken coop. He folded himself back to the ground, unwilling to even crawl along on his knees for fear of having his head blown off.

With the AR-15 cradled in his arms, he crabbed along the contours of the earth like a centipede. After fifteen minutes of slow, fruitless slithering, he came upon a helmet on the ground and a bedroll beside it. He ignored the supplies, strewn about, and followed the tamped grass away from the sleeping place. He kept his belly tight to the nap of the ground with his dick dragging behind it. The adrenaline came in waves and he forced his mind to slow its mad churning.

A shape materialized in a shaft of light, five yards ahead. The bottom of a boot. It shifted, tilted, then returned to upright.

*Alive!*

The adrenaline hit hard again, like a miserable drug trip that refused to end. He could see no other boot, which made no sense to his addled brain. A man—probably wounded—lay on the ground, the sole of his boot pointed toward Cameron. But he could see nothing else.

If he came up to his knees, the third guy might shoot him. If he shot at the boot, the other guy might rush him. Cameron should've taken the redhead's big knife, but even if he had, how would he kill a man from under his foot?

*Screw it,* Cameron surrendered to the adrenaline.

*Blam, blam, blam, blam!*

He riddled the bottom of the boot with bullets, probably sending lead up through the guy's ballsack. The echoes died and the copse of trees returned to silence. The boot stilled. A bullet had punched a hole in the middle of the tread.

"Cameron?" Isaiah moaned.

He ignored the plea. Cameron's every sense tuned to the minuscule sounds of the thicket. The fall of a stick. The chirrup of a bird. The susurration of the cottonwood leaves. Nobody came to kill him.

"Cameron?"

He had no idea what ground he'd covered and what ground he hadn't. From face-in-the-dirt, he had the opposite of a bird's-eye-view. He'd been slinking around for thirty minutes. He had no better plan, so he slid toward Isaiah's voice—fifty yards away.

"Cameron, is that you?"

It dawned on him that his biggest threat, at this moment, was probably Isaiah. His compatriot was undoubtedly pointing a gun in his direction.

*Two down. One to go.* If he found one more guy, he'd be good.

Cameron loud-whispered, "Don't shoot Isaiah. I'm coming to you. Cover me."

He army-crawled into a dried-out side stream of the river, carved in the sand and lately filled with Indiangrass. He slid through a wet patch, reached for the edge of the depression and touched cloth. The gun scrabbled into his hands and he shoved at the body with the flash suppressor at the end of the barrel. The corpse budged, then rolled back to its resting position. Cameron exhaled and wiped his forehead with his arm. It was the third guy, dead.

"Isaiah, I'm right here. Don't shoot."

"Okay. I got two of 'em," Isaiah yelled back.

Encouraged, Cameron climbed up into a crouch, then onto his feet. His head spun round-and-round as blood rushed to his legs and away from brain. He staggered up, focused his eyes with effort, and took in the thicket.

The rifle flew to his shoulder even before he knew why.

Another raider.

This man, in camouflage like the others, sprawled backward over a huge, fallen log. Some greedy monster had taken an immense bite out of his neck. Wet blood coated the cottonwood log. He lay back over the log an impossible, gymnastic contortion.

The adrenaline receded and left behind a fierce ringing in Cameron's ears.

There'd been *four* raiders, not three. There must've been a man hanging back, shadowing his friends. Searching for followers. Covering their movement. It explained why they'd been so cavalier about making noise.

Fear induced vertigo struck Cameron and somewhere his body found reserves for yet another adrenaline dump. By some miracle the marauder following the group last night had not detected him and blown out his brain stem. His scheme to push the risk onto Isaiah had been a joke. He was alive by sheer, dumb, luck. He grabbed at a tree trunk to keep his feet under him.

"Cameron, I'm hurt." Isaiah's voice shook him out of his terror. He'd come very close to dying in the last twelve hours. He'd never been safe. Not for a second.

"They shot me. Twice, I think. Where's Leah?"

Cameron slung the rifle across his back and looked Isaiah over. He was sitting up in a slump, against a dead log that smelled of mildew. There was a hand-size blood patch above his hip and blood dripping down his left pant leg. The gray tint to his face made his blond hair seem almost orange. He'd lost a lot of blood, probably out the back of the gut wound.

"Find Leah, now, please," Isaiah plead. "We'll take care of this later." He waved the back of his hand across his belly and leg.

Cameron didn't want to look for the girl. He was frankly afraid of what he might find. He shook his head, brought the gun around, and began to search the copse of trees in a more-or-less systematic fashion.

*What if there were five of them?*

He shook away the worry. A fifth guy would've fled.

*What if Rockville heard the shots and sent a posse?* Shots were common along the highway, and they were at least a half-mile from the town.

He couldn't let minor threats paralyze him. He needed to get food in his gut before someone else came. He could accomplish anything with a little food in his belly.

Each raider had slept beside a rucksack loaded with food and critical gear—an inconceivable treasure. The packs had the look of well-oiled systems, perfected over the course of many raids, dozens of gunfights and lots of killing. These guys were all about "speed over security" as he'd once heard a Navy SEAL say in an action show. Cameron had won this conflict through sheer luck.

"And your luck tapped out, buddy," he mumbled to the dead mens' gear.

He consolidated the packs in the center of the sleeping area, not wanting to get the bounty too close to Isaiah. He tore into a package of fancy, health-nut fig bars and folded one into his mouth. Blueberry-flavored. The sugars and carbs caused a pain storm on his teeth and tongue. He swallowed. The pilot wave of energy traveled down his esophagus and hit his stomach like fireworks. He could feel calories pulsing into his bloodstream. Moments later, the tiny packets of energy set his cells on fire. Arms, legs, chest. His head buzzed with ragged power. *Calories!* His body trembled.

"Did you find her?" Isaiah's shout broke with a cry.

"I'm still looking," Cameron answered. Searching for gear was the best way to search for the girl, too.

"Daddy?" the girl's voice called out.

"I'm here, darling," Isaiah shouted with relief. "Come to my voice. Hurry."

Cameron unslung his rifle and moved to intercept her. Maybe she was being followed. He paused, turned back to the pile of packs and grabbed two more fig bars and stuffed them in his pocket with the energy bar from earlier.

The girl thrashed through the underbrush. Cameron crouched and listened. No one followed.

He found her at her father, fretting over his wounds. Isaiah lifted his shirt and she stared at the small hole, pulsing slightly in a fleshy pool of watery blood.

"I think it'll be all right. It barely hurts," Isaiah comforted his daughter.

"Eat these. Both of you." Cameron handed a fig bar to Leah, then one to Isaiah. Leah took hers and held it in front of her with stunned confusion in her eyes. Isaiah didn't reach out for his. He regarded Cameron with sadness.

"I'm afraid I'll throw up if I eat anything right now," he explained.

"No. You both need to eat. Right now." Cameron didn't know if he spoke from wisdom or shame. "Your bodies can't recover, heal or...anything without some energy. Force yourself to eat." Cameron unwrapped the fig bar for Isaiah. Leah tore into hers and ate in great, greedy swallows, barely chewing. Isaiah took his in a bloody hand and nibbled, chewed, then swallowed.

"You were right. That hit the spot," Isaiah muttered around bites. It was a discordantly-cheerful thing for a gut-shot man to say. Cameron grimaced. He truly wanted to hate Isaiah because he would not be carrying him back to the homestead.

Cameron decided when he heard the wounded man call out: Isaiah was a played-out hand of cards. He'd drawn twenty-two in the blackjack game of life and death. Dragging his gut-shot ass back to the homestead would wipe out any survival advantages from the little pile of food and the big pile of guns. Cameron was the sole survivor of this battle. This was his stuff. The spoils of war go to the victor, not the casualties. Survival went to the hard case, not the sob story. He'd not allow the group to waste focus and calories tending to Isaiah. They must prepare themselves for the next band of marauders.

"Cam..." Isaiah must've sensed the internal monologue. "I know it looks bad but I've got to get back to the homestead and heal up." The poor bastard actually managed a smile as he said, "Ruth Is pregnant: we're having another baby. She's going to need me."

Cameron looked away to hide the crush of feelings. "Well,

congratulations," he mumbled, looking off into the forest.

"Thanks. And, thank you, Brother Cameron, for getting her back."

It took Cameron a second to realize that Isaiah meant the daughter.

As soon as he could, he escaped them and returned to the pile of gear. Even with fresh calories pumping him full of life, he couldn't sort the feelings. He retreated to the granular arithmetic of survival: four AR-15 rifles, fifteen magazines, a hundred and ninety-six rounds of rifle ammunition. Four handguns, two revolvers, nine magazines, two pipe bombs. Knives, paracord, fire-starters. Two pump-style water filters and one gravity-style filter. Very little in the way of medicine or first aid supplies.

There wasn't as much food as he'd hoped. The raiders traveled light: Top Ramen, backpacker meals, survival rations, processed foods and cereals. It might be enough to get the clan healthy for a couple weeks, but not enough to get them to Spring. Not even close.

The guns and supplies would be game-changers, though. No longer would they be helpless mice, victims to passing hawks. Cameron would've traded all the water filters for a battery-powered DeWalt drill and a solar panel, and he'd definitely swap the handguns for food—which might be a possibility if Rockville had any food left.

They'd been so helpless, these past two months, that they'd been forced to maintain a no-contact rule with the warring towns. Better to keep their heads down than stick them up and get them shot off. Maybe with this level of firepower, they could trade even-Steven with Rockville or Hurricane.

He glanced over at Isaiah and his daughter. She nursed him with a water bottle. Cameron came over and made a show of checking out the gunshot wounds.

The gut wound had entered Isaiah's belly near the belly button, but had exited out the side. There was a chance it hadn't ripped a hole in his actual guts, but Cameron had no way of knowing. He knew enough to know that infection was likely in any case. It'd be certain death if the contents of the intestine blew into the body cavity. He'd watched enough Western movies to know a gut-shot wound was a slow, but inevitable death.

The calf wound hadn't bled very much, but might've been the worst of the two. The bullet went in-and-out, but the exit wound had chips of bone sticking out. The bullet had struck one of the lower leg bones. Cameron couldn't imagine how a blown-apart leg bone would be set, even in the best of times.

He needed time to think. The adrenaline rush had gone fetid and rank in his stomach, and the dry Top Ramen he'd wolfed down felt like it'd expanded to the size of a beach ball in his belly. The girl would be mewling over her doomed father until he died, so Cameron was on his own, schlepping newly-acquired gear back to the clan. He could use that time to plan.

Instead, he used the time to worry, and twist himself up in guilt, like a panicked rat in a beach towel.

*There was no way Isaiah was the father of the baby. Cameron had been screwing Ruth for two months. That baby had to be his.*

Ruth hadn't said anything to Cameron about being pregnant, but that didn't surprise him. He and Ruth never talked and they certainly hadn't discussed what their coupling meant. He assumed it meant nothing, which suited him fine.

*Now there was a baby. Didn't these polygamists understand birth control?*

Cameron hadn't thought about the women getting pregnant until this very moment. It wasn't something grown adults worried about in the modern world. It was something the women handled, medically, and needn't be discussed until someone *wanted* to have a child. This was fucking ridiculous.

Tough decisions needed to be made, and this time, Cameron would make them alone. First, he would get the supplies completely under his control. With Isaiah dying and the girl—possibly—lost to her family, he could return home and tell whatever story he chose, but he needed to cache the supplies in a secret spot, half-way home and well-concealed.

He knew of a jumble of logs, far enough from the homestead that Isaiah's other kids wouldn't happen upon them. Cameron shrugged into the straps of two, consolidated backpacks—both packed with food—picked up one of the AR-15s, and trudged toward his hiding spot.

He'd always imagined that survival would be a ruthless, dog-eat-dog affair and that he'd do whatever he must to safeguard his family, like all the apocalypse shows he'd watched: Mad Max, the Postman, The Road, The Walking Dead. He'd shout at the TV screen when they put emotion ahead of brute survival.

*"Comeon Rick! Why'd you tell those sonsabitches where you hid the cans of beans!"* He'd yell with the fourth Michelob Ultra in his hand. *"Lettum starve, you sappy idiot. They're gonna die anyway!"*

Yet when faced with a zombie apocalypse of his own, at every turn, Cameron had played it like one big, happy family. A hundred times he could've screwed the polygamists but he shared instead. He'd done, for the most part, his half of the work despite knowing damn well he shouldn't.

*But that ends now,* he scolded himself as he reached the log pile. The polygamist was not going to survive his wounds. Without iodine, antibiotics and a surgical team, Isaiah would never be anything more than a black hole where they sent calories to die.

Cameron cleared out the river sand and tumbleweeds from the stack of logs. He set the tumbleweeds aside to serve as camouflage later. He slid the backpacks into the cavity, then moved a log over the gap. Then he shoved tumbleweeds into the cracks.

"Are we going for help?" the little girl's voice shattered the silence.

Cameron startled and dropped the tumbleweeds. The rifle sling slid off his shoulder and into the crook of his arm. "What?" he said like a fool.

"Are we getting help for my dad?"

She'd followed him halfway back to the house. She looked at him with big, green eyes, like she could hear his thoughts.

Maybe kids always knew. Maybe they just didn't know how to say what they knew.

As a boy, Cameron had always known his dad was a prick—at least that's how he remembered it now. "Never a borrower, nor a lender be," his dad always said, as though it was in the Bible. When Cameron or his brother asked to stay the night at a friend's house, that's how his dad always said no—as if they'd be in debt to little Jimmy Whatshisface's mom if Cameron ate her ketchup meatloaf.

But kids always knew. Cameron had known, even back then. When you're a real prick there's no hiding it from the kids.

The girl stood still and watched as Cameron finished the camouflage job. He hadn't answered her question. Instead, he worked on his supply cache, despite the fact that it was no longer a secret.

He'd avoided thinking about his own dad these months of apocalypse. Cameron left Southern California in a mad rush on the precipice of chaos. He hadn't spared a worry for his dad. His old man didn't hit his mental radar until he and Julie reached Las Vegas. Cameron assumed he died in his carbon-copy bungalow in Pasadena, California, on his half-collapsed couch, surrounded by Louis L'amour books and cheap scotch.

His brother, Tommy, lived in Phoenix and the last time they spoke, while the world crumbled, Tommy was high-tailing it to their sister's survivalist compound in Utah. As far as Cameron knew, their dad died alone.

"But doesn't everyone die alone?" he thought he heard the little girl say.

"Huh?" Cameron pivoted back to her. *Had she read his mind*

*again?*

"Are their kids alone? Where are they?"

"What kids?" Cameron asked. He suddenly remembered why this little girl struck him as being so creepy. She was like the little blond in the movie Poltergeist who showed up silently behind her mom and stared, then said the damndest things.

"Their kids," Isaiah's daughter replied, pointing back to the thicket at the dead marauders.

At first, he chalked it up to her Quaker worldview. Every man she'd ever met over twenty-five years old had at least one wife and children. But then again, *where were their children?* Other than the redhead, all the marauders had been in their thirties or forties. Cameron had gone through their gear, so he knew them from the inside out. Porno mags, jewelry, booze, playing cards—he had a window into their cauterized souls and there hadn't been a single family picture.

*Neither a borrower nor a lender be.*

As he recalled the dead men's faces, he formed first an idea, and then a certainty: every one of the dead men had children, once upon a dream. When faced with the choice, when the shit hit the fan, they'd packed up and struck out on their own. Their kids had probably been at the ex-wife's place, doing small time in juvenile detention or running amok with the rioting masses when time came to pull stakes and make their way in this fucked up world. They'd left their kids behind. That's what a piece of shit does.

That's what his own dad had done. Sometime in the 1990s, his mom had gotten a little thick around the middle. Her womanly curves settled into Russian blockiness, as was the way with her people. She always came home smelling like Mexican food after shifts at the restaurant. Even as a boy, Cameron found that smell off-putting. His dad must've found it downright disgusting. *Fajita-fucking, every night. Take it or leave it.*

Family life in a three-bedroom in a cookie-cutter neighborhood in Anaheim must've caught up with the old man. He bailed.

There were other women, but probably no one specific. He'd thrown in the towel. He packed up his shit and moved to a one-bedroom in Pasadena where he didn't have to smell stale Mexican food in his bed.

Cameron finished hiding the cache, stopped and stared at her. She was a pretty little girl; green doe eyes, a pleasant face, glowing, ruby-tinted hair. He wondered if she had any Russian blood. Maybe she had the expanding-hip thing in her future like a genetic time-bomb. More likely she was English. Most of these religious nutjob-bers got their crazy from Puritan ancestors, at least that's what he'd seen on the History Channel.

"I think those men ditched their kids, sweetheart."

The girl—Leah—shuffled her feet. "A family stays together forever, unless someone commits a sin against the Holy Ghost. Committing a sin against the Holy Ghost is like spitting on God's wife. That person goes to Outer Darkness. Are we going back to get my dad?"

Cameron thought about his dad. Dead, on his precious couch, decomposing in the California heat, his cells collapsing one-by-one, dripping into that unsightly swale in the collapsing middle. His dad and that couch would be together forever, now, until Judgement Day, sins against the Holy Ghost or not.

Cameron's mom had inherited an expanding waistline from "her people." He wondered what he'd inherited from his dad. A lonely, meaningless death, most likely.

He reached out, put his hand on the girl's head and smiled. The calories had kicked in and he felt better than he had in weeks. She wasn't his daughter, but she felt like family anyway. Like a niece or a cousin's kid.

"Let's go get him," Cameron said. It sounded galactically stupid, but it felt like Christmas morning.

He slung his rifle and followed her back to the thicket.

# 14

## SAGE ROSS

**Donna Butterton Residence**
**Elgin, Oregon**

Sage laughed and tossed down the last of his beer. It was getting warm, anyway. The girl had been poking fun at Enterprise High—the only high school over in Wallowa County. Apparently, La Grande had beaten them in football ten years running. To call it a rivalry might be overstating things. Enterprise High pulled from three thousand residents and La Grande pulled from twenty-seven thousand. Raw math was on La Grande's side.

Talking to the girl—she'd said her name was Aimee—felt like taking a shower after working in the dust. She even smelled like civilization. Sage could listen to her prattle of local gossip for days. When she talked, he forgot about freezing to death up on Blue Mountain. He forgot about killing those men. Sitting with Aimee on her mother's couch felt like returning, finally, from war.

When he first came back from his recon mission into Wallowa County, Captain Chambers hailed him as a conquering hero, like a special forces soldier embedded in the captain's department for "high value missions." Apparently, they'd expected him to get picked up right away and sent directly back. The fact that he'd lasted three days, then returned with information on cattle numbers and general intel, catapulted Sage into the inner circle of the police department. When he reported about his meeting with Commissioner Pete, Captain Chambers leaned over his desk in disbelief.

"That self-righteous sonofabitch had a meeting with you?" Sage nodded, not sure what it meant. "I haven't been able to get him to talk to me since the meltdown—that stuck-up prick. Cattlemen are all like that." He sat back abruptly in his chair. "They think they're the only true cowboys. Unless you have a hundred head or more, you're not even a man to them."

After his successful recon mission into Wallowa, the department moved Sage into the town of La Grande, to a room at the Best Western hotel. They took him off the security duty roster. Instead, Sage worked out of the police station, though they hadn't given him anything specific yet to do. For the time being, he went for coffee and food from the town square, where the ladies ran a soup kitchen. The higher-ups in the department took Sage with them on important calls as a back-up gunman, like when they got reports of theft or trespassing by out-of-towners. They even issued him a Glock 17, nine millimeter sidearm.

The hundreds of rank-and-file officers—really more of a militia —called the captain and his close confidants "The Five." The Five were all high school buddies, had gone to La Grande High School, and had served in the La Grande police department for a decade or more. Sage became their mascot.

Sage's acquaintances from the militia started calling him "Number Six." Sage preferred that to "Stack," but it made him nervous when they said the "six" thing around one of the actual Five. He wasn't there to rock the boat. He'd promised his dad that he'd do whatever it took to survive, and serving, heads-down, loyal to the La Grande police department was as close to a sure thing as he'd probably find in America. He was not going to screw it up.

The fringe benefits, as it turned out, were out-of-this-world, and they included Aimee Butterton.

The Five, plus Sage, had taken their Sunday afternoon jaunt over to the town of Elgin, as was their custom. There, they visited the home of Donna Butterton and her daughters. The man of the house had passed away years before Black Autumn in a four-wheeler accident, but he'd left behind a beautiful wife and five gorgeous farmer's daughters, each with chestnut hair and sparkling green eyes. The youngest, Aimee, was still too old for Sage, but she seemed like she was into him, so he sat back and enjoyed the ride.

Sage had never had much trouble with the ladies. He was a trim, corded-arm teenage stud with a winning smile and a devil-may-care whip of the hair. His good looks and his dad's mansion bought him entré into any social circle he wanted, back in Utah.

Like every high school boy who won at the game of popularity, Sage knew deep down it was all bullshit. He hadn't done anything to be esteemed by anyone, and the ladies who flocked to him were seeing what he wanted them to see—decent genes and his dad's money.

Back then, he wasn't about to turn his back on a good thing, so he enjoyed rolling around with the hottest chicks; turning and burning through the Instagram Hall of Fame in his hometown of Oakview.

Then, one day, the cleaning lady found weed in the bottom of his dresser drawer. The maid belonged to some kind of uptight religion, so she went to Sage's dad with his baggie of skank. His dad freaked out, Sage cut loose, screaming obscenities at his old man, and got his ass packed off to the Olympic Peninsula to cool his jets with his grandma and grandpa. That's when Black Autumn put the smackdown on America and ruined it all.

Sage had long ago forgiven his dad for overreacting to the weed. He'd learned a lot about how the world really worked while surviving the mobs and the weather. Those days of being a rich prick with a pimped-out truck were ancient history. He missed his mom and dad so bad it made his bones ache.

Sitting on the couch with Aimee Butterton brought back the feel of home—those carefree high school years at the top of his game. She wasn't the hottest girl he'd been with, but her green, cheerful eyes made up for a lot.

"Where'd you get this beer?" Sage asked just to make conversation. He held up his bottle of Bud.

"The Captain had them brought by yesterday." She smiled. "Membership has its privileges." She waved her hand at the living room, but Sage didn't know what she meant. It seemed like an average living room in an average, rural home. Then he noticed: The Five had all disappeared.

They had been hobnobbing with Mrs. Butterton and the older daughters, but now the house had gone quiet. He heard a titter of laughter somewhere in the back of the sprawling ranch house.

They were all married men—The Five. They'd invited Sage, saying they were "dropping by the Buttertons'" to get an end-of-the-week drink. Rolling back the tape in his mind, each man had gravitated to his own young lady, almost like assigned seating. Captain Chambers drifted off with Mrs. Butterton. She'd met them at the door wearing the hell out of a pair of Levi's and it hadn't been long before she and the captain took their leave.

Men in power enjoyed the fruits. It'd probably been that way since mankind built a circle of huts and then asked the biggest man to stand guard. Undoubtedly, the big guy got a bigger share of lovin'.

The Five worked hard and took personal risks to keep Union County from flying off the rails. Sage had seen every one of them in physical confrontations, and he'd seen them kill men in the line of duty. It was a violent world, with dire consequences, and captain's men were the hard line between order and chaos. They deserved the chance to cut loose every now and again.

Aimee slid over on the couch, took Sage's beer out of his hand and set it on the glass-topped coffee table. Mr. Butterton, may he rest in peace, must've been a fly fisherman, because under the glass a wood-carved brook trout snapped up a blue-winged olive fly in a pretty, little diorama. Sage wondered if Mr. Butterton had carved it himself.

Aimee put her hand on his cheek and kissed him. Combined with the tang of the beer, her mouth tasted like a coconut chocolate bar. Her skin smelled like honeysuckle.

Sage's head swam. He put his hand on her waist and gripped her soft hip. She deepened the kiss and moaned. Her tongue reached in and traced the top of his mouth, hunting farther, tasting him.

She pulled away and smiled. She had perfect teeth—still some baby fat, even in her early twenties. He reeled a bit, imagining her naked.

She leaned back and tugged his hand, drawing him on top of her on the couch. Sage resisted, and looked around. None of The Five were in the living room or kitchen. He didn't want to cause problems. His gig with the police department was literally life-or-death for him, and Sage had flirted with death enough. The girl must've sensed his apprehension.

"They're with my sisters. I'm here for you. It's okay."

*What was the deal here?* Sage almost asked her, but thought better of it.

She eased him past the silence. "We're friends of the police department. We party a little at the end of the week. It's okay." Aimee pulled his hand down and set it on her ample breast. Sage let himself go but stopped in the middle of the kiss.

"Is there someplace we can go that's not so...open?" he asked.

She laughed again, stood up, straightened her blouse over her jeans, and led him by the hand out of the living room and down a hall.

---

AN HOUR LATER, Captain Chambers rapped on the door of the bedroom. Sage had already dressed. He and Aimee were chatting about his job with the department. She seemed fascinated with local gossip; who was being robbed, who was making trouble for the department, who was beating their wife. In a county barely over twenty-five thousand people, everyone eventually knew everyone.

"Time to get back to work," the captain spoke through the door.

"Yes, sir." Sage wondered if he'd done something wrong.

The Five plus Sage had driven in the same unmarked Chevy Suburban to the Buttertons. Now, Sage understood why they'd left their cruisers and personal cars at the office in La Grande. They couldn't park five squad cars in front of the Butterton ranch house on Sunday night without generating buzz among the locals.

On the road back to La Grande, the men laughed and joked about the Butterton girls.

The night was black as asphalt. The moon wouldn't be up for another two hours.

"I gotta tell you," Bill Raff bragged, "That Terra—she's a damned wildcat. Nothing like a young girl to get an old soldier like me upright and standing at attention. I mean, she gets turned on faster than a light switch. She's slicker too, right from the first. Zero foreplay. Right to business. More time for more that way, she says."

The men in the Suburban laughed and Sage laughed with them. Truth was, he'd felt awkward with Aimee. It was far from his first time. He'd lost count of how many by sixteen, but the setup at the Buttertons made him jumpy.

Other than laughing along with their stories of sexual conquest,

Sage remained silent. He'd never been in the military, or even worked in a crew of rough men. He'd heard his brother talk like these guys—he was a Marine Corps veteran—but the obscenity and carnality was unfamiliar ground. In a way, it liberated him, to hear men cut loose and speak like men; with no women to hear them, and no shame to fear.

The captain was obviously drunk, but he drove the suburban anyway. He didn't contribute much to the boasting and joking. Behind the wheel and in-charge of the department, he was above it all. When he finally spoke, the guys switched gears.

"We're doing pretty good on food," Chambers began, inter-rupting one of the men in the middle of regaling the others about how "down to get down" some local girl had been in high school. Captain Chamber's steady voice made it clear that this was going to be the only staff meeting that really mattered. "But we won't be good for long. We can't count on the Professor and his greenhouses to save us this winter. A lot can go wrong with greenhouses—my mom had one for years."

The men settled down and flipped into business-mode. Bill Raff offered a solution. "We can run more Klingons out of the county. You know—reduce our consumption to match our supply."

Captain Chambers raised a finger off the steering wheel. "We could, but every time we walk someone to the county line, we piss off more locals. Even a Klingon has a mom and dad, sisters, cousins and brothers. We can force people back into line, but it gets riskier the more we do it." It seemed clear he'd already made a decision and he wasn't really looking for suggestions.

"If Wallowa kicks in with their cattle, we'll have plenty, and there will be enough to jumpstart breeding in the spring. With Wallowa's cattle, we're all set. If they horde their cattle like they're doing now, they'll get stronger while we get weaker. By spring, we'll be half-starved rag dolls. They'll be fat and happy."

Reggie Fletcher snorted. "Yeah, but Wallowa can't never take us down. They're pissant-small. They can barely field a defensive line."

Sage realized he was talking about high school football, not combat. Everything with these guys seemed to come back to football.

"You need to think bigger," the captain corrected Reggie. "They won't have to take down Union County. They only need to take *us* down." He made a circle in the air with his finger. "From what Stack here tells me, Pete Lathrop over in Wallowa is telling people we're un-American, that we don't follow the Constitution. He sounds like he's getting ready to stage a mutiny against us, over here in Union."

"Commissioner Pete's got a lot of family in Union County. That's true," Reggie said, bootlicking his boss.

The captain continued his train of thought. "If they wait until we're suffering over here, and they're healthy over there, people will begin to think that maybe Pete Lathrop's got it right; that we're un-American for defending our county."

"That's easy for them to say," Bill Raff nearly shouted, "we do all their fighting for them. We sealed off Union County to outsiders, so they ain't got no problems with trespassers. There's no way for outsiders to get over the mountains and fuck with their cattle. They should pay us for doing their policing, instead of paying that fat prick Tate. They owe us!" he roared. Bill Raff had been drinking a lot more than just beer, Sage concluded.

"Yup," Captain Chambers agreed. "they don't have to invest much in defense because we do it for them. They have it easy, tucked in the back of Wallowa Valley, while we deal with the interstate, cutting across us like a clothesline."

"They should pay us in cattle," Kevin Tursdale chimed in.

The captain shook his head, backlit by the suburban's headlights carving the road. "They're not going to do that so long as Pete Lathrop is the King of Wallowa County. He's the reason they sealed off the road and he's the reason they won't talk to us about trade. He sits on his high throne at the back of the valley, surrounded by fifty-thousand head of cattle and he watches us eat ourselves into oblivion. All he has to do is wait us out, and he wins. No doubt, he plans to take over Union too, and he'll do it when our people are in a bad way."

The men fell silent. The road clicked by under the tires and the alcohol-fogged thoughts coalesced like a virus gathering itself for an onslaught. Even a newcomer like Sage could follow the captain's logic: a lot of people in Union County were already hungry. Not the farmers or the ranchers, but the city people had been on rations for weeks. They stood in bread lines and soup lines or they didn't eat. It was a hell of a lot better than in Portland, but the kind of people standing in line for food weren't the kind of people who counted their blessings. They complained, given half a chance. They were fertile minds for revolution. They couldn't do much, the Klingons, but they could agitate.

"We should hit him while we're still strong. Hit Commissioner Pete, I mean."

Reggie said the words, but Captain Chambers had all but put them in his mouth. Sage saw now that the conversation had been a carefully scripted, meandering journey to reach this conclusion: they needed to remove their rival, and they needed to do it soon.

Sage felt a chill go up his spine. He remembered a moment, while he ate his burger in Lostine. He and Commissioner Pete shared a laugh with the lady setting up the tables. Joan, Sage remembered her name. She'd made a comment about how men thought they ruled the world, but women ruled the men. Pete had given Sage a goofy, knowing look that seemed to say, "someday, you'll understand."

Sage almost spoke up in the Suburban—almost said something to slow the freight train of indignation that'd overtaken The Five. Then, he remembered the promise he'd made to his father.

*He would do everything necessary to survive and make it back home.*

Pete Lathrop, over in Wallowa, could tend to his own survival. Truth and justice were not Sage's job. Keeping a promise to his father trumped all questions of truth and honor.

He'd grown up enough, in the last two months, to understand he couldn't right the wrongs of this grated-flesh world. A man couldn't throw a stick in America without hitting a kid dying of dysentery or an old lady being raped. A tidal wave of defilement had washed over the once-pristine land, and now the most noble pursuit was to breathe another day, eat another meal.

In Sage's case, he would keep his promise to his father, and keep his damned mouth shut.

## 15

MAT BEST

**Creek Camp**
**Outside McKenzie, Tennessee**

The Creek Camp founders arrived, and Mat asked them for a private audience.

"I have information for you—something that I won't be telling the other camps. They lack the leadership to take advantage of it, and this opportunity should not go to waste," Mat said, rolling out his best CIA-inspired performance.

"You have our attention, Sergeant Best," said a man with unkempt hair and a ragged, handlebar mustache.

Mat fired up the engine on the Bullshit Express. "I first heard this story back when I was at Basic in Fort Knox. I assumed it was one of those army legends that gets repeated one grunt generation to the next, but then I started to see a consistent pattern. I actually did a little research at the base library and I was surprised to find out it was real."

Mat launched into the story he'd concocted with the help of

Deputy Rickers. Mat told of a trail of military depots dating back to the beginning of the twentieth century. As the tale went, the U.S. Cavalry positioned supply depots every twenty miles to support army mule trains crossing the Old West to San Francisco. They passed through Tennessee and Fort Knox before venturing out over Indian lands.

The next part would be the pitch; the mule train bit was weird enough to create a hook—to generate intrigue. But he needed to put meat on the bones of the fable.

Mat dropped his voice to a conspiratorial whisper, "I heard versions where the depots, at one time, held thousands of gallons of whiskey or bars of gold. One guy claimed the depots hid bales of confiscated marijuana." His audience fidgeted. He was in danger of losing them. "When I mentioned the story to one of the McKenzie deputies who also served in the Army, he said, 'Those depots are real, and they're in places nobody would look. Small towns and out-of-the-way side roads. The closest one is thirty miles north of here outside a one-horse town called Sedalia. We should go up there and clear it out,' the deputy said."

Mat had their full attention.

"The depots belonged to FEMA before the economy collapsed. It's where they stored the government reserve; supplies hidden away for local disasters. They're in nondescript, heavily-secured warehouses, packed to the rafters with dry food, HAZMAT suits and medical supplies."

Mat took a breath and forced his shoulders to relax. "Crazy story, right? Mule train supply depots still operational in the twenty-first century? I was skeptical myself." He paused and let the drama build. "Three days ago, I checked out the depot in Sedalia with Rickers. It was there. Untouched. Dry food. Water purifiers. N95 masks."

Mat paused to let it sink in. "We brought back all of the medical supplies for our town clinic. We have our own pig farms, so it's not worth the exposure to make multiple trips with semi trucks to bring back the food. Plus, a lot of it's expired."

Dr. Hauser looked unconvinced. "If you can't transport the food, what makes you think we can?"

Mat looked at each of them. They were good people. These were the rats who cooperated, which was why they were more likely to buy his story.

*I'm killing them with a story. It's slower than botulism, but I'm killing them just the same.*

It was better than poisoning, and better than starvation, and he wasn't lying about one thing: there was food there. Mat had gone to Sedalia and placed the food on the racks himself. Alongside the food he left maps, FEMA brochures and fake evidence that the next warehouse was twenty miles away. By the time the rats figured out the story was fiction, they'd be marooned fifty miles from McKenzie and too hungry to walk back.

"You can move your camp to Sedalia until you exhaust the warehouse. Your base of operations is mobile. Ours isn't. But let me know by dusk if you're going. If you're not interested, I'll pass the word to the Buford Woods camp."

Mat struggled to read their faces. He closed his argument by adding, "Send scouts to the first depot. See for yourselves. I brought five gallons of gas so a couple guys can drive there, and maybe bring a truck load back for you to test." Mat shook the red, plastic gas can that he'd brought with him.

The rats exchanged glances: their faces filled with trepidation and hope.

Hauser spoke. "Thank you, Sergeant Best. We'll get back to you by nightfall."

CANDICE STARED at the bloody mess until her eyes got dry and sticky.

The rabbits in the glass cages were twisted into knots. The blood from their mouths and anuses striped their white, fluffy coats. Candice's stepfather had left the dead rabbits in there, now going on three days. There was no reason to remove them, he explained. The fan loop was air-tight and the experiment had been successful. The mustard gas worked. The dead rabbits could rot in their cages forever.

Inside the HAZMAT suit, her stepfather couldn't see her gnawing fear. She'd been trapped alone with him for forty-eight hours. They slept only in snatches, waking every two hours to climb back into the HAZMAT suits and start a new batch of poison.

They worked together to combine the sulfur dichloride with ethylene in a gentle heating process that required a two-hour ramp up to temperature. The sulfur came from the lumber yard, and her stepfather had the ethylene in barrels from his days pretending to cook meth.

As the solution warmed, the reddish-amber sulfur dichloride climbed up a spiral glass condenser and dripped into a bulbous flask of ethylene. Heated slowly enough, the two chemicals didn't react. They combined gently into the yellow slurry that they poured onto cookie sheets in a plastic-sealed room Jensen had divided off from the rest of the basement. Several times a day, the pair suited up and scraped the dry mustard dust into glass jars.

They were both so exhausted, after the two day marathon of lab work, that Jensen didn't even take time to put his hands down her pants. When the HAZMAT suits came off, they both went directly to sleep. For Candice, the terrifying, sweaty work inside the rubber suit was almost worth the reprieve.

IT WAS a little before midnight and Mat stood in the front yard of his house speaking with Carlos Cabrera and a member of the perimeter team, Mary Tribble.

Before the collapse, Mary had shared mechanic duties with her husband at the town auto repair shop. Two days before the nuclear attack on Los Angeles, Mr. Tribble had taken their son to Atlanta on a father-son trip, with the intent of visiting parts suppliers to make the trip tax-deductible. When the bomb hit, they cut the trip short, but never arrived home. Her last contact had been a selfie of her husband and son, via text message at a service station outside of Murfreesboro, Tennessee. She ended her story looking at the south-eastern sky.

"Google said they'd be home in three hours. Just a little traffic, it said."

*Crack! Crack!* Two gunshots echoed, almost on top of one another.

Mary started to say "Did you hear that?" But Mat had already keyed his radio.

"All checkpoints report in. Where did those shots come from?"

Eight checkpoints reported. The gunshots didn't come from their locations. Each checkpoint offered a guess as to the direction of the gunshots. The consensus clarified. The shots came from the south end of town. Reedy Grove again.

Mat called up the QRF then ran inside for his kit.

"Where are you going?" William asked from the gloom of the living room. The boy always asked, as though by asking he could prevent Mat from leaving someday.

"Um. We're headed to check out a couple gunshots on the south end of town. Did you hang out with Candice today?" Mat made conversation while kitting up.

"Nope," William replied tersely. "She says she's working on a lab project with her stepdad. She's bailing on me too."

Mat hated it when the boy played the victim card. He had every right to paint himself as a victim, but it wouldn't serve him well as a man. Not in this brave, new world.

"Hmpf." Mat knew what Candice must be doing. She and Jensen were making poison gas. The days when teenagers were spared hard, dangerous work had vanished in the rearview mirror like the blank side of a sign. "It's true—what she told you. She and her dad are working on something important for the town. Give her a couple days. She'll come up for air soon."

The poison gas drew Mat's thoughts back to town security and the gunshots.

Mat rattled his plate carrier vest in the dark. "Gotta run."

"Okay," William muttered.

Six minutes later, Mat jogged into the parking lot of the Walgreens. Eight men from the QRF arrived a minute later on foot, and a minute after that, two deputies on horseback. Sheriff Morgan had converted the empty lot next to the sheriff's department into stables.

"Why only two horses?" Mat asked one of the deputies.

"Only these two have been re-shod for paved roads."

"Alright," said Mat, while motioning the mounted deputies over. "There've been no additional shots. It might've been a negligent discharge or someone killing a possum." People weren't supposed to discharge firearms in town, not because of gun safety concerns, but because it forced town security to mount a "where'd it come from" poodle circus every time someone torched off a round.

Even with the outer town consolidating inside the HESCO line, a lot of homes in McKenzie were vacant. People had combined households with kin or friends for mutual protection; they preferred to share resources, security and heat. Having your "own place" wasn't the advantage it'd once been. Privacy was a luxury nobody could afford.

In their downtime, the QRF went around town and tied yellow ribbons outside occupied homes, but they hadn't been particularly systematic about the process. This side of town hadn't yet been marked. They'd have to check every house's front and rear yard, knock, then enter if there was no response.

After clearing just three homes, Mat decided to wake up the rest of the QRF. It was going to be a long night.

Before he could call it in, his team radio barked. "Sarge, we found 'em. 421 Whittle Lane."

Found *them* he'd said. That wasn't good. "Do we need the medics?" asked Mat.

"No survivors."

"Fuck," Mat swore. "On our way." Mat's team of four broke into a jog toward Whittle Lane.

421 Whittle Lane was at the end of a cul de sac. One of the QRF and two deputies stood outside with the horses.

"How many dead? Do we know who lives here?" Mat asked Deputy Wiggin who stood outside holding the reins of his horse.

"Five dead. Monroe and Davis families were here together, but..." The deputy went silent as Juan Cabrera's QRF team exited the house. They stormed down the porch, gripping their ARs like pitchforks.

"Raiders," Juan Cabrera seethed.

"Have you cleared the neighborhood?" Mat asked, business before fury.

"Yes. Only one other family—at the far end of the street." Cabrera pointed.

"Who's inside? Five dead?"

"Seven dead, actually. Kids too." Cabrera agitated in the spare light of the overcast night. The "battle rattle" of his plate carrier jostled with pent-up ferocity. The heat of vengeance radiated off him like a pulsar. He had kids of his own.

Cabrera described four dead adults and three dead children. The bodies lay where they were killed. Two of the adults were in bed, and all the children were in bedrolls on the floor. Dan Monroe was the only victim found out of his bed. The fourth adult corpse was filthy, and it gave off a corrupt odor, more than blood and the stink of bowels and bladder—one of the murderers.

There was one missing adult from the dead family. In old America, an investigator's first thought would be that any missing adults would be prime suspects for the murders. But the house had been ransacked. It'd clearly been raided from the outside; murder by strangers, not a family member on a domestic violence rampage. Somewhere in McKenzie there was a man or a woman working at a clinic, or helping a friend repair a water pipe and that person had just lost their entire family. They didn't even know it yet.

Mat went inside and surveyed the scene. "This guy's a rat," Mat said as he kicked the reeking man over. "Looks like the raiding party bludgeoned the family in their sleep. Mr. Monroe got to his gun. He killed this one and another rat shot him. I guess they were hoping to kill them all quietly, then take their time looting the house."

"QRF Four to Sarge," the radios growled.

"Go for Sarge."

"The other three houses on the street are empty except, well, we're at 427 Whittle. It's the Simms. It's bad." Mat knew Marjorie Simms from security committee.

One of the QRF inside the Simms place inadvertently "stepped on" his push-to-talk button. Everyone on the channel heard his ragged inhale and a shuddering exhale. It sent a chill down Mat's spine. Then the guy continued. "They killed them all. All of them, even the baby."

———

WITH THE COMING of the wet, steel-sky morning, word of the murder of the Simms, Monroe and Davis families flushed throughout the town. Around nine a.m., an agitated crowd gathered outside of the McKenzie Sheriff's office. News traveled even without cell phones and internet; the small town "wireless" had hummed for a hundred years before electronics, and murder most foul sent neighbors scurrying to their mutual defense.

Mat Best stood next to Sheriff Morgan on the front steps of the station, looking out on two hundred angry citizens.

"They want blood. We need to come up with a response, or one of these hotheads is going to lead a mob against the Brashear Camp."

"Maybe we should let 'em," Mat said, deadpan. Anger was the only thing keeping him standing. He'd been awake for sixty hours. "Me and my boys could use the break."

The sheriff didn't bother to reply. They both knew Mat wasn't going to allow pissed-off vigilantes to do his job. Half of them would accidentally shoot the other half in the confusion of battle.

The closest camp, and the most likely culprit, was squirreled away in the middle of the Brashear woods, a quarter mile beyond the south edge of town. Mat didn't think there was any question what they should do. His QRF was gearing up for an assault. "We have to hit them—if for no other reason than to show the refugees what happens when they murder our people. They have to know that hunger is better than bringing down our wrath."

"Wrath?" The sheriff tucked in the front of his shirt. "I don't condone revenge missions."

"Whatever you want to call it, the rats need to know we're pissed. The HESCO's only one-third done. We can't protect the town from night raids. We gotta show them that we hit back *hard*. We're Israel and they're Palestine. We're screwed if they don't fear us. Deputy Stamets traced the raiders back to Brashear Drive and that's where we should strike."

"What if Stamets is wrong? What if we shoot up a bunch of families that had nothing to do with the killings?" Sheriff Morgan countered.

"We'll never know, and the message will still be sent." Mat

shrugged. "Intel is never ironclad." Mat knew it was his exhaustion talking, and his anger.

*But fuck it.* War and anger went together like pizza and beer. There was a yawning gulf between law enforcement and war—the difference between violence dolloped out like castor oil medicine and violence heaped upon your enemy to make them rue the day they picked up arms against you. The defense of the town was never going to be a law enforcement gig. It was always going to be war.

"What are your rules of engagement?" the sheriff asked with resignation in his voice.

"We'll kill whoever passes for leadership in the camp. We determine who's responsible for the raid and cut them down where they stand. This won't be investigate-arrest-convict."

"And the rest of the Brashear wood refugees?"

"It would be nice if the bad guys wore name tags, but this is war. We'll try to limit the mission to leadership, or what passes for leadership. But lines blur and the enemy gets a vote as to how things go down. What I know: we have to put the fear of God in them. That's a given."

Sheriff Morgan looked out over the crowd. It had swelled to three hundred, and more streamed down the streets toward the station.

"The fear of God," Morgan said in a low voice. "I wonder who will learn that lesson." He took a deep breath and held it for a second, then released it with a sigh. His sad, jowly face hardened as he turned to Mat.

"Okay. But help me preserve the heart of this town."

"The inner town?" Mat asked.

"Not the center of town. The *heart* of the town. We will not survive if we become frightened, vicious animals. We're trying to preserve civilization here, not just our lives."

Mat hadn't been hired to preserve civilization. He'd been hired to keep citizens alive and to protect assets. Part of him knew the old lawman was right—the part of Mat's mind that noticed the women in battle and saw imaginary, colored shawls and windswept burkas where none existed. But Mat had no idea how to accomplish the two opposing goals: preserving civility and crushing aggression. He settled for soothing Morgan's concerns.

"I hear you sheriff. We'll make our statement, eighty-six the murderers and get back to town."

The sheriff nodded. "I'm coming too. Stick me with a team—low man on the totem pole." The sheriff turned and vanished into the station, probably to gather his fighting gear.

---

TWO HOURS later Mat stood in the Walmart parking lot in front of fifty men and one woman. Gladys Carter was the only woman to volunteer for the strike mission. Mat had declined over a hundred men from town, and opted instead for a smaller fighting force with more control and experience.

Mat split his force into two with a simple plan. They were too tired for L-ambushes or complex flanking maneuvers. They'd come at the camp from two fronts, set at forty-five degrees from each other, and they'd become a single firing line when they hit the edges of the camp. He couldn't afford much of a blocking force. If their blood got up, a blocking force would shoot their own guys coming through the trees. It was better to flush the camp like a pheasant hunt.

Mat posted two of the town's best marksmen with scoped hunting rifles overlooking the highway. They would take down armed targets that attempted to cross. Those had been Mat's orders: "Shoot refugees who look like they probably attacked the town."

Mat's forces had yellow caution tape tied to their hats and around their necks. It looked patently uncool, but would look cooler than a bunch of body bags from friendly fire incidents.

They entered the woods from Hansen Lane at two o'clock in the afternoon. Fifty yards into the forest, one of his men slipped and fell.

"Damn rats don't even bury their shit."

"Quiet," Mat ordered.

The "go signal" would be the bullhorn. Team One, led by Juan Cabrera, radioed that they'd reached the fringe of the camp. Mat signaled the man on his team with the bullhorn to get ready. The two flush lines met in the middle and everyone came on-line for the final assault.

"All stations, this is Mat. Execute, execute, execute."

The bullhorn blared, "This is punishment for last night's attack on town. Stay away from town."

Even before they reached the tumbledown camp, the snipers over the highway boomed. The rats must've heard them coming—had probably expected the reprisal. The overwatch hunters called out their hits over the radio with precision.

"Overwatch one. One target down."

"Overwatch two. Two targets down."

Mat hadn't asked them to do that. The hunters racked up kills on the highway like culling a deer herd.

Team one on Mat's left opened fire, first a trickle, then a roar. The woods exploded with rushing people. They were in the refugee camp proper now; drooping lean-tos, ragged latrines, and smoldering fire pits.

Mat had pictured a slow drive, converging on the camp, then pushing toward the highway. With the constant radio call outs of enemy casualties, and the chaotic melee of human shapes darting through the trees, the plan came undone in the first three seconds.

"This is punishment for last night's raid. Stay away from town," the bullhorn hollered.

Refugees sprinted in every direction—men, women, children. Almost everyone had something in their hands. The strike team opened fire at anything that looked like a weapon, which was pretty much everything. Mat stepped over the motionless body of a teenage boy gripping a folded-up camp chair.

A cluster of tents came into view as Mat stepped around a huge beech tree. Rats ran for the thickest brambles, or bolted down muddy paths toward the highway. Some ran in circles. Others snatched at belongings.

Return fire pattered from the camp, weak and sporadic. A hurricane of fire rained down in response from the strike team, hacking the brush to bits and sawing off branches from the trees. A tent collapsed. A metal pot on a campfire exploded.

*"This is punishment for last night's raid. Stay away from town."*

A group rushed toward Mat's team, probably running away from the snipers on the highway. Mat put a handful of rounds into the front-runners—they were carrying sticks and knives. The rats attempted to scatter but none was still standing after half a second of sustained gunfire. Two more rats popped up off the ground, ran away and were shot in the back. One looked like a teenage girl.

"Let them go!" Mat screamed, but he hadn't clicked the push-to-talk on his radio. He couldn't call a cease fire while anyone in the camp was still shooting at them. They were taking incoming gunfire.

Mat despaired and finally radioed, "Hold fire!"

A few on the channel responded, but the gunfire continued—rifles and shotguns in the woods, and the booming long guns on the highway.

*"This is punishment for last night's raid. Stay away from the town."*

"Robert's hit! Shit-eating rats!" someone on Mat's team screamed.

"Light 'em up!" the college kid next to Mat yelled and rushed into a cluster of ramshackle tents.

"Hold fire! Cease fire!" Mat shouted. They'd overrun the campsite, but kept pushing through the swampy, filthy hovel and into the surrounding forest.

"Fuck these guys!"

"Hold! Hold!" Mat bellowed. "Cease fire."

Finally, gunfire slowed. Mat made his voice heard. "*Cease FUCKING fire!*" he screamed into the pause. Other than the booming hunting rifles, the strike team quieted their guns.

Two minutes later, it was over. Finally, the rifles on the road either ran out of ammo or the snipers came to their senses. Mat's teams milled around, hiding behind tree trunks, pointing their guns into the now-quiet woods. Few looked back at the camp.

Mat turned and looked. It was a massacre. At least two dozen men, women, and children lay strewn across the camp. A lot of them cried in pain and writhed on the wet ground.

Gladys Carter slung her rifle and ran back into the camp. She scooped up a crying little boy next to a woman's limp body. He screamed and fought in her arms until she set him back down on his feet. He clawed at his dead mother, patting her face, running his fingers through her dark hair. A bloodless, fist-sized exit wound gaped where her right eye had been.

"Report," Mat keyed his radio.

"Rickers is dead. Friendly fire," Cabrera replied over the radio. "Two others wounded."

Mat's team was okay, other than a grazing wound and what looked like a sprained ankle. Mat plowed through the woods to Cabrera. He stood over the corpse of Deputy Rickers, shot through the liver and bled out in the muck. His skin was the color of chalkboard dust. Mat turned and stormed back to the center of the refugee camp.

They hadn't planned for what to do with enemy wounded, and there were a lot of them. Six, at least. Gladys darted among the shredded and sagging shelters, organizing whomever would listen to collect the wounded. Mat had no idea where she planned on taking them.

He still couldn't bring himself to think about the highway. There would be a bumper crop of dead and wounded on the road.

He keyed his mic. "This is Actual. Overwatch One and Two, come in."

"Copy," they chimed overtop of one another.

"Return to town." Mat hoped the order would be enough. If they could all just walk away from this, that might be best. "Everyone return to town. Now."

Juan Cabrera waded toward Mat through the underbrush.

"Sergeant Best. I have four guys who pursued rats to the south. I can't raise them on their radio."

As if on cue, rifle fire crackled in the distance.

Mat sighed. "Fuck 'em. They can find their own way home. Tell everyone to RTB. Return to base. Regroup at the sheriff's station."

Mat hoped that'd end the conundrum about the enemy wounded, but Gladys still darted around the camp, giving orders. She had no rank, but people listened to her. Some of the strike team had begun to come down off the rush and they were doing whatever she told them. Sheriff Morgan shuffled his bulk around in her wake, gathering up the broken remnants of the refugees.

"What're we gonna do with those guys, Sarge? What are your orders?"

"Go home. RTB." Mat didn't wait for acknowledgement. He'd done his job. They'd obliterated the camp. Questions of decency were not his to answer. "RTB." He circled his finger in the air. "RTB, folks!" Mat shouted as he walked toward town. He didn't turn around to see if anyone was following.

He breech-checked his rifle, shuffled through a tactical reload, inventoried his magazines, yanked out his radio earbud, and trudged alone toward the Objective Rally Point.

"Sarge?" Wiggin called over the dangling earbud. He sounded like a mechanical spider on Mat's shirt. "Sarge? You okay?"

There were questions within the question. *Am I okay? Are any of us okay?*

Mat didn't answer. His thoughts felt heavy, sluggish. This was not the first time an operation produced collateral damage. But in his mind, a trollish thug in a suit and tie made the case prosecuting Mat for the massacre at Brashear wood.

*Cue the video...*

People running for their lives, some shot from behind.

Mat defended himself in the mock court in his battered cerebellum. *"They killed our townspeople! They killed Marjorie Simms. They killed a baby, for God's sake."*

Mat remembered the open, sightless eyes of Bob Rickers, killed by his friends.

*"That's not my fault. There was no time to train."*

He remembered his girl, Caroline, dead in a hospital bed, one leg missing under the cruel, flat sheet.

*"I did everything I humanly could to save her."*

Mat stumbled on a root and went down to one knee. In an instant, the wet ground soaked through to his skin. His head felt like it might explode. He squeezed his eyes shut and covered them with his hands, pressing in with the heels of his palms so hard that purple lightning bloomed behind his eyes.

The images stopped, but there was little relief. They were replaced with one, constant refrain. Two words, relentlessly in their finality.

MISSION FAILED.

"I can't protect these people," he said out loud to the dead leaf litter and the soaked, mossy tree trunks. "I can't protect anyone. Caroline is gone. William's parents are dead. Rickers is killed," he babbled out loud, to himself.

This was not what Mat had been trained to do. He was an attack dog, not a guard dog. A missile, not a shield. A fighter, not a savior.

"I don't know how to do this. I don't know what you want of me," he despaired at the forest canopy.

Mat waited for an answer from the sky. All he heard was the quiet dripping of the forest and the distant sounds of his men bearing the aftermath of the strike. He was alone. So utterly, profoundly alone.

Later, Mat wouldn't remember his route back to town, or how he avoided confrontation with refugees in the woods. He wandered, circumnavigated a swamp, passed through a three-mile gap in the HESCO, drifted through neighborhoods, then arrived at his doorstep. It was a wonder he hadn't been bitten by a cottonmouth. At some point, William silently prepared him food and Mat ate mechanically.

He fell asleep before dark and he dreamt of assaults.

---

SERGEANT MATHEW BEST raised his binoculars and glassed the mountain village from his position 700 meters on a ridge above. He and Airman Perez, TACP, were tasked with confirming the presence of an Al Qaeda HVT for a Predator strike. The winged missile platform circled on station where the late afternoon sun would conceal it.

In the compound, they celebrated a wedding. Some chieftan's cousin's sister was marrying an elder's brother's son. Most of the males from the village were in attendance, and the men served food to one another. Mat was focused on the guests who traveled to the wedding.

Six small pickup trucks and one incredibly-dusty sedan were parked a short walk outside the compound.

The "compound," as described in his briefing, consisted of a

larger house than the rest of the village homes with a few outbuild-
ings huddled inside a wall. Mat couldn't see any women, but they
would be inside tending to the bride and following the required
traditions.

"Fuckers eat well," Perez commented as he munched on a
Powerbar.

"You're not wrong," Mat replied. The serving tables clustered
against the inside wall of the compound. The food filled Mat's
binos. Men buried a meat dish under heaping scoops of rice
flavored with carrots and spices from twenty-gallon pots. The dark
specks looked like dead flies, but they were raisins. Afghans did not
fuck around when it came to food. Their grub made the military
MREs and energy bars seem like processed cardboard.

The Afghan men dipped from communal plates. Oranges were
served whole, peeled and shared. A young man Mat took to be the
groom drifted among the other men, greeting them and laughing.
He held hands with an older guy. Maybe the father or the best man.

Mat and Perez could've brought a hellfire down on the
compound and not kill a single person who wasn't a Taliban sympa-
thizer, but that wasn't the mission. Their orders were to take out a
single guy and his security detail, and not waste another soul if
possible. Still, they were so far into Zabul Province, they could erase
an entire village and it probably wouldn't catch print in the
newspapers.

Mat and Perez watched and waited. After a time, the bride made
her appearance. She walked slowly, demurely; her henna-tattooed
hands clasped in front of her. Her attendants carried a decorated
cloth awning over her head. It hid her face from Mat's position, but
he was surprised by the beauty of her gown. The gold and red
edging caught the rays of the setting sun and twinkled like an aura.

She moved more gracefully than her attendants, and the awning
undulated as they walked with her. Mat caught the profile of her
face. On any other day, the bride was a six-out-of-ten. Pretty, but not

hot. To Mat, watching from half a kilometer away, with the low sun caressing her with its final rays, greater beauty could not be imagined.

"We're Mission Incomplete," Mat said, his eyes fixed on the young woman. "He ain't coming."

Perez wasn't convinced. "He could show up late."

Mat checked the road again and a wisp of dust rose from behind the rolling hills.

"Vehicles approaching."

Perez scrambled for his binos.

They'd have a narrow window for the strike, if this was their guy. They'd provide the cake eaters at the TOC with eyes-on confirmation of the target, then the head shed would green-light launch, then a UAV driver, stateside, would pull the trigger. All those steps had to happen in the time it took the HVT to step out of his vehicle, but before he entered the compound. It was like shagging two sisters in the same house without either finding out, and without making the dog bark.

The TACP spoke up, "Three vehicles. Two technicals with crew-served and one sedan. With a parade like that, that is our dude."

The Air Force required one of their own guys to be present on a strike like this one. Mat was there to back Perez up in a shooting situation, even though Mat out-ranked him. In any case, the TACP was a solid warrior. They were a good team together.

Perez lowered the binos. "You ID the target and I'll make the phone call."

"Roger that."

Mat settled on his ruck, prone, with his elbows resting comfortably on his sleeping pad. The binoculars steadied. The trucks pulled into the dusty parking lot, the gunners swiveled to-and-fro, hunting for invisible threats. Neither looked into the sun, where the Predator swam on air currents, happy as a falcon.

The sedan parked. The dust swirled, then cleared. Mat recognized the HVT, rising out of the back seat.

"HVT identity confirmed," Mat said.

The TACP rattled off confirmation into the radio.

Mat's job was done. He swiveled his view back to the compound. They must've heard the vehicles arrive. The bride and her entourage stopped floating among the crowd, and all eyes turned to the open gates of the compound.

The bride's face lit up and she gathered her skirts.

"No, no, no, no. Be smart. Stay put," Mat muttered.

She bolted from under the awning. The bride broke decorum and rushed toward the gate, her face radiant. There hadn't been any intel about a personal relationship between the bride and the HVT, but his arrival turned her into a bubbling schoolgirl.

"No, no, no. Stay inside," Mat hissed. He glanced over his binos. The target and the security team had circled up in the parking area. The HVT checked his hair in the driver's side mirror.

"There's a civilian running toward the target," Mat told Perez.

"No authority to cancel the Reaper for collaterals..." Perez stated the obvious. Their job was to call the arrival of the HVT, not to sweat a couple civilian casualties. Some collateral damage was "baked in" to the plan. Vaporizing the whole compound was to be avoided.

"We could call it in again when they go to leave," Mat squabbled. He knew they wouldn't do it. By then, it would be dark, and target ID would be impossible.

"Negative," Perez replied.

The bride ran through the gates, her bright orange shawl and brilliant, yellow dress flowed around her legs like pooling ephemera. One of the bridesmaids followed close behind.

They made it half-way to the grinning Taliban chieftain when the hellfire missile turned the ground into a tower of dirt-vapor. A full second later, the concussion hit Mat's face like a sand blaster.

The wave passed and Perez radioed, "Target eliminated."

Mat caught a flash of color in the roiling dust and returned to his binoculars. A brilliant, orange, flickering ghost rose above the churning mushroom. It danced on the air currents; twisting, reaching, rising above the death below. The soul of the bride, stripped of her body, pirouetted into the evening sky.

"...the fuck was that?" Perez uttered.

———

"SERGEANT BEST," a man's voice jostled Mat from sleep. Mat cracked his eyes. Sheriff Morgan hovered over him with a thin smile. "It's morning," the sheriff said.

Mat moaned, then rubbed his face.

"Bad dreams?" the sheriff asked.

Mat turned away so he wouldn't blast the man with his morning breath. "Something like that."

Mat felt a strange compulsion to talk about it this time. "Yeah," he continued. "I was remembering a bad Predator strike in Afghanistan. I mean, it was a good strike—by the book. But a couple girls ran onto the X at the last second. It happens."

The sheriff nodded. "Just because it's by the book doesn't mean it doesn't hurt."

"Yeah. True dat. I ran into Perez before the shit hit the fan—the TACP who was with me on that mission. I ran into him at a bar in Landstuhl. He was all strung out on oxy and booze. He couldn't talk about anything else. He'd done a million of 'em, but it was that strike that ate his lunch; the one with the orange shawl."

The sheriff nodded and kept his mouth shut, which was smart. There was no way he could understand or commiserate. Civilians just didn't get it, no matter how hard they tried.

"I'm going to brush my teeth," Mat made his excuse, climbed off the couch and walked to the bathroom. When he got back, the sheriff waited on his couch.

The sheriff shifted his butt nervously. "I've got some shitty news. I couldn't find you last night, so I held off till this morning," the sheriff said.

Mat's stomach flipped. "What's that?"

"Parker shot himself."

Parker had been one of the overwatch guys, blocking for the Brashear camp assault.

"Parker went down to the road for some reason, after the...thing," the sheriff explained. "It was a mess. He and Bergman really got into it. They hammered anyone who stepped onto the highway. I'm talking boxes of shells. Anyway, Parker went down to see his handiwork, saw a dead teenager or something, and he shot himself right there on the road. He has a wife and a baby—Parker does. Well, Parker did."

Mat slumped on the couch next to the sheriff. He rubbed his eyes again. "I don't know how to do this. I don't know what you want from me," Mat agonized.

The sheriff tried to make it better. "Yesterday got crazy. I was there. I took part. This is the shitty hand we're being dealt. It's nobody's fault."

"Every time we defend ourselves," Mat grieved, "We're snuffing out the town. We can't kill our way to safety. No matter what, we can't use that fucking gas. Promise me we won't use the WMDs. If we use mustard gas or anthrax on refugees, this whole town will commit suicide." Mat's eyes burned into the sheriff. He was fully aware that he was being melodramatic, but the truth wasn't far from the worst case scenario. "I don't know what I'm doing here. This is not what I was trained to do. I fight bad guys, not infestations. Nobody commits mass murder and shrugs it off, least of all a bunch of Midwestern pig farmers. Parker is just the first from that strike team to off himself. He won't be the last."

The sheriff sighed. "No matter what happens, we'll get through it together. We bear the sin together. You. Me. Everyone in Brashear wood. This isn't on you, Sergeant. We chose to hit that camp *together*."

"You think that *kumbaya shit* is going to save us? Because it didn't save Parker, and it didn't save Perez."

"No. It didn't save Parker," the sheriff admitted. "This is death by a thousand cuts. You're right about that. We have to find a better way."

## 16

CAMERON STEWART

"Ah how shameless—the way these mortals blame the gods.

From us alone, they say, come all their miseries, yes, but they themselves, with their own reckless ways, compound their pains beyond their proper share."

— ZEUS, THE ODYSSEY

**Grafton Ghost Town,
Southern Utah**

Two weeks after being shot, Isaiah hadn't yet died. Miraculously, Cameron didn't regret bringing him back to the homestead. Maybe it'd been the warm spell in the weather, or maybe it was the restorative power of calories, but Cameron felt almost cheerful.

The last of the raiders' food had been eaten—shared equally among the group—and they'd resumed their desperate rationing of the last scrim of red winter wheat in the five gallon bucket. But the captured, nutrient-dense calories had served them well. The children even played a little in the dirt outside the house.

Isaiah's boy, baby girl and Cameron's boys acted out a Bible skit with figures made of sticks. From what Cameron could gather, it was a conflation of Daniel in the Lion's den and John the Baptist. He assumed the polygamist kids had come up with the plot because his boys sure-as-hell didn't know the Bible.

Beside their "lion's den" carved in the earth, the cold frame grow-beds had finally sprouted, and all manner of tender greenling peeked through the ocher soil. There was nothing yet to eat, but the little shoots had survived more than a dozen frosty nights beneath the plastic enclosures.

While studying the sprouts, Ruth devised a sprouting tray for the wheat berries that, hopefully, would add a bit of the sun's energy to the wheat's calories. With a little water and a couple days' sun, the wheat kernels shot up grassy tentacles and reached out with twisting roots. She didn't know if there was any increase in nutrition, but the matted mass of the sprout tray certainly satisfied the stomach more than wheat alone. They'd grown utterly weary with the starchy flavor and gummy consistency of raw, boiled wheat. Any variety dazzled the palate.

The grandest ray of hope came in the form of a note tied to a road sign on the highway across the river. From his sickbed, Isaiah had suggested they make careful contact with the town of Rockville, and even writhing in pain, he devised a clever plan to trade with the besieged town.

Rockville's reply on the road sign read, "Let's meet up. Tuesday. 10am. This location. —Rockville P.D."

It'd been posted in response to a note scrawled on the back of a porno mag page from the marauders' packs, written in coal by

Isaiah. His invitation offered, "Mesquite, Nevada militia with hand-guns and ammunition to trade for bulk food. Interested? Leave reply here." Isaiah hoped that the porno page would convince the stodgy people of Rockville that they really were dealing with bad guys from Nevada, instead of a hapless family from Southern Utah.

Rockville P.D. had written their reply on a torn-out page from a Mormon hymnal. It was clearly a moral rebuke, so they had likely bought the ruse.

The song was "Reverently and Meekly Now" and the lyrics made no sense to Cameron. He couldn't tell if it was a funeral dirge or meant to scare the hell out of kids. If there was a message in the gruesome description of crucifixion, Cameron didn't understand it. When he'd asked Isaiah, he'd shrugged. Apparently, "regular" Mormons were just as strange to Isaiah as they were to Cameron.

The Rockville reply launched a debate about the day of the week that never reached a satisfactory conclusion. No one had kept track of how many days they'd lived in the Grafton ghost town. It might've been a hundred days or more. The day of the week was a complete mystery.

After the Rockville reply appeared on the "Speed Limit 55" sign, Isaiah and Cameron stayed awake into the night discussing the trade meeting and the myriad of risks involved. If Rockville figured out who they were and what they had, nothing would stop them from taking all the guns and ammo by force. They were too weak and too close. After watching the town do battle with the town of Hurricane for months, the clan couldn't assume civility.

Undoubtedly, the town knew that a family occupied the Grafton homestead. They were too close to town for their presence to have gone unnoticed. Rockville might've discovered the stripped-down bodies of the raiders they'd killed. Cameron had done nothing to move or bury them. Rockville might even suspect that they were involved in the killing.

Or, Rockville might conclude there was another militia roaming the countryside—it was a reasonable possibility since people with guns could be expected to range out in search of resources, and Southern Utah had historically been littered with polygamist clans and survivalist retreats. Claiming that they were the "Mesquite, Nevada Militia" would generate doubt. Just over the mountains, Mesquite, Nevada was thirty times the size of Rockville.

Rockville might also suspect a trap set by the town of Hurricane. The fighting had drawn down between the towns in the last couple weeks, but bad blood could still run hot. Rockville would suspect subterfuge. They might not even want guns. It might be a trap inside a trap.

No matter the truth, they would have to be extremely careful. The more Isaiah and Cam thought about it, the more they wished they could lay low and skip out on the whole thing. Trading was perilous business, but starvation again lurked in the shadows of their homestead.

Isaiah was laid up in his sickbed, his belly healing but his shattered leg wracked with pain. It was decided that Ruth would make the trade and Cameron and Julie would cover her with rifles. From the dead marauders, they'd scavenged six handguns—four automatics and two small revolvers. The men had carried only nine millimeter ammunition; 157 rounds, both loose and packed in nine handgun magazines. Cameron and Isaiah decided to keep all four AR-15 rifles, magazines and ammunition, and trade all the rest, including the Mosin-Nagant and the pump-action twenty gauge shotgun.

Isaiah came up with the plan and Cameron found himself again grateful he'd brought the man back from the cusp of death in the wilderness. The big nerd had a penchant for meticulous forethought.

Cameron had seen plenty of action in the apocalypse. He knew he was better for devil-may-care fighting than careful planning.

When it came to the upcoming trade with Rockville, everything looked like a possible trap. They had to assume a town that'd been fighting for its life would take advantage where they could find it. They couldn't afford to run-and-gun on this one. Isaiah's mind, even laid up in bed, served them as a weapon.

Completing a trade was a chess game—survival wizardry that depended on moves and counter-moves to defeat the nuclear option of stealing all goods and murdering all players. The only thing keeping the trade from going off the rails in a storm of gunfire was the promise of future trade, and of course, the mutual risk of getting shot.

As per Isaiah's instructions, they set the meeting place on the highway with open ground all around. It'd make life hard on the snipers that'd undoubtedly be placed on overwatch around the site.

If Cameron had been in charge, he would've carried all their trade goods to the meeting, haggled over a price, then took the payment or not. If the Rockville militia tried a double-cross, then so be it. There would be blood.

But Isaiah insisted they not expose the totality of their trade goods in one trade, but settle into a string of smaller trades. Instead of one, hell-bent-for-leather swap, they'd dole out the marauder's supplies in four or five installments.

Cameron would've sent everyone who could shoot into the trade with an AR-15 as a show of force: Julie, Ruth and himself. Isaiah suggested they send only Ruth, and send her in unarmed. Cameron and Julie would hide in the tree line and provide rifle cover. If they sent Ruth to trade with a gun, it might be tempting to kill her and add the gun to the booty. If she carried an AR-15, killing her would be even more tempting. If she carried the Mosin-Nagant or the shotgun, it'd make them appear weak and maybe encourage the traders to welch on the deal. Better to carry no firearm at all. It sent the message: *we have enough guns to trade them and enough riflemen covering our negotiator that we don't need to arm her.*

Cameron would've carried the trade goods to the spot, but

Isaiah counseled him to send Ruth with a written list instead. They'd hide the booty at the edge of the river, and Ruth could retrieve it if they reached terms.

Cameron had reservations about allowing Ruth to conduct the negotiation. She'd grown up in Colorado City, and to say she was naive to the ways of the world would be an understatement. Isaiah countered that nobody in their group knew the value of raw food-stuffs better than Ruth. She'd been born and bred into mastery of the kitchen. She'd know good food from bad, and there were strong odds that Rockville would try and deal in bad food. Isaiah's wife was the obvious, best choice.

In Cameron's mind, the notion of "wife" had fogged over, like the memory of a Pink Floyd concert he'd gone to in high school after his first run in with a bong. He remembered marrying Julie—the white dress, tuxedoes and the cake with two tiny figures that looked nothing like him and Julie—but he couldn't put his finger on why marriage had been such a big deal.

In the now-and-foreseeable reality, there were two basic functions of adults: surviving and rutting, and the second one only rose to consideration when the harsh edges of hunger had been knocked off by a bite or two of food.

He and Ruth were still fucking, but Cameron was no longer sure why anyone would care. Isaiah couldn't even get out of bed lest his leg crumble, and Julie had become an apparition who did little more than make sure the kids' food made it to their faces. He still humped his wife on occasion, but it was a joyless, perfunctory affair, and he told himself she needed it as a link to the old life—an artifact to give her hope. She consented to sex without the slightest moan or sway from her hips, and every time Cameron came away telling himself it would be the last time with her. Any fool could see the signs; his "former wife" was sinking away in an ocean of depression. But who wouldn't? Their life sucked.

One night, Julie stumbled upon he and Ruth screwing on the edge of the tree line. Julie had been collecting tinder to restart the fire. It was dark, but without batteries or candles, they'd learned to get by without light. Everyone went half-speed at night to avoid bumps and bruises that would take weeks to heal, given their malnourishment.

When Julie came upon them screwing, Cameron held Ruth's skirt up over her shoulders while he massaged her breasts and entered her from behind. Ruth's mouse-like moans squeaked to a stop, and Cameron looked up to see Julie staring straight at them. She paused for a moment, then turned and moved off into the night, plucking up twigs from the forest floor.

He finished with Ruth, then went back to the homestead to face Julie's wrath. But Julie never even brought it up. She went about her slack-faced duties like ever before. If there was now more distance between he and Julie, he could barely perceive it.

And that was pretty much the long and the short of how Cameron became a polygamist. There might've been some odorless contagion in the sand and the red rocks of Southern Utah, or perhaps the rudimentary addition and subtraction of survival in a clan led to one man and several wives. If another wife or two added themselves to Cameron's family unit, he could envision that working out too. The women did most of the work, now that the irrigation pipe was built, and Cameron's job—standing ready to protect them—arose only on rare occasion. By killing the troop of marauders and a half-dozen snakes, he'd done almost everything expected of him by the clan. He roamed the pasture, repaired the impoundment dam and cured leaks along the corrugated pipe. Otherwise, he ate and screwed.

Since the captured food from the marauders had run out, they were being forced to take risks by trading and he would, once again, be called upon to work a gun. He couldn't help feeling more god-like behind the bright, red-dot scope of the AR-15 rifle. He didn't know much about the range or accuracy of the black, metal gun, but it was certainly much deadlier than his Mosin-Nagant.

The next morning, he went with Ruth and Julie for the first face-to-face trade meeting, but Rockville didn't show. Someone must've gotten the day of the week wrong. It could easily have been them.

The morning after, they tried it again. Ruth carried a note with a list of offerings: one Glock 17, the Mosin-Nagant, a gun cleaning kit, twenty rounds of nine millimeter and a bowie knife. They hoped to score at least two week's food in exchange.

Rockville showed up at ten a.m. sharp. A pickup truck rambled down the road and stopped three hundred yards from the speed limit sign where they'd exchanged notes. Ruth stood beside the sign and Cameron and Julie waited in the trees. Cameron felt like he could hit the man walking up to Ruth if he had to, but the truck seemed awfully far. Three Rockville men held back at the truck— the driver and two with hunting rifles aiming over the cab to cover their negotiator.

Ruth and the man, a small, pot-bellied yokel under a huge cowboy hat, talked for a few minutes. Ruth handed him the note, they exchanged a few more words and the man walked back to the truck. He climbed into the passenger seat, the truck did a three-point turn, and drove back to Rockville. Five minutes later, Ruth stepped under the cover of the tree line along the river.

Cameron slid through the brambles over to the trail and caught up with Ruth. "What happened?" he asked.

"They said they'd bring some food tomorrow at the same time to trade for the guns and stuff."

Ruth wasn't always the sharpest beak in the chicken coop. She hadn't provided any interesting details.

"What exactly did he say?" Cameron made his question more specific.

"He wanted to know who we were and where we were from. I told him that I wouldn't discuss that. He said that not telling them who we were gave us an unfair advantage in the trade since we already knew that they were from Rockville. I said nothing, so then he asked what we wanted to trade. I gave him the list. He said 'Okay. We'll come back tomorrow with some food.'"

"He didn't say what guns they wanted from the list?" Cameron asked.

She shrugged. "That was everything he said."

"What was your impression? Will they give us a lot of food for the guns?"

Ruth shoulders hunched. "I don't know. He didn't say anything about how much food they had."

Dealing with Ruth in the light of day was infuriating. Cameron should've done the negotiating himself, but then who would cover him? Neither of the women could shoot, and he didn't want to waste the ammo to train them, if training them was even possible.

The three trudged silently back to the homestead. As per Isaiah's instructions, Cameron stopped at the halfway point and doubled back, quietly, all the way to the edge of the trees until he saw the speed limit sign again. They were alone. Nobody had followed them.

The next morning, they left an hour early for the trade. Isaiah insisted they watch the road for a long time before the meeting, keeping an eye out for Rockville spies or snipers who might come before the meeting to ambush them or follow them home. Cameron and the two women waited for an hour in the bushes and saw nothing.

Right before 10 a.m., the pickup truck shimmered into view on the gray ribbon of highway. Ruth stood under the speed limit sign. The clouds sulked across the sky, maybe a rainstorm in the making. At his feet, Cameron kept the guns, ammo, knife and cleaning kit wrapped in a plastic sheet. If the deal went through, Ruth would come for them.

The truck stopped, three hundred yards out and the short, portly guy stepped down, walked around the truck bed, and retrieved a pair of white buckets from the riflemen in the back. He lumbered over to Ruth under the weight of his cargo and plunked the buckets onto the pavement with a thud that carried across the sage flats.

Ruth struggled with the lids on the buckets. The man pulled a screwdriver out of his pocket and pried both the lids off. She stabbed her hands into the buckets and let the grain run through her fingers. She held something up to her nose. Inaudible to Cameron, they spoke for several minutes, with the man gesticulating ever more emphatically with his hands, and Ruth keeping her hands folded neatly in the fabric of her voluminous dress. At last, Ruth said something, turned and walked off the road. She stopped and glanced back. The man was already returning to the truck with the buckets.

"Fuck," Cameron swore under his breath. *No deal.*

Ruth stopped in the middle of the clearing and waited for the truck to disappear over the horizon before resuming her walk to the tree line.

"What the hell happened?" Cameron whispered when she reached him in the brambles.

"It wasn't enough grain, and it smelled stale to me," Ruth held out her hands in supplication. "You and Isaiah said at least two weeks of fresh food. That wasn't two weeks and it wasn't fresh. The wheat was stale and the oats smelled like cardboard—not sweet like they should."

"Oats?" Cameron repeated. "They had oats?"

"Yes, but I think they were at least thirty years old. There's lots of old food storage like that floating around Mormon Country. The Mormons started stocking up for the apocalypse sixty years ago.

The old stuff has a smell to it, and it's lost most of its nutritional value. That's what they tried to give us—somebody's old stuff from the 1970s. Isaiah said that if we take a bad deal the first time, we'll never get a good deal from them, ever again. He said we should probably turn down this first trade—no matter what they offered."

Cameron knew she was right. Isaiah had told all three of them, and it'd made sense at the time. Awash in visions of sweet oats, Cameron had lost track of the big picture. Maybe Ruth was the perfect person to negotiate after all. She had no inclination to get creative in the clutch. She didn't care that they were hungry. She did what she was told.

But then why was she screwing Cameron? It wasn't predictable, or even particularly stable.

Ruth stood in the brambles, empty-handed and quiet. Julie was still in her assigned overwatch post, across the path, holding the AR-15 like a wet towel.

"Let's head back," he said with a wave. He didn't bother to explain to Julie and Julie didn't ask.

"When do we come back, then?" Cameron asked Ruth.

"I dunno. I walked away. We didn't set up a next meeting."

Cameron swore and waved the women ahead of him. Trading was their only shot at cheating starvation. The garden vegetables were taking forever to mature, probably because of the shitty winter sunlight. Even if the plants suddenly exploded with life, the truth was slowing dawning on him: at best, the garden greens would offer a few vitamins and almost no calories. The turnips would fill their bellies when at last they matured, but the tubers would be mostly water. Even after planting every seed in the survivalist seed vault, they could expect *maybe* a few thousand calories from the cold frame garden. They'd invested tens of thousands of calories in the dam, the pipes and the cold frame greenhouses. Without starches, like wheat, rice, oats or corn, they were going to perish long before the skylark days of spring.

Cameron turned around and stumbled back to the tree line to watch for pursuers, as per Isaiah's instructions. All the cleverness and tactical-whatnot sounded really cool when Isaiah laid out the plan for the trade. Doubling back on "rear security" was a Navy SEAL thing, and Cameron had loved the thought of it. Now, after doing it twice, it already felt like work.

Nothing was easy, not even a simple trade. They'd already wasted hundreds of calories walking back and forth to the highway, and they had absolutely nothing to show for it. Maybe Rockville had nothing to give them but nutritionless buckets of chaff. Maybe they'd been barking up a dead tree from the get-go.

Cameron already knew what Isaiah was going to say, and as much as he wanted to tell the cripple to shove it where the sun doesn't shine, he knew Isaiah would be right: they should come back every morning until a good trade materialized, no matter how long it took. It was either that or death by starvation. They didn't have a choice at this point.

---

Two mornings after the trade deal went flat, the truck and the portly man in the cowboy hat returned to the speed limit sign. He brought four buckets—the same two buckets of old wheat and oats, plus a bucket of only-slightly stale rice and another of fresh wheat.

Ruth struck the deal and carried two of the four buckets to the tree line, retrieved the guns and ammo, and delivered them to the Rockville negotiator. He gave her the last two buckets, retreated to the truck and rolled back the way he'd come. The trade finally went down just like Isaiah predicted.

"We'll meet them again, here, in three days," Ruth reported at the tree line. "Today's Saturday, the guy told me. So, ten a.m. Tuesday. He said to bring more guns and ammo if we have them."

"What's his name?" Cameron asked.

"He didn't say."

Cameron stared up the highway toward Rockville. He couldn't see the town, but he could imagine it in the distance, curled at the foot of the towering red rock mountains that marked the entrance to Zion National Park.

His brows furrowed. It irked him that the stout man hadn't given his name, or asked for Ruth's. Manners counted for something, but Cameron couldn't say what it meant. He just knew he didn't like it.

Cam collected two of the buckets and let the ladies trade off with the other two. As was his custom, he left the heavy buckets at the mid-way point, doubled back and "checked their six."

Starvation, once again, retreated into the ominous shadows, at least for the moment. He'd sleep that night with a full belly and without waking to the moans of his hungry children.

They were probably nearing the middle of January, if Cameron were to guess. It would be a long road to April, when Isaiah said the days would grow longer and the night frosts would meander north.

Isaiah's intestines hadn't been pierced by the bullet or he would've died from infection by now. The slug must've circled around his belly, slipped through loose flesh and glanced away from the abdomen. On the other hand, Isaiah's lower leg looked like a hairy salami, hanging from his knee and hardening in an angry, red shank. Where the bullet passed through the bone, a series of porcine lumps had formed around the bone, none of them clearly infected, but not appearing in any way human. The pain had only intensified. Isaiah insisted they carry him to the porch at night, to weather the cold night alone so he wouldn't wake them with his restless agonizing. Part of Cameron wished Isaiah would die, and the other part knew he would miss the man. Cameron knew he would've made a long and dangerous series of mistakes without Isaiah as a second opinion. Even crippled and crushed in a vice of pain, Isaiah saw things in a way Cameron never would. In another befuddling irony of the apocalypse, the two men actually made a pretty good team.

One horrifying truth plagued Cameron, so vomitous that he dare not speak it, and every day the truth stalked closer, like a lion in the tall grass. For a short while, Cameron took courses at the local community college to become a paramedic. He went on some ride-alongs with the ambulance, and discovered that his stomach did barrel rolls every time he saw gross human injury. Guys who puked at the sight of compound fractures and arterial bleeding weren't a good fit for pararescue, his instructor told him with a hand on his shoulder. Thus ended Cameron's short time as a paramedic.

Before changing career course, He sat on the edge of his chair during a night class that taught "traction in-line" or TIL as the gleeful instructor called it. TIL wasn't in the course curriculum, but the teacher described the procedure "in case you have a bone break deep in the wilderness, where there is no surgical center."

The usual first aid for a bone break was to immobilize it and transport to a trauma center, but in case a trauma center couldn't be reached in twelve hours, the first responder would need to set the bone before splinting. Leaving a bone crooked for more than twelve hours risked further tissue damage. The instructor had demonstrated the TIL by holding a student's arm, yanking the shattered bone straight, then setting it back "inline" where it ought to be. *"Then, it can be properly splinted,"* the instructor pronounced. Cameron felt like he might puke on the linoleum.

The specter of traction in-line had haunted him since he first saw the bone fragments sticking out of Isaiah's shattered shin, back in the thicket where he'd been shot. Ruth had carefully removed the exposed pieces of bone and they'd hoped the leg would heal on its own. It hadn't.

It'd been two weeks, and the leg looked like it might require amputation. It simply wasn't healing. The infection came and went, but the limb would accept no weight or movement without sending jolts of pain into the man. Cameron hadn't even mentioned traction in-line to Isaiah, but unless he wanted the man to die from gangrene, he would have to reset the leg. With new food in the larder, now would be the time.

By the time Cameron shuttled the buckets to the homestead, Ruth was cooking sweet, fresh rice over the cook fire alongside the porch. Isaiah lay in bed on the porch obviously in pain, but happy the trade had finally come through.

"No trackers?" he asked Cameron.

Cameron shook his head, set the buckets beside Ruth, and climbed the steps to Isaiah's bed. He lifted the sheet back and smelled the raw, not-quite-rotten odor of the leg. Isaiah had been the brains behind the trade, and he'd sacrificed himself against the marauders. Cameron owed him this much.

"We need to reset the leg," Cameron said. "Now."

Isaiah's eyes widened. "Can I have a bowl of rice first."

"No." Cameron shook his head. "You'd probably just puke it up. Let's do this now while both of us have empty stomachs."

"Do what, exactly?" Isaiah worried.

"You're going to have to trust me on this." Doubt flashed across Isaiah's face. It made Cameron wonder: *does he know about Ruth and I?*

Cameron closed his eyes and explained. "I'm going to pull your leg in-line, straighten it out, try to push all the pieces where they belong, then re-splint it straight. I can see that it's crooked and I doubt it'll heal like that. It needs to be re-broken and re-set. I'm sorry, bro, but this is your best shot at ever making it out of this bed."

Isaiah hesitated, then nodded. Cameron hurried to remove the splint around his leg—a hasty amalgam of boards and rope. He needed to do this fast, before he lost the nerve.

"Ruth!" Isaiah shouted. "My bride. Come hold my hand. Gosh

darn it." Even the removal of the splint caused Isaiah's eyes to roll back in his head.

Cameron steeled himself for the big moment. He'd be lucky if he didn't faint. Ruth ran to her husband's side and glanced from one man to another, confused.

"Just hold my hand, please," Isaiah repeated. "Cam's going to fix my leg."

Cameron wrapped one hand around the lower calf and the other hand around the ankle. Then he pulled hard and steady toward the foot of the bed.

The rotten flesh and chips of bone tore free. The lumpy meat around the wound undulated like a troubled sea. Isaiah shrieked to raise the rafters and the children rushed in from the pasture. The boneless leg popped and ground, shattered bone against gristle. Hidden cysts of watery blood and pus gave way inside the wound and on the surface. The sound of evulsing tissue didn't so much reach Cameron's ears but radiate up through his hands. Wet bone, scarcely healed in a gnarled caricature of a leg, tore apart like cooked sockets of barbecue ribs.

Cameron swooned.

Isaiah went suddenly silent.

Cameron watched in a fugue state as his hands shoved knotty lumps back into place. His hands worked on their own recognizance, reshaping his friend's shin bone. They finished, as best they could, and went to work re-tying the splint. His hands cinched the compression rope tighter than before, but hopefully not so tight as to cut off circulation.

With the operation complete, and Isaiah passed out, Cameron staggered down from the porch, around the corner of the homestead, and retched. His head lolled on his shoulders and his stomach heaved, over and over and over. He puked up a thin, acrid bile that burned his throat on the way up. It felt like the bile had been with him a long time, maybe since escaping Los Angeles three and a half months before.

Eventually, his stomach quieted. Cameron wiped his mouth with the back of his hand and stood upright.

The clouds overhead had thinned, and some slight blue sifted through the gaps. The sun was still obscured by the rainless gray, but a little color filtered down upon the ghost town and its desperate, barely-living guests.

## 17

SAGE ROSS

**Border of Union County and Wallowa County**
**Wallowa, Oregon**

S age led The Five into Wallowa County on the same route he'd used before. He could even see his old snowshoe dimples from the last time under the new-fallen snow. The six men waded across the Minam River, dried their feet, replaced their socks and cut across the foothills of Sacajawea Mountain. It wasn't long before they ran into trouble.

All wore snowshoes, and Sage compacted the trail ahead of the group. Depending on the freshness and structure of the snow, cutting trail meant about thirty percent more work, but it left a much easier path for the rest. Even so, on the first big rise out of Minam River, Sage dropped all five behind. The fattest guy, Reggie, fell back more than a hundred yards. He heaved for air with his hands on his knees.

Captain Chambers had called their visit into Wallowa a "look-see" but every man carried an AR-15 on his back, except for Sage, who carried his 30-30. The plan was to scout the southern edge of Wallowa Valley to prepare for a snatch-and-grab mission in the near future. The solution to their woes would be to kidnap Commissioner Pete. With Pete out of the way, safely locked up in La Grande, Captain Chambers could roll Union and Wallowa counties up into one, big, happy family.

Captain Chambers caught up with Sage, on the rise overlooking Minam Canyon.

"Sorry about this," he apologized to Sage, which seemed a strange thing to do. "Too much coffee and donuts." He looked back over the struggling men on the climb.

Chambers had climbed the hill without a struggle. His deputies looked like they might have coronaries. Sage had seen Captain Chambers jogging the streets of La Grande, just as the sun came up, many times on his way to work. The captain had been breathing heavy on the slog up the mountainside, but he'd kept within a few dozen yards of Sage. His respiration recovered within a couple of minutes. It reminded Sage: this was a formidable man. He had the force-of-will to stay in shape, even late into his forties. This "look-see" would undoubtedly turn into something more serious. If not today, then soon.

"Don't let yourself get out of shape, son," the captain advised. "It's a sonofabitch to get back, especially in your forties."

Sage had no worries about staying in shape. Unless Cheetos and Taco Bell made a roaring comeback, he wouldn't probably have to worry about getting fat. Ever.

"There's a long way to go, still." Sage watched Reggie stop for the fifth time on the climb. "This is just the first rise. There are five or six more before we reach the valley."

The captain nodded. "I'm glad we did a dry run. I didn't realize how out-of-shape the guys were. They used to be monster athletes —every one of them."

"Have we crossed the county line?" Sage worried.

"Barely. It's up here somewhere."

Sage hazarded an opinion. "It seems like a lot of risk." When the captain didn't respond, Sage continued, "Hiking all the way to the back of the valley, where Commissioner Pete lives, is going to be a challenge. Getting back out will be even worse. The residents have vehicles and can cover a lot more ground than we can on snow-shoes. If we have a prisoner, that'll make us even slower."

Again, the captain didn't answer. He looked lost in thought. The deputies were finally catching up to them.

"Hey-o," Kevin Tursdale said as he reached them. He choked on the cold air and fell into a coughing fit.

"You're right," the captain said, turning to Sage. "This isn't going to work. We're going to turn back here. I'd like you to do me a favor. Do you have enough food to continue on for another couple days?"

Sage nodded. "I'm good."

When he left the room at the Best Western that morning, Sage had loaded up his full survival kit. It made him nervous to be in the wild without it. He'd spent months living out of the bug-out bag.

"Great. Pete Lathrop's ranch is past Enterprise but before Joseph. It's close to the airstrip by Hurricane Creek."

Sage jiggled his backpack. "I have a map."

"Okay. Do you think you can avoid getting caught?"

Sage nodded. He would circle higher up the mountain where nobody could see him in the pines. It'd be a tougher march, but it was nothing compared to the climb up the Blue Mountains.

"I can make the hike, but it'll take me a few days. If someone cuts my back trail and puts dogs on me again, there's nothing I can do about that. But I'll do my best to avoid detection," Sage said.

"Good." Captain Chambers clapped him on the shoulder. "I need to know where there's a barn full of snow machines nearby Lathrop's. The ranches along the foothills should have their snow machines out. They'll be tuning them up for winter. Snow machines are a way-of-life up here once the snow starts to pile up. Find me at least six snowmobiles that look new-ish and ready to run."

Sage nodded. "How do I know if they're good?"

"Should be obvious. They'll be the snow machines that aren't all busted up." The captain smiled. "If we come in here with a team that's not so damned fat," he said loud enough for three of his guys to hear, "we can snowshoe in, grab snow machines, then ride out. There's nothing that can keep up with snow machines other than other snow machines. You locate the machines and we'll make it happen."

It sounded like a crazy plan to Sage, with lots of moving parts, but it wasn't his job to poke holes in the captain's ideas. So, he nodded agreement and restated his mission.

"You want me to get to the back of the valley, and find a ranch near Lathrop's with at least six snowmobiles that look well-serviced. How're we going to get the keys?"

The captain laughed. "In this part of the world, people leave the keys in the ignition. Hell. Half our keys are probably rusted in place. Just find me snow machines and we'll take it from there."

"You want me to recon Commissioner Pete's ranch?" Sage didn't know which ranch belonged to the Commissioner. He'd yet to see the back half of the valley.

The captain shook his head. "Naw. I've been there more times that I can count. His dad used to be the hunter safety instructor when we were kids. We've all been to his ranch. Don't worry about that. Just find me six snow machines. I don't want to scoop that bastard up and be forced to run around, hunting for a way back out. The Potbelly Patrol and I will go back to La Grande this morning and put together a better assault team. I'll leave a cruiser for you on the Minam River. We're running out of time. We need to get this done before big snow falls."

Sage could think of a million ways the plan could go wrong. He could get arrested again, skulking around Wallowa, for starters. They probably wouldn't give him a burger, this next time. But if he stayed under the heavy pines, he felt confident he wouldn't be seen from the valley. He didn't think people roamed around the mountains now that there was more snow.

"Okay, Captain. I'll radio you from the cruiser when I get out, but it'll probably take four days."

The captain exhaled, and nodded his head. "It'll probably take me that long to get a team figured out, anyway. I'll train them and lead them myself. You get the recon and the snow machines lined up and I'll handle the rest."

Sage couldn't think of any other questions, so he hitched up his pack and tightened the belly band. "I'll see you in four or five days. Whoever comes with us next time will need to be in pretty good shape. I think it's twenty-five miles to Lathrop's ranch. We've only gone two miles."

Chambers nodded. "War's a young man's game. We'll get it figured out." He turned his snowshoes around and plodded toward Reggie, who still hadn't made it to the top of the hill. "Let's go boys. That's enough for today."

Sage hung his hand on his rifle sling and charted a course up the mountain and into the trees.

*War's a young man's game,* the captain had said.

Sage hadn't signed up for a war. But, he supposed he might've signed up for just about anything, that day coming down off the Blue Mountains with frost-nipped toes. War was better than a world of scavengers, psychopaths and cannibals.

---

Sage reached the back of Wallowa Valley two days later. By his calculations, he covered twenty-five miles, which in snowshoes on virgin trail was no small achievement. He was in the best shape of his life, and it felt good to do battle with the altitude, the cold and the snow. As the sun set on the second day—Friday, he figured—he could see the tiny airstrip from his vantage on the tree line. He backed up half-a-mile into the pines and laid out his low-profile bivouac shelter.

He'd modified his two-man camo tent so it functioned like a bivy sack. He'd never actually camped in a bivy sack, but his dad once showed him one and explained the concept. At this point, Sage probably had more practical knowledge about snow camping than anyone he'd ever met, including his dad.

He scraped out a flat in the snow with his glove, then stomped it down. He laid down a small tarp, then unrolled a fat, rectangle of egg-crate foam in the depression. The trampled snow might as well have been an ice slab, but the layer of foam would slow the sapping of his body heat.

He set the tent on top, but didn't raise the full dome. Geometric lines in the forest stood out like a porno billboard. The tent would be harder to detect uneven and lumpy instead of tight and tidy. He repurposed two of the fiberglass rods to go between the stake pockets. The flexible rods would hold a hoop of open air over Sage's head as he slept. He positioned the zippered door on the up-sloping side, so he could open or close the zipper to allow more airflow into the tent during the night. He knew from experience that he'd alternate between seething-hot and iceberg-cold all night long, and he'd adjust the zipper thirty times throughout the night. There was no other way. That was the nature of winter camping. The deflated tent added tremendous warmth to the rating on his sleeping bag—at least ten degrees with the zipper closed, by bottling up his warm, moist body heat. It also made his sleeping bag damp by degrees; a little more each night.

The bag his grandfather had given him was a zero degree bag, which had seemed like overkill back in October when Sage first used it to survive. Now in early December, he was forced to employ every trick in the book to keep from freezing at night; his tent, ground insulation, and full clothing. Sage didn't wear his boots to bed, and he preferred to take his rain shell off, but otherwise, he slept with every stitch of clothing he owned. Insulation was insulation, and the more clothes he wore in his sleeping bag, the less often he'd wake up freezing.

There was no silver bullet to sleeping outside in the winter. It was a bitch. The vapor barrier trick would eventually come full circle and bite him in the ass. By the end of four nights, Sage's warm sleeping bag would be wet with accumulated perspiration, and it would no longer be a "zero degree bag." Not by a long shot. To make matters worse, the inside of the Franken-tent would be like a sauna —literally dripping with the moisture he exhaled in the night.

It was Night Two and Sage could already feel the slick on the inside of the tent, even before sleep time. By the next morning, it'd be a serious issue. He dug out the chamois rag, and painstakingly wiped down every inch of the tent wall. He wrung out the chamois outside over the snow, and draped it over his pack. It'd be frozen solid in an hour.

Sage looked up through the pine boughs at the stars overhead. He couldn't see a cloud in the sky. The half-moon would rise in five hours, and there would be a four hour window of working moonlight.

He could either skip sleep and make it a night mission, or he could recon the ranches for snow machines the next morning with binoculars. If the snowmobiles were stored inside barns, which seemed likely, he'd be shit-out-of-luck. With the clear sky came the biting cold, and he figured the ranch dogs would be hiding inside tonight.

Night would be his best play if he wanted to get close to the snow machines. He didn't want Captain Chambers to rely on his intel only to find out he'd been guessing based on thousand-yard spotting. He preferred to see the machines, and the keys, firsthand.

Sage squirmed all the way inside his bag, reached over and laid two pine branches across the hoop of the tent. He scooted to where the moonlight would strike his face when it rose. That'd wake him for sure—that and the damned cold.

---

WHEN THE MOONLIGHT splashed over his eyes, Sage was dozing restlessly. He wasn't sure troubled sleep counted for much, but his aching leg muscles from the twenty-five mile trek felt a lot better. He was fully dressed already, so he slid out of the tent, popped on his boots and swished some snow around in his mouth to wash out the worst of the morning breath. He figured it was about two a.m..

He stuffed his backpack inside the tent and opened the zipper all the way in an attempt to let the humidity vent a little. In the bitter cold, it'd probably freeze before it evaporated. He remembered that much from high school science: water didn't both freeze and evaporate. It did one or the other.

Sage set off in the light of the half-moon, just now peeking over Sacajawea Mountain. The valley sparkled below in the light of Mother Moon. Not a single electric light burned in the valley. Like everywhere else, they'd lost electricity when the grid went down in early October. Unlike everyone else, the Wallowa Valley didn't seem to care. They'd switched over to oil lamps and solar camping lights, and carried on. At two in the morning, even those lights were extinguished. The valley probably didn't look much different than it had a hundred years before.

The moon painted the fields of snow-dappled prairie in sapphire blues, interrupted only by the black speckles of thousands of cattle, motionless in the cold night. Sage breathed in the cleanness of the scene.

He'd asked Aimee Butterton a lot of questions about Wallowa. It'd become an obsession with him—a romantic affection for them after having a burger with Commissioner Pete. It was likely three parts personal uneasiness over the mission, and one part hope for the future.

The people of Wallowa lived in quiet balance with their mountain home, Sage had learned from Aimee. They raised cattle amidst a tremendous herd of elk, trading range lands, hunting and beef harvest in a careful dance that preserved the prairie, their livelihood and the elk herd. Under the winter moon, Sage sensed the people and the land, linked together through generations like star-crossed lovers.

His mission felt like the opposite of that. He came as a thief in the night, seeking to take—to reap where they hadn't sown. Yet, he'd made a promise to his father: he would do everything necessary to survive, and this reconnaissance fell neatly on the list. It was survival—serving a police captain and a county that had its share of corruption; Sage couldn't deny it, not in the honest moonlight and not standing in this valley, cloaked in its naked grandeur. The city of La Grande had side-stepped chaos, but it echoed the brokenness of Seattle.

La Grande P.D. walked the same paths of old government. Reaping where a man hadn't sown had been the disease, and someday, honesty might be the cure. Sage knew Mother Earth well enough now to say for certain, she would not stop her onslaught until men won back their souls. For him, that meant keeping his word to his father, whatever the discomfort.

With that thought, he trudged down out of the foothills, toward the ranch he thought belonged to Commissioner Pete. If he could locate the family snow machines, it'd make for a lightning-fast getaway when they came to ambush the Commissioner.

The next nearest ranch was a quarter mile away. It'd be lots easier if they could just take Commissioner Pete's snowmobiles.

The snowshoe down from Sage's camp seemed like a couple

miles, but snowshoeing downhill was almost like skiing. He closed the distance to the ranch in less than twenty minutes.

The snow didn't thin out until Sage reached the prairie flats. He found a prominent pine, shucked off his snowshoes and stabbed them into the snow that'd tumbled off the boughs. He walked the rest of the way to the cluster of barns in his boots.

Sage passed by the tall barn and headed straight for the low barn he took as the motor pool. The big, sliding doors were open, and nothing stirred as he slipped inside. He stopped and waited, just inside the doors for his eyes to adjust. He carried a head lamp in his pocket, but he dare not use it, now just a hundred feet from the ranch house.

A dozen snow machines sat in rows along both walls of the motor pool. He retrieved his headlamp and cupped his hand over the bulb, then turned it on. With the thin light shining between his fingers, he looked over each machine, checking for a key and examining the gas gauges. They all had keys in the ignition and none had less than half a tank of gas. Sage had no idea how much gas it'd require for a snow machine to run twenty-five miles back to the county line.

He noticed many of the machines appeared to be old, the vinyl on the seats cracked and brittle, with the rotting, yellow foam poking through. There were eight, though, that looked like later models—maybe no more than a couple years old. Sage recounted the machines, and re-checked the keys on each of the newer machines. He clicked off his light. Mission accomplished.

The screen door of the ranch house banged shut. Sage froze. A dog woofed, then a man mumbled.

Sage picked his way to the edge of the sliding doors and peered around the rolling door toward the house. The figure of a man stood at the edge of the porch, staring out at the half moon.

The dog woofed again, and a stream of piss pattered off the porch into a pile of snow. The man mumbled again to the dog and chuckled, low and quiet. He finished peeing, zipped up his pants, and sat down on a wooden bench. The dog thrust his head onto the man's lap and the man chuckled again, lavishly scratching the dog's furry head. The dog whined, pulled away, then looked directly at Sage and the motor pool.

The wind blew down-slope and would carry his scent away at a ninety-degree angle from the ranch house. But breezes swirled and did funky things around buildings and stands of trees. The dog must've caught puffs of Sage's scent on the wind's unpredictable dance.

Sage could tell from the voice that it was Commissioner Pete, but the man obviously thought himself alone and safe. He ruffled the dog's head and spoke nonsense to it.

It wasn't much of a dog—one of the breeds his own dad called "useless, old lady dogs." Maybe a Maltese. Sage imagined that the dog belonged to the Commissioner's daughter. The more useful dogs would be inside, sleeping off the cold. Sage could see that Pete had a secret adoration of the tiny dog, expressed only during TV commercials and the middle of the night when his bladder woke him up to watch the prairie moon.

"Daddy's boy...my happy baby...you know who loves you the most..." the words waxed and waned on the breeze, drifting from the porch, then dribbling away with the Commissioner's open-hearted chuckle.

Sage's face warmed with shame. He was a villain to intrude on the rancher's private moment with the stars, the moon and the puppy. Sage despised the world and his place in it. He wondered if his own father's heart ever paused to lavish affection on a silly dog. Sage had never seen it happen.

Who was his father, anyway? He couldn't say he really knew. Would his father have survived all that Sage had survived? He assumed his father was a survivor, but he'd learned that the mountain and the snow revealed a man in a way nothing else could.

What did he really know about the man who had locked him into a promise—a promise that led to this moment of ignobility?

The rancher got up from the bench, took a last look at the moon-stroked prairie, and went back inside. The screen door clicked shut, then the main door thunked closed.

Sage took inventory of himself and his surroundings, waited five minutes, then picked his way back to the hills. He didn't bother covering his tracks. There were so many animal tracks criss-crossing the patchy snow that he hoped it wouldn't matter. He collected his snowshoes and raced the coming dawn up the mountainside.

By the time he reached his bivouac, the sun colored the eastern horizon a milky gray. Exhausted by emotions and the climb, he let his moist skin dry in the cold as long as he could stand, then climbed back into his sleeping bag. It wouldn't be long before the stark light of day.

He knew better than to make decisions in the middle of the night, muddle-headed and full of worry. He hoped that a couple days' sleep would bring him back from his emotions to the cold reality of his mission. He worked for a man, who served a county, who fought for survival. Maybe it was just that simple.

---

THE NEXT DAY, after a sleepless night, Sage stumbled twelve miles back toward Union County. The next night, he slept like the dead in his ever-more-humid sleeping bag. The clouds filled in over Wallowa Valley, and nighttime temperatures warmed under the floating cover of fluff. He slept a good night, woke with the sun, and faced the rest of the long hike out.

It was Sunday morning and Sage felt fueled by a singular cause: to make it back in time for the Sunday visit to the Butterton home. As hammered as his body felt from traversing fifty miles of snow, his yearning for Aimee's soft hips, candy lips and lilting, country-girl voice drove him hard. He had thirteen miles to cover—half the length of the valley—if he was going to reach the police cruiser and have a roll in the hay with Aimee Butterton, he'd have to haul ass.

He pounded mercilessly up the inclines, then glissaded down at a jog. He was making good time, snowshoeing smoothly along, weaving through the pine trees, and following his trail back.

Snowshoeing was like jogging, but without the impact. He drifted along in a mind-numbing cadence of exertion. *Swish, swish. Swish, swish.* The cold was a forgotten uncle, and the brisk wind on his face whisked away the sweat with only a slight crust of salt left behind.

Sage flounced into a canyon when he heard a branch crack like a rifle shot. He slammed to a stop and flopped sideways behind a big pine. He rolled his rifle from his back and into his hands. He racked a shell and listened.

Another crack. A thunk, and the thud of snow falling from a tree. A huge, dark form burst from the tree line. Then a dozen more. Elk.

They skittered in circles, unsure where his scent and sound had originated. Sage watched them whip left and right, confused at the interruption to their midday nap. They must've been dozing in a copse of dark pine when the swish-swish-swishing of the snowshoes startled them. The wind whistled down-canyon. They probably couldn't smell him well, and they'd likely barely heard him over the rustling of the pines. The elk settled, then returned to their bedding area in the black pines. Sage eased the cartridge out of the chamber, reloaded the bullet into the tubular magazine, then returned the rifle to his back without a round in the chamber.

He wasn't in Wallowa Valley to fight. He didn't like running overland with a round chambered. It was an artifact from the combat rifle course he'd taken as a teenager. Maximum safety.

With the wild vision of the elk, his world had brightened. The clouds from the night before had drawn back without dropping snow, and the morning sun cast across the snowfields, making the cold-hardened flakes glitter like stardust.

The rifle was slung over his backpack, which tightened the sling and minimized the bouncing as he, once again, flew over his old trail. He probably shouldn't have brought the gun in the first place. There was no turn of events in Wallowa Valley that he could imagine, where he'd defend himself with a rifle. If they caught him, he'd let himself be arrested. As it was, he had a hard time stomaching the thought of reporting back to Captain Chambers. His promise to his dad had grown thin in the clean air of the Wallowa Valley. From the snowy crags of Sacajawea Mountain to the rising prairies that skirted the Zumwalt, it was a beautiful, open range, as though God made it to shelter a favored breed of bright ones. The people acted as though they knew they were blessed. It seemed to humble them; make them kinder and slower to anger. He'd only been with them for a few hours, but their grace and generosity had stunned him. The land, it seemed, had leaked into their souls.

As he made the last climb back to Union County, Sage thought about Commissioner Pete and the little dog. It was a sacred thing, to see a man before God on his porch. The commissioner had worn his flannel pajamas, but his soul was naked in the moonlit hours before dawn. The man, lavishing affection on a ridiculous dog, had been the same person who arrested Sage and fed him a burger. There'd been no difference between the two—no fakery, no pretension, no phony friendship. Commissioner Pete—the man he would help capture or maybe even kill —was undeniably good. The truth made Sage a villain in this story. Could he live with himself, knowing that he'd brought down a good man?

Sage pushed into the climb and let the sweat and the cold numb him. He decided to take it one-thing-at-a-time, and now, he knew what was next: the arms and lips of Aimee Butterton.

SAGE REACHED the police cruiser with time to spare. He didn't bother driving into La Grande. He needed her touch and he could shower at her house.

He parked the police cruiser around the corner from the Buttertons, then walked the last quarter mile on the gravel lane. There wasn't nearly as much snow in the town of Elgin as Wallowa Valley, a thousand feet higher in elevation.

Sage knocked, and Mrs. Butterton showed him in. He was the first to arrive for the Sunday visit. His eyes followed the swing of her ass in her customary denim, and he almost missed the loaded glance that Mrs. Butterton shot Aimee as she showed him into her room.

*What was that?* he wondered.

Then, the sight of the girl swept away any rational thought. She was dressed in cut-off shorts with the fringe hugging the line where her ass met her legs. On top, she wore a perfectly-crisp, white T-shirt that rode the curve of her breasts like the snowfields he'd just crossed to get here. He could almost see her nipples finishing the perfect curve with a "screw-you" to gravity.

He blinked, wordless. She laughed out loud.

"Don't just stand there." She flashed her bright smile. "Go shower."

Sage realized he still wore his snowshoeing getup: layered, merino wool top, fleece mid-layer and a wind shell. He'd worn his snow pants to the house because he had nothing else to change into.

"Does your dad's closet have, um, a pair of sweats or something I could borrow? Maybe a T-shirt, too?"

The mention of her dad sent a cloud across her face, but her smile returned. "Yeah, but you're going to be swimming in them. He was a big guy. I'll find you something. They'll be outside the bathroom door." She pointed toward the hallway. "To the showers, Soldier."

*Soldier?*

Sage tore his eyes away from her breasts and headed out of her room. It took a second for him to identify the door that must be the bathroom—the slightly narrower one. He didn't want to wander into her mom's room by mistake. She'd probably be getting made up for the captain.

Sage dreaded the coming debrief with Chambers. Once he told the captain what he'd seen, there'd be no way to stop the coming conflict.

*Heck*, he thought as he dug through the cupboard for a towel. *There probably wasn't anything he could do anyway.* Captain Chambers had his cap set on taking down Commissioner Pete. Sage was just the new guy following orders.

He hurried through his shower because the water was ice cold. The natural gas lines had died long before Sage had arrived. After the miserable shower, he reached blindly into the hallway and felt a stack of fabric. Indeed, it was a pair of unfamiliar underwear, some gray sweats, and an "Elgin Eagles" T-shirt.

Aimee laughed when he returned to her room. "We need to fatten you up, young man." She reached over and pulled him close by the waistband of the sweats.

He let himself be tipped off-balance, and fell on top of her on the bed. He was freezing and needed her warmth. They toppled into a deep kiss, and from there, directly to the good stuff. Sage abandoned his worries while they had sex, but afterwards, his grinding guilt returned.

As much as it seemed like a bad idea, he couldn't stop himself from talking to her about his misgivings. The flush of hormones swamped him and his mouth proceeded without checking itself. He knew he should minimize risk of something bad getting back to the captain, but he had an agonizing need to sort this out.

*Could he trust her?*

Aimee took it surprisingly well—the story of his recon into Wallowa. He told her about Commissioner Pete and his dog. Sage admitted that he was having second thoughts.

She listened in silence until he finished. "You're not from around here," she stated the obvious. "You don't know our history, and you don't understand the rivalry between Wallowa and Union. We share a lot of family ties. Ranch land has gone back and forth, split so many different ways between siblings, cousins and distant relations. Today, there's bad blood everywhere you look. Pete Lathrop and Wallowa County screwed us over, big time, when they deeded the Zumwalt prairie over to the Nature Conservancy. In one stroke, those tree-hugging assholes sold out the elk hunting land we'd used for the last hundred years. You don't understand, Sage. Trust me—Commissioner Pete is NOT who you think he is. He's a dirty, double-dealing bastard. If you get the chance to knock him down a peg or two, you take it."

Her eyes burned with fury—an anger that'd probably been passed down through her DNA. When she said the words "ranch land" it almost rhymed with "holy ground."

Then, she flashed back to her effervescent smile and his apprehension melted away. "I'm just saying," she reiterated, "you're doing the right thing, helping Captain Chambers. One word of advice, though: you can talk to me about this stuff, but don't *ever* talk to anyone else. That's how you get hauled to the county line. Right?" She smiled again, as though she'd just told him her favorite band was *Fallout Boy*.

Sage nodded. He was in over his head. He had no idea what was going on here. Telling Aimee had convoluted the situation even further. What in the *literal fuck* was up with these people? He resolved that his best play was to follow her lead.

He nodded again, and packed his regrets away in a box in his mind labeled "She Said." His shoulders released some of their tension and came down from up around his ears.

Aimee took his head in her hands and laid him down on the bed. She massaged the back of his neck for a long time. Then they went for a second go-round.

## 18

MAT BEST

**McKenzie City Hall**
**McKenzie, Tennessee**

Another rat raid, more deaths. This time on Joy Drive in the northwestern corner of town. They were up to thirteen murders in town at the hands of desperate refugees, and that was aside from the hundreds of thefts. The town had experienced more crime in the last three months than in the previous thirty years by a factor of ten. Mat suspected the refugees numbered over twelve thousand now—four times the population of town.

McKenzie City Hall buzzed with the security and food committees. The latest murders on Joy Drive refreshed their terror. An elderly couple had been stabbed to death in their bed.

The massacre at Brashear wood camp hadn't been widely gossiped. Those who participated in the killing weren't bragging. Some had vanished from sight. Very few of the strike team came to Parker's funeral.

Mad Scientist Jensen showed up to the committee meeting with another milk crate of jars, and a massive, white gun that had to be some kind of pneumatic launcher. Mat kicked himself for not insisting the science teacher come on the strike at Brashear wood. Maybe that would've pulled him up short.

Sheriff Morgan began the meeting and turned the podium over to Mat.

"During the strike on the camp at Brashear wood, we lost one man, Deputy Rickers, plus three wounded, all expected to fully recover."

"How many'd we kill?" a man from the food committee interrupted.

"There were forty-six enemy casualties." Mat looked down at notes he didn't have. The room went still.

"At least now they know we mean business," the same guy interjected, this time at half volume.

"Yes, to the extent that other refugees might learn what happened there, and if they know why we did it, they know we're capable of wiping out a camp. But conducting military strikes against the camps is like swatting mosquitos on a dog. The more we swat, the more we're going to get bit. If we try to put a bullet in every refugee, we'll run out of bullets long before we ran out of refugees." His last sentence hummed with frustration.

"So, then what the hell we gonna do?" the guy blurted out.

"Finish the HESCO barrier and continue to patrol, assess and strike—mostly around the corridor to the town of Henry. We're being ambushed along the highway again, almost daily."

"What about our neighborhoods?" the woman who'd replaced Marjorie Simms on the security committee asked. Gwen Sizemore —Mat remembered her name because she was a thin, older gentle-woman. The exact opposite that her name implied..

Mat held out his hands as though he wished he had a better answer. "We need to get that wall done and we need to increase our neighborhood patrols."

It'd rained every day since Brashear wood. The townspeople had slacked off on HESCO work and on neighborhood patrols because of the discomfort of being outside in the weather. Mat and the team had a devil of a time getting people to work security in the rain.

"So, you're saying we need to keep doing more of the same? The same thing that's getting half-a-dozen of us killed every week?"

It was an exaggeration, but a fair assessment. Their town wasn't secure. That was a fact.

Mat ticked off what they had accomplished. "The HESCO's almost half done. We haven't lost hogs in weeks. We've rounded up a dozen possible HVTs—rat leaders likely to start something against us. The Creek Camp has moved on, en masse, for greener pastures, many miles from here."

The FEMA camp trick had been kept a secret—only the security and food committees knew Mat was responsible for drawing away Creek Camp. His trick worked, but only because Creek Camp and Dr. Hauser were so cooperative. The committee had talked about doing it again, but other camps were too hungry to travel even ten miles.

Mat ran out of things to count on his fingers after four, and he'd been standing in silence for a few seconds. He wanted to talk about his new camp spy initiative, but he hadn't decided if he should keep it secret or not. He'd been recruiting informants from the camps by trading food for information. *Would it leak back to the camps if he talked about it in committee?*

"Um, Sergeant Best? If I may?" Mad Scientist Jensen stepped beside him with a jangling crate of ugly jars.

Mat would've rather dealt with a hundred angry hecklers than this guy. Mat normally carried himself with the confidence of a warrior, but he came off as flat-footed around Jensen. Whenever Jensen stood up in a meeting, Mat felt like he'd stumbled into an ambush.

Mat wanted the town to accept their losses and be patient. He wanted them to knuckle down, work harder, endure the rain and finish the damned wall. They were not quick, sexy solutions, but that was all Mat had. Mad Scientist Guy, on the other hand, could trot out weapons of mass destruction and monstrous guns.

Jensen set the milk crate down on the table. "Gwen, would you please pass me the launcher?"

The egghead had literally brought a bigger gun to the meeting. As much as he wanted to tell the town that whiz-bang technology could work out to be a very dirty means of victory, he didn't have the words. *Should he tell them about Perez and his oxy habit?*

Jim Jensen jumped into the gap left by Mat's hesitation.

"Of course, you're right." Jensen gestured toward Mat, now standing beside him. Mat didn't know about what he was right about, but Jensen nodded at him with an unctuous smile. Gwen Sizemore passed Jensen the plastic, PVC cannon.

Nobody would be satisfied until they knew what the big gun did. A new weapon was a hell of a lot sexier than building a wall out of junk in the freezing rain. Mat meandered around the table and dropped into the closest chair, helpless to stop the tide of Jensen's oratory.

"Again, thank you Sergeant Best. Without you, we wouldn't have made it this far. Now it's time for the town to really dig in and support you." Jensen then talked about how the town's ingenuity was its strength—about how they'd solved a water quality problem thirty years back using science.

It was an exhibition of carefully chosen words and phrases designed to gather the committees to Jensen's way of thinking. He talked about their shared fears, and the staggering number of the refugees around them—12,000 and growing. He stoked the revulsion, outrage, and fear the townsfolk already felt. He preyed upon their fatigue. He feasted on their frustration.

When Jensen shifted to the "science" of leaving food, poisoned with botulism, for the rats to find, Mat saw way too many heads nodding agreement.

Mat wanted to stand up and scream, *so now we become Nazis?* But before he could find the words, Jensen bent the room to his artful turn.

He held out his hands and offered reason to go with the science. "These people are dying. For all intents and purposes, they're dead already." Jensen talked about the "peace of death" in one's sleep as the botulin toxin slowed the responsiveness of the diaphragm.

It was Susan Brown, the biology teacher, who finally interrupted his roll. "Mr. Jensen, I believe you may be exaggerating the peaceful nature of death by botulism poisoning."

Jensen didn't miss a beat. "Well, Susan, I can't deny we're discussing death, and death is certainly unpleasant. But avoiding death, for the refugees, is not a reasonable possibility. We're all logical people, here. We understand facts. Winter is far from over and the desperation and peril that surrounds us will double, then double again. Eventually, refugees will swarm over our wall. Eventually, they will cannibalize us. They will eat our children. I'm not exaggerating."

Apparently, Susan Brown couldn't disagree because she said nothing in response.

Jensen continued. "I propose we task Sergeant Best's night patrols with depositing food laced with botulism in the woods surrounding our town."

"What's the cannon?" Mat blurted out. He didn't have the words to stop the inevitable vote on mass poisoning, so he tried distraction instead.

"This," Jensen said, and hefted the white, bulbous gun, "is an air cannon that launches glass jars. It's the solution to your bullet shortage, Sergeant."

The gun was five feet long, made of heavy, plastic irrigation tubing. Underslung beneath the main barrel, a compression tube gathered air pressure from a compressor to launch a glass jar. The "trigger" was some kind of pneumatic ball valve on the knuckle between the compression tube and the cannon barrel. Mat had seen the same design for potato guns when he was a kid back in Santa Barbara. Somebody on the committees gasped, but with a thrill instead of a shock.

Mat knew he had lost the fight against WMDs.

"We can launch canisters of anthrax, or better yet, mustard gas, at anyone who approaches our town perimeter." Jensen patted the barrel of the cannon like a good Labrador retriever. "If a refugee camp commits crimes against our town, we can surround them and bombard them without ever stepping foot into the danger zone."

"I'm sure you'll address issues of wind, and the risk of gassing the town," Sheriff Morgan spoke for the first time. "You're getting to that part, right?"

Jensen smiled and nodded. "I still have a battery of tests to perform before I can present anything solid. I brought the cannon to show you my progress."

"Are we going to vote on the botulism thing," the loud guy from the food committee said.

Sheriff Morgan interrupted, and his voice carried great authority. "Beatrice asked me to share something with you, and now's as good a time as any." Sheriff Morgan unfolded a half sheet of paper he'd been gripping the entire meeting, and read with a voice that made it instantly obvious: he was reading words from the Bible.

"His disciples came to Him and said, 'This is a deserted place, and already the hour is late. Send all these people away, that they may go into the surrounding country and villages and find bread; for they have nothing to eat.' But He answered and said to them, 'You give them something to eat.' And they said to Him, 'Shall we go and buy two hundred denarii worth of bread and give them something to eat?' But He said to them, 'How many loaves do you have?

Go and see.'" The sheriff finished reading the passage and sat down without explanation.

Silence hung in the room, broken only by one member whispering to another. "*That doesn't make any sense.*"

Another low voice countered, "Thank you, Sheriff."

Both committees voted on the botulism plan, and while not everyone agreed, it passed.

---

CANDICE HAD JUST FINISHED a sponge bath when Jim Jensen burst into the house with his ego smoldering. She heard him coming and wrapped a towel around her body before he stormed into her bathroom.

"Your little friend's adopted father, or whatever he is, wasn't even a speed bump. We were worried that he'd try and stop our innovations, but I blew him away like flatulence in the proverbial wind."

Candice had no idea what Jim was talking about. She was having trouble concentrating on anything other than the fact that she was naked, wet and vulnerable. An excited Jim was a dangerous Jim.

"What happened?" asked Candice as she considered whether there was enough room to slip past him without making it obvious she was fleeing.

"The rifle jockey voted against our botulism plan."

"Oh," Candice said, and edged closer to the door. "That's terrible."

Jim seemed to notice her near nakedness for the first time. His speech slowed as his eyes ran down her body.

"I won, of course. He can barely string two sentences together. The committees are all behind me now."

Jensen smiled as he caressed the terry cloth towel where Candice had tucked it near her left breast.

"I'm the only one who can save this town, Candice," he said with a husky edge. "Right?"

"Yes. We need you."

Jensen gazed through her, lost for a moment. "Yes, the town needs me. And I will save them."

Jensen's fingers plucked at the tucked corner of the towel. It came free and fell.

Candice had learned how to minimize the pain and humiliation of his advances. She did what women in her circumstance had done for thousands of years. She complied with her body and pushed her mind far, far away.

---

TWENTY MINUTES LATER, Candice ran down the middle of the street, the nighttime rain mingling with her tears. She often exercised at night. It was how she decompressed after being touched by him.

After a time together in her bedroom, Jim had left her for his lab. She had thrown on sweats and bolted from the house.

Only a few lights burned in the homes of McKenzie, mostly candles. Almost every night for the last week, it'd drizzled a cold, sallow rain, tainted by smoke from the big cities and the refugee camps that surrounded them.

She left her normal exercise loop and followed a series of turns that would lead her, inexorably, to the home of William and Mat.

She lived two lives: one of a girl and the other of a woman. She only, really belonged to one, but the flavor of smoke on the rain demanded she bow to the reality of this tortured world. Thirteen years old or not, they all lived in a time that ate young ladies for dessert. Gone were the lipgloss days when a newly-minted teenager was still years from womanhood.

Jim Jensen was indeed her lifeline, but to die an orphan might be better than to live like this. In the night rain, she ran toward the boy, and away from the secrets.

———————

"Sergeant Best. May I have a word?" The sheriff waited for Mat in the foyer of the city building. Mat had just finished his nightly team leader meeting. He was bone-tired, but the sheriff never wasted his time. If he had waited around to talk, it must be important.

"Mrs. Morgan and I are leaving." It was the last thing Mat expected to hear. "Now I can see that you're upset, but hold on a moment." Sheriff Morgan raised hands, palms out, urging Mat to calm.

Mat didn't wait. "If you're bailing on this town, what the fuck am I still doing here?" He bristled.

"No, no, no. It's not like that. We're not running out on the town..."

"...because I wouldn't blame you if you bailed. We're like those German towns near the death camps—those people who stood around while the SS genocided the Jews. Except we're the ones with the poison gas this time."

"It's not necessarily about that," the sheriff explained.

Mat exhaled his frustration. "If you leave, there'll be no stopping Jensen."

"Jensen's poisons are part of a bigger dilemma; questions of survival and morality. For Beatrice and me the answer has become clear: we're going out to help the refugees. We need to do all we can for those who suffer. It's the oath we took when we chose to follow Christ. The collapse didn't change that. This badge didn't change that."

"And the town? What's the answer for the town? We can't all

follow you to join the fucking Peace Corps. They'll overrun the town in a day."

"Yes, you're right," Morgan agreed. "But when I ask God what I should do I hear the same answer again, and again. It's the refugees, Mat. The people you call rats. That's where God wants Beatrice and me. I don't think he's going to answer any of our other questions until we keep our word and obey His commands. You see what I'm saying, Mat? Bea and I aren't abandoning the town. We're keeping our word of honor. There's no way we can stay here while the town poisons those who suffer. We can't be party to it."

"You'll die out there," Mat argued. "She will die. Your wife will die, probably while you watch."

"I know that's what it looks like. She knows too. But a promise is a promise. And our faith isn't just for good times. We leave tonight. We're all packed. We're going out to look for Dr. Hauser's group. I'll keep my radio on me and, of course, my truck's got the high power mobile transceiver."

Mat surrendered to the inevitable, his hands on his hips. He seized the big man's shoulder. "I'll pray for you, I guess."

"You will?" The sheriff grinned. "I didn't peg you for a praying man."

"I'm not. But I'll make an exception for you."

―――――――

WILLIAM'S WORLD wobbled in a weird, drunken spin while Candice spoke. She said words like "*touched me down there*" and "*made me promise not to tell*" but he couldn't put the words in an order that made any sense to his twelve-year-old mind. They struck him as gobble-de-gook; an acidic, word soup that burned a festering fissure across the face of William's world. The words seared into one another, smoked and fumed, then poisoned all hope left in the world.

At first he felt confused, but the more she mumbled at him, in front of his pathetic fire as the rain pattered outside, the more his anger rose and clarified.

He'd been angry before. Heck, he'd been angry ever since Mat told him the plan to pawn him off on Gladys Carter. But this was a different color of anger. This was carbon, light-swallowing, voracious rage.

"Fuck all of them." William fed the tempest in his belly. "I'm taking you away."

The two sat next to the fireplace, drying her sweats and her waterlogged sneakers. Her sweet, feminine smell surrounded William. It overcame the smell of smoke from the fireplace. She was like cookie dough and fresh laundry. Her tears seasoned her breath with nutmeg. He would fight the world for her. He would die for her. He would kill for her.

She nodded and wiped her nose. William burned to get her a tissue, but they'd run out of tissues weeks before. He didn't know how to touch her, now that she'd been touched by evil. He didn't know how to love her, now that her love had been tainted with arsenic.

"Wait here," William said, and went to gather supplies. He might not know yet how to fight for her, but he knew how to rescue her. They would run, tonight.

---

It was very late—well past midnight as Mat wandered the streets, alone in the rain. He told himself that he was running a one man, unscheduled night patrol. He wore his rifle and his plate carrier vest, of course. He never went anywhere without them, as was the rule for QRF fighters. He looked the part of the soldier and the town defender, but really he was just a wanderer—a gunfighter with no idea where to point his gun. If someone had leapt out in front of him, brandishing a weapon, he wouldn't know whether to piss himself or dance the hula. He couldn't identify tonight's enemy on a bet.

*Was it the committee? The mad scientist guy? The rats? The sheriff? Was Mat the enemy?*

He found himself in front of the home of Gladys Carter, and lo and behold, she sat on her porch, in a wicker chair in the dark, enjoying the rain.

"Well I feel safer already." She chuckled. "Patrolman Best walks the streets at night, soaking himself to the bone."

He tipped his bump helmet like a top hat. "Good evening, Miss Carter."

"Get over here and out of the rain," she ordered. "You should be resting, not wandering like an alley cat."

He plodded up the walk, up the steps and dropped into a chair beside her. His kit rattled and he adjusted the pockets on his belt so the various bits of metal didn't stab him in the butt.

"Tell me why you're walking the streets like a fool," she said. "Then, I'll get you a nice, hot tea. I already got water goin' on the stove."

Mat tried to gather his thoughts, but gave up. Instead, he blurted the first thing that bubbled to the surface. "There's no way I'm ordering my men to deploy poisoned food outside the wall."

"Mm-hm," she agreed, though she clearly had no idea what he meant. Gladys wasn't on the committees. She didn't know about the bio-chem weapons. "You definitely should not do that."

"You really think so?" Mat stared at her dark face across the pitch-dark porch.

"I don't really know the ins-and-outs of what the hell you're talking about, but I'm a reasonably-educated, sensible woman and I can say with total certainty that you should not put poisoned food where people will find it. That's just crazy."

"Yeah, but it might be the only way," Mat said, airing the debate inside his skull.

Gladys chuckled again. "It never ceases to amaze me how quickly people abandon hope and focus on one bad option or another. It's a big universe, with thousands of solutions to every problem. Scared people are stupid people."

"When I'm a hammer, everything's a nail," Mat heard himself agree.

"Yessir. When you're a hammer, every damned thing's a nail. That's the God's honest truth."

"You're saying I should refuse the committee's order to place poisoned food near the camps?"

"Of course you should." Gladys laughed. "You were never going to do that anyhow."

The tea kettle whistled. She raised herself out of her Adirondack chair and moseyed into the house. As she passed Mat, her hand touched his shoulder.

The screen door creaked open, then clacked shut. Mat was alone with the rain and the night, but her touch had landed on him like a blessing, and his shoulder buzzed with the ghost of her hand. The feeling spread, like a warm, summer wind in the face, fresh with the scent of lilac.

In that moment, Mat didn't feel so alone.

# 19

## CAMERON STEWART

"... as a blacksmith plunges a glowing ax or adze
in an ice-cold bath and the metal screeches steam
and its temper hardens—that's the iron's strength—
so the eye of the Cyclops sizzled round that stake!"

— ODYSSEUS, THE ODYSSEY

**Grafton Ghost Town,
Southern Utah**

Cameron and Julie hid, burrowed at the base of a knot of blackbrush. Ruth stood on the highway, beneath the speed limit sign, trading with Rockville for the third time. Cameron's clan had enough guns and ammo to trade one more time after this. Isaiah insisted it was less risk to dribble out the trade goods in multiple deals, never giving any indication of when they'd run out.

Once the other side knew the trade was over, they'd have no reason to cooperate. They could shoot Ruth and seize the final delivery. The only reason for Rockville to trade in good faith was to keep the trades coming. They had no way of knowing if the supply of guns would continue for a week, a month or a year, so fair dealing made sense—for now.

The swap had settled into a routine, with the short, fat man and one of his gunmen bringing four buckets of grain to each meeting; two fresh and two stale. Ruth checked the food for quality, walked two buckets into the tree line and returned with the guns, ammo and survival gear. Then, she'd return to the treeline with the final two buckets.

This time, Cameron asked Julie to sit with him in his blind rather than sitting in her own blind, fifty yards away. Originally, he'd thought it better to separate overwatch so that they'd have two angles on the target, but given two successful trades, he figured he could fudge security this time. He wanted a minute alone with his wife. They needed to talk. He needed to come clean with her about some things.

There'd been enough food at the homestead for once—boring food, to be sure—but enough food to ease them back from the edge of desperation and toward some form of normalcy. It was time to become a proper clan, and that couldn't happen with unspoken schisms and broken loyalty.

Julie lurked behind a solid wall of depression since escaping the polygamist town over two months before. She spoke very little, and mostly just to the children. She did the minimum to survive, and often stared at the mountains of Zion for hours. It hadn't seemed strange before, because they'd all been doing the minimum to conserve energy. They'd all done a lot of staring off into the distance, dozing in the daylight. But now, with food in their bellies and energy coursing through their veins, Julie was the only person still listless.

Cameron didn't begrudge her depression. Julie's world had gone from decorating turkey-themed cupcakes for the boys' pilgrim festival to being shot at, forced into marriage and then starvation. She'd come face-to-face in the night with her husband screwing another woman. She hadn't said a word about it—Julie hadn't said anything about anything—but the time had come to make things right. Plus, there was the question of Ruth's pregnancy to discuss, with both Julie and Isaiah. The clan would need to strike a new accommodation, if only to drag the truth into the light. At least Isaiah was a polygamist, and he'd been "eternally married" to Cameron's wife in a weirdo ceremony back in the polygamist town. Isaiah would probably understand that relationships in the red desert wastelands weren't always tidy.

Isaiah's leg had responded well to the traction in-line. Coupled with a diet of carbohydrates, he was on-the-mend. He couldn't stand on the leg yet, but the pain had backed off thirty percent, he said. The shin had gone from the dark red of simmering infection to the yellow and purple of a healthy bruise. With a crutch fashioned from barnwood and a tight splint, he could hobble to the privy under his own power.

The seedlings under the cold frames had exploded in green, and they now pressed against the glass in a profusion of growth. The new, daily challenge was to replace the covers each night without breaking stems or damaging leaves.

The Grafton clan, as they called themselves, was healing, and after a couple more trades, they'd be provisioned well enough to survive until the green grass of springtime.

Cameron's attention snapped back to Ruth, on the highway with the traders from Rockville. She hovered over another bucket, checking the contents. There appeared to be no surprises. She lifted two buckets, climbed down the highway embankment and trudged across the field toward the big cottonwood where they'd stashed the guns. Everything was going according to pattern.

"Jules," Cameron called his wife by her nickname. "I wanted to say: I'm sorry for all of this."

"Huh?" she looked up from studying the grass.

"I'm sorry for how this turned out. I've been a shit husband, I know."

Julie's face turned in his direction, but he couldn't read her expression.

"I mean," he stammered, "I'm sorry about Ruth. I don't know what happened. I don't love her. The hunger had me in its grip, and I wasn't myself. I've made some awful decisions."

"Ruth?" the question floated in her eyes.

"Yeah. I'm sorry. I'm ending it."

"What are you talking about?"

"It was never love. Just sex. And not really even sex, per se. There were no feelings, you know?" He was rambling.

She blinked three times. "Wait. Are you telling me that you had sex with Ruth? You cheated on me with a horse-face polygamist?" She went to stand up.

Cameron grabbed her belt and pulled her under cover. "Stay down, Julie. They'll see you." Apparently, she had *not* seen he and Ruth that night in the trees. "You don't get to tell me what to do, you...pig." Julie broke free and pushed her way up through the blackbrush. It was more words than she'd said to him in a long time, and he was astonished at the sudden intensity. He hadn't thought she was capable of it anymore.

"You fucking asshole," her voice launched into a high warble. "You screwed her in the same house with our sleeping children? Do they know?"

"No. I mean we never...did it in the house."

"You cheated on me with *her*?" Julie shrieked.

"Lower your voice and get back down. They're going to see you."

"You don't ever get to tell me what to do *ever again*." Julie was on her feet now, and her rifle barrel drifted in his direction. He had bigger problems than screwing up the trade.

"Point that rifle away from me. Julie—stop and think."

The corral that'd penned in her anxiety, terror and cataclysmic loss seemed to burst its fences all-at-once. The wild-eyed ponies of her ruined wonderworld caromed onto open ground, and bolted for the horizon. She arched her back and howled with rage.

Halfway across the clearing, carrying the last two buckets, Ruth froze. The fat cowboy and the men in the truck jolted toward the scream. Cameron sprang at Julie's rifle barrel and batted it aside.

*BOOM!*

The round from her rifle went into the ground. Cameron lunged at the barrel, yanked it out of her hand and stumbled into the clearing.

*Boom, boom, boom. Zzzzt-crack.*

The men in back of the truck from Rockville opened fire. Cameron's own AR-15 jumped out of his hand like it'd been smacked with an aluminum baseball bat. He threw himself sideways into the blackbrush and scrambled to his knees.

An invisible golfer hit Julie in the head with a golf club. Her head cocked at an unnatural angle, like lifting her ear to the sky to identify a strange sound. A bloody divot of scalp chipped off her skull and cartwheeled into the underbrush. Her scream died instantly in the breeze. Her legs crumpled and she folded sideways to the ground. Slumped against the blackbrush, the fury in her face gave way to mute amazement. Her sightless eyebrows lifted as if to say, "What's that you said, Cam?" She lay motionless, like a boneless puppet of herself.

Cameron's brain ceased to function. He was buried in the blackbrush, ass-over-tea kettle. He was eye-to-eye with his dead wife. She didn't blink, just stared, an eternal question setting in forever across her eyes.

*What's that you said?* her face wondered.

Part of Cameron's brain wanted to continue the argument. It needed to explain. *"I'm sorry for shtupping the horse-face polygamist. Don't worry about that. It's not like I got her pregnant or anything."*

*Boom, boom, boom....Boom, boom.*

Cameron's fear dragged him back to the violent present. He scrambled to the edge of the briar and gazed at the highway. Bullets sizzled through the air, but they no longer seemed focused on his position. Julie—their primary target—had disappeared from view. Now their bullets hunted phantoms along the tree line.

Ruth low-crawled under the sage toward where she'd left her rifle. New waves of gunfire erupted from the hill on the opposite side of the road. Men scampered down the hillside, running from sagebrush to sagebrush, firing into the riverside bramble. Cameron counted the men as they rushed forward. He thought there were a dozen. It was an ambush, and it was probably always going to be an ambush. Rockville had been poised to screw them this morning. By freaking out, Julie sprung the trap early.

Cameron crawled past his rifle in the brush. A bullet had sliced through the aluminum breach. It looked like someone had taken a welding torch to the upper receiver. That rifle was finished.

He grabbed Julie's rifle, hanging from a dead branch, and scrambled deeper into cover. He left her body in the blackbrush, her blank face still working through the confusion of a world catapulted into the absurd.

*I don't understand. What did you say? You cheated on me with a polygamist chick?*

———

CAMERON RETREATED fifty feet from the clearing before climbing to his feet and running. Bullets sluiced through the thicket, burning holes in the underbrush and knocking chunks off the cottonwood bark. Ruth appeared ahead on his path, gathering her rifle and backpack. She grabbed the two buckets she'd dropped earlier.

"No, no, no. They're coming. More than a dozen. Leave the food," he shouted.

She did as she was told and ran behind him in a crouch, her huge, polygamist dress swirling around her feet.

They waded the Virgin River and struck out directly for the Grafton homestead. The *pock-pock-pock* of gunfire across the highway slowed, then stopped. The ambush had paused for the moment, probably regrouping before pursuing them into the thicket. Cameron had no doubt they would follow their trail. Why prepare an ambush if not to pursue and take back all they'd traded?

Cameron waved Ruth forward.

"Where's Julie?" Ruth heaved for breath.

"She's dead." He shook his head. "They'll follow us for sure. We need to get back to Isaiah."

As they ran through the trees and broke into the open pasture around the cabin, Julie's voice echoed in his head.

*What did you say?*

They'd been together fifteen years, and now they'd never be together again. All those long years keeping house, raising kids, arguing about bills. A lump of lead, a chip of skull and it was gone.

Their life together was over. Compulsive, reckless sex had ended it—or had it been a bullet that ended it? His mind reeled. It had happened so fast. But he knew this for sure: her death was on him, as sure as if he'd pulled the trigger himself. He'd pulled it with his dick and a thoughtless treachery. Julie had deserved better. Depressed or not, she'd deserved better than Cameron Stewart.

Even with her surging skirts, Ruth pulled ahead of him across the pasture around the homestead. Isaiah stood on the porch, holding himself up with one of the posts. The children gathered beside him, terrified by the sound of gunfire. Cameron poured on the speed. He needed to get to Isaiah. Isaiah would know what to do.

"They're coming!" Cameron bellowed as he ran. "Right behind us."

Isaiah shouted something to the children and they rushed inside. Ruth fell behind Cameron's exhausted sprint. Cameron needed Isaiah—needed to know what to do next.

"How many?" Isaiah asked as Cameron closed the distance.

"Fifteen, I think," Cameron heaved as he took the steps two-at-a-time. "More than we can fight. Julie's dead." He bent over and struggled for breath.

Pain wrestled on Isaiah's face. His leg must've been on fire.

"Get the kids in the truck and get out of here," Isaiah said. He choked on the pain, swallowed and said again, with resolve, "You take Ruth and the children. I'll make a stand."

"That's stupid. We all get in the truck and go," Cameron argued.

Isaiah shook his head emphatically as he battled personal tides of agony.

The boys and Leah rushed out of the cabin carrying buckets of food. The little ones had bedding in their arms. They ran to the truck, threw everything in the truck bed and ran back inside for more.

Isaiah spoke with unaccustomed authority. "I'll make a show of defense. The Rockville militia needs to think we're pinned down, or they'll cut you off on Wire Valley Road. If they have radios, they'll call back to town. They'll ambush you as you go past. They're after our guns and the food. The only way out of here is to go past the back side of Rockville. It's the only escape route over the butte. Cameron, you need to go now and let me do my part. Get Ruth and the kids out. Save my family."

"That's stupid," Cameron repeated, but he knew Isaiah was right. They were on the opposite side of the river, and the only road out of Grafton doubled back past Rockville. If the militia knew they fled with the supplies, they'd ambush them and shoot them to pieces. The truck could probably blow past, right now, but only because Rockville thought they had them cornered. The jig was up.

"Cameron, there's no time to debate. I'll tie them up here. Take Ruth and the kids, and everything we have, and go. Run toward Saint George. It's your best chance. *You* are this family's best chance." Isaiah put a hand on his ruined leg. "*You* are their father now. Her *husband*. Promise me."

Ruth overheard, sobbed in agony, but worked feverishly inside the house, nonetheless.

"Promise me," Isaiah asked him again. "Be her husband. Their father."

"I will." Cameron looked into the eyes of the man he'd once planned to kill. "I promise."

"Brothers in Christ," Isaiah said, and held out his hand to Cameron. "Husbands unto the Lord."

Cameron took the hand and pulled himself into Isaiah's chest. He hugged him hard. He would've liked to crack a joke, but the sob trapped in his throat wouldn't allow it.

Isaiah pushed him back upright. "Go, before they see you drive away. Go now."

Cameron ran inside, grabbed the heavy pack with the survival supplies, and sprinted for the truck.

---

CAMERON, Ruth and the five children pulled over in the truck after they flew past Rockville and reached the top of the butte. They stood where they could see into two valleys—the Virgin River and Colorado City, both. Cameron got out and leaned against the truck, and watched through binoculars as their homestead was overrun by riflemen. The crackle of gunfire reached two miles, delayed and echoey.

Rockville men fell in the pasture. They fell surrounding the cabin. They fell on the porch as they kicked in the door of the cabin.

Isaiah made a good showing for himself—a man's man, when it counted. He exacted a steep price from the Rockville thieves for their trespass.

Cameron turned the binoculars on the town of Rockville. The truck had made it past before the assholes could block the road. The militia was probably just now realizing that Isaiah had been alone in the cabin—that the clan had fled with the guns and supplies.

Still, Cameron knew they were the furthest thing from safe. They'd slipped the noose of Rockville only to throw themselves onto the mercy of the angry, red desert. There was only one dirt road and it'd take them back toward Colorado City—the polygamist enclave where Cameron had killed over a dozen men to free his family.

Isaiah once told him that this dirt road emptied onto Highway 59, north of Colorado City. Hopefully, it was far enough north to avoid a confrontation with the colony. The last time Cameron drove through Colorado City, they'd shot him in the throat.

It was early afternoon. Colorado City—the polygamist town— was a gridwork of homes painted across the red sands. Parts of the town belched black smoke. Tanks—actual army battle tanks— stood in a mile-long column through the center of town.

A shiver ran up Cameron's spine. He hated that town, and all the polygamists of Colorado City. In his book, they deserved to be crushed by the Army. But his hate paused mid-flush, and he checked himself: one of their favored sons had just given his life to save Cameron and his boys.

Perhaps the United States Army had come up against the road-block outside of town—the same one that'd put a bullet through Cameron's throat. Maybe the Army had smashed it flat and set fire to the town. Maybe the polygamists had reaped what they had sowed; unforgiving, mechanized death. Yet he couldn't celebrate the destruction of his enemies—not with Isaiah dead and his wife standing beside him against the truck, between their children and death. He could only bear witness.

"I don't think that's the American Army," Ruth muttered, perhaps reading his mind.

She watched with the same, shared binoculars, but she saw with different eyes. She probably didn't see a cult. She probably saw her home and her religion in flames.

"Look." She pointed. "The soldiers aren't wearing uniforms. They're regular guys. Maybe...Mexicans?"

Cameron didn't know if Mexico had tanks, but she was right about the uniforms. The men milling around the column of parked tanks weren't wearing camouflage. He couldn't tell what nationality they were, just that they weren't behaving like American army. If they weren't the government, who the hell were they? If they were the Mexican Army, wouldn't they be wearing Mexican uniforms?

It didn't matter if they were U.S., Mexican or Martian, Cameron would avoid them at all costs. He'd avoid everyone. Their clan were now refugees, with barely enough food to make it to spring. The food and guns made them strong, but it also made them a target; a neon sign saying "*Look at Me. I'm not Starving. I have stuff.*"

They needed a place to hide, to sit out the winter. That meant getting down off the butte before the column of tanks moved north and cut off their escape. He had no idea what they'd find north of Colorado City on Highway 59, but it couldn't be worse than the Rockville militia or a column of plundering tanks.

*What's behind Door Number Three, Bob?*
*Throw it open, Cam, and find out! It could be a brand new car, a wash-*

*er/dryer or a roadblock bristling with cannon. Try your luck! Spin the big wheel!*

"WE NEED TO GO," Cameron said.

"Yes." Ruth climbed back in the cab of the truck. The children were piled on top of each other in the back seat. Ruth pulled Cameron's youngest son onto her lap. Cameron wondered if the passenger side airbag had been disabled. It could be dangerous in a wreck.

He looked one more time at the smoldering town through their binoculars.

Tanks. Airbags. Starvation. Crucifixion. Marauders. The many faces of rollicking death. He'd lost his wife and his friend so far today. Who else would die before nightfall? One of the children? All of the children?

The pickup truck's gas gauge was almost on empty. Saint George wasn't far—maybe thirty miles as the crow flew—but he'd have to take detours to avoid the armed patrols of the town of Hurricane, and then he'd need to figure out how to get through the roadblocks keeping people out of Saint George.

"Run for Saint George," Isaiah had said. Isaiah had believed running was better than hiding in the desert, but Cameron didn't know why. They'd been hiding in the desert for months, and it hadn't ended well. Maybe Isolation meant vulnerability. Hiding was great until someone found you, which they inevitably would. Scavengers picked across the land like locusts. The only real safety was a town, civilization, if any still existed.

*Run for Saint George.* Isaiah had implored him. He'd promised to do it.

Highway 59 would take them back through Hurricane, which Cameron thought might be as dangerous as Rockville. He'd find a dirt road around the town, then loop west toward the big city of Saint George. There, he hoped to slip in and take up residence without raising a fuss. They didn't need anything from the city— just a buffer zone of watchful humans to blunt the predations of marauders and militias. The clan had enough food for the rest of the winter, but they needed protection from predators. They needed a community to watch their back. A bigger clan.

The truck rolled down the dirt road on the south side of the butte, following an old two-track that had probably been used by polygamist kids to escape out from under the watchful eyes of their priesthood.

Cameron would gladly submit to a few priests at this point, if it meant being surrounded by a community. He'd run fresh out of individualism. After living in a bolt-hole, under the starry skies, away from the comforting lights of town, he no longer took good neighbors for granted. The Grafton bug-out location had chewed every ounce of fat off his body, taken his wife's life and killed his friend. At this point, he'd trade his dad's sterling, American individualism—*"neither a borrower nor a lender be"*—for a half-decent Neighborhood Watch.

The truck reached the highway at sunset. The tanks still hadn't rolled out of Colorado City. Cameron stomped on the spongy accelerator and put distance between the clan and the armored column. Hopefully, by this time tomorrow, they'd be tucked away in an abandoned house in Saint George, no longer refugees. Having no place to hide, no home base, left them vulnerable to threats from every point of the compass. He longed to have his back against a community, with allies surrounding him, facing threats head-on instead of over his shoulder. Being a refugee felt like a three-hundred and sixty degree ring of death.

They drove fifty miles on blacktop, through the coming night, and descended toward Hurricane. The dark closed in on all sides and the gas gauge ceased its bobbing and stuck firm to the red post.

Ruth drifted to sleep in the dark of the cab, as did the children. Looming death had dried up any lifeforce energy in the cab of the truck. They slept while Cameron drove, and communed with ghosts.

As the half moon hovered overhead and flickered between the banks of clouds, ghastly figures glowed in the bed of the truck. Cameron watched them in the rearview mirror. If he didn't look straight at them, they appeared in the edges of the gloom of the taillights. His dead wife, Julie, sat on the driver's side, perched on the wheel well, leaning back against the sidewall. Her arms reached wide, relaxed and wind-blown. Her golden hair whipped in the slipstream, clean and intact. She luxuriated in it, grinned and laughed like the girl he'd met at a party, fifteen years before. Across from her, the big, easygoing polygamist sat on a pallet, younger-faced than Cameron had ever seen him. Isaiah pontificated to Julie about some factoid—the stolid young man, religious and sure. Hardworking and fair.

Cameron knew they weren't really there. His mind was making its allowances for the injustices of the day. He'd played his guilt-stained part in the play, and the other protagonists had suffered for it. They'd been taken up to heaven, now away from this world of terror and pain. Julie was no longer depressed and Isaiah was free of pain, but for a moment, they tarried in Cameron's truck bed.

The ghost of Isaiah looked straight at him in the rearview mirror and pointed a thick finger. He grinned, as if to say, "I see the same thing you saw when we first met: the back of the head of a weirdo, his polygamist wife and bundle of kids, in a pickup truck in the southern desert, running for their lives."

The ghost said something to Julie in the whistling wind. It sounded like "Look! Cam and I traded places. Ain't God a darn joker?" The ghost raised his eyebrows and poked his finger ahead, into the night. "Lookout, brother," the ghost mouthed.

Cameron stood up on the brakes and the truck howled to a

sliding stop. Ruth and the children jolted awake with screams and cries. Red bonfires burned on both sides of the highway, a mile down the road: the Hurricane road block. The town, once a sparkling pool of electric light, barely twinkled beyond in a dark valley, with a few campfires and a hundred wispy candles.

Cameron made a three-point turn and drove back the way they'd come. His terrified family settled with each new thump-thump-thump of the reflective bumps in the road. Cam found the dirt road Isaiah had described to get around the roadblock. If it was the right one, it'd circle the town and drop them at Sheep Bridge, at the edge of the tiny town of La Verkin. Hopefully, La Verkin hadn't militarized like Hurricane and Rockville.

Every move, for refugees, was fraught with risk. They just had to survive the night, Cameron urged himself and his ghosts. Just this one night.

---

THEY CROSSED THE SMALL, concrete bridge and rolled through the town of La Verkin. It'd been rendered black, toothless and burned out. Charred posts and soot-plastered chimneys were all that remained of the farming hamlet. Some past evil had chosen the town for immolation. Cameron rolled through the graveyard and toward the interstate.

They would attempt entry, that night, into Saint George. It was a plan crafted by Isaiah, many weeks before—a plan barely remembered. Cameron had never seen the mountains at the back of Saint George. He'd only ever motored past the city, flying along the interstate toward Salt Lake City to visit his sister.

Isaiah had cavorted around the little city of Saint George as a teenager, no doubt hoping to glimpse the lives of "normal" high schoolers. He'd known the roads, lanes and dirt tracks in and around the once-neon boulevard. The way he'd described it, Saint

George sounded like a throwback to the nineteen fifties, straight out of *Happy Days*. Now, that same boulevard would be chained-up pizza joints and dusty milkshake shops. It'd be a sad, rusting monument to the heyday of middle America. The boulevard would be surrounded by thousands of brick bungalows, and most of them would be occupied by frightened, resolute Mormons, each with their food storage and maybe a few boxes of hunting rifle cartridges. To Cameron, it sounded like paradise. The lawns would be overgrown, but streets would be safe—at least until that column of tanks came to town.

Saint George was only a dozen miles away, now. But they couldn't approach directly on the interstate. They'd have to circle around. Without a doubt, the city blockaded the main approaches. Cameron would have to probe to find a way under the watchful eyes of the community guard.

The truck drove slowly through another smoldering town. The winter mists rolled off the snowy plains of the valley and curled into cloud banks along the dark ramparts of red rock. The chill night air flattened the clouds to earth and splashed them against the buttes and gravelly escarpments. Cameron flicked the switches on the dash, but the aging truck had no fog lights. The engine missed a beat as they passed through a cut in the hills and descended toward the junction with the interstate. The engine sputtered, coughed then resumed its growling when they hit flat land. They weren't going to make it to Saint George in the truck and they were too far to walk, at least not carrying their food.

Cameron quietly cursed himself. *If I had looked for gas in the burned-out towns.*

Without Isaiah, he felt like a hammer without a hand.

The engine sputtered, then cut. The silence of night enveloped the truck. Ruth and the children slept with quiet murmurs and troubled dreams. The tires hummed against the roadway. The headlights pierced the fog, but it was a sham. The light would only last as long as the battery, now. They rolled downslope by gravity for the moment, but hundreds of bearings, gears and shafts bled momentum away into a stubborn universe that preferred stillness to life.

Ahead in the distance, the fog glowed. The apparition of head-lights pinpricked the haze and lit the fog banks. Cameron strained to see what lay ahead, but it was pointless. Six pairs of lights—probably the same marauders who'd burned the towns—waited up ahead. He groped the dashboard for the switch and killed the truck lights in a desperate, if too-late attempt to save his family from the hell that would soon eat them alive. The truck rolled to a stop with the squeal of brakes. The clan was doomed. Cameron sighed. His instinct to give up rose on a ground-glass bed of frustration.

Ruth woke up, rubbed her eyes and craned her neck forward to stare into the impenetrable fog.

"What're those lights?" she asked.

"They've seen us. We're out of gas," Cameron explained. Ruth was usually content to leave decisions in the hands of others. It was a nice quality: being a good follower. That quality alone should've guaranteed her survival, but she'd hitched her wagon to the wrong star. Cameron had been the wrong man to award sex. He was no husband—no sheepdog at the gate. He ran like an aimless mongrel, snapping at flying birds and chasing jackrabbits he would never catch. Without the steadiness of Isaiah, Cameron couldn't shepherd a family. He had no business leading a clan.

The mongrel knew what to do, now. *Run.*

The marauders would want Ruth, and maybe they'd want the little girl, Leah. They might not kill Ruth's other kids to keep her from going insane. The killers up ahead would want the two women for sex, of course, but that was better than death, wasn't it...*was it?*

Either way, Cameron and his two boys were dead. The marauders would cut their throats on this very spot and leave their bodies for the turkey vultures. But they could run, and leave Ruth behind to occupy the horde. Maybe that'd satisfy them. Maybe they wouldn't see the need to chase after three tracks in the snow. If Cameron and his boys didn't run, the killers would surround the truck in two minutes, and after that, he'd be a trussed hog. A leashed cur. A dead man.

Cameron jumped out of the truck and snatched the backpack of ammo from the truck bed. He flung open the rear door of the crew cab and woke his son.

"Come on, Denny, we gotta run," he said to the boy. "We need to go. Ruth, give me Paulie. Give me my son."

Ruth opened the passenger door and hurried around, the four-year-old boy in her arms. Cameron slung his rifle around to his back and scooped up the child.

"What're we doing?" she asked. Her own rifle dangled from its sling.

"You're better off with them. You'll be okay with them," he said, flicking his head toward the lights.

But her eyes reflected the withering truth: she and the girls would *not* be okay. They would be better off dead. They needed a family in order to survive. Her hand gripped the front of Cameron's shirt and wouldn't let go. When he went to pull away, she pulled the handful of cloth and buttons back toward her.

"We are a family," she hissed.

Cameron closed his eyes and exhaled. His resolve evaporated. The headlights in the fog rolled forward, slowly. The rumble of engines and men carried on the fog. The truck would soon be surrounded. Cameron shucked off his backpack and let it fall to the pavement. A new, cleaner resolve formed within him, a dogged resolve in the face of futility. Ruth was right. They were a family, and they could still die like a family.

"Leah, take a gun," he said. "You too Denny. Get in the bed of the truck and get ready to shoot anyone who isn't us." Cameron wrapped a free arm around Denny and hefted him over the side of the truck bed.

Denny began to cry. "I don't know how to shoot."

"I know. I know, Denny. It's okay. Just do your best. Here, take your brother." He passed the child to Denny and gathered an extra rifle from the truck. He ran the slide on an AR-15 and passed it to Leah, then lifted her into the truck bed too. Denny sobbed quietly. The fog around them carried a timeless truth, plain to all, young and old—this was where everything ended. This is where their light would finally bleed away into the mist.

"You get in too." Cameron pointed Ruth into the truck bed. "I'll be over here, to get an angle on them. Don't shoot until you see the men. Don't shoot at the lights."

Ruth stepped onto the bumper, swung her skirt over the tailgate and settled in for the fight. They were all crying now. Cameron too.

The headlights were no more than a hundred feet out now, and Cameron heard the rumble of heavy equipment. Tanks, maybe.

Before his last stand, he held Denny's chin in his hand, leaned over the wall of the truck and looked him eye-to-eye in the dim. "I love you Den-ster. You're a man now. This is what men do. No matter what happens, we protect them. Okay?"

The boy sniffed back his tears and nodded in the dark. "No matter what," Cam repeated.

*I guess this is what we have left,* Cameron thought. *We keep our word to the dead.*

"Occupants of the truck, come out with your hands where we can see them," a bullhorn blared out of the mist. "We will open fire if you do not." The vehicles crunched forward on the pavement. The shapes of men passed in front of the headlights, like a pack of wolves circling.

"This is your last warning. Surrender your arms and step out in front of your headlights."

Cameron stepped to the hood of the truck, leaned over and took aim at the shadows. With everything he had left, he bellowed, "Let's dance, motherfuckers."

*One last jackrabbit to chase. One last bar brawl. This was something Cameron knew how to do.*

The bullhorn crackled. Another voice took over.

"Who is that? Tell me your name or we shoot."

Some faint hope rattled in Cameron's head, like a memory of a dream of a time that existed before memory.

"I'm Cameron Stewart and I'm about to kill a stack of you assholes, so shuttup and fight," he yelled.

"No shit?" the bullhorn answered. "I'll be da—" the bullhorn cut out. Another man's voice continued without the bullhorn. "Don't shoot." It shouted. "Cameron. Don't shoot. It's Tommy. It's me, Tommy."

Cameron's mind stutter-stepped. A shadow grew before the headlights; bigger than a man, monstrous in the fog. The towering shadow threw off spectral rays of light around it. "Don't shoot me, Shithead. It's your brother, Tommy."

Cameron clicked his gun to safe and fell back to the truck bed. "Put down your guns. Denny, put it down. Carefully. Leah, Ruth. Put your guns down. Lay them down." The truck bed clattered with rifles. The sobbing and muttered questions continued. Cameron ignored them.

"Don't shoot. It's me, Tommy." Cameron's brother materialized from the fog and into the thin light around the truck. He wore military camouflage and had a big rifle slung across his back. He held his hands up. "Is that really you, Cam? I'll be dipped in shit. We found you. Out here in the middle of fucking nowhere."

Cameron had been lost, but now he was found. The brothers hugged; their own, lost clan restored.

# 20

## SAGE ROSS

**Chambers Ranch**
**La Grande, Oregon**

C aptain Chambers tasked Sage to work with the 'arrest team' on combat training. That's what he called the ten high-school-aged boys chosen to slip into Wallowa County with Sage and Captain Chambers. The plan was to arrest Commissioner Pete off his porch in the dead of night—when he went out to pee.

The captain chose the boys from La Grande High's receivers and backs. He whisked them away to his ranch outside La Grande, telling their parents they were 'training to defend Union County.' Once sequestered at the ranch, they learned basic combat firearms and put a finer edge on their cardio fitness. The captain armed them with department AR-15 rifles, and kitted them out in assault vests.

"This county leaks gossip like a rusty bucket," he told Sage. "Nobody can know what we're doing until it's over."

They'd been at it for two weeks, and the boys were probably as solid as they were going to get. If Sage had been the golden child of the La Grande P.D. before, after his last mission into Wallowa, he was their patron saint. The captain treated him like the son-he-never-had.

Sage had traversed twenty-five miles of wilderness and infiltrated to the Commissioner's doorstep, even checking the gas levels and keys on the snow machines. It didn't seem like a big deal to Sage at the time, but the captain talked about it as though he'd crept into Hitler's Eagle's Nest and secretly impregnated the tyrant's girlfriend.

Armed with Sage's intelligence, they had a clear plan to infiltrate and exfiltrate, and they knew when the Commissioner got up to take a piss. From that point, things moved down the tracks like a locomotive with a drunk conductor and a tender full of dry coal.

"Old men are like clockwork," the captain explained. "If he got up at 3:30 a.m. one night, he'll get up at 3:30 a.m. every night. If he pissed off his porch once, he'll piss off his porch always."

It made sense, but Sage disliked it—arresting a man outside his home while he peed. But the die was cast. Sage consoled himself with the knowledge that he would be asked to make peace with many evils in this new world.

He'd shot men before. Their faces had filled his scope and their guts had blown onto the snow, red as Christmas. Someday, he hoped to stop having nightmares about those men. He would welcome the day when he didn't wake up in the witching hour and see their slack faces against the snow.

Snatching up a county politico and throwing him in jail shouldn't be a big deal after the killing he'd done; it would be just another burr under his saddle.

He was tempted to join the high school boys in their five mile afternoon run, but with the mission coming, he opted to conserve his energy. Captain Chambers called it "tapering," which had something to do with storing up glycogen in the muscles prior to a triathlon. Sage wondered how many years it would be until the world hosted another triathlon, or the Olympics.

It wasn't like the world was starved for exercise. People hadn't been in better shape in a hundred years. Everyone worked, all day, with their bodies and hands. Nobody worked strictly with their mind anymore.

He and the high school boys were the same age, but running laps with them felt like child's play. The boys left from the bunkhouse, and the same daily competition heated up: some boys lit out like they were running the quarter mile, going balls-out to be first. Those same guys would be dragging ass by Mile Two and would barely make the finish line at Mile Five. Even after weeks of running five miles, they couldn't help themselves. They sprinted and then paid the price. Everything was a competition for these numb nuts high schoolers, but Sage knew better than to get sucked in. Even around other seventeen year-olds, he'd seen too much bad shit in the world to squander his energy on gamesmanship.

He'd been seeing a lot of Aimee Butterton. The captain didn't ask him to sleep over on the ranch with the high school boys, so he drove out to Elgin every evening, curled up in Aimee's lap and let the stress of the coming mission bleed away into her sweet smell.

Union County had a lot of gasoline from a storage facility Sage had never seen, and no one seemed to be conserving fuel. The unleaded would go bad in another eight or ten months. So, they didn't begrudge him the gas to drive thirty miles to see his girlfriend.

Sage had begun to wonder if Aimee might be too old for him, but that didn't stop him from gravitating to her like a puppy to its mother. Sometimes, as she swept back his hair and rubbed his neck, she felt more like a big sister than a lover.

Once, he picked her pants off the floor when he reached for his own, and based on the feel of them, he guessed hers might be an inch bigger around the waist. She was no bikini model. She looked great naked, but she was twenty-two years old, and while he'd seen the dark side of the world, she was the adult in the relationship. She was wiser in the ways of north-eastern Oregon, and she corrected his mistaken assumptions about town and county. If she came off as a little motherly, that could be forgiven. Sage needed a mother, he supposed.

He'd never been with a more physically affectionate woman. She rarely stopped rubbing his shoulders, scratching his back and straightening his hair.

His nightly appearance at the Butterton home became routine. He got to know the older sisters, and even kissed Mrs. Butterton on the cheek when he came through the door. The smell of comfort food usually swirled around him when he stepped over the threshold, redolent of potatoes, casserole, cheese and cabbage. The captain kept the Buttertons in food and drink, and their home welcomed Sage, every evening, like the prodigal son. After he got over the newness of sex with Aimee, he couldn't tell if he was going every night to see his girlfriend, or just going home.

Captain Chambers never spoke of Aimee Butterton to Sage. He and the captain spent most of their days together at the Chambers' ranch, around the captain's wife and children. It was the wrong place to mention the Buttertons. He took his cue from the captain and kept his mouth shut.

Sage spent less and less time in his hotel room in La Grande. He'd found a home with the Butterton ladies and they treated him like a beloved pet—five pretty girls and their smoking hot mom. After two weeks, he settled in as a member of the family. Occasionally, one sister or another would breeze through the living room in panties, or with her breasts out, while Sage ate leftovers or enjoyed a cup of coffee with Mrs. Butterton at the kitchen counter.

The more comfortable he grew with his new, all-girl family, the more he regretted ever thinking of the place as a whorehouse.

That'd been his first impression, but he'd judged them unfairly for "entertaining" The Five. The longer he stayed, the more he understood: they were guilty only of coming to terms with the new world faster than others. Trading companionship and sexual congress for food and protection had always been the way. Modern society briefly interrupted fifty thousand years of sexual transaction, only for it to come rushing back. It wasn't as simple as prostitution, and it probably never was.

Aimee told him that her mom and Captain Chambers had been a thing before the apocalypse—even before their father died. Mrs. Butterton had been unfaithful to the girls' dad, and he'd died, leaving the breach unresolved. It was a sullen cloud that drifted over the house from time to time; a rare bit of enmity between mother and daughters.

The high school boys were returning from their run, much reduced in piss and vinegar. Sage snapped out of his daydreaming and pointed them back to the bunkhouse to get their guns. They returned at a sloppy jog and Sage ordered them to set up and resolve Type One, Type Two and Type Three malfunctions on their ARs. They were blown out from the run, and Sage walked up and down the firing line cajoling their messy performance.

The captain cut a beeline across the pasture from the house.

Sage smiled. "Good afternoon, Sir."

The captain pointed at the boys. "Are they ready?"

Sage shrugged. "When I can get them to stop playing grab ass, they do okay."

"We rounded up snowshoes for everyone. If you think their snow boots are adequate, then I think we're set to go. We've got a small storm tonight. There'll be a window of good weather after that."

"How do you know the forecast?" Sage asked.

The captain pointed at the building clouds atop the Blue Mountains. "Your best weatherman is what your eyes tell you. That one's a small storm. It's not dark and towering like the heavy ones. But a big one will come soon. After that, even the snow machines will have trouble bogging down in the canyon bottoms. This is our window. We go tomorrow, weather permitting."

Sage had been secretly harboring hope that the weather would stop the mission. The ranch was tucked so far back in the valley that it'd soon become difficult to reach, even on snowmobiles. Unless Union County plowed the main road right up to the Wallowa roadblock, the smaller county could soon lock itself in a snow fortress for the duration of the winter.

Sage turned to the high school boys and shouted like an angry drill sergeant, "Pack it in. Head to the bunkhouse, get a meal and prep your packs to head out tomorrow. Open chambers on those rifles while you're in the bunkhouse! I want to see nothing but air in there. No brass. If you shoot a hole in the captain's place, we shoot a hole in you. That's the deal."

But he was no drill sergeant, Sage knew. He was just a boy like them. He'd gone to one, two-day training on the AR-15, and that made him the most-expert guy on the force when it came to running gun drills.

Sage would be late to the Buttertons' tonight. He'd need to drive by his hotel and pack up his own kit so he'd be ready the next morning. The extra drive time would chew into his sleep, but he needed the smell of Aimee. He needed her assurance that he was doing the right thing.

Packing wouldn't be a problem. Every item in his winter survival pack had proven itself useful or been discarded. After crossing the Blue Mountains and conducting two recon missions into Wallowa, Sage knew exactly what to expect. His gear was like a second skin, and it was all dried out, which felt like a new lease on life.

He got the boys settled in for supper, said his goodbyes to Captain Chambers and his wife, and headed to his hotel. He put all thoughts of Aimee aside while he ran a mental inventory of what he could leave behind, given he'd be spending a single night in the snow. When covering that much ground—twenty-five miles each way in snowshoes—ounces became pounds and pounds would eat you alive. Anything he could ditch, he'd ditch. He wasn't worried about beating the high school boys on the trail, but he needed every advantage to make sure he didn't lag behind the boss.

The cold and the wind had burned hard lines into Sage's face. He could see it when he looked at himself in the rearview mirror of the police cruiser. The world-weariness of surviving outdoors had etched into his soul. He would never again be a carefree high schooler like the boys at the ranch. He'd never again sprint the first quarter mile of a five mile run.

He wished the hardness had sunk deeper. He wished it'd cauterized more of his soul because no matter how much he focused on his backpack stove and whether to bring a bigger knife, his heart quailed at the thought of putting hands on Commissioner Pete.

Aimee's touch would make it okay, at least for tonight. She'd steady his resolve; remind him that he knew nothing about the area's history, or about Commissioner Lathrop and his family. She'd punctuate her words with caresses and cooing singsong, and he would drift off to sleep in her arms.

Sleep was the only peace he could hope for in this fucked up world.

---

**Lathrop Ranch**
**Outside Enterprise, Oregon**
**Wallowa Valley**

LUCKILY, the arrest team from La Grande P.D. had spent only one night sleeping in the snow. The boys were wet and freezing, and they bitched about it non-stop. Keeping them quiet through the cold, dark night had proven nearly impossible. Captain Chambers threatened to shoot the next boy who spoke out loud.

A malevolent, churning snow cloud had poured over the top of the Blue Mountains as the team of twelve men snowshoed through the pines that afternoon, following the same trail Sage had cut on his recon mission. Other than hundreds of elk tracks and a few coyotes, nothing had cut across the sign of his passing. Preparing cattle for winter probably occupied the people of Wallowa Valley. They hadn't turned their sights on hunting elk yet, so no one appeared to have ventured into the forests.

The arrest team arrived at final camp after covering twelve miles of trail that day. The boys had been well-prepared for the trek, and other than a lot of blisters—and the bitching— they'd comported themselves well enough. Tonight, they'd stage their ambush, and not a moment too soon.

Pregnant, lofty snowflakes drifted on the breeze. It'd be a night of unsteady winds. A serious snowstorm often did that—halted the other functions of weather until it had its way. Heavy, quiet snow would mute sound, but it would confuse the winds; send them swirling like ballet dancers across the prairie.

A steady wind would've been better. Sage worried that the little dog might scent them outside the ranch house and alert the Commissioner. He fretted it might end in violence, with the Commissioner or his family getting hurt. Despite their folksy demeanor and family ties, this mission was still an armed incursion. Sage knew from experience: bad things happened fast when guns were involved.

"It's a good night for an arrest," Captain Chambers whispered to Sage.

"Good night for dark deeds," Sage answered without weighing his words.

It'd been a mistake to say that. He didn't turn to look at the captain, hoping he hadn't heard him. Turning to look at the captain would only make it weirder, plus it was utterly dark beneath the cloak of clouds. Not a scintilla of moon showed.

"They're asleep. We can leave soon," Sage added to cover his gaff. He'd been watching the house through binoculars. The back corner bedroom, where he assumed the Commissioner and his wife slept, had gone dark.

"It should only take half an hour to get down," Captain Chambers said.

The urge to turn and check the captain's face was almost too much, but Sage resisted.

Chambers continued. "Let's wait until two o'clock before we roll out. I don't trust these boys to stay quiet, not when they're cold."

Sage focused on the tactical issues. "We'd probably be better off making them run laps in their snowshoes because they're going to freeze their balls off waiting for two a.m."

The snowflakes were fat and heavy. They floated aimlessly, like children wandering home from school. Too much snow might bog down the snow machines the next morning, but this amount of snow would quiet their footfalls and cover their tracks. It was good weather in which to operate, and in truth, it wasn't that cold.

A chunk of bile had lodged in Sage's gut, and it ground at the cold, freeze dried meal he'd choked down for dinner. He hadn't taken a shit in two days.

On the eve of the mission, he should've felt tense, or even excited. He was doing his part in a law enforcement action—like a SWAT team in snowshoes. He had no idea how county lines worked when arresting someone across boundaries. He was following the orders of a police officer, and beyond that, he hadn't a shred of legal understanding that hadn't come from watching re-runs of the Dukes of Hazard.

But in his gut, he knew this arrest wasn't legit. If Commissioner Pete had done anything wrong, he deserved a day in court, not to be swept off his porch with his dick out. Swooping down on a home carrying rifles wasn't how good men resolved issues of property and cattle.

*Captain Chambers wasn't a good man, no matter what Aimee Butterton said.*

Sage had given the man the benefit of the doubt. He'd done his best not to judge the man for shagging another woman. He could even forgive the captain for hoarding food and playing favorites with the locals.

But this raid seemed like a power grab—like a desperate warlord playing out his land-envy using younger men, rifles and a badge.

Sage was in over his head, and the realization felt like an anvil hitting the floor. At seventeen years old, he had plenty of opinions and very little experience. How could he be expected to navigate the dealings of men who owned tracts of land and thousands of head of livestock; men who'd been elected to public office?

He decided: the chunk of bile in his stomach would have to be tolerated. He'd have to follow orders and live with the outcomes. He was a pawn in this game. He didn't rate an opinion. If he got uppity, odds were good he'd make a bad situation worse. He'd hunker down and keep his promise to his dad, and that meant doing this damned job.

Sage walked circles in the snow. He could feel the captain watching him in the dark. The blood flowed back into his legs and the exercise warmed him. The knot in his stomach loosened a little. He dug out the insulated hose from his Camelbak and sucked down some water.

"You okay?" the captain whispered.

"Yeah. I'm just cold. I'm good to go, sir," Sage lied.

---

AT TWO O'CLOCK in the morning, they rallied the boys and padded downhill single-file.

They left nothing at camp. Their plan was to snatch up the Commissioner and have him out before the roar of the snow machines echoed across the valley: clandestine incursion, lightning-fast exfil. They'd whisk him back to La Grande and stick him in a cell until the winter played out.

They bet everything on the snow machines. It'd taken them two days, and all their physical reserves, to sneak into the far reaches of the valley on snowshoes, but the snow machines would cover the same distance in two hours.

If something went wrong, Plan B was to hide the Commissioner in an outbuilding on the edge of the airfield, then steal snow machines from nearby ranches. That'd be Sage's mission should all else fail, and it'd set them back a couple hours. In either case, they'd be long gone by daybreak—before the commissioner's family could raise the alarm. Telephones were dead and, most likely, nobody monitored radios through the middle of the night. Even if the family discovered their missing father and reached another house by radio, the ranch houses were all at least a half-mile apart. It'd take at least an hour to go door-to-door raising enough men for a rescue operation.

The snowshoes floated over any ankle-busters that would otherwise imperil their passing in the night. Sage's blood was up, to be sure, but he couldn't enjoy it. The mission felt cursed.

Sage stopped abruptly. The captain bumped into his pack. Sage held up his fist, but it was unlikely anyone could see the fist in the black of the cloud-covered moon.

Directly in his path stood a dog. Sage could barely make it out, silhouetted against the snow. It wasn't the little lap dog that belonged to the commissioner. This skinny, mangy mutt let out a low growl and its back arched with menace. Sage's rifle drifted into his hands, sliding on its sling, following the movement he'd practiced a thousand times. If he fired his rifle now, the mission would get hairy. The whole section of the valley would hear the gunshot. Sage felt the hand of the captain on his shoulder, steadying him.

The dog growled for a full minute. Sage kept the gun between them, more as a spear than a firearm.

"Coyote," the captain whispered in his ear.

Sage had always thought of coyotes as being afraid of men, but maybe the wild dog couldn't see them, or smell them in the snowfall.

The coyote finally went silent, then padded off across the plain. It vanished into the fringe of the storm. Sage sighed and the captain patted his shoulder, apparently eager to get moving again.

Ten minutes after the coyote, they arrived at a cluster of buildings: three barns, a large chicken coop, a smoke house, and the main ranch house. Sage knew from his recon there weren't on-site quarters for the ranch hands. The arrest team didn't stop to coordinate. They'd planned this and even practiced it back at Chamber's ranch. Everyone knew their role.

Sage took ten of the boys and split off toward the motor pool barn. Their job would be to load up the packs and double-check the snow machines.

Captain Chambers headed toward the house with the two biggest boys. They dropped their packs on the trail, and two of Sage's team snatched them up.

If Commissioner Pete didn't come out to pee, they'd be forced to go inside and roust him out of bed. Sage prayed that it wouldn't come to that.

*Please, Lord, wake him up with a full bladder and a hankering to check on the snowstorm.*

Sage was glad he hadn't been asked to lay hands on the commissioner. All thin muscle and no fat, he wasn't nearly as solid as the fifty-year-old rancher. Old man strength was not something to underestimate. That, and Sage had no desire to look him in the eyes.

Once inside the motor pool, Sage flicked on his red headlamp and hung it from the handlebars of one of the snow machines. The machines appeared to be exactly where he'd left them. In an abundance of caution, he checked every gas gauge. Only one of the snow machines was below half-tank, and it was one of the beat up old ones they weren't taking. He hung the red light on the handlebars and left the boys to strap down the packs.

Every boy went to work, and none of them made the slightest sound. They were probably too scared to dick around for once. For his part, Sage had never been so terrified, not even when he'd been in a gunfight against a mob at the Holland farmhouse. Skulking around another man's homestead made the hairs stand up on the back of his neck.

He sidled over to the sliding door and looked toward the ranch house porch, where he'd seen Commissioner Pete take a piss. In the snow-speckled pool of light given off by the solar floodlight on the livestock barn, he could make out the shadows of the captain and his football linemen standing to each side of the door.

Sage checked his watch. It was three a.m..

Time passed slowly, like watching a pond freeze over. The snow fell, heavy and weightless at the same time. The fat flakes soaked up all sound, rendering the night mute and dumb.

Sage checked his watch a hundred times between three a.m. and three-thirty. Almost to the minute at three-thirty, the screen door opened, and the commissioner stepped onto the porch. A scuffle ensued, muffled and dense. The little dog barked once, then squeaked as someone kicked it off the porch. Sage watched it tumble in the snow, then bolt for the motor pool, running for cover.

As it flew past his feet, Sage scooped it up. The dog was both startled and comforted. In the red light, Sage could see only the wet eyes and nose, but it squirmed quietly—nothing likely broken.

There was no time to fret over the dog. The captain and his henchmen struggled across the yard and into the motor pool. The commissioner was wrapped up between them. Strangely, he was mostly-dressed. Perhaps he'd intended to check his livestock after his piss. Sage had carried a pair of over-boots in his pack in case the commissioner was taken shoeless.

Sage set the dog down. It bolted under a stack of boxes, alarmed by the scuffle.

One of the big boys had a hand and a wad of cloth clamped over the commissioner's mouth. The captain whipped out duct tape and did a proper job of gagging him. They zip-tied his hands in front of him with three, heavy ties.

Sage averted his eyes from the struggling man, and watched the house for light. The yip of the dog might've woken the wife, daughter or son, and it was his job to deal with them if they came to investigate.

In the gloom, he couldn't tell if the door had been left open or closed. The screen had closed by itself, but the front door couldn't be left open. The icy draft would eventually awaken the farm dogs, at the very least.

Sage crossed the yard, his rifle at the low ready. He crept up the porch and his eyes adjusted. The door was indeed wide open.

He eased the screen door open, reached inside, and pulled the heavy, wood door closed. The final click sent a bolt of adrenaline up Sage's spine. He waited and listened for movement inside. After a minute, when nothing happened, he guided the screen door closed, and backed away from the porch toward the motor pool.

The captain met him at the rolling door.

"Everything good?"

"No movement," Sage replied.

"We're loaded. We can drive the snow machines out the back."

Sage followed the captain inside, found his headlamp and pulled it over his head. Inadvertently, the light passed over the handcuffed and gagged commissioner and a flash of recognition passed between he and Sage.

Sage had never felt such shame. This was a man who had treated him with respect and kindness, even as a trespasser. In the black of night, he had returned the man's goodwill with villainy. Sage dropped his eyes and looked at the commissioner's feet. The commissioner was wearing boots.

The arrest team mounted the snow machines, and as planned they fired them up at the captain's signal. The roar in the barn was deafening after the silence of the raid. They were thirty yards from the farmhouse. The snow muted all, but it seemed very unlikely that eight howling machines wouldn't roust the sleeping family.

The snow machines roared out the back door of the motor pool. Sage followed, erupting into the brisk night air in the wake of the pungent two-cycle oil. The boy most experienced with snow machines cut the trail in front, followed by the captain with the commissioner tied behind him. Sage was the last in line. The next few minutes would determine whether or not they'd face resistance.

Snowflakes slapped against his cheeks, but it felt like a liar's freedom; like succumbing to fate. They'd taken the commissioner and they were getting away with it.

It was going to be a long, cold few hours, racing through a snowstorm toward their home county, but the die was cast. No matter how gently the snow fell or how the clouds warmed the earth, the speed of the snowmobiles blew the chill right through Sage's clothes.

Four of the machines carried two high school boys each. Sage was the least experienced with snowmobiles, so he'd been assigned rear security, and he was alone on his machine. He followed in the groomed tracks of the seven others.

There was no reason to expect the Lathrops to follow. The boys had pulled the keys from the old snow machines and tossed them away. Sage stopped anyway, at the distant edge of the family ranch, and looked back toward the house. The snowfall obscured everything, but he could barely make out the white-blue glow of the barn light. He saw no other lights.

*Would he see kerosene lamps burning inside the house this far away through the snow?*

The family had to have woken to the sound of the snow machines, but it would be some time before they figured out that Commissioner Pete was overdue back to his bed. By then, the arrest team would be ten miles away.

The captain and the boys were driving the snow machines like Grand Theft Auto, so Sage couldn't linger on rear security. He popped his goggles back on and chased after the fleeting taillights of his companions.

By the time he caught up with them, three machines were stopped, waiting in a line. They'd traveled maybe five miles from the ranch in just fifteen minutes. At this rate, they'd easily cross the county line before dawn.

Sage pulled alongside the last snow machine in line and shouted over the rumble, "Why'd we stop?"

"Burton's having trouble with his machine," the kid shouted.

Halfway up the line, one of the boys madly yanked at the pull start rope. Sage pulled up alongside.

Sage yelled at the boy. "Grab your backpack and leave it. The rest of the group is dropping us. Get on the back of Sherman's sled."

The boy complied, and the four sleds at the back of the team were underway again in thirty seconds. The front half of the group had stopped to wait for them on the next rise in the snow-covered county road.

But when Sage's group reached them, two snow machines had their hoods up, and those boys were hauling on the pull start ropes too. All these snow machines had electric starters. Pulling on the start rope meant they couldn't get them to catch spark, which made no sense, since the machines had started like eager lions back at the barn.

Captain Chambers bellowed from the lead, "Leave them and double up. Now! Let's go."

Boys rushed to collect their bags and jump on the backs of the machines that ran. When they'd consolidated, Sage's was the only sled left with just one rider. They were now down three machines. Sage searched his mind for answers: what had he missed when he checked the snow machines? Why were they failing?

The team launched forward and covered another mile before the captain's snow machine sputtered to a stop. The point man looped back when he noticed he was alone. All the machines circled the captain and his captive.

"Mine just died too," one of the boys yelled.

"Mine too."

Sage's own snow machine sputtered. He listened with dread as it hitched, coughed and went silent. His gas gauge showed full.

Sage shook his head in disbelief. Something was profoundly wrong, and it couldn't be happenstance. After three minutes of panicked shouting, all the snow machines had gone quiet. They were just ten miles from Pete Lathrop's ranch, on an ice-covered county road, deep in enemy territory. They hadn't seen another barn in miles.

The captain unstrapped Commissioner Pete and dragged him to his feet. He ripped the duct tape off his mouth with a savage yank.

"Ow," Pete said. He sounded remarkably composed for a kidnap victim.

Captain Chambers drew his sidearm, a nickel-plated 1911 hand-gun, and put it to the commissioners chest.

"What the fuck is going on with your snow machines, Pete?" he fumed at his rival.

"Well," Commissioner Pete drawled, "I'm guessing you guys are doing some kind of Guns of Navarone thing where you nab old men while they piss off their porch. I still need to pee, if you don't mind giving me a moment."

Captain Chambers poked him hard in the chest with his handgun. "I'm going to blow a hole in you right here, you sonofabitch, if you don't start talking. Where's the nearest ranch with snow machines?"

Pete Lathrop looked around as though seeing the place for the first time. "It's kinda hard to tell with all this white fluffy stuff in my eyes."

"You think you're so clever," Chambers seethed. "You think you've got this county wired—wrapped around your devious, little finger. I'm going to count to three and I'm going to blow a half-inch hole in your lying heart."

Sage's rifle slithered down and around on its sling, and before he knew it, his 30-30 was in his hands, pointed at Captain Chambers. His hands racked a shell of their own accord.

"This is over," Sage boomed. It took a Herculean force-of-will to make his voice work, because his throat had almost entirely closed up in terror. "We walk away now and we leave the commissioner here. I can lead us back through the forest on foot. We still have our snowshoes. We can make it out, but we can't make it dragging him."

The captain laughed, but his handgun remained jammed into Commissioner Pete's chest. "So does this mean your balls finally dropped, Sage Ross? Good for you. We'll dump you in the same snow bank as Commissioner Rattlesnake, here. Arrest him too." The captain pointed a finger at Sage. Half the boys aimed their AR-15s at Sage, then the other half followed suit.

Sage was close enough that he didn't need to look through his scope to know his bullet would go through Captain Chamber's chest. "They shoot me. I shoot you. This is where it ends, either way," Sage said. He sounded a lot more confident than he felt.

"Hold on now, boys," Commissioner Pete patted at the air with his zip-tied hands. "Sage, lower your rifle." He rubbed the side of his neck, then unwrapped a red scarf that'd been tucked under the collar of his jacket. "Just calm down everyone." Pete worked the wrap up and around his ears.

"I'm not going to ask again: where's the nearest ranch?" Captain Chambers hissed.

Sage hadn't lowered his rifle, and the boys hadn't lowered theirs either. The high school boys darted glances around the circle. Their jaws gaped. They looked at Sage, the captain, the commissioner, then each other. Then, they repeated the process, each on his own circuit. They looked like a gaggle of confused roosters. Sage knew they'd shoot him for no other reason than they didn't know what else to do.

"Seriously, Sage. Sling your gun," Commissioner Pete ordered. "It's over, Ron. Holster your gun. It's over boys," Commissioner Pete called out to the high school boys standing in the circle. "You're surrounded and everyone but Chambers can go home."

"What're you talking about, *surrounded*?" Captain Chambers spat, but Sage saw realization dawn in his slack cheeks and wide eyes.

"You don't think all those snow machines ran out of gas at the same time by chance, do you, Ron? And why did the gauges show *full* back at the ranch? Hmmm. Makes you wonder." Pete Chambers tapped his chin with his bound hands. "Makes you think maybe I knew you'd do something desperate to hang onto your little fiefdom over in Union. Makes you ask yourself if little, ole Wallowa County didn't already know you were planning this escapade." Commissioner Pete nodded while the truth settled. "Sheriff Tate," Pete shouted into the night. "Come on into the light. Show yourself."

The snow rustled outside the circle of snowmobile lights. From the gloomy edge, the portly figure of the Wallowa County Sheriff appeared, wearing his uniform, his revolver drawn.

"Holster your gun, Ron Chambers. You're under arrest." Sheriff Tate reasoned with the team, "All you boys, put your guns on the ground. Don't give our men any reason to shoot you. Half of them are still pretty sore about the lickin' you gave them last time on the football field."

Commissioner Pete smiled and held up his hands. "That's right. Set the guns down. Half the men of Wallowa have you in their sights. Just set your guns down and go on home, boys. Nobody needs to bleed tonight."

"Steady, boys," Sheriff Tate yelled over his shoulder into the dark-curtained snowfall. "Don't shoot unless they shoot first." He crunched over the snow toward Captain Chambers. Chamber's gun barrel wavered like a divining rod of his confusion and unwillingness to quit. It struck Sage: it'd probably been a long time since anyone had told Chambers "no."

"You too, Sage," Pete said. "Put your gun down."

Sage snapped out of his adrenaline-drenched fugue and complied. He untangled his sling from his backpack and set the 30-30 on the snow.

Sheriff Tate reached up and slipped the web of his thumb between Captain Chamber's 1911 hammer and firing pin. He lifted the gun gently out of the stunned captain's hands.

Chambers stood in the circle of snowmobile lights, mute and lost, while Sheriff Tate cuffed him and recited his Miranda rights.

Men with hunting rifles appeared from of the edge of the night and closed the circle around the arrest team. Sage raised his hands and the boys followed suit. A bearded, bear of a man collected their guns. Headlights flickered on the county road ahead and trucks appeared out of the drifting static of the snowfall—a dozen or more.

Wallowa County men helped the high school boys into the back of the trucks and tossed their backpacks in after them.

"Not him," Commissioner Pete pointed his bound hands at Sage. "He comes with me. Give him back his rifle."

One of the men whipped out a Leatherman tool and cut Commissioner Pete's bonds with pliers. A man Sage had never met handed him back his 30-30.

"Come on." Pete motioned Sage toward one of the trucks. The driver behind the wheel looked like he might be Pete's son. "Let's get coffee."

---

SAGE WATCHED the dawn as it colored the sky behind Sacajawea Mountain. He sat at Commissioner Pete's breakfast table while his wife and pretty daughter made breakfast in the kitchen. Pete's son was away recovering the snow machines.

The Lathrop breakfast table was what Sage would imagine—big enough just for the four of them and covered in a red-and-white gingham tablecloth. Commissioner Pete's wife came with a smile stretched from cheek to cheek and set a cup of coffee in front of each of them.

"She's gloating. I hate it when she gloats," Commissioner Pete chuckled. "Damned woman."

Sage had no idea what he was talking about. He felt like he'd been teleported from the set of a James Bond movie straight into the kitchen of Family Ties. He woke up an evil soldier in a military thriller to being served a country breakfast in a Hallmark holiday special.

"Sir, I'm so ashamed of my actions. I can't tell you how awful I feel about what I did. I disrespected your hospitality and I violated your trust, and I committed a crime. I deserve whatever punishment you throw at me. I won't complain."

Pete chuckled again. "I'll grant you, it might be a while before you can show your face in Union County again. They're going to need some time for new elections, and we're hoping none of Chambers boys make it into office, ever again. But, democracy is democracy. You never know what you'll get. But some folks over there will blame you for betraying Chambers, sure as the Pope wears a fancy dress."

Sage stared into his coffee. He didn't feel like he deserved to enjoy the sunrise.

"I'll just tell you plain," Pete sighed. "You were working for us, almost right from the start."

Sage looked up.

"Well, actually, you were working for Aimee Butterton and *she* was working for us. More accurately, you were working for Aimee Butterton and she was working for my missus. My wife, Veronica— the one burning the bacon right now—she was U.S. Army intelligence back in her heyday, and she loves these mind games. She played Union County and Captain Chambers like she was the CIA and he was a North African warlord. I swear to the Maker, she's as crooked as a three dollar bill. The only reason I'm a county commissioner is because of her finagling." Pete took a sip of his coffee and collected his thoughts. "So, I'm saying she sorta put you up to all this, with Aimee's help."

"Aimee?" Sage parroted back. He still wasn't tracking. "Butterton?"

Pete closed his eyes and sighed. "Yes. Aimee Butterton. Son, I tried to tell you before. Well, it was Joan Schlacter who told you— that day at the Blue Banana in Lostine. Do you remember? She read you in on the natural order of things? *Men run the show and the women run the men?* she said."

Sage didn't know if he remembered anyone ever saying that, but he could barely remember his shoe size right now. He had a very unsteady grip on reality at the moment. He nodded anyway, and picked up his coffee to have something to do other than sit with his jaw open.

"The Buttertons are second cousins to my wife's family. The Butterton girls aren't actually big fans of Ron Chambers on account of him having *relations* with their mother under their papa's nose, may he rest in peace. The girls have been network assets for us from the get-go. Not Mrs. Butterton—the mother—but the girls."

Sage's face must've looked a-mess because Commissioner Pete tried to explain again. "We needed that corrupt sonofabitch Chambers removed for his crimes of corruption. He and his band of merry men have been robbing that county blind while some people went hungry. We could've helped Union with beef, but there was no way we could do that with the amount of graft Chambers would've charged us. You see?"

Sage nodded. He knew Chambers was crooked. He'd witnessed it, even gotten used to the idea. He still didn't understand how they'd been led straight into a trap.

The commissioner continued. "This is about democracy. Chambers is arrested now, and will stand trial in Wallowa for kidnapping. It's all legal and on the up-and-up. La Grande will have to choose a new police captain and probably reinstate the Union County sheriff that Chambers silenced. After that, we can go forward as one valley, Wallowa and Union. At least, that's my wife's plan. So far, she's called it on the nose, one hundred percent. I ain't never gonna live it down. She's going to be fuller of herself than a homecoming queen after this." As much as he complained, even a fool like Sage could see how proud Pete was of his wife.

"What about me?" Sage held out his hands. "I'm as guilty as anyone for your kidnapping."

"I think you and I both know where your heart landed on this thing. We set you up, Aimee Butterton kept you on-track and you did what was right when push came to shove. At seventeen, I wouldn't have done half as well. Chambers wore the badge and our daddies taught us to respect the badge. As far as Wallowa County is concerned, you're welcome to abide here." Pete held out his hand. "And you're welcome in my home until this thing blows over."

Sage shook the proffered hand. He felt like he might be getting a lot more grace than he deserved.

"Sir, I won't let you down again," he offered.

Commissioner Pete raised an eyebrow. "Well, I'm glad you said that, because there's a lot of work around here before the real snow hits. All this goofing around has set us back."

## 21

MAT BEST

**Reever Street Pork Drying Facility**
**McKenzie, Tennessee**

Buddy Lansing needed a drink. His flask was empty and he hadn't had a nip in over an hour. His whiskey supply was back at home, and he'd been stuck in the pork shed for hours, babysitting 300 propane barbecues as they slowly dried 1,000 pounds of thinly-sliced pork.

"This is bullshit," he told his shift partner, Lee Billings.

When Buddy took a volunteer slot at the hastily-organized pork shed, he imagined it would be like staying up all night drinking beer with his buddies while occasionally tending the barbecue. He'd done it a thousand times. But this was entirely different. This was like a damned job—a shitty job, too.

They'd lined up hundreds of scavenged, home barbecues in the old lumber curing shed and piped them to the lumberyard's 5,000 gallon propane tank. His job was to mind the meat.

Buddy didn't have a problem doing menial tasks. He'd worked

in the back end of a kitchen since he flunked out of high school, but he always cooked in the haze of a whiskey buzz. Working sober royally sucked.

"Stop your bellyaching," Lee Billings jeered. "Shift's almost over. Finish packing up today's batch. I'll go shut the valves, and we'll be outa here in twenty minutes."

Buddy was trying to remember whether he'd hidden a whiskey bottle in the lumberyard or if he'd only thought about doing it. While he considered it, his gloved hands shoveled dried pork into plastic tubs, snapped their lids tight and stacked them on industrial shelving on the wall of the curing shed.

Billings headed to the exit and called over his shoulder, "Finish cleaning up for me will ya? Wendy's cooking a real breakfast this morning."

"Yeah, yeah." Buddy didn't have a family waiting for him, just a half-empty bottle.

"Come on over to our place," Billings invited. "There'll be plenty."

"Thanks. I'll think about it." Buddy could think of little except how soon he could get the next slug of whisky into his belly. As Billings walked out the door, Buddy turned the wrench on the six rows of ball valves to shut off the propane supply. If he'd been paying attention, he'd have heard Billings say that he'd already done it.

The hoses from the rows of barbecues snaked across the floor to the propane tank outside. The shed had once been used for a lumber oven, but now it powered every barbecue in town. To make it easier to add or subtract rows, they'd split the main hose at a hose manifold C-clamped to a heavy wooden workbench. They used surplus ball valves from a bin at the back of the hardware store, and the handles had been swiped for some dude's sprinkler system back before the crash, so they had to use a crescent wrench.

Buddy turned the last of the six valves with the wrench. He

saluted the barbecues, like rows of soldiers, and headed for the door. He trimmed the kerosene lantern by the exit down to a dull glow and left.

The door clicked shut and physics ran its course. The propane gathered in an invisible layer on the floor until it flowed across the entire footprint of the warehouse, then it seeped between the floor slats into a long-forgotten storage basement, where they'd once kept coal for firing the lumber ovens. For two hours, propane shushed from 300 barbecues, cascaded through a thousand gaps in the rough-hewn floor and mingled with the hundred-year-old coal dust.

When the basement filled to the brim, the lapping pond of colorless gas filled the warehouse: six inches, eighteen inches, thirty inches. By the first light of day, the propane reached the guttering flame of the kerosene lantern, and the structure had become an enormous fuel-air bomb.

In a *ka-whomping* flash, the explosion killed every living thing in the warehouse, even the cockroaches feasting on pork drippings. The fireball vaporized the windows and ignited mountains of left-over sawdust and a hundred trillion particles of coal dust.

A dust explosion can blow the top off of a grain silo. A propane fuel-air bomb mixed with coal dust and sawdust can send a man to the moon. The roof of the pork shed didn't stand a chance. The primary fireball and secondary dust explosion hurled the roof 300 yards in six pieces. The flaming warehouse walls collapsed on 2,000 pounds of dried pork.

---

ALAN STOKES LAY awake on his rotting cot as the the sky above became too light for sleep. His morning wood was painful, but he was too tired to jack off, or make a move on Janice, his end-of-the-world-hookup sleeping on the other side of his plastic lean-to tarp.

The word "girlfriend" didn't make sense anymore because nobody even pretended there was a future, but the word "hookup" fit. She hated it when he called her that, but the options for a grimy brunette with teeth coming loose from starvation were markedly limited, so she tolerated his vulgarity.

Life in the mud camps didn't leave much for courtship. Before they grew too weak to care about sex, he and Janice couldn't get enough of each other's unwashed, malodorous bodies. One type of hunger took the edge off another, it seemed.

But not anymore. The hunger had taken even that. Alan lay still, waiting for his dick to get the memo, when a pair of near-simultaneous explosions slapped at his lean-to.

*Ba-boom-boom!*

The explosions came from the direction of the town. Janice rolled over, startled, then went back to sleep. Alan stayed awake and pondered his boner. Janice probably wouldn't turn him down, now that she was probably awake. By the time he thought it through, he was soft again, which was probably for the best. It occurred to him that he may have done the deed in this life for the last time. He was too weak and hungry to care about such a minor tragedy.

Ten minutes later, the smell of cooked meat ran over him like a dump truck.

"Oh, my God!" Do you smell that?" Janice sat up ramrod straight, like she'd taken an enormous coke hit.

"Dear Lord, where is that coming from?"

"Fuckers are having a cookout in town," Alan spat.

The couple scrambled out from under their clumpy sleeping bags, pulled on pants and stumbled out of the lean-to. The cluster of tents around them sprang to life. Some people staggered directly toward the scent of roasting meat without bothering to put on shoes. Others paused to pick up possessions so they wouldn't be stolen in their absence.

Alan grabbed the heavy stick he used for defense, slipped on his boots without tying the laces and shuffled southwest. Throughout the woods and across the highway, desperate thousands of insidious, human beasts converged on the town of McKenzie, Tennessee.

---

**Dr. Abraham Hauser**
**Sedalia, Tennessee**

DR. HAUSER HAD TRUSTED the wrong people. He'd been taken in by Sergeant Best's lies and the seemingly-kind acts of Sheriff and Beatrice Morgan. He'd been fooled into a pipe dream—an unlikely tale of food to feed his people through the winter. All they had to do was walk thirty miles and take it, the Army Ranger had said. It was a tale they'd yearned to believe.

Three days and thirty miles later, 800 people gathered in campfire groups in and around a rural warehouse outside Sedalia, Tennessee.

Dr. Hauser regarded the now-picked through shelves along the walls of the warehouse, and he knew they'd been betrayed.

At first, when they arrived, they'd celebrated. The shelves looked stocked, just like the Federal Emergency Management Agency might've done. But as Hauser's friends unpacked the shelves, devoured the dried meals, and took a hard look at what was left, they realized the shelves had been shallow, with empty boxes instead of heavy, preserved calories. Much of the dried and canned food was expired. Though it turned out to be edible, they began to suspect FEMA had nothing to do with the warehouse. Too many details failed to line up: the empty boxes, the too-perfect map of FEMA locations, the lightweight padlocks on the doors.

The food would barely get them to the next warehouse on the

map, which was supposedly another thirty miles north in a town called Hillerman on the far side of the Ohio River.

One of their group had grown up near Hillerman, and she was absolutely certain there was no FEMA warehouse, nor a warehouse of any kind.

They'd been duped, and the realization steadily dawned that they were marooned in Sedalia. Soon, they'd begin starving again.

Hypothetically, they could *drive* back to their camp outside McKenzie. There were plenty of vehicles around for the taking, but nothing to put in the gas tank. Every car, everywhere, had been driven until it ran dry.

"It was all our mistake, Doc. We're in this together," Jeanine Barlowe reassured him as she put her hand on his forearm. "We'll figure it out."

"Vehicle approaching. Defensive positions!" a sentry on the roof shouted through a skylight.

The refugees responded by forming circles, with fighters and melee weapons facing outward. The vulnerable members moved to the centers of the phalanxes.

"One pickup truck. Driving slow. Two pax," the sentry shouted again.

His people clutched clubs, axes, and spears, poised for another sad turn in their parade of misery. Dr. Hauser hurried out, through the front office of the warehouse and into the parking lot.

A truck turned the corner, and Hauser recognized Sheriff and Beatrice Morgan in the front seat. Hauser almost signaled "all clear," but hesitated. The Morgans had certainly been party to his deception.

*What was going on?* His shoulders hunched in anticipation of coming conflict. If they didn't bring the conflict, Hauser certainly would.

Sheriff Morgan pulled in, got down from the cab and looked

Hauser in the eyes. Hauser curled his lip and signaled an all clear with his finger in the air.

"You've got some nerve, coming here," he sneered.

Mrs. Morgan walked around the fender and joined the two men. Shame painted her face red.

"That's true," Sheriff Morgan agreed. He didn't extend a hand.

Hauser jammed his fists on his hips. "You lied to us. My people could die here. There's not enough food. We're too far now to make it back without people dying along the way."

"Yeah. That was the plan," the sheriff confessed.

"And the next warehouse?" Hauser asked.

"Doesn't exist."

"What in God's name are you doing here, Sheriff? Do you think I can stop these people from stomping you to death when they find out?"

"Bea and I made peace with that possibility, if the Lord wills it. But if you'll hear us out..."

Beatrice Morgan interrupted her husband, "Dr. Hauser, the Lord told us to be your Esther." She smiled like a penitent and quoted, "Do not urge me to leave you or to turn back from you. Where you go I will go, and where you stay I will stay. Your people will be my people, and your God will be my God."

Hauser felt nonplussed. "Our Esther?" He knew next-to-nothing about Bible stories.

Sheriff Morgan interjected, "When I agreed to be complicit in lying to you, I thought I was choosing the lesser of two evils. I told myself that the town was giving you the chance to move on before you became too desperate and we had to shoot you. But my better half had other ideas—more faith than me. She was right and I was wrong. The town was wrong. I see it now. We've come to ask you back, to find a way to survive together."

Hauser suspected another deception. "You mean to tell me the same town that sent us on a death march has had a change of heart? I don't believe you."

"We weren't sent by the town," Beatrice answered. "We've come to share your fate, one way or the other."

"That's it? That's all you have to offer? Two more mouths to feed?" Hauser looked around at his people, milling about the parking lot. He shook his head.

Sheriff Morgan smiled, and flipped back the tarp covering his truck bed. "We bring two more mouths to feed, plus eighty gallons of unleaded gasoline. That sound any better?"

---

**William and Candice**

**Abandoned home on Kemp Street**
**McKenzie, Tennessee**

WILLIAM PULLED the heavy handgun from his backpack and studied the mechanism. Mat hadn't let him shoot this gun yet, and yet William planned to kill a man with it.

He and Mat had done four gun range sessions since the collapse, and they hadn't been long ones. There was precious little ammunition, and Mat was working overtime on the HESCO barrier and night patrol. Organizing a mini-Ranger School for William hadn't been a top priority.

In those shooting sessions, Mat taught William the Glock handgun, not the shiny, heavy pistol William had taken from the house. He wasn't a hundred percent sure how the handgun functioned. It didn't look anything like the Glock.

He found the magazine release and dropped the gleaming,

silver mag into his hand. The bullets were thicker than Mat's nine millimeter rounds.

With the magazine out, he tried to pull back the slide. By jamming it against his hip, he managed to get it back until it clicked open, just like the Glock. The breach was clear of brass, but William still handled the firearm as though it was loaded, pointing it in the opposite direction of sleeping Candice.

"Where'd you get that?"

He startled, but quickly covered it with a grin. "I stole it from my dad's workbench."

"Your dad, huh?"

"I stole it from *Mat's* workbench."

"Don't be too hard on him." Candice sat up from the sleeping bag and leaned on an elbow. Her naked clavicle showed under the collar of the too-big T-shirt she'd found in the closet of the abandoned house where they'd come to hide. "He's doing the best he knows how."

They were both runaways now, and William didn't care. Whatever happened, they'd be together.

"What're you planning on doing with that?" she stared at the big handgun.

"Erm. Nothing. It's just to protect us from rats," he lied.

She lowered her brows and gave him a look that said *baloney*.

"Mister Jensen needs to be stopped," William sputtered, then felt foolish for saying anything so dramatic. He hadn't even figured out the gun yet.

His heart galloped like a runaway horse at the thought of pointing a gun at Mr. Jensen; a willowy, twelve year-old child facing down a grown man. In the movies, that scene rarely worked out in a boy's favor.

Candice would see it too—the foolishness of a boy bringing justice down upon a man respected in the community. She'd see him for the unsteady child he really was. Candice was no thirteen year-old girl. Not really. She'd been through stuff. He could see the question in her eyes—like when he would tell his mom that he was going into the backyard to practice sword fighting. Candice knew the embarrassing truth: he was just a kid.

The pistol was almost as long as William's forearm, and he could barely get his hands around the grips. Candice's eyes tracked from the gun, up his arms, to his face.

He clamped down hard on the slide release and it clacked shut with authority. William slid the magazine into the mag well and ran it home with a loud *click*. The metal-on-metal action sent a shot of adrenaline up his spine.

"If no one else will do it, I will," he said. "Let's go."

"William, stop. Don't do this," she cried.

He stood and struggled to maintain balance with the handgun in both hands.

"You stay here. I'll be back later."

Without waiting for her to answer, William turned and walked out of the house. The screen door slammed shut behind him.

---

THE TOWN TORNADO siren began to howl as William passed in front of Casey's Takeout. For a moment, he imagined Candice had called the police, and the town was coming to arrest him. He imagined, for a moment, that the tornado siren was for him.

A knot of people ran past him in the middle of the street, but nobody spared him a second glance. He tried to hide the gun, but it took both of his hands to carry it without pointing it at his own leg. Mat had taught him never to point a gun at himself.

"William!" Candice called to him as she ran down the sidewalk after him. "Wait."

He stopped and turned. "It's not murder if he's a bad man."

"Yes, but he's not... I mean, he is. But the town needs him. The town needs him to make chemical weapons."

"That's just some B.S. he told you so you wouldn't tell on him." William shook his head. "He's a liar and a peedo-file."

Confusion blew across the smooth silk of her pretty face. William turned and continued down the sidewalk.

"He protects me," she said, but this time without conviction.

William kept walking and she hurried to catch up.

"When you use someone in a bad way, you're not protecting them," William said. "You're hurting them. Only a bad man hurts young girls, and you know it."

"Yes, but things changed. The world's different now."

"Not that thing. That didn't change," William said, and he was pretty sure he was right on that score. He'd found an absolute truth in a world of uncertainty. He clung to it as his lodestone—that and the heavy handgun.

They turned onto Forrest Avenue. The tornado siren grew louder as they faced downtown. Two more groups of townsfolk ran past them. They carried guns, and the smell of smoke swirled down the avenue.

Something had happened in town, but if he didn't keep marching toward Mr. Jensen's house, he'd lose his nerve. What he was about to do was *right*. He was sure of it.

Candice trotted beside William, struggling to keep up. She offered no further argument. Jim Jensen was in the front yard, running back and forth between the garage and a van—big and white like a FedEx truck. Mr. Jensen held a milk crate in his hands. The radio on his belt chattered with panicked voices.

"Stop!" William shouted and pointed the hulking gun at Jim Jensen. The teacher's eyes darted between William and Candice and comprehension dawned on his face.

"William. Candice," Mr. Jensen said. He carefully set the milk crate on the cement. "Hold on..." he stammered.

Gunsights wavered in front of William's eyes and he willed his arms to be stronger. He realized too late that he'd yelled at Mr. Jensen too early. The distance was much farther than Mat had taught him to shoot—all the way across the grass. Still, Mr. Jensen seemed to take the gun seriously. He held up a hand and stepped toward them.

William pressed the trigger.

*Clack!*

The handgun's hammer came down like a lightning bolt, but without the thunder. Nothing happened. The gun wavered in front of William's face. Mister Jensen smiled, reached around to his back and brought out a gleaming revolver.

William's arms dropped and he stared at the gun, trying to understand why it had failed to fire. He'd done everything right, *but maybe not in the right order.*

Mr. Jensen pointed the snub-nosed gun at William and took three steps forward. Then he looked over his shoulder at his open garage and appeared to reconsider.

Jensen waved them away with his gun. "You kids run along now. The rats are attacking *en masse* and I'm the only one who can stop them. Take refuge at the middle school. Go on." He stomped menacingly, and William's legs betrayed him by faltering backward. Candice tugged at his arm.

"Come on, William. We need help. Where's your dad?"

William had no idea where Mat was. His head swam with fury and humiliation. Mr. Jensen had gone back to loading the van.

William tossed the pistol in a bush, and they both ran back the way they'd come.

---

**Mat Best**

**Smith Street HESCO barrier**
**McKenzie, Tennessee**

THE MCKENZIE COMMUNITY college and Smith Street met in an inverted corner cut out of the northeast perimeter of town by a huge hayfield. It'd been easier to place the HESCO barrier on paved road than setting the foundation across a muddy field.

The smoke-and-pig aroma drifted over the college, into the gaping field and northeast through the bustling woods around Caledonia Creek reservoir.

The Paw Paw Lane neighborhood had been lost to the town when the perimeter left out over a hundred homes as well as the Christ's Temple Apostolic church. It would've required another two miles of HESCO barrier to protect them. The residents and the pastor relocated to the community college campus. Refugees instantly squatted in the cluster of starter homes on the edge of town.

Now the rats emerged, like creatures awakened from rain-soaked hibernation. The smell of cooked meat and charred wood drew them onto the overgrown lawns and trash-strewn streets where children once rode scooters and played frisbee. They carried weapons, most of them. Nobody seemed to go anywhere outside the town perimeter without a weapon of some sort.

Mat watched from atop the Smith Street HESCO barrier, panning his binoculars up and down the four-lane highway that separated the Paw Paw neighborhood from the rest of town.

The rats had no way of knowing the smell came from inside the town perimeter, nor would they care. Mat learned the over-whelming power of smell when he'd half-starved during field exer-cises in Ranger School. After a few days of starvation, even the slightest food smell struck like rebar upside the head. It caused physical pain in the nasal cavity and dragged a man forward like a nose ring on a rope.

The rats moved like zombies, driven by their gnawing hunger and weakened by atrophy—stumbling, sniffing, abandoning their mewling children. Mat watched in wonder as the wind dragged his enemy from their hovels and drew them toward murder. He guessed there were a thousand of them, and the woods hadn't begun to empty yet. This was just the three streets of split-level homes.

Mat marveled at the power of smell—it could've been such a simple weapon. If only he'd considered using it before, it could've helped the town. He could've lured rats away.

With wind sweeping across McKenzie, the scent of cooked meat pulled an army of desperate souls toward the wall, and toward a do-or-die, winner-take-all clash with the townspeople.

His mind swirled with visions of bullets, poison gas, cannons, and walls. Like so many commanders before him, he struggled against fighting the last war in his mind instead of *this* war.

Today, he didn't face an enemy army, or insurgents bent on toppling a government, he fought locusts. They would gobble every morsel of food, ruining what they could not eat. Mat remembered seeing rats "butcher" a captured pig with pocket knives, bare hands, and teeth. In their desperation, they wasted most of it.

"Cabrera. This is Actual. Report," Mat spoke over the radio. He'd already called in all available perimeter guards, and everyone in town who could wield a gun, or even a bat. This fight would be for all the marbles. The town would live or die right here on the Smith Street HESCO, in the next thirty minutes.

The tornado siren continued its doleful wail. It was the pre-set signal for everyone to rush to defense, but it would take time to get the word out as to where. *Where would they make their stand?* On the other side of McKenzie, the townspeople would have no idea of the crushing masses hurdling themselves across the fields.

"Sergeant, this is Juan. We're moving out now. ETA five minutes."

"Bring everyone you see on the street. Everyone," Mat ordered. "This is *all-hands*. I've got over a thousand enemy combatants converging on my position."

"Fuck me," Cabrera swore over the radio.

Gray, cotton swirls of smoke drifted over the college, across the field and into the woods. Mat didn't know if the smoke was a sign that they were getting the fire put out, or if it meant the surrounding neighborhoods had caught fire too. The town could easily burn from the inside out, but that wasn't Mat's problem. The fire crew wasn't even on the same radio frequency as him.

---

THE REFUGEES POURED across the highway like a flood. They plunged off the edge of the blacktop and into the fringe woods around the Carroll hay farm.

The highway was over a mile away from Mat's position on the HESCO barrier, and the rats disappeared as soon as they hit the trees. They'd cross a half-mile of pasture, another windrow of trees, and then they'd appear on the edge of no man's land, south of the Carroll's cluster of homes. Mat prayed Old Man Carroll had evacuated ahead of the wave of zombies. The Carrolls had been unwilling to abandon their family homestead to the predations of the refugees. They'd been fending them off for months, on the wrong side of the HESCO.

The first rats surged onto no man's land just as the QRF arrived.

"Spread out along Smith Street," Mat ordered on his radio. "Be prepared to displace along the barrier wherever the fighting gets heaviest. They'll hit us in five mics. I have eyes-on across the field. Use the poles whenever possible. Shoot anyone carrying a firearm. Good copy?"

His team leaders acknowledged and sprinted to their positions up and down the four hundred yard stretch of wall.

Luckily, the pork-laden wind cut across one of their best sections of HESCO; their most-defensible position. They'd stacked logs from the lumber yard, wired them together with bailing wire, then piled vehicles behind the logs to stabilize them. The logs would be easy for a healthy man to scale—eight feet tall at the most —but atop the logs was a wobbly, six foot chainlink fence. The starving rats could scale it, Mat had no doubt, but his defenders would ram them with the greased poles through the holes in the chainlink. So far, he could see less than a hundred defenders atop the Smith Street HESCO, but more were coming. A hundred or two against thousands.

Mat scanned the tree line. Hundreds of rats surged into no man's land, then lurched into the swirling scent of cooked pork. Mat picked out a man with a double-barrel shotgun, wading through the muck with the rifle at port arms. Mat slid the barrel of the SCAR heavy through the chainlink alongside a post.

The wind sighed against the fence, sending a gentle sway along its length. Mat let his sight picture undulate with the post. He waited for the glowing red chevron of the ACOG to pass over the man's torso and he timed his trigger press to match.

*Whoom!* The SCAR barked. The man fell face down in the mud. Two men following flipped him on his back, and one snatched up the mud-caked shotgun.

*Whoom!* Mat blew a hole in his chest.

He couldn't allow himself to get tunnel vision this time. The moment he turned his attention elsewhere, another rat would pick up that shotgun, but Mat was in command, and he had to watch the whole battlefield.

He keyed the team radio. "The tree line is five hundred meters. Hold fire until they're under two hundred meters. Acknowledge."

*Range by fire,* Mat thought grimly. His AR would've struggled with this distance and the crosswind. This was no urban gunfight. This was a *siege*—a merciless ocean of desperation against whizzing bullets and a few hundred defenders, if they even got to Smith Street in time.

Mat had killed the only two guys he could see carrying obvious firearms. At least six hundred rats stumbled in the field, through the mud toward the town. When they got another hundred yards closer, Mat and his men would have to shoot anyone who looked threatening, which would be everyone, and then they would run out of ammo.

Inevitability swamped him. The weight of the six remaining magazines in his vest felt like a stretching length of paracord, holding him dangling over the abyss. When those mags ran dry, the sea of enemy would overwhelm his position, and whether they killed him or not, he and William, and everyone in the town, would starve.

Hundreds more crossed the highway in a mighty wave. The smell of pork would empty a thirty-square-mile swath of woods. The *pock-pock-pock* of his men firing into the ranks of rats picked up tempo and Mat's worry rose with it; a savage, clawing futility.

"Save your bullets for people with edged weapons," he coaxed over the radio. "Use the poles on everyone else." At most, there were two thousand rounds of ammunition along the half-mile of wall. He could see almost that many enemy, at a single glance.

Another three hundred rats staggered out of the woods and onto the field of battle as Mat dropped his transmit button. "Save your ammo for people with serious weapons," Mat spoke to himself. He didn't bother to push transmit. The rats were upon them.

---

**Gladys Carter Home**

## McKenzie, Tennessee

"Miss Carter! Hold on. Miss Carter."

The voice of one of her P.E. students shook Gladys out of her call to arms. She bounded off her porch, dressed in full military kit, on her way to the rally point at the baseball diamond.

"Miss Carter, help!"

It was Candice McClaughlin, Jim Jenkins' step-daughter. She was with Sergeant Best's son, William.

"Miss Carter. We need help. My step-dad—*er* Jim—is doing something he shouldn't. He's going to shoot the poison gas."

Gladys stopped on the sidewalk and looked at the kids, not understanding. "The town mucky-mucks said okay to the poison?"

"No, I mean the other stuff. The mustard gas. He's loading it into a van right now," the girl explained while her hands flailed at the air.

Gladys wasn't at the top of the information food chain. It was entirely possible that this morning's mass attack on the north HESCO called for such weapons. She would never use mustard gas on people, but her vote barely mattered.

"There's an attack across from the college. You two need to get to the school to shelter until this passes."

"No, Miss Carter," William barked. "You don't understand. Mr. Jensen's been touching her. He's been touching Candice." The boy turned to the girl. Her eyes fell to the sidewalk.

"Mother of God," Gladys muttered. The truth clarified, suddenly. Her head raced forward to catch up with something her gut already knew.

"And he's going to do something bad with that poison gas. I know it," William said. "Mr. Jensen was acting weird. And talking weird too. He pointed a gun at me and said that he was the only one who could save the town. He's a *psycho*, Miss Carter. And he has poison gas. Lots of poison gas, and cannons to shoot it."

In her rational mind, Gladys knew that using poison gas without the town's say-so and committing pedophilia landed on two unrelated squares. But in her human mind, she felt the two things criss-cross like French cheese and bad breath.

Something clicked in her brain, like the last tick of a grandfather clock before the bell goes *gong-gong-gong*.

*Jim Jensen is a motherfucking sociopath.*

She knew something was off about the man. She'd seen his shuffles and half-steps on the high school campus, like the feet of a basketball player hankering to step back for the three-point shot. She'd watched him do his little dance in the staff room, and while passing through clusters of kids. Something had been *off* about the man. Something just wasn't right, but it hadn't been until the girl's eyes dropped to the concrete that Gladys fully understood.

*Click.*

*That dude's a true-blue psycho, and he has weapons of mass destruction.*

"Does anyone else know?" she asked the kids.

They shook their heads.

"Find your dad. Find Mat. Tell him what you told me. *Hurry*." The former WNBA player launched from her yard in a ferocious sprint—a pace she could maintain all the way to that cocksucker's house on Forrest Avenue.

---

JIM JENSEN WASN'T HOME. Gladys turned in circles on the sidewalk in front of his house.

No van. No jars of poison gas. No ego-maniac pedophile in the yard or in the house.

While Gladys spun, she caught snippets of info from her QRF

team radio on the wall, six blocks north of Jensen's house. All the town's defenders had dashed to Smith Street to fight off a huge attack. She'd been called to join them on the HESCO, but now she had bigger possums to fry.

*The explosion. The column of barbecue smoke over the town. The tornado siren. The rattle of gunfire.*

She put it together bit-by-bit. The pork drying facility at the lumberyard burned, and the clouds of pork smell had stirred the refugees into a frenzy.

Jim Jensen probably planned to counter-strike the mob with poison gas. He might see it as a way to prove to the town he was a hero, someone special—someone who could abuse his step-daughter while the town looked the other way, as though that was ever going to happen. Gladys had been molested by her dad's friend, and that's exactly the kind of shit that sonofabitch would've come up with in his twisted head.

*Where had Jensen gone?* She forced herself to slow down and *think.*

Jensen had poison gas and a cannon that launched jars. Her combat team was lined up on Smith Street. The best place to launch gas into the mob would be the community college football field. Maybe.

"Gladys to Sergeant Best," she radioed for the tenth time. *Nothing.* Either his radio was out-of-range or Mat was busy fighting for his life. Gladys fingered the short antenna on her radio. She'd forgotten the longer one on her kitchen counter.

Gunfire rattled to the north. Smith Street. Her team.

*The football field.* That's where Jensen would go, she felt certain.

She ran north up Nolan Street and cut across a backyard with a pretty white gazebo and another yard with a truck up on blocks. It was a mile to the football field, give-or-take. She'd be there in less than eight minutes.

Gladys heard a sonorous thumping, like the first bars of the song *Stand By Me*—like a rhythmic mortar, firing six shots in a row. She'd never heard anything like it, but she knew in her gut: the town of McKenzie, Tennessee had just joined Sadaam Hussein and Benito Mussolini in using chemical weapons against their own citizens. She poured on the speed and fired herself like a missile toward the sound.

---

THUNK, *thunk, thunk, thunk.*

Mat Best hadn't ever heard that sound on a battlefield, but within a few seconds realization dawned: Jensen was launching poison gas into the rats.

*Thunk, thunk.*

It was Jensen's pneumatic cannon. He'd built a multi-barrel version.

During the time it took for Mat to reach a conclusion, he'd killed two men and a handgun-wielding woman churning across the field of hay stubble and mud. A few rats turned back in the face of the rifle fire, but for every rat who faltered, ten more appeared on the edge of the woods.

The Carroll farmhouse had been completely overrun. The woods teemed with a human flood that reminded Mat of rats he'd seen overflowing a burning field in Iraq. Rank upon rank of desperate people drove each other forward, pushing, shoving and lurching into the wind. Mat was already down to three mags.

The first wave hit the HESCO barrier at the eastern end of Smith Street. Mat didn't dare shift resources in that direction. The human tidal wave would strike along the entire half-mile-long stretch in the next thirty seconds.

"They're getting through!" one of the Cabrera brothers screamed into his radio.

"Monica, this is Mat. Send all newcomers to the east end of the line. Repeat, have the townspeople head to the east end. If the rats get over, the townies have to beat them back." Mat knew it wasn't going to happen, even as he ordered it. Ninety-nine percent of the townspeople weren't capable of the level of violence required to survive this. It was a scrambled egg mess of a battle. The rats on the east end didn't even pause on top of the HESCO to fight the defenders. They leapt over and ran for the smell of barbecue. Mat's men were little more than speed bumps.

Up and down Smith Street, townspeople fought, wrestled and clung to the rats that'd made it over. The townies were five times as strong, because they'd been eating actual food, but they had none of the desperation of the rats. The refugees fought to get past, and when they did, they disappeared into the neighborhoods like filthy water down a drain.

The rats that lost their fight with the townies either stayed down or crawled back to prop themselves against the inside of the HESCO. But even then, half of them caught their breath, then made another run for it. Once a rat was over the wall, there was no way to get them back on the other side.

Mat watched an elderly lady with a revolver hold six men and a girl captive against the town side of the barrier. Five more rats flew over the top and bolted for the cover of the homes. The lady blasted one of them, maybe by accident. Half the people she had "arrested" got up and ran for it while she went to see if she'd killed the guy she'd shot.

"Hold the line," Mat ordered into his radio. "We'll deal with the ones that got past later."

Mat had seen at least a hundred rats make it over into town. If enough of them got in, the town would be done. He had no idea what that number might be. But if they overwhelmed them, the HESCO wouldn't matter. The rats would eat everything not protected by a gun, and all the guns were on the wall.

"Hold the HESCO. Even if they're getting past. Slow them

down." Mat didn't know if it'd work, but he began to think of the HESCO, not as a medieval wall, but as a semi-porous barrier, like a fleece jacket in the rain. It wouldn't keep out the weather, but it might be just enough to keep from getting drenched. The rats weren't turning to attack his men once inside the wall. They ran for the pork instead.

*Thunk, thunk, thunk, thunk, thunk, thunk.*

Mat's attention turned back to the sodden hayfield. He expected to see flying missiles, arching over the battlefield, then wispy clouds of yellow smoke. Instead, he saw nothing; just rambling, clotting masses of filthy people.

*Maybe the jars didn't break when they hit the mud.*

That wouldn't surprise him. Random shit happened all the time in war, even with a multi-trillion-dollar military-industrial complex. With Kerr jars and potato guns, who could say?

Then, a knot of twenty rats wavered in the middle of the field. They stumbled, fell to their knees, then pitched over. Some writhed in agony in the mud, others went still.

Another patch opened in the sea of rushing rats, then another. There were no explosions, no smoke, no sign of poison gas except men, women and children scythed down to the mud.

Mat slung his rifle and snatched his binoculars.

A ten year-old boy went down, clutching his throat. A woman rolled in agony in the filth, coating her hair with sludge. An old man fell to the ground, like a chopped pine and didn't twitch a muscle; dead upon impact.

Mat dropped the binos and whipped his head left and right, giving the sensitive skin on his ears and cheeks a chance to test the wind. It was still blowing from the southwest, at about five knots. But he knew from long-range shooting school that the wind in one part of the field didn't guarantee wind in another part. Wind swirled. A lot.

*What would happen if the wind turned? Could the poison reach the*

*HESCO, or the town?* The prevailing wind would definitely carry the poison across the Carroll's homestead.

There were no hills or trees in no-man's land—just tilled mud—so Mat prayed the wind would behave and not blow it back across his men. But a five knot wind was close to no wind at all. Light wind had a mind of its own and could whirl around at the slightest provocation. Gas attacks were notorious for killing "friendly" forces. Mat kept one eye on the waves of starving rats and another on the fickle wind.

*That psycho motherfucker, Jensen. He'd gone kinetic without even a by-your-leave from Mat or the security committee. He'd taken it upon himself to bring the whole town with him on his little journey of mass murder.*

But they might just win. Mat's eyes narrowed to see if the tide of oblivion could be turned.

*Thunk, thunk, thunk, thunk, thunk, thunk.*

Jensen had dialed in his pneumatic mortar because the next wave of death cut across the heaviest wave of rats. Mat saw several of the jars flying through his binos this time, falling from the heavens like tumbling capsules of malevolence. They slapped to the ground and blew into fragments. Thirty seconds later, men, women and children began to drop like flies passing through the flame. Mat sagged, jerking his binos away from another child strangling on her own vomit.

The battle wavered as the possessed mobs stumbled over piles of their dead. Newcomers inhaled the gas, twisted, and added to the twitching layers of bodies. Thirty meter-wide sweeps of the rough-turned hayfield twisted with the struggle of the doomed.

The mass of rats finally reckoned with the invisible destroyer in their midst and slowed their advance. Thousands tarried, screamed terror, then choked on the swirling, silent, chemical weapon.

For a moment, it looked to Mat like the poison gas might stem the tide. The overwhelming thousands flooding across the field thinned and slowed. Rats poured back across the field toward the tree line, like vermin caught between the brushfire and the exterminators.

Hundreds, maybe a thousand refugees contorted, screamed and thrashed in the mud. Mat's radio had gone silent. Every man on the HESCO line stood, mute and boneless, as they watched the destruction of their enemy.

Tears welled up in Mat's eyes, finally overcoming his adrenaline. *The town might be saved. All it'd cost them was their immortal souls.*

---

*THUNK, thunk, thunk, thunk, thunk, thunk.*

Gladys Carter pushed into a balls-out sprint, turning into the final mile to the football field. Her tactical vest clanked and bobbed on her thin frame. The AR-15 pumped in her hands. She caught glimpses of the Carroll hayfield, and she turned away from the sight of it. People were dying en masse. There was no time to lament. Her run would end face-to-face with a mass murdering motherfucker. What happened next would be up to Jensen. Either way, he was going down.

The football field lay in a depression; better for the halogens to shine those Friday night lights. But Jensen wasn't on the football field. It was empty and overgrown.

Gladys veered away from the entrance to the fenced stadium and angled toward the raised roadbed of University Drive—toward the thumping rhythm. On the side of the road facing the hayfield, she spotted a white van. As she flew toward it a man climbed on top of the van and gazed east.

*Thunk, thunk, thunk, thunk, thunk, thunk.*

From a few hundred yards, she recognized Jim Jensen, wearing his saggy-ass denim pants and yellow golf shirt. He always tucked in his polo shirts, making his belly protrude like a volleyball. She pictured his naked, skinny ass on top of the thirteen-year-old girl, his pathetic, white belly smashed against hers.

*I'm gonna fuck a brother up,* she decided. Her legs pumped harder, pushing her into a ferocious sprint.

As she dashed onto University Drive, she saw the whole of the Sprinter van. A ladder leaned against the side and the rear doors hung open. Jensen climbed down.

Her right hand slid to the tang of the pistol grip on the AR-15. Her left hand ran the charging handle like it had ten thousand times in training. She glanced down to see brass in the breach and she let the charging handle fly. The bolt sprang forward with a satisfying *snick*. She looked up just in time to see Jensen's startled expression. He held a jar in each hand, three-quarters full of yellow powder.

She must've looked like she felt—like the Goddess of Vengeance —because Jensen began babbling before she could even hear him. The barrel of her rifle made her emotional state abundantly clear.

"I'm saving the town," he screeched. "Just look. Look at the field. Stop! Wait!"

Nothing would brook her fury, but she couldn't help but look where he was pointing. Then she looked again. All the fire went out of her legs and her sprint became a jog, then it became a walk.

The Carroll's hay field flooded over with thousands of refugees, stumbling, running, laying in the muck. It was as if she witnessed Dante's Inferno alongside University Drive. Her brain vibrated in her skull with the horror of it.

"I did that. I stopped them," Jensen whined. "I formulated the mixture of mustard gas and anthrax. I invented the launchers. I pulled the trigger. It was *me* who saved this town."

A corner of her mind rolled below an avalanche of emotion: thousands of refugees threatened her town. Some terrible evil was eating them from the inside out. This animal...what he had done to the girl.

*His cold, sweating belly pressed against her pubis.*

The rifle snapped to her shoulder. The sights centered on his chest.

"Whoa," he held out his left hand, like a magician drawing a bird from the air. His other hand appeared with a revolver. The jars had disappeared while she was stunned by the mayhem of the battlefield. The jars of putrescence must've gone down the white, yawning mouths of the up-angled tubes in the back of the Sprinter van.

Gladys' radio blared to life. On top of the road, she had line-of-sight with her QRF team. "All stations, this is Mat. Hold what you've got. Repeat, hold what you've got."

"What's happening, sir?" another voice cried in her earbuds.

"Just hold what you've got. Mat out."

Jensen's revolver was out, but not pointing directly at her. His other hand wandered to a milk crate on the tailgate. Her rifle hadn't drifted a centimeter from his chest.

"Break, break, break." Gladys keyed her radio with her left hand while the right kept the rifle aimed at Jensen.

"Go for Mat."

"I've got Jim Jensen in front of me getting ready to launch some kind of poison gas into the refugees. This is Gladys."

She wasn't asking for orders. She just didn't know quite what to do. Should she drill this fucker or contain the launcher-weapon. She felt totally overwhelmed. The little, shiny revolver in his hands barely merited consideration. Not from where she stood. Not with people dying in the hundreds.

Jensen's free hand drifted toward a bright red lever poking out of a cluster of white tubes. He was going to fire the launcher again. He'd send more people to a twisting, tortured death.

"Acknowledged," was all Mat Best replied.

*What the hell was that supposed to mean?*

BECAUSE OF THE POISON GAS, he was going to win this battle, and it'd probably be the final battle. After this, the WMD genie would be out of the bottle. The clutching horror of mass murder would be knocked off the town like dust off an old golf ball. The town would take Jensen's murder wagon on tour, around to the camps, and by-hook-or-crook, the refugee threat would go somewhere else; either to the Great Beyond or to the next, hapless Tennessee town. For Mat, it would be *mission accomplished.*

*Welcome to the long, lonely road,* Mat pictured himself saying to the people of McKenzie, Tennessee. *It was kill or be killed and you chose to kill. That was the cost. So, pay up, bitches.*

He'd been clutching his binoculars like a grenade with a lost pin. The radio shushed in his ear. He could almost feel Gladys Carter on the other end, waiting.

He pictured William, growing up in a town with mass murder scrawled in the Book of Life.

He pictured himself leaving them all behind; William, Gladys, the Morgans—McKenzie town vanishing in the rearview mirror of his Ford Raptor as he rolled west. Forever west.

"No," Mat said to gentle breeze. "Win, lose or draw, that's not me. That's not them."

Mat keyed his radio. "Gladys, this is Mat. He doesn't fire that thing again. Not at any cost. Do you copy?"

"Good copy. Cease fire the cannons," she replied.

THE CHILD MOLESTER lurched toward the van when Gladys said, "Cease fire the cannons." His hand hit the red lever at the same moment she pressed the trigger—twice in quick succession.

*Pop-pop.* Jensen fell back against the white doors.

Instead of *thunk-thunk-thunk*, the six gaping mouths of the launcher coughed. Six glass jars puffed out of the tubes, flew four feet and crashed to the gravel. Four of the jars shattered.

Jensen tipped sideways into the Sprinter van and fired his revolver.

*Blam, blam, blam, blam, blam, blam, click, click, click.*

A bullet punched Gladys below the collarbone. Jim Jensen slid down the door, leaving a bloody smear.

She stared at her former colleague. He wheezed, then hacked; his eyes welled with copious tears.

*The gas!*

She dropped her rifle and ran. Her clavicle howled in pain. Her lungs were suddenly seized by fire.

Gladys made it a hundred yards before she collapsed onto the asphalt.

---

"All stations. This is Mat. Consolidate ammunition. Prepare for the second wave."

This half-mile of HESCO barrier was their last stand, and it'd be Mat, his forty-man QRF and a few hundred lightly-armed townspeople against thousands of desperate, starving barbarians. He had one mag left.

Mat had probably killed them all with his decision to end Jensen's death cannons, but serenity flowed around him; over his shoulders, through his hair, and it caressed his arms. It smelled a lot like barbecue.

The apocalypse would kill them all eventually, but it'd be on terms Mat, Gladys, the Bible-thumping sheriff and his rosy-cheeked wife could abide. They would hold to their humanity, even in death.

This time, on this field, Mat had the authority to stop the Reaper drone from raining death on the young bride, and he had done it. This would be his own final entry in the Book of Life. He wished he could have Perez here beside him—that his old buddy could die with redemption on his head instead of oxy strangling his soul.

The invisible gas must've thinned and blown northeast because another thousand rats surged onto the field from the edge of Carroll's wood, and these rats knew nothing of poison gas. All they knew was that someone, somewhere was cooking hundreds of pounds of pork. The dead and dying that littered the hayfield meant nothing to them.

*Why haven't they gotten that fire under control?* Mat fretted as he went through his magazines and shuffled every bullet into one and a half, twenty-round SCAR mags.

The few hundred rats that'd crossed the HESCO barrier and run into town would've reached the source of the smell by now and realized their mistake; the pork was all burned up. Now, they probably rampaged across town, raiding homes for food.

Sporadic gunfire popped and crackled from town proper, but Mat couldn't allow that fight to distract him from the stunning threat he now faced: two thousand refugees, churning toward him and his hapless cohort.

"All stations, this is Mat. Shoot only those with weapons. Stop everyone you can at the wall, hand-to-hand. This is to-the-death, folks. May God help us. Mat out."

The first ranks of the rats reached mid-field, where a gravel service road cut across, east to west. They loped up and over the road and poured into the last three hundred yards before the HESCO.

A low rumble built on the wind as the thronging mass of desperate zombies bore down on them. Out of the north, a line of speeding pickup trucks burst onto Carroll's field, racing down the access road along University Drive, then angling out across the gravel service road, cutting the field in half.

At least twenty trucks of all makes, models and colors cut across the mid-field service road and plunged into the mass of refugees. The trucks smashed through them like ships plowing the sea. Rats dove out of the way as the convoy stretched across the breadth of Carroll's field. Men and women poured out of the trucks, and leapt from the truck beds, and went instantly to battle with sticks, baseball bats, shovels and rakes.

The fight for Carroll's field flipped from a siege to a melee in an instant, but it was still thousands of rats against hundreds of defenders, and Mat had no idea who had just thrown themselves into their fight.

"All stations. Reinforcements in mid-field. Move up to the center road. Get off of the wall and help them! Give them cover fire. Go, go, go, go!"

Mat slung his rifle around to his back and climbed over the side of the HESCO. He scaled down the unsteady chainlink, dangling like a sail. He let go and dropped the last ten feet to the muddy field. All the defenders followed. Up and down the HESCO, townspeople slopped across the mud and into the melee.

They charged forward, ignoring the rats that'd made it past the service road. Mat burst onto the gravel road first, punched a rat in the nose, and scanned. He saw Sheriff Morgan below in the field, shoving a woman back the way she'd come. The sheriff stood a head taller and was a fair-sight cleaner than the refugees. He wore a chunk of neon orange survey tape around his head. So did many others—all the others fighting with their back to the town.

"Friendlies are wearing orange tape. All stations acknowledge," Mat radioed. A refugee raised a knife. Mat shot him through the chest. Another man swung an ax. Mat blew the top of his head off into the hay stubble.

"All stations, look for weapons. Clear shots only. Friendlies are wearing orange marker tape," he repeated.

Rats charged the raised road bed. Mat butt-checked a guy in the face with the stock of his SCAR. The dude went down with his nose smashed flat. Mat searched the crowd and shot a woman swinging a shotgun like a club, then he shot another man with a hatchet.

All along the service road, town defenders picked their targets and added gunfire to the fist fight. It was impossible to read the tide of battle, but the flow of rats had halted at the melee, and few crossed the gravel road. Fewer still made it across the stretch of churned-up mud to the foot of the HESCO.

Thousands of starving rats had been fighting for fifteen exhausting minutes and, all-at-once their will broke. Whatever spare calories they had in their bodies gave out, like a switch had been flipped. Hundreds folded to the ground like wet paper dolls. Others staggered back the way they'd come. Some fell unconscious from exertion.

"Morgan!" Mat shouted over the din. The sheriff looked up from a fist fight he was winning against a bald man with a goatee. The sheriff delivered a gut punch, the man collapsed forward, then toppled into the mud.

"Can you get your people to pull back to the HESCO?" Mat shouted.

The sheriff bent over his knees, heaving for breath and flashed a thumb's up.

"All teams, this is Mat. Pull back to the HESCO barrier. Disengage."

## 22

### CAMERON STEWART

"Trust me, the blessed gods have no love for crime.
They honor justice, honor the decent acts of men."

— EUMAEUS, THE ODYSSEY

**Main Street,
Saint George, Utah**

The milkshake joint on the main drag of Saint George wasn't shut down after all. Quite the contrary.

Cameron, Ruth and the kids sat under the awning on the half-rusted picnic tables eating sandwiches and fries for breakfast. The parking lot milled with men and women in camo, and a small tank covered them from the high point on the boulevard where it went over the I-15 freeway.

"I still can't believe we found you." Tommy Stewart shook his head. "We were out on patrol to get a look-see at the enemy in the desert. Lo-and-behold, we find your sorry ass with a bunch of polygamists. Um, no offense, ma'am," Tommy said to Ruth.

"It's okay. It's true," she said. "We're from Colorado City. We're polygamists. It's not offensive to us."

Tommy nodded. "Where's Julie?"

Cameron shook his head. "She didn't make it. They shot her during a trade."

"Who shot her?" Tommy tensed.

"Rockville. Their town militia. They ambushed us when we traded guns for food."

"I'm so sorry, Cam." Tommy reached across the table and put his hand on his brother's arm. "We were thinking about scouting along the Virgin River today. Maybe we get a little payback on Rockville."

Cameron shook his head. "I just came from there. I can tell you what's up. There's no reason to go there. Rockville will pay for their sins in time. Colorado City, over on Highway 59, is full of tanks. Maybe fifty of them. The Mexican Army, I think."

"It's not the Mexican Army that's in Colorado City," Tommy corrected. "It's the cartel. They captured abandoned American tanks and have rolled up all of Arizona, half of New Mexico and everything that's left of Nevada. We're holding them at the outskirts of Saint George for now, but they could roll right through us, any time they like. They stopped after annihilating our roadblock in the Virgin River gorge. They're probably waiting for those other fifty tanks to come up through Hurricane so they can hit Saint George from two directions at once. We don't have anything that can stop them, and I think they know that. Today, we evacuate. That's why we're eating up all the perishable food this morning."

"So where's your family?" Cameron asked his brother.

"They're at Jenna's place in Salt Lake City. That's the base of operations for the Mormon Church. General Kirkham's cobbling together an army to stop the narcos. We're down here on reconnaissance. The whole state's rallying to the church banner, Mormon or not. Maybe the whole Intermountain West."

"A Mormon Church army?" It sounded absurd to Cameron.

"They're the biggest show in town since the government fell."

Cameron chuckled. "Like a big Neighborhood Watch, huh? Are they making everyone join the Mormons? Should I call you Elder Tommy now?"

"Yuck it up. At least I didn't become a polygamist like some people." Ruth looked up from her fries. "I'm sorry, again, ma'am."

She smiled and waved it away. She still wore the long skirts and kept the towering hair of a fundamentalist woman. Cameron felt strangely unconcerned about what his brother might think about him having two wives. After a fashion, he had. In the apocalypse, polygamy might be a survival strategy. A clan was a clan was a clan. Who slept with whom was less important than watching each others' backs. Even coming from "civilization" in the north, Tommy would probably understand that. Things had gotten weird.

A new reality had been imposed by Mother Nature. Religious differences would get sorted out, but probably not until they figured out how to feed the survivors. Until then, the bigger the team, the better the chance of seeing spring.

Tommy crumpled the wax paper of his sandwich. "The Mormons don't care if we're Mormon or not. We're all in this together. It's Utahns versus drug dealers, and it's the Super Bowl of the survival finalists."

"You guys are going to need lotsa Jesus to beat those tanks." Cameron shoved the last bite of roast beef sandwich in his mouth.

"That's the damn truth. I hope General Kirkham has another rabbit up his sleeve."

"What was the first rabbit?" Cam asked.

"It's a long story. I'll tell you about it on the way back to Salt Lake City. We'll escort you and your family to Jenna's place. We're done here for now. I assume everyone's going with us?" Tommy waved a fry at Ruth and the kids.

Cameron saw the scene for a moment from his brother's point of view; Cameron was with a strange woman and her strange kids. Julie was gone. Tommy wouldn't know if Cam and Ruth were together or "together."

Cameron looked his brother in the eye. "This is my family now. Ruth and all five kids. I made a promise."

Tommy nodded. "Maybe you'll tell me your long story too. Honestly, brother, I'd given you up for dead. The kind of man you were when you left Anaheim...that kind of man doesn't last long out here."

The words stung, but the sting meant little against all he'd lost, and all he'd seen destroyed.

"I'm not that man anymore," Cameron admitted.

Tommy stood up from the metal bench. "I can see that. Unfortunately, all that grit landed you in the middle of an even-bigger shit-storm. Sorry 'bout that."

"Don't apologize. Nothing's guaranteed anymore. We eat sandwiches when there's sandwiches. Tomorrow, maybe there's nothing. Every day is a gift."

Cameron helped Ruth untangle herself from the metal picnic bench and round up the kids and their mess. He herded his family toward the pickup truck, now full of gas.

He wondered what it all meant. All of the children had survived. His and Isaiah's. Every one.

For thirty thousand years of human survival, protecting the children had been enough. As Cameron climbed into another man's truck, with another man's wife, he regarded the kids crammed into the old pickup. At last, their bellies were full, and for the moment they were safe.

He counted that as a win.

# 23

---

## SAGE ROSS

**Zumwalt Prairie**
**Wallowa County, Oregon**

It was the brightest morning Sage had ever seen, and he'd forgotten his sunglasses. The snow sparkled for ten miles in every direction.

Aimee Butterton stood by his side, dressed in a snow suit and wearing snowshoes. They'd been working their way close enough to the elk for Sage to attempt a shot with his 30-30, but so far, they'd bumped the herd twice without getting within three hundred yards.

Their next gambit would be to push the herd toward another hunting party farther up the slope of the Zumwalt to the north. Maybe the elk would hit those guys' wind, double back and run past Sage and Aimee. There were six elk herds they could see from their location and ten hunting parties working them. The elk would eventually get harassed enough to filter into the forests at the edge of the prairie and disappear for the day.

He and Aimee had permission from Wallowa to hunt the morning, so it'd be now or never. It was mid-January and Wallowa County had graciously offered permission for Union County hunters to cull the elk herd to reasonable numbers. Union County needed meat to hold them over through winter and spring, when their own cattle would be ready to butcher, so Wallowa gave them permission to take a thousand elk. It'd put a big dent in Union County's need for fat and protein.

"You're going to have to shoot," Sage said. Aimee's father's rifle could reach a lot farther than the 30-30.

"You sure?" Aimee asked with a tilt of her head.

"Yes. Obviously." Sage couldn't entirely conceal the irritation in his voice.

"You okay?" she asked as she shucked a round into the 30-06. She handled it with ease and familiarity—glancing down to check for brass as the cartridge slid home. He hadn't asked, but he was sure she'd killed deer and elk many times before.

"I'm fine," he said, his voice flat.

The elk turned when they caught scent of the other hunting party, and they angled back across the rolling prairie. They looked like they might come within four hundred yards.

"If they come close enough, you take the shot," she said.

That wasn't going to happen. The elk had seen them before and elk weren't stupid.

Sage, on the other hand, still felt pretty stupid. He'd been used by a crooked cop, a disgruntled daughter, a housewife spy mastermind and an affable rancher. As down-homey as they all seemed, they were all serpents and he had been their prey. He understood why they'd done it, but it was a thing, now, between him and Aimee. Deep down, he found that being played like a wandering puppy did not make him hot like a hound dog. Quite the opposite.

Commissioner Pete had used him for good cause, but Sage's life had been on-the-line the whole time, and it'd been without his consent. If they'd told him what they were up to, he might've helped. At least, he'd like to think he *would've* helped. To say he felt butt-hurt would be an understatement.

"I don't think this is going to work out, Aimee." Sage didn't know how else to express his feelings of helplessness and betrayal.

Aimee looked him in the eyes with sadness, but not surprise. She nodded and turned back to the approaching elk. They'd picked their path and the herd was committed. They'd give her an opportunity.

Sage and Aimee slid out of their backpacks and set them on the snow as a bench rests for her to steady her rifle. It'd be a long shot —at least three-fifty. She'd take it prone.

"I don't blame you. What we did to you wasn't cool," she whispered. The elk already knew they were there, but they'd cut close enough anyway. They had no other option.

Sage grunted. It didn't really matter. He couldn't go back to Union County without risk of reprisals from what was left of The Five. He wasn't welcome in the Butterton home now. Mrs. Butterton blamed him for Captain Chamber's arrest. It wasn't clear if she knew about Aimee's part. Mrs. Butterton would forgive blood a lot faster than she'd forgive him.

Sage lived with the Lathrop family now on their ranch in Wallowa, and he'd be there through the winter. The big snows had begun, one or two a week, and the risk of travel toward Utah had escalated beyond reason. He could set off again in the spring— strong and healthy.

The elk spread out in a single-file line and side-hilled across the slope between the couple and the other hunting party.

When the elk reached the closest point, Aimee settled into the scope, let out a slow breath and squeezed the trigger.

The rifle roared, then settled on the packs. A cow elk stumbled, turned around once, then fell sideways onto the snow. The herd danced in circles, confused, then the lead cow tucked her head and trotted forward, continuing on their way. The others stepped around the fallen companion. The diminished herd loped toward the tree line, then disappeared.

Aimee looked up and smiled. The elk was her family's only meat for the duration. It was fortunate she'd put one on the ground, given that their former patron was now locked in the Wallowa County jail.

"Please tell your mom I helped with this," Sage said. "I care about you. Your family's hospitality meant a lot to me."

Aimee nodded. "She'll come around. Chambers wasn't good for her."

Sage nodded. One part of him wanted to argue—to rail on her for not trusting him with the truth. He felt like he'd played the part of one of the bad guys, but he should've been one of the good guys. He blamed Aimee, partially, for him coming down on the wrong side of the raid.

The other part of him knew they'd been struggling for their own survival and using any means necessary to achieve it: Chambers, Commissioner Pete, Butterton, and even Sage Ross, none had behaved with any particular nobility. They were all serpents when it came down to it.

Sage would have to live with his doubts and his guilt. Arguing with Aimee would achieve nothing. All that mattered, really, was the meat.

Nourishment. Survival. Spring.

"I'll bring up a snow machine," Sage said, instead of arguing.

Aimee smiled. "I'll get to work quartering her out."

Sage snowshoed toward the machines. They'd dragged an empty sled behind for just this purpose. When he got a hundred yards away, he turned around and watched her. Aimee hung the rifle over one shoulder, her pack over the other, and her slightly-larger-than-his ass worked hard, stomping up the rise toward the dead animal. She reached it, set down her pack and gun, dug into the bag, then plunged her knife into the hide, unzipping the belly like a duffle bag.

He would've loved to stay and watch her—a woman only a few generations removed from the women who settled this valley in the wake of Lewis and Clark. Aimee would need his help in a few minutes to roll the elk over to get to the other side, so he couldn't tarry. He set off again for the snow machines, thinking about the women of the frontier. He'd always imagined them as beasts of burden, doing the homestead work, caring for the children, and keeping house while their men hunted, fought and lead the way, but now he wondered if that was even remotely true.

How many times had those frontiersmen looked up from their adventures only to realize they'd been nothing more, really, than puppets on a string? Servants to a wiser clan?

Sage stopped again on the next hill. Aimee wedged her shoulder under it's blood-streaked rump, pushing with her legs to get the three hundred pound beast rolled over far enough to pull back the hide covering the elk's rear quarter. She struggled competently in her own world of hide, snow and blood.

He shook his head in amazement. She'd lied to him, cajoled him and kept him on track with a plan only she and her aunt fully understood. She'd taken down a powerful man, with a militia army of hundreds. Then, just now, she'd killed an elk twice her weight and set to quartering it without even glancing around for help.

*Would he ever be that strong?*

He knew that he probably wouldn't. But the human race would go on—carried on the shoulders and in the hearts of the true warlords.

## 24

MAT BEST

**Clear Lake Bog**
**McKenzie, Tennessee**

F *our weeks later*

IT LOOKED LIKE COLD, miserable work to Mat. Two hundred of Dr. Hauser's people stood butt-deep in the bog, pulling cattails up from the roots and loading them onto rafts made out of empty milk jugs. Every so often, they shouted and flailed after dislodging yet another cottonmouth. The swamp must've been infested with them.

"Can they eat those?" Mat asked Gladys Carter.

"The snakes or the cattails?"

Mat smiled. "I know they can eat the snakes, but is there really any nutrition in the swamp reeds?"

"Some parts of the cattail, sure. They can eat it raw or dry it, grind it and make flour." She shifted around on her walking stick. "It makes more sense to feed the cattails to the pigs, though. The pigs eat the whole thing—root, leaves and all. A human can only digest the tender center of the root."

"Look who's becoming the resident biologist," Mat joked.

"Naw, that'd be Susan Brown. Biology was my minor."

Mat had come out from town to visit the swamp lands to see how Gladys was healing. Her breath came with obvious difficulty. She moved like a fawn with a broken leg. It was anyone's guess if she'd recover from the lungful of anthrax and mustard gas.

"So, we trade the refugees our pigs for their cattails? Explain that to me. The Tosh Farms guy told me, but I didn't quite follow."

Gladys smiled, obviously proud of what they'd worked out. "We trade them five piglets on credit. They raise them on cattails and give us back a two hundred pound pig—or they *will* when they have them fattened up. Then Tosh farms finishes the pigs with a couple weeks of grain."

Mat understood but felt like he should keep her talking. He'd heard somewhere that having a purpose gave sick people a reason to heal. Gladys had taken the Rat War harder than most, and she'd paid a bigger price as well.

The townspeople buried almost a thousand dead refugees in a mass grave on Carroll's field. The guilt and the shame of it was almost more than the town could bear. Down in the bog, many of the cattail pickers were townsfolk practicing a wet and painful redemption for Jim Jensen's sins.

Gladys had taken part in both the Brashear wood massacre and the Rat War. She wasn't about to blame it all on the pedophile. They'd all lost their way, to one degree or another.

Gladys must've read his mind. "I still can't figure out how our imagination so utterly failed us," she lamented. "We were surrounded by tens of thousands of acres of wetlands, chock-full of cattails. We had the piglets. Tosh euthanized an average of fifteen percent of their piglets because they didn't have the space in their barns to bring them up. Refugees were starving and raiding while we were sitting on a calorie machine. An acre of cattails raises up *forty* pigs, and we have thousands of acres of the stuff. The swamps are so hard to harvest, we never considered it. The refugees could've been considered an under-utilized workforce instead of a threat. Piglets plus cattails plus refugees equals survival—for all of us."

Mat overheard a lot of hindsight lately: *we should've thought of the cattails before. We should've known that Jensen was molesting his step-daughter. We should've put down our guns and seen the refugees as human beings.*

"Us and them," Mat agreed.

"What's that?" Gladys asked with genuine interest.

"Us versus them. It's easy to see the world like that. It feels kinda right, but it gives a person tunnel vision. When you're a hammer, everything's a nail."

Gladys inhaled, closed her eyes and nodded. Mat wondered what effect remorse had on her healing. At least she was moving around outside, in the winter sunshine, breathing fresh air, and *doing something* about her personal guilt.

Mat saw a flash of color down in the swamp, among the slogging, heaving workers.

*An Afghan wedding gown? A bright orange dress?*

No, he decided. It was just a guy in an orange road worker's jacket. The people around McKenzie struggled together to survive. At least for the day, nobody would be killing anybody.

Gladys described the work, "Susan thinks they'll produce a hundred pounds of pork to every seven hundred pounds of cattail. Hauser's people are eating the center part of the shoots for now, and feeding the rest to the piglets. We're advancing the refugees ten fattened hogs per week, just so there's a little meat in their stewpot.

That's what passes for a *small business loan* these days." Gladys smiled at her own joke.

"How many refugees are in the program?" Mat got to the second reason he'd ventured three miles outside the HESCO barrier. He wanted to understand the threat. They were far from being out of the woods.

"Dr. Hauser says five thousand have taken the oath. They keep a pretty good record of it. They make them sign their names in a book —give their word of honor not to steal. Even the kids sign it."

Mat nodded. It still terrified him; being surrounded by thousands of organized refugees. If Hauser decided to screw them over, it'd be a serious war this time.

But so far, the raids on the town had dropped to almost zero. Hauser's ring of organized refugee camps had accepted responsibility for patrolling and turning away refugees who refused to conform to the treaty between the camps and the town of McKenzie. Mat thought of Hauser's refugees as a three-mile buffer zone of semi-pacified aboriginals. Historically, that hadn't always worked out for the British Empire, but Mat was willing to give it another try. The Creek Campers had definitely proven themselves worthy.

Hauser's group had come through for McKenzie when push came to literal shove, and many of those folks had died or were maimed from exposure to the anthrax and mustard gas lingering on the battlefield. Some of Mat's men had been struck as well, but nothing like the Creek Campers that fought the refugees hand-to-hand. A quarter of them had gotten sick.

"Where's Susan Brown? Is she helping with the pig enclosures?"

"No." Gladys began the slow walk to her electric golf cart. "The Tosh people train the refugees on how to raise pigs. They're trying to remember the old ways of fencing in an austere environment. Susan is in Jensen's lab synthesizing more penicillin."

"Does it actually work?" Mat hadn't heard good things.

"It saved my life." Gladys shrugged. "We used up all the real antibiotics the day Jensen gassed us. Since then, Susan's been making it out of bread mold. It's not a strong antibiotic, but it holds the anthrax at bay long enough for the immune system to do its job. Most of the time, at least."

"How're you feeling about Jensen?" Mat probed. He meant, *how are you feeling about ventilating that sonofabitch?*

"I wish he'd survived my bullets and the poison gas so I could beat the shit out of him." She smiled, but the bravado played across her face like eternal sadness.

"Candice is going to be okay," Mat reassured her as he helped her into the driver's seat of the golf cart. "She's got a good family now. So does William."

"Is that why you came all the way out here? To say goodbye? Mission accomplished for Mat Best?" Gladys' face showed her disapproval as clearly as if the words were stamped on her forehead.

Mat chuckled. With this lady, what you saw was what you got.

He slapped his thigh. "Nope. I'm staying. Through the first of spring, at least. I have brothers and my folks on the West Coast, and eventually I need to go to them. For now, McKenzie's my home."

Gladys smiled, this time for real. Her approval landed just as quickly as her disappointment had fled.

"Welcome home, Mat Best. It's about damned time.

---

**Would you enjoy seeing Honor Road,
and the Black Autumn series made into a movie or show?**

*(There's something you can do to truly help make that happen. Rate it a fair five stars!)*

**Rate the book a fair Five Stars on Amazon.**

Much appreciated!

## MEANWHILE...
### NOAH MILLER

Noah Miller would either disintegrate in a mile-high fireball or wake up in another life with his wife and daughter. Either way, in the next few minutes, his story would end.

He revved the 650 horse engine of the dune buggy and it growled like a two hundred pound panther. Even in the face of oblivion, he grinned. A man couldn't help but rejoice in fine machines. Like a Greek hero, he would cross the river between life and death surrounded by treasure: a $130,000 carbon-fiber dune buggy, a $50 million tactical nuke and a half-full bottle of Lead-slingers whiskey.

The carbon-fiber, supergrade plutonium, kamikaze dune racer would fly off the mountain, into the heart of Flagstaff and vaporize the enemy forever.

Noah wasn't concerned with his own death. No thoughts of his own fate tormented him as he thumbed the red, plastic cover on the detonator, up-down-up-down-up-down. There were hundreds of American slaves in Flagstaff and his brother-from-another-mother, if he was still alive, would be down there.

Noah had duct-taped the detonator to the chrome-plated stick shift of the Tatum Dragon—an immense dune buggy once the privilege of men with more cash than good sense. He'd traded fifteen gallons of gas and an MRE for the buggy.

The taped-up detonator was the size of a paperback novel, with a red, plastic cover over a toggle switch. The switch woke the detonator and the clacker-bar grip made it go "boom." Noah had been fiddling with the red cover as he hauled ass across the Arizona desert, circling the town of Flagstaff like a vulture hunting for a way past the coyotes.

Up-down-up-down-up-down. *Click-clack-click-clack-click-clack.*

Three days before, Noah and his men smuggled the cylindrical, three-foot-long Tomahawk nuke from Ellis Air Force Base, where the U.S. government had hidden it in an underground bunker. The remnants of Ellis command had joined the Arizona resistance after the battle of Dry River Refinery. They'd followed the cartel army back to Flagstaff, and later sent Noah to collect the tactical nuke from the Air Force base.

With the warhead and the buggy, Noah would slag the narco invaders, garrisoned in Flagstaff, along with hundreds of innocent Arizonans. It wasn't the first city Noah had annihilated, but it would be his last. At least this time he'd die with them.

Up-down-up-down-up-down.

*Click-clack-click-clack-click-clack.*

There had been a lot of hoopla about which lives mattered, back in the Stupid Days before the collapse.

*Black Lives Mattered. Blue Lives Mattered. Trans-pedo-nose-pierced Lives Mattered. All Lives Mattered.* Noah couldn't remember the whys and wherefores of the ceaseless, clickety-clack arguments on the internet. He did remember the fat, comfortable fools who argued. Half of them were dead now, at least in the Southwest. He didn't know how many had died in the cities back east. Maybe all of them.

In the Stupid Days, they'd all but forgotten about slavery—consigning it to the wood pile of history. But just four months after the world face-planted into its own briar of selfishness, technology and limp-dick comfort, slavery came flying back into vogue, like the Bee Gees and bell-bottom pants.

An off-color crop of freedom fighters had sprung up in Arizona and they chased the slavers into the soon-to-be-radioactive heart of Flagstaff. Now, Noah and hundreds of others would die to end slavery. Hopefully, the next time America wrote history, it would remember better.

In the immortal lark of the movie *Team America, World Police:* "Freedom isn't free. There's a hefty, fuckin' fee."

Indeed.

Noah gunned the engine, punched the shifter into gear and popped the clutch. His head slammed into the headrest. The tires clawed at the dirt and the front end danced with ferocious power, threatening to take flight. In a fury of gravel and dust, Noah Miller *yee-hawed* as he rode the warhead toward both victory and death.

---

*Nine Weeks Earlier*

**Black Panthers**
Nackards Corner
**Phoenix, Arizona**

> *"I don't see no white militia, the boogie boys, the three percenters and all the rest of these scared-ass rednecks. We here, where the fuck you at? We're in your house… let's go!"*
>
> — BLACK PANTHERS, FACEBOOK POST,
> OCTOBER 6TH, BLACK AUTUMN

Willie Lloyd had no clue why he was shooting at the cops, except that they always shot at the cops and the cops always shot at them.

Hell, he wasn't even sure the dudes across the boulevard, hiding behind the CVS Pharmacy were cops at all. They used to be able to tell the cops apart because of the chunky mustaches and the 1950s haircuts. Now, two months into the Boogaloo, everyones' hair and beards were shaggy. It was like Bible times. But Willie could tell which dudes where his brothers, 'cause they were black, shaggy or not.

That pretty much summed it up. His boys were black and the boys on the other end of his gun barrel were white. Not that the cops had much to fear from Willie Lloyd—bossman of Black Panthers, Phoenix faction; Willie Lloyd couldn't shoot for a damn. He'd been a felon since he was nineteen, but he was no hard-ass gangbanger criminal. He'd gotten rolled up in some trouble with his big brother and that'd been enough to give him a criminal record. When you had a felony record, carrying guns became as risky as carrying dope. After his short stint in prison as a kid, he pretty much followed the instructions given by his parole officer, which included *no guns*. Willie had joined the apocalypse not knowing a mag release from a meatball.

In the last two months, that had changed. He had a lot of guns now, plus a couple hundred soldiers. Willie and a handful of his men were in another skirmish with the cops—the kind of firefight where nobody really focuses on killing the other guy, Bullets fly like insults; lots of noise but not a lot of physical contact.

Six shaggy-faced white men busted out from behind the CVS and ran full-tilt across Southern Avenue. They ducked behind the burrito joint and bullets chewed at the tan stucco behind them.

They were definitely cops. They sprinted like a bunch of defensive linemen—short, fat and squatty. All butt, no body—as his boxing coach used to say. Phoenix cops had either been pumping a lot of iron or taking 'roids. Most of them were fire plugs with shoulders that ran up to the bottom of their jaws instead of stopping at the base of their necks.

Willie waved five of his guys back to the Ranch Market. When they dipped through the the store, they'd grab a few more brothers and head off to flank the burrito place. This wasn't the first time they'd done this dance with the cops. They did it every two or three days. The cops wanted to push the Panthers out of the Ranch Market. It was an attempt for supplies, like every skirmish these days. Willie sheltered twenty families in the Ranch, along with fifty black soldiers. They weren't going to be driven out by a handful of cops. The cops were wasting their time.

Little by little, Willie's men came out to join the fight. In no version of this story were a dozen cops going to overrun them. His boys would trade rounds until the cops got the picture. Nobody needed to die to figure that out, but accidents happen when guns are involved. He wished he could just tell the cops and save them the bullets and the grief. Cops were suckers for doing things the hard way.

Willie and the Panthers owned the CVS pharmacy as well as the market, but it was lunchtime and all but one of his lookouts had beat it over to the Ranch for lunch. His last remaining dude on top of the pharmacy lobbed rounds over the side of the roof, but three of the cops were keeping his head down pretty good. Willie would have to position a guy on top of the strip mall behind the pharmacy after this skirmish—another ring of defense.

Willie countered every move the cops made. It was like playing rock-paper-scissors with guns. He'd win again, and then they'd come back three days later with *"Okay, best out of seventeen?"*

Each day, he and his Black Panther boys strung out further around the neighborhood. They currently held down four little malls, a school and a water tank over on Baseline Road. His men and their families had already eaten up most of the food in the Ranch Market. They'd soon need to find another place to scavenge. Willie worried that they wouldn't find it this time. In Phoenix, two months after the collapse, scavenge had become scarce, and there were a lot of dead bodies to prove it.

Most died inside their homes instead of in the streets, which didn't make a lot of sense to him. Phoenix homes were hot-as-hell without air conditioning. Even with all the windows open in December, they were hot boxes during the day. People had resorted to removing big chunks of their roofs so their homes could breathe. These days, most anyone still on their feet had fled the city seeking water. Those who had stayed were bulging corpses, splayed out in their beds, naked and stewing in their juices. There wasn't anywhere in Phoenix a man could go without smelling them.

The Harbor Freight next door to the Ranch Market had been pretty damned useful, and Willie would hate losing it when they moved on. The cops had no way of knowing the market was almost tapped out. They risked their lives over empty shelves.

"Yo, dawg." Will's nineteen-dollar WalMart radio beeped then chirped. They still hadn't figured out how to get the radios to stop chirping before every transmission. They'd thrown away the instructions.

"How many times I gotta tell you: we don't know who you mean when you say 'dawg.'" Willie explained into the radio. A smattering of rifle fire popped around the burrito joint. Gunfire was so common these days that it'd become like a barking dog; no big deal.

"Well, whatcha want me to call you? You are da Big Dawg." *Chirp.*

"Just call me Willie." *Chirp.*

"Then dey know your identity."

Willie sighed. He had twenty IQ points on most of these guys. That's why they'd put him in charge. But, sometimes, it was painful being the smartest guy. "What do you want, Mo?"

"Them cops is backing off."

"Good. Send someone for your lunch, and hole up inside the Harbor Freight in case they rally."

This was getting old. Even the adrenaline of a gunfight barely got his blood moving. It'd been weeks since anyone had even taken a bullet.

They skirmished with the cops. They skirmished with the Arizona State Militia. They even skirmished with the damned Neighborhood Watch, before they split out of town. Food was running out and the threat of the Mexican cartel hung over all of their heads. It'd been weeks since they'd seen a convoy through their hood, but that didn't mean the cartel was gone. They'd come back, and he wouldn't stop them with his ragtag bunch of brothers. Aside from Terrence and maybe Mo, there wasn't a street soldier in the whole group. They'd all been workaday, middle class black Americans when everything went to shit. Willie drove a forklift for Costco. They called themselves Black Panthers because what the hell else were a bunch of black guys supposed to call themselves? Willie had voted for Trump. Twice. But that was then and this was now.

"Yo. Boss Dawg," the radio chirped again. It was Mo. "One of 'em is comin' out with a white T-shirt tied to a pipe."

"Hold up, Mo. I'm coming. Don't shoot him." Willie jumped up and trotted back toward the Ranch Market. He used the tire shop like a bullet shadow between him and the pharmacy, where the cops were still trading rounds with his man on the roof. He ducked into the Ranch, went out the back door of the breakroom and ran around to the side of Harbor Freight. Mo was there, beside the tan-painted cinderblock wall, watching with suspicion.

Mo pointed toward the burrito joint. "He stepped back behind the Mexican food place, but he's still hanging that T-shirt out. You see?"

Willie used to eat at that place at least once a month. He loved their smoked chicken and cream half-pounder.

"Come on out. We ain't gonna shoot ya," Willie shouted. "Tell your guys at the pharmacy to stop shooting."

The cop holding the pole with the T-shirt leaned out then ducked back, probably trying to tease a shot if one was coming. Nobody fired. The skirmish died down and the corner quieted. After a few seconds, the cop stepped all the way into the clear. He waved the flag, as if to punctuate the sincerity of the truce.

Willie stepped out from behind the Harbor Freight and pointed the barrel of his gun at the ground. They walked slowly toward one another and met in the middle of Central Avenue.

"What makes you think you can loot the market?" the cop argued when he reached the yellow line in the middle of the street.

Willie barked a laugh. "That's what you start with? Bitching at us for looting?" He wiped the sweat off his forehead. "Brother, you need to get with the times. There's those who get and those who get got. That's it. There ain't no more *looting*."

The cop shook his head as though Willie was a disappointing teenager caught smoking weed behind shop class. "Those supplies are needed for the war effort. You and your Nubian warriors are burning them up, partying like it's nineteen ninety-nine."

"Oh, dawg. You going *waaaay* back with your racist smack and your music references. You're like the *un-cool* cop on Starsky and Hutch. I'm gonna let it pass because I'm only half black myself. If I was full black, I might have to knock out a few of those pearly whites that make yo mama proud." Truth was, Willie didn't give a shit about racism. It didn't get under his skin. He knew racism when he saw it, and he'd seen plenty, but he wasn't compelled to correct ignorance. They could just keep on keepin' on being ignorant motherfuckers for all he cared.

The cop shifted on his feet, and in that moment, Willie knew everything he needed to know about the two-hundred and sixty pound man. He knew he could do anything he wanted with him.

When a man got set to fight, he either went heavy on his feet or he went light. This guy planted his feet like an oak tree, and that meant he wasn't within a country mile of Willie's fighting class.

Reflexively, Willie was already light on the balls of his feet, his knees flexed, his hips fluid and ready to dip and dodge. If Officer TrunkDick took a swipe at him, Willie would drop the gun and have some fun. He'd allow a couple haymakers from the cop, duck around them, do a little dance. He'd bounce around to the big guy's right—the cop already telegraphed that he was a righty—and then he'd fire off a Willie Lloyd Special. Not that it was all that special; just a three punch combo that ended with a lightning jab to the throat. In ninety-nine-point-nine percent of street fights, the jab to the throat was the spunk-taker, rage-shaker, and friend-maker. Plus it had the added advantage of not jacking up his hand. After ten thousand hours in the boxing ring—in Philly as a kid—street fighting was like cheating to Willie. There were no rules, and the other guy almost never had more than a few fights under his belt. Willie had hundreds. After a fast-as-a-blink combo with the jab to the throat, all but the most skilled boxers would be at Willie's tender mercy, and he could help them up off their knees, offer a few soothing words, slap them on the back while they tried to breathe and establish brotherly relations.

Nothing made Willie happier than dominating a man, and then offering him the hand of fellowship. It was where the two sides of Willie Lloyd met: the vicious street thug and the Warrior for Christ. He never felt as at-home as when he was knocking the shit out of a dude then apologizing after.

But not today. There were too many guns around. There were more cops behind his favorite burrito joint, and there were Panther brothers watching them from behind the Harbor Freight. Either group could punch a hole in Willie, standing in the middle of the street, if things got violent.

So Willie soothed the angry cop. "Settle down, Hoss. You don't want to do what you're thinking about doin'. It won't end like you think it's gonna end." Willie said the words with a confidence born of taking a thousand punches and delivering at least that many in return. Apparently, the cop heard it as intended and his feet unrooted themselves from the asphalt.

"What do you mean when you say *war effort*?" Willie asked.

"We're taking the fight to the Mexican cartel in Flagstaff. We're filling a semi trailer with supplies and meeting up with the resistance north of here. They've enslaved the population of Flagstaff, and once they get their footing, they'll enslave all of us too. That probably doesn't matter to you, though. I bet you're on the beanslinger payroll."

"Oh, I see what you did there." Willie clicked his tongue and saluted. "You pulled a double racist slur—that takes talent. Your momma must've taught you well. So you figure all the mud bloods are working together, because we're all criminals, and we all don't give a shit about slavery, so long as we're not the slaves. That's some high level intellect at work, Dog. They teach you that strategical thinking in community college, or did you come by it watching CSI?"

"So you're asking me to believe you're not with the drug dealers?"

"We're not cartel. Would we be barricaded in a Ranch Market eating cornflakes for dinner if we were cartel?"

The cop snorted.

Willie's mind churned. He'd heard rumors about the cartel wintering in Flagstaff, but this was the first he'd heard of a coordinated defense mounted by American patriots. Truth was, his group was running out of options. The markets would run out of food in a couple weeks, give or take. Every new market, distribution center or restaurant they'd probed recently had been ransacked or was occupied by another gang. It'd been ten weeks since the stock market crash and Willie could see dark at the end of the tunnel. He had a lot of mouths to feed, and the city was nearly scavenged out. He needed a longer-term solution.

"So are you going to let us into the market or not?" The cop stabbed a thick hand toward the front door of the Ranch.

"Naw. That ain't going to happen. Our families are in there," Willie said. "Tell me where the fight against the cartel is going down and we'll think about it, but we definitely ain't fighting under no cops. I need to know what you boys got planned and we'll do what we're gonna do. Tell me where and when we meet up."

"I'm not telling you where. You'd sell us out to the cartel for a dime bag and a reach around."

Willie sighed. Fifty-fifty the cop was manipulating him—filling him full of bullshit just to get his hands on the Ranch. There probably wasn't "a resistance" or a meet-up. Willie had his master's degree in getting manipulated. His short stint in state prison taught him everything he'd need to know to avoid the traps. But he was desperate for options. He had a wife, a ten year old girl and a six year old boy. In a little more than two weeks, he'd start seeing hunger in their eyes. He'd do anything to prevent that. Even take a chance on joining up with a bunch of peckerwoods.

"Leave one of your boys with us," Willie floated an idea. "Leave someone who knows about the meet-up. He can guide us there when we're ready."

The cop cocked his bald head. "How do we know you won't just kill him? Or torture the information out of him?"

"If we wanted to kill a cop, we would've shot you holding the white flag. I could shoot you right now." Willie hefted the AR-15. "You're going to have to take some calculated risks if you want to add two hundred black soldiers in the fight against the cartel. And, we're going to want something else, thrown into the bargain for good faith."

"Yeah, what's that?" the cop asked.

"I'll tell you when the time comes." Willie smiled. "It won't be anything you'll mind giving. Word-to-the-mother."

At the end of the day, what Willie wanted was help learning

how to grow food. He'd never felt more vulnerable than this moment, seventeen days from running out of supplies for his kids. In his life, he'd never grown so much as a tomato.

None of his people—not a single one—had ever planted a garden. In the Phoenix African-American community, there were no farmers; not even an enterprising pot grower. They must reach outside their community in order to gain that knowledge. He and his brothers would be happy to do the work. They just needed to know where to dig and where to get water in the desert.

The cop had been mulling over the idea of leaving a guide. Willie could almost hear the buzzing and clinking of the slow, cast iron machinery inside the cop's head. He seemed to reach a decision. "Alright. I'll leave someone, but you have to let us inside to load up on supplies."

Willie shook his head. "No deal."

The cop drilled into Willie's eyes with his own, as though his whiteness was going to make Willie swoon. It was the face of a slave master staring down a slave, or just a big man accustomed to getting his way by threat of violence. Willie chuckled.

"What's so funny?" The thick-necked cop spat.

"Nothing. History trying to repeat itself, I guess."

The cop swiped the statement away and Willie could see in his face that he didn't get it. "I'll leave a man here, and if you princes of Wakanda decide that protecting America means anything to you, show up at the meet—with supplies."

Willie had no intention of taking food away from his wife and kids and giving it to white men, but that was a fight for another day. "Groovy," he said.

"Wait here," the cop ordered.

Ten minutes later, another cop crossed the parking lot of the pharmacy and joined them in the street. This one was a Latino.

"Saúl Calderon," he reached out a hand to Willie and smiled. His accent was too thick for a Phoenix cop.

"You don't look like no cop and you don't sound like no American."

"I'm not. I'm ex-military—on-loan from the Mexican government to help you put down the cartel."

"Well, Champ." Willie stepped forward and put his hand on the man's shoulder. "That sounds like the biggest crock of bullshit yet today. But I like you." He laughed and clapped a hand on Calderon's shoulder. "You're not white. You got that going for you. Come have lunch. Do you like cornflakes?"

---

### Thin Blue Line
Bridlewood West Ranches
**Tucson, Arizona**

> *"Police should flex their muscle nationwide and put a stop to all this bullshit protesting by any means necessary. Bust out the AR-15s and the MRAPs. Rack 'em, stack 'em and pack 'em, boys! Let's see some blood in the streets. It's time!"*

> — THIN BLUE LINE, FACEBOOK POST, OCTOBER 2ND, BLACK AUTUMN

*Tat-a-tat-tat-tat-tat. Tat-tat-tat-tat-tat.*

Chisholm ignored the machine gun fire and kept his binoculars on the M1 Abrams clanking down the middle lane of I-10.

A fusillade of AR-15 gunfire silenced the belt-fed, but the roar of the engine of the Abrams turned his blood cold. They had ten minutes to make it to the foot of the mountains before the giant lumbered into range. They were like junior high kids trading punches. Then, the big brother banged the screen door open and ran out of the house to settle matters with authority.

"Come on the run, boys," Chisholm radioed. "The beast just crossed Twin Peaks Road. Exfil, exfil, exfil."

Scattered throughout the neighborhood of abandoned ranchettes, OHVs and motorcycles sprang to life and raced for the sanctuary of the Saguaro Mountains. The partisans had just shot the ever-living shit out of a cartel fuel convoy, and the unstoppable counter-attack would begin with the main cannon of the M1 Abrams tank. By the time the beast got close enough to Chisholm's position, they'd be long gone, blasting up the dirt roads of the Saguaro State Park, then looping south to the safety of the partisan base at the Sandario Water Treatment Plant.

Chisholm took one last count: they'd destroyed three of the five tanker trucks. The I-10 flooded with thousands of gallons of unleaded fuel and three of the trucks belched black smoke. Amazingly, the roadbed hadn't gone up in flames. Next time, Chisholm would make sure to assign one of his cops to shoot tracers. They could've doubled their cartel body count if they'd lit the interstate on fire.

*Ka-whomp!*

One of the smoldering tankers erupted into a massive mushroom cloud, followed by a skyscraper column of black smoke. The flames shot out from the truck and consumed the other six vehicles on the roadway. Men ran in flaming circles, slowed, then crumpled into a lake of fire.

One more tanker caught fire underneath. The driver and his co-pilot bailed and ran for the riverbed. The fire climbed up the tires, into the engine compartment, up the back tires and licked the bottom of the fuel storage tank.

*BOOM!*

The storage tank blew and that sent another however-many-thousands of gallons of unleaded in a flash flood of greedy, fiery death.

Other than one narco Jeep that chased them into the neighborhood and the Abrams, they'd killed the entire convoy. The tank wouldn't wait to consolidate. He'd come straight at them. Chisholm needed to get his ass in gear.

*KA-DOOM!*

Something whistled overhead and a gout of rock erupted from the mountainside. The Abrams was firing on them on-the-run. *Time to go.*

He kick-started his motorcycle and gunned it, spewing sand and dust behind him as he whipped around and pointed the nose of the bike toward the hills. Another high explosive round whistled overhead, this one much closer, and blew apart one of the ranch houses two streets over.

His smile widened with each boom and whistle as the cartel Abrams fired haplessly at his fleeing troop of insurgents. He whooped into the tearing wind.

Truth was, he loved this shit. He regretted going to the academy instead of joining the Army. This was his jam, no doubt about it. But he'd gotten his second chance—his life do-over—with the apocalypse and the rise of the Mexican cartel, God bless 'em. He could kill these fuckers all day long and twice on Sunday. If they wanted to invade his country, he'd happily blow 'em up, shoot 'em up and cook 'em like a rack of ribs.

He didn't technically belong here, but Tucson had become his new, post-apocalyptic home. When the collapse struck, he'd been enjoying guns, booze and all-you-can-eat buffet at a cop convention at the Indian casino south of Tucson. His department in Colorado Springs had sent him as a perk. At the time, he was a newly-minted captain, and the cop convention was time off without chewing into his PTO.

He'd been getting his ass kicked at the craps table when the shit hit the fan. His dying, alcoholic pappy always said that Chisholm "couldn't win for losing." But this one time, he'd proved his old man wrong. He pulled an apocalyptic victory out of the jaws of a five grand losing streak at dice. One moment, he'd been teetering on a gambler's depression, and the next he was running and gunning in battle.

The partisans saw the double bars on his uniform and gave him the same rank in their army. Over the last few weeks, Chisholm delivered for them. Yes, indeed. This was his third ambush, and it'd been a doozy.

He sped up the mountain like a fleet-footed cougar, never looking back. The shadows of the mountain canyons closed in on the dirt road, and the thundering of the Abrams muted a bit with each turn in the canyon road. Chisholm's men reported in, safe and sound. He hadn't lost a single guy.

He'd held off hitting the twice-daily fuel convoys for seven days, until the Norteño soldiers grew lax. Instead of four Abrams tanks down the Alburquerque stretch of I-10, they'd dialed back to just two: one at the south end of Tucson and one at the north.

The Mexicans employed the tanks as pop-up garrisons—miniature forts to control the entrance and exit to the city. The buildings made it easy to conceal an ambush in town, and several partisan factions hit convoys inside the city limits of Tucson over the last two months—the Three Percenters, Arizona State Militia, and his own troop, Thin Blue Line.

It was a dumb war. Chisholm didn't know why they were fighting, other than the obvious intrusion of a Mexican drug cartel on American soil. The Mexicans weren't doing anything other than passing through with fuel tankers and a couple Jeeps. He wasn't sure why they bothered fucking with them.

The brass said the tankers were running to and from Flagstaff and caching the gas in water tanks. It was some kind of build up for an offensive campaign, probably after the snows of winter pulled back up north.

None of that mattered to Chisholm. He'd probably be dead by spring, so why should he care? It was the beginning of December, according to the camp cook. It wasn't even Christmas yet. A lot could happen between Christmas and Spring Break. The government could come back. The Russians could invade. A damned asteroid could strike. In the dirty hands of fate, nothing was off the table this year. Black Autumn: the year of shitty luck.

America had saved up all its bad luck since the Civil War and shit it out in a two month span. Terrorist attacks, stock market crash, power grid failure, riots, looting, then radio silence from the government, state and federal.

The deathly silence had been the real head trip for Chisholm. America had once been so full of noise, twenty-four-seven. Then it just stopped. It reminded him of when he was a kid and he and his brother would spend the night in the family camper out in the driveway. Friday night, their dad would let them play Monopoly and watch TV as late as they wanted in the cab-over camper he kept rusting away in the side yard, waiting for the family camping trip they never took. The boys hooked up a dinky black-and-white TV in the camper. His older brother would crush him in Monopoly while they watched Miami Vice, Fantasy Island, then The Benny Hill Show. It was the closest thing they had to porn back in those days. He and his brother watched with wide eyes as the big-breasted British ladies bounced around in cockneyed skits that neither of the boys understood. It kept them up late—late enough to see the television go off-air. They'd watch the last of Benny Hill, the closing credits, then the national anthem. At the end of the Star Spangled Banner, the television toned, then a rainbow pattern of columns appeared, then the screen winked out to static. He and his brother had stared at the screen, the snow and hiss mesmerizing their sleep-gummed eyes. They'd pack up the Monopoly board, climb into their sleeping bags, and fall asleep within five seconds.

America had gone to static in early October. There'd been a frantic skit with bomb blasts in the sandbox, gas shortages, a Russian hack, then race riots in virtually every town, including

Colorado Springs. The National Guard rushed around for a week or so, trying to pen the mayhem in, but with the banks closed and the mail no longer running, the slide into chaos felt inevitable. The closing credits rolled. The national anthem played. The colored columns flicked on, with an irritating howl that sounded like the Emergency Broadcast System.

Then static.

That's what it had been for two months, now.

Static.

When morning came, there were no Saturday morning cartoons. No American Bandstand. Just static, static and more static.

For now, he could fight the druggies, and that was a pretty solid silver lining, if you asked him. He had no kids. His mom had died of lung cancer ten years before. His dad was an asshole. His sister lived in some New Age crystal-loving village in the Blue Ridge Mountains. He didn't waste any brain juice worrying about his family. All he had was the here-and-now, just how he liked it.

The Thin Blue Line army fed him okay, and there was an ever-growing tent city full of hungry ladies—both physically and emotionally—around their camp. Life was pretty good for a wandering gunman, and life was downright *outstanding* for a gunman with a silver bar on his uniform.

So what if he didn't entirely understand what'd happened in the world?

---

**United States Air National Guard**
*162nd Fighter Wing*
**Tucson, Arizona**

*"Having safety nets in place can be priceless when the unexpected strikes. All Airmen enjoy excellent benefits, ranging from low-cost health insurance to eligibility for VA home loans."*

— AIR NATIONAL GUARD RECRUITING POST,
FACEBOOK, SEPTEMBER 26TH.

*"REALLY??!! What do we do now that the Postal Service isn't delivering our checks? How are we supposed to feed our families, Army? Get your soldiers f\*\*cking paid! Then we can talk about VA home loans and all that other shit."*

— FACEBOOK COMMENT ON OCTOBER 4TH OF
THE BLACK AUTUMN COLLAPSE.

Jessica "Jazzy" Padilla had been asked to get a squadron of A-10 Warthogs combat-ready and airborne. The order was from the Colonel himself, but it made about as much sense as asking her to bring Bruce Lee back from the dead. She'd been trained to work on F-16 Fighting Falcons, not Warthogs. They hadn't been able to flush a toilet for seven weeks, much less order parts for scheduled maintenance. A half-mile across town, she could hear the *pock-pock-pock-BOOM* of partisan groups battling drug traffickers with tanks.

And for all that, she'd done it. She'd busted into the abandoned Air Force base with her team, wrangled the JP-8 fuel over to the Hogs, gassed them up, turned over their engines and rounded up three pilots to make the bunny hop over to the 162nd airfield. One of the pilots hadn't flown in twenty years. In all their battered glory: three A-10 Warthogs, as menacing as ever, sat on her tarmac in the desert sun, poised to strike.

Alas, it wasn't to be. The Warthogs were like ugly prom dates waiting on the porch for a skinny, tuxedoed boy who would never arrive. They had everything they needed except the bullets, and without armor-piercing rounds for the Avenger cannons, the Warthogs were paperweights holding down an airfield.

*Armor-piercing*, that was the whole mission these days. The only mission: to kill tanks.

The northern Mexican drug cartel had come upon a hundred American M1 Abrams tanks in the desert. Jazzy had no idea why they'd been abandoned and why they were pre-loaded with ordnance. She couldn't find a live round for the Warthogs in a deal with the devil. How a hundred tanks had appeared out of the New Mexico desert, loaded for bear, was one of a thousand fresh mysteries in tumbledown America. All Jazzy knew was that she'd been ordered to produce a weapon that'd kill those damned tanks.

The Warthog could do it—that wasn't the problem. Without air cover or surface-to-air missiles, even the mighty M1 Abrams would be a lamb to the slaughter against the 'Hogs. With enough fuel and ammo, they could turn the tank brigade into a smoking heap of slag.

Between the Air Force base and the 162nd Fighter Wing, she had enough fuel for fifty sorties, give or take. Pretty soon, though, the targets would move outside the 'Hogs operating range of two-hundred fifty nautical miles—the distance they could sortie and safely return to base. As of this moment, reconnaissance placed the majority of the tanks in Flagstaff, which barely fit inside their flight envelope.

The tanks had already taken a beating over in Nevada. There were only seventy or so in and around Flagstaff, and they bore the marks of combat: scorched black and dinged-up. Word from partisans in the north was that local irregulars from Ellis AFB had brought down an oil refinery on top of the *narcotraficantes*. It sent them scurrying back to northern Arizona to lick their wounds and wait out the winter before rolling north into the Rocky Mountains.

Colonel Withers appeared in the door of Jazzy's hangar. "You asked to speak to me?"

"Yes sir. But I could've come to you, sir." She stood at attention, as did the three mechanics in the bay.

He waved for them to stand at-ease. "I have nothing more important on my to-do list than these Warthogs. Report, please."

"We're fully operational, sir, but we've got no teeth. We've recovered a hundred and fifty thousand training rounds from the Air Force base, and no penetrators. The dummy rounds won't penetrate the hull of the Abrams. They're copper-coated lead. No depleted uranium core."

The colonel looked at the waxed concrete floor. "I was afraid that might be the case. Have you searched the entire base?"

"Yessir. Also, we rounded up a munitions airman hiding in his apartment. He confirmed: the air base hadn't stockpiled armor-piercing rounds for decades."

"Did he say where they were stockpiled?"

"Yessir. McAlester Army Ammunition Plant, McAlester, Oklahoma. There's a closer depot in Hawthorne, Nevada, but we don't think they kept thirty-millimeter penetrators there."

"Without ordnance, the Warthogs are no more useful than dog tits."

"What're your orders, sir?" Jazzy resumed standing at attention. The conversation was above her pay grade, but these days, airmen did all jobs.

"You've done your part, Sergeant. Now it's time for me to do mine. I think I'll pay the local militia a visit. Let's see how seriously they take the Constitution."

"The militia, sir?" Jazzy cocked her head. "I thought that was *our* mission. To protect the skies over the CONUS."

"Yes?" The Colonel chuckled. "I thought so too. Then why the hell did they store our bullets a thousand miles away from our fighter jets?"

**Arizona Three Percenter,**
**United Patriots Encampment**
*Forty-niner Country Club*
**Tucson, Arizona**

> *"They have no idea the storm that comes their way should they choose to cross the line, but we stand at the gateway to civil unrest and the next civil war. It is past time to prepare. It is time to **patriot up**."*

> — *FACEBOOK COMMENT, THREE PERCENTER,*
> *UNITED PATRIOTS, ONE WEEK BEFORE THE BLACK*
> *AUTUMN COLLAPSE.*

"Are you in command?" Colonel Withers asked the man in camouflage. He wore the twin stars of major general, and Withers' first impulse was to salute him, but that would've been ridiculous. The man looked like Santa Claus put on a uniform and rolled around in the ball pit at Chuck-E-Cheese. Colonel Withers shook the militiaman's hand.

The scraggly general returned the handshake. "What can I do for you, Colonel?"

"I'm sorry. I'm at a loss how to address your rank. I apologize," Withers stammered.

"That's understandable." The militia man walked around his desk without further comment. "Please sit." The name strip on the uniform said "Conners."

Colonel Withers was a direct man, so he came right out with it: "We need a detachment of men to go to McAlester, Oklahoma and return with two million rounds of thirty-millimeter for our Avenger cannons."

"What for?" the self-appointed general asked.

They met in a pro shop on a dried-up golf course. The uniforms were almost right, but everything else was wrong. Between any other two National Guard officers, there would be no need for explanation—the man with the higher rank would tell the other man what to do. End of story.

"The A-10 Warthog close air support aircraft fires the thirty-millimeter armor-piercing round with its Avenger cannon. We have three Warthogs ready to fight, but we have no armor-piercing rounds on base. They're in Oklahoma."

"You don't have bullets for your weapons?" the general asked, incredulous.

"No, I do not. The Army consolidated munitions for budgetary purposes a decade ago. I'm requesting that your militia unit send a detachment to recover the rounds so we can take the fight to the Mexican cartel. *Please.*" The Colonel had never followed an order with "please," but strange times made strange bedfellows.

The militiaman looked across the desk with inscrutable, dark eyes. Colonel Withers assumed he was considering the request.

"We're not militia. We're Three Percenter patriots. The Arizona State Militia's hiding out somewhere south of town. What you're requesting isn't our mission set."

Colonel Withers yanked off his cap and scratched the top of his head. "Could you please explain the difference?"

"We're not an auxiliary military force to the federal government. We're like the three percent of patriot farmers who fought the British in the Revolutionary War. We don't defend the federal government or take orders from the Army. Our primary mission is to protect our families."

Withers had seen the families as he drove across the golf course neighborhood. The militia had taken up residence in the spacious, abandoned homes ringing the fairway. There were hoses criss-crossing the streets as families drained the swimming pools of the estates higher up the hill, presumably for drinking water.

Colonel Withers exhaled. "You needn't worry about the federal government. You got your wish. They're gone. All that remains are

American soldiers opposing an invasion by a Mexican drug cartel. We could use your help. We have weapons, but inadequate personnel, and no ammo."

The Three Percenter shook his head. "Like I said, our primary mission is to protect our own families."

"If one of their Abrams tanks drives up this road, your families will be destroyed. We're enlisting your help to neutralize that threat."

"We'll take our chances. I'd say our odds of avoiding a confrontation with the Mexicans are a hell of a lot better than our odds of surviving a trek across the apocalypse to pick up a load of bullets." He sighed. "We'd love to help, but we aren't young soldiers. We have families to consider."

Colonel Withers stood up and extended his hand again. "Thank you for your time, Conners. The three percent in the Revolutionary War fought against the crown, family men or not. Good day and best of luck." The Colonel stomped out of the pro shop.

---

**Arizona State Militia**
*Pima County Fairgrounds*
**Tucson, Arizona**

> *The Arizona State Militia is a body of armed American citizens committed to defending their Constitutional liberties and serving their communities. We are free and independent from the control of any local, state, or federal government, except when called to service by the State Governor. Our intentions are constitutionally legal. "A well regulated militia being necessary to the security of a free state, the right of the people to keep and bear arms shall not be infringed."*
>
> *— FACEBOOK PAGE, ARIZONA STATE MILITIA*

The Arizona State militia commander greeted Colonel Withers with more respect, but reluctant to take any unnecessary risks. They were barely surviving.

"Colonel—why haven't you sent Arizona National Guardsmen to retrieve the munitions?"

Colonel Withers choked on the question, not because he hadn't thought of it, but because he still couldn't believe the answer himself. "We did. A month ago. We lost comms with them a week later." Withers shifted in his seat. The two men sat at a dinette table in an RV, parked at the county fair campground. The fairgrounds had its own well and a huge solar bank. From that foundation, the Arizona State Militia had built an operating base. Two thousand men, women and children lived like refugees in tents, campers and recreational vehicles, spread across the fairgrounds like a Boy Scout Jamboree.

"Was the unit attacked?" The militia commander showed genuine concern. The reception was markedly warmer than the Three Percenters.

"We don't know. They might've encountered comms problems. It's quite possible they went AWOL. They were having...personnel issues on their last check in."

"Why not send more men?"

"We abandoned Papago Park HQ when the inner city rioting overran the grounds. Then the cartel seized our readiness facility in Buckeye. Without facilities, most of our servicemen and women vanished. I assume they're with their families. Some are probably here with you. A uniformed national guardsman walked past my Humvee when I pulled in. He even saluted."

"The militia had a contingency plan, as I'm sure you did." It sounded a little like an accusation. "Our people knew what to expect when the shit hit the fan. They knew we'd meet up here. It was in the plan."

"I'm afraid the vaporization of the United States Government wasn't a planning contingency on our list." Colonel Withers had been as guilty as any for assuming the government was ironclad.

"Mighty Zeus," the militia captain said. "…with gaze so powerful and distant he cannot see the earth beneath his feet."

"Is that Shakespeare?" Colonel Withers asked.

"No. It's something a friend said. He's Police Chief over in Window Rock on the New Mexico border. Navajo." The militiaman waved out the window at the bustling camp. "Some of us saw this coming. We were dubious of the government and saw the cracks in the foundation. Militia. Constitutionalists. Native American nations. We saw the signs before the stock market crash. Only the 'crazies' could see what was happening, I guess."

"It was unimagineable." Colonel Withers accepted the lecture. The militia commander was obviously taking some small enjoyment from being proven right. The old world—just two months before—regarded these militia people as tinfoil hat loonies. Colonel Withers had a hard time shaking that prejudice even now —even with this encampment well-defended and standing while many of his National Guard bases were smoking ruins. The only armored vehicles intact in the state might be here on the Pima County fairgrounds, operated by militia.

The militia leader, Paul Hargreaves, interrupted the Colonel's thoughts. "Have you spoken with the Navajo Nation? They're the largest functioning government in the region."

"The Navajo?" Withers hadn't considered the reservation. They were remote enough they might not have entered into conflict with the cartel, nestled away in the four corners area of the states.

"Yes. Not counting the Hopis or the Utes, they're over 170,000 souls. I'm told their government hasn't skipped a beat."

Withers hadn't factored them into his thinking. "I'd appreciate a letter of introduction, if you'd be so kind. Do they have representatives in Phoenix?"

"I doubt it," Hargreaves chortled. "They're probably staying as far from our population centers as possible. They closed their borders at the first sign of civil disorder. They practiced during COVID. According to my friend, Chief Descheny, they stood up defensive paramilitary units to reinforce their borders. That's how I met the Navajo police chief. He asked me for advice about interfacing with Arizona state government. I told him not to bother—that you guys wouldn't take that kind of end-of-the-world hypothetical seriously, even after COVID and the riots."

Colonel Withers sighed. He didn't enjoy the brow beating, but he deserved it. In truth, three months ago, he wouldn't have taken the Native Americans seriously. He would've thought the idea of a total collapse crackpot—unlikely in the extreme.

"Back to my original question." Colonel Withers sat up straight in his chair. "Will you send a unit to Oklahoma to recover thirty-millimeter ammo for our 'Hogs?"

The militia commander wore no rank insignia, but based on how the others in the camp regarded him, he was the primary decision-maker. He sat back in his chair and scratched his five o'clock shadow.

"We do have a unit that's chomping at the bit to fight the narcos. They're younger men and veterans. I might convince them that an ammo supply mission makes more sense than throwing themselves against tanks. They're a small unit—a reinforced squad really. Twenty-five men, more or less. I'll send them to Oklahoma if you can add thirty more men from one of the other factions—the Navajo, the National Guard, the Frats, the Three Percenters. My men will command the group."

"Who are the Frats?" Withers asked. He hadn't heard of a partisan group by that name.

"Arizona Fraternal Order of Police."

"I thought they were the Thin Blue Line?" Colonel Withers had uncovered six partisan groups so far, and Hargreaves had just added two more to the list.

"Thin Blue Line is Phoenix PD. Frats are Tucson PD plus the cops who got caught at the Blue Sky casino when the shit hit the fan. They're based in the mountains west of Tucson and they make their living robbing narco supply convoys."

"Is anyone considering a coordinated offensive?" Colonel Withers asked.

"Against Abrams tanks? I hope not." Hargreaves laughed. "You're the first to bring up the idea. Do you think three A-10s can kill all those tanks?"

"Unless they have air cover or missile batteries, I don't see why not. That's what the 'Hogs do. They're tank killers."

Withers wanted to nail down the militia's commitment, so he repeated it back. "If I can find thirty men for the mission to Oklahoma, you'll add your twenty-five? I'll be sending a veteran Army officer to command the unit, by the way. That's non-negotiable. I'm not losing another unit to a breakdown in comms." Colonel Withers stared across the desk mustering all the latent authority of the United States of America and channeled it into his unblinking stare.

"Okay, Colonel," the militiaman relented. "Your man can command the unit if you dig up thirty men and muster them here. Out of curiosity, who will you send to command?"

Withers smiled. "An old Green Beret vet. He's a tracker and a guerrilla fighter: Master Sergeant Bill McCallister. You'll like him. He killed an entire narco unit in his front yard at the start of all this. He's a batshit crazy prepper just like you."

*[Excerpt from **America Invaded**, the sequel to both **Honor Road** and **Black Autumn Conquistadors**. Continue reading on Kindle, paperback or free on Kindle Unlimited]*

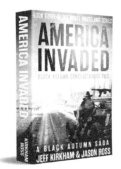

# ALSO BY JASON ROSS, ADAM FULLMAN & JEFF KIRKHAM

The first five books of the *Black Autumn series* rampage through the seventeen days of the Black Autumn collapse, chronicled coast-to-coast through the eyes of thirty-one desperate survivors.

*Series in order:*

*1. Black Autumn*

*2. Black Autumn Travelers*

*3. Black Autumn Conquistadors*

*4. The Last Air Force One*

*5. White Wasteland* (same characters as Black Autumn)

*6. Honor Road* (same characters as Travelers)

*7. America Invaded* (same characters as Conquistadors)

*8. President Partisan* (same characters as The Last Air Force One.)

*9. Blood Spring* (all characters from all books.)

*10. Fragments of America* (short stories)

While the unique book order can be a bit confusing, it helps to think of the five "black cover" books as a single, epic novel covering the same seventeen days of collapse, then the four "white cover" novels telling the story of the following, impossible winter. Then, Blood Spring culminates all storylines and characters. Like *Game of Thrones*, or *The Stand*, the Black Autumn series breaks down an epic tale with dozens of characters, fighting for their survival.

Our apologies for any head-scratching that may ensue. We couldn't think of a better way to tell the massive, 2,000 page tale bouncing around in our brain buckets. As usual, I blame it all on Jeff.

— Jason

# ABOUT THE AUTHORS

**Jason Ross** has been a hunter, fisherman, shooter and preparedness aficionado since childhood and has spent tens of thousands of hours roughing it in the great American outdoors. He's an accomplished big game hunter, fly fisherman, an Ironman triathlete, SCUBA instructor, and frequent business mentor to U.S. military veterans. He retired from a career in entrepreneurialism at forty-one years of age after founding and selling several successful business ventures.

After being raised by his dad as a metal fabricator, machinist and mechanic, Jason dedicated twenty years to mastering preparedness tech such as gardening, composting, shooting, small squad tactics, solar power and animal husbandry. Today, Jason splits his time between writing, international humanitarian work and his wife and seven children.

**Adam Fullman** is an American attorney and entrepreneur. He and his three siblings were raised in California by their American father and Dutch immigrant mother. After spending two decades building a successful law practice, Adam rediscovered fitness, dropped 100 pounds and began his pursuit of preparedness, bushcraft and physical competence. His current favorite interests are minimalist wilderness survival and his fruit tree orchard. Adam lives in Ogden, Utah with his wife and three children.

**Jeff Kirkham** (editor/consultant) served almost 29 years as a Green Beret doing multiple classified operations for the US government. He is the proverbial brains behind ReadyMan's survival tools and products and is also the inventor of the Rapid Application

Tourniquet (RATS). Jeff has graduated from numerous training schools and accumulated over 8 years "boots on the ground" in combat zones, making him an expert in surviving in war torn environments. He spent the majority of the last decade as a member of a counter terrorist unit, working in combat zones doing a wide variety of operations in support of the global war on terror. Jeff spends his time, tinkering, inventing, writing and helping his immigrant Afghan friends, who fought side by side with Jeff. His true passion is his family and spending quality time with his wife and three children.

*Check out the Readyman lifestyle*...search Facebook for ReadyMan group and join Jeff, Jason and thousands of other readers in their pursuit of preparedness and survival.

**Honor Road**

**Black Autumn series Book Six**
**& Black Autumn Travelers Book Two**

by Jason Ross & Adam Fullman

Made in the USA
Las Vegas, NV
25 June 2024

91492814R00233